TRILOGY
THE FREQUENCY

I0682403

Janja Srečkar

THE FREQUENCY

If you had a supernatural power –
what would you do with it?

(1st book)

THE FREQUENCY, JANJA SREČKAR
Title of publication: The Frequency
Subtitle of publication: If you had a supernatural power - what would you do with it?
Original title of publication: Hitra frekvenca
Original subtitle of publication: Če bi prejeli nadzemsko moč - kaj bi storili z njo?
Author of publication: Janja Srečkar
Publisher: selfpublishing (Janja Srečkar), Ljubljana
Edition (printed): First edition
Year of printed edition: 2016
Printed by CreateSpace, An Amazon.com Company – Print on demand

Year of first publication (e-book): 2011
Year of second publication (e-book): 2013
Year of copyright protection: 2010
Pictures and ornaments: Pia Rihtarič
Design and layout realisation: www.leparec.si
Translation and editing: Mojca Lorber and Alan Horvatič
This text is copyright protected in accordance with the provisions of 174. article of the copyrihgt law.

CIP - Kataložni zapis o publikaciji
Narodna in univerzitetna knjižnica, Ljubljana

821.163.6-312.9

SREČKAR, Janja
    The frequency : if you had a supernatural power - what would you do with it? / Janja Srečkar ; [pictures and ornaments Pia Rihtarič ; translation Mojca Lorber and Alan Horvatič]. - 1st ed. - Ljubljana : selfpublishing, 2016

Prevod dela: Hitra frekvenca

ISBN 978-961-94018-0-4

284539392

TABLE OF CONTENTS

To Jan Sebastian.

I STARTED TO SHIVER. I knew that the invisible thing was there, that it was watching me, studying me, and that it's not going to leave at all. I lay in my bed. Suddenly I felt the thing had sat on the edge of it... *What shall we do now?* I thought. *Am I going to die?*

I felt pressure on my chest as if somebody had placed a hand there. The same as before, in the car, when that thing hit me on the head. Suddenly I felt peace descent on me. I started to disappear. First I lost my legs. Then arms. And before I could start panicking, my torso was gone. I felt how different my soul was from the body to which it has been attached for the entire 17 years.

Was that – *it*? Was I going to die? Luckily I had written a note and left it on my desk, just in case…

> *Please let my parents Zoran and Amalija Kralj and my sister Ela know that I love them very much and that I am extremely grateful for all the support they have given me in my life. I am sure I am in a better place.*
> *Best regards, Ina Kralj.*

It had to happen.

Suddenly an even stronger whirlwind came over me. The only thing I felt was the weirdo beside me…I knew it…

Obviously I was leaving.

I. THE BEGINNING

IT BEGAN EVEN BEFORE I STARTED ELEMENTARY SCHOOL. Although I was of a rather slight built, my mother would tell me I was pretty smart and sensible for my age. I didn't feel like that especially when I would observe the enormous people around me who were moving like giants and knew things, secrets that I was not privy to. I always felt that the adult world was big and mysterious and that I was never going to gain access to it. So I got along with my friends much better than with the adults.

There were so many of them! My room was always full of people and everyone had a great time in my company. They were young, beautiful, smiling and of a slightly darker complexion than my own, but only by a shade. They brought me gifts. Some of them could even fly. Their only fault was that nobody else beside me could see them. So my mom always became upset when I talked about them. And also when I asked her to tuck in and kiss goodnight thirty other people in my room whom she didn't see and I did. It was fun at the beginning but later on she became more and more angry and anxious. I couldn't see why.

I had such a great time with my friends! I felt closest to the boy with dark brown hair and golden-bronze brown eyes. His name was Ravi. He was the same age as me but he was a bit taller and he liked to believe that he was also smarter. I suppose he really was. He had a handsome, boyish heart-shaped face with a small dimple in his chin and when he smiled, you had a feeling that the whole world was smiling. He knew better than anybody else how to cheer me up. He spoke slowly and eloquently and he always told the truth. Everything that came from his mouth sounded so simple, as if lying didn't even exist in this world. Like everybody else, he always wore white clothes. I never asked him why. It seemed natural and self-explanatory. Since they were always smiling, I couldn't picture them wearing black. White seemed totally appropriate.

Because there weren't any children my age in the neighborhood (we lived in a house and there was only my sister Ela who was five years older than me, but this doesn't count because she didn't want to have anything to do with me), I really enjoyed playing with him. He had the most beautiful dark brown curls that drooped over his forehead. When I looked at him for some time, I felt as if I was in another dimension. Of course I was not able to put all this into words at that time. But I remember precisely the feelings I had when I was spending time with him.

We did everything together. He was my best friend. We often watched the colorful haze that surrounded people. Ravi told me that was the aura. I was very amused to see the yellow glow around the people who expected you to tell them a joke. Or the soft pink reddish glow people get when somebody gives them a hug. And I was sad to see the black smog around the people who were sad. Sometimes I would run over to them and start waving my hands and blowing to make the smoke go away. My mom was very embarrassed in such moments – she would grab my hand and while she was pulling me away, she would utter an apology: "You know what the kids are like…" Ravi only smiled.

Sometimes it seemed he understood more than I did. That he knew the world better and more profoundly. He taught me many things. He taught me how to draw, how to watch the sunset, he liked playing with me and many times he flew around me and I had to catch him. Ravi called this game "catch the butterfly" (he was the butterfly) and it is only now that I realize why the name of this game was so convenient at the time. If my mom asked me what I was doing on the lawn behind our house and why I was jumping so much, I would answer, "I'm catching the butterfly." And everybody was happy. Mom was happy thinking I was catching a real butterfly like a million other little girls around the world. She somehow resented all my imaginary friends, which I understood only later. She simply didn't understand it. But I was happy because Ravi was always making funny faces, which made me laugh very hard while I was chasing him.

I have always wanted to fly. Don't understand me wrong. I didn't jump from rooftops or anything like that. I just wanted to fly, upwards. To jump from the ground, catch the air with my arms and…fly. Like Ravi. I used to dream about flying every night. Sometimes I even dreamed I was teaching others to fly. One day I made my own pair of wings – from cardboard boxes. I cut off two pieces – the two you use to close the box. I fastened two little strings on the edges of each piece. Then I tied them around my wrists and shoulders. I went to the top of the hill behind our house. I ran down the hill flapping my arms. When I was pushing myself from the ground, I noticed that it took a bit longer for me to touch the ground again than it did when I was running on flat ground. I was sure that my wings did the trick and that it had nothing to do with the fact that I was jumping down a hill (where it's logical your jump is longer).

I really believed I could fly although only for a split second. But of course this was nothing in comparison to the somersaults Ravi was performing the day before while we were playing "catch the butterfly". It also didn't help that he was hovering before me and trying to stop me while I was running downhill. I was sure I had made a giant contribution to the development of aviation in the world. I called my parents to corroborate my theory on aerodynamics. When they saw me running down the hill, my dad started to laugh and my mom started yelling to come down. I didn't know why dad was laughing. Was it because he was making fun of me or was it because he was so happy that his daughter had defied the laws of gravity, which many had tried for thousands of years? I liked to imagine that the second option was the right answer.

My pre-school years passed in this way very quickly! I would wake up and go to sleep with a smile on my face, and in the meantime – beside a few moments when I had to be told off because of some small mischief – I would have fun without any worries whatsoever. I could be totally relaxed with Ravi. In summer we often played outside. Because the front door was open we heard everything my mom said to my dad. They fought a lot and I couldn't understand why they couldn't work things out in a calmer and more reasonable way.

"Feelings are not always simple", said Ravi. "Especially when you get used to them and they get under your skin. And then, before you know it, you are angry and hurt. And it gets even more interesting when you hear only the things you *want* to hear." I didn't agree. "I will never be like this", I replied. "If we ever get married, I will never yell at you."

Ravi smiled sadly. There was a glitter of something in his eyes, which I could best describe as 'a complicated story with a sad ending'. As if he felt something approaching that was to influence all events that were to follow. Something unavoidable. He shoved his curls out of his eyes and chased away black thoughts, "Let's talk about something else."

And so we did. We talked a lot in those last days of summer. About everything! About plants and animals; about school, how I was created, what the space looks like, why people argue, why love and happiness are so important. Looking back, I learned more in those 14 days before starting school than in the rest of my life put together!

I could hardly wait for my mom to leave for work every morning. Dad didn't pay much attention to Ela and me anyway. Ela liked going out with her friends and always when she came home, her nails were a different color or there was a new, freshly acquired lip-gloss glistening on her lips. When peace descended on the house I called Ravi. It was very easy. I would think of him or say his name silently. He was usually hiding behind the door anyway or was swinging lightly from the chandelier waiting for me to call him.

The last week of summer, my mom gave me an old camera. Because I had something valuable, even Ela forgot about the irreconcilable differences between us that week and her thousands of friends and went out with me every afternoon. Ravi stayed at home.

I felt very important when we were taking pictures of ourselves and posing in front of the camera. I identified with the role of the model completely. I posed by a low windowsill and pretended it was very high and I was utilizing my last atoms of strength to hold on to it, I climbed on the fence and spread my arms (I shouted to Ela not to take the picture of the fence so that the clouds in the background would be in the picture and it would look as if I was in the air)...As far as posing went, she didn't hold back either. It was only that her poses were always more boring and model-like, she always smiled, she only fluttered her eye-lashes differently.

It was so exciting because that week I was collecting the things that were to help me with studying the following year. The bag which was bigger than me with big red reflectors to be more visible in the street; a big pencil case with pencils and color pencils; triangles and squares in bags, big sheets of paper for drawing...

I was so busy that I didn't remember to call my best friend till that fateful September morning...And when I did it was too late.

II. THE FIRST SCHOOL DAY

IT WAS SIX TWENTY-FIVE WHEN I WOKE UP. It was one of those days when you wake up before the alarm goes off. My head was still empty and the birds were chirping outside. My first thought was, "Finally I'm going to school." I had really wanted to go to school in the last year. All the older children went to school and it seemed to be the place for important, more mature people. I got up and started to get dressed. I put on each piece with great care. I thoroughly washed my teeth in the bathroom and it was the first time that even Ela had to wait for me to emerge from the bathroom dressed up to the nines.

I had my favorite cereal for breakfast (chocolate with banana). My heavy bag was waiting for me at the door. Luckily we lived quite near the school. It was just a 5-minute slow walk. So my mom decided to take me there only on the first day. Of course Ela was supposed to accompany me every day.

I was so excited that I was urging both Ela and mom to go quickly. When I had given up on them, I took my enormous bag, left the house and set down on the stairs in front of the house. Ravi came towards me.

"Hello Ravi," I said distantly. "I'm sorry I haven't called you so much recently, I had to prepare for school, you know."

"I forgive you."

Silence. What should I say to him?

"I must be organized and grownup there. My mom told me to be friendly and do what I am told."

"OK."

"I won't be able to play so much anymore."

"I know. That's why I'm here."

I could see an unusual calmness and sadness on his face. Suddenly I felt sorry for not playing with him more. I felt I was loosing the most important part of me and that everything I had worked so hard for – the lovely dress, big bag, school, adulthood, friendship with Ela – was just a dream in comparison with the friendship Ravi stood for.

"Will you walk me to school?" I suddenly exclaimed.

"I don't know if that's a good idea," Ravi said seriously.

"You are my friend," I objected stubbornly. "We do everything together."

"If you want me to go with you, you must pretend you *don't see me*. As if I didn't exist."

"Why should I do that?"

"Don't ask too many questions", he said. He looked down and then away from me. He took two steps away and covered his face with his hands. Then he straightened and faced me again. "Now you will have more important things to do."

I didn't manage to ask him what he meant by that because mom and Ela came out.

"So, shall we go, first-grader?" mom said proudly and patted me on the shoulder. Somehow we were no longer on the same side. Half an hour ago I was burning with desire to be ready to go, but now my head was full of thoughts and strange premonitions.

Why should I pretend that I don't see Ravi? Why was I the only to see him? How come he was so calm and at the same time so obviously sad? What did he think when he said I had more important things to do? Does that mean we can't be friends anymore? Doesn't he like school? Why do I have the feeling that I'm standing on both sides of a big crack in the ground? As if I had to decide on which side to jump so as not to get sucked in by lava. I was pulled to one side by everybody: school, society, mom, dad…and on the other side there is Ravi. And he isn't even trying to pull me to his side. He is just sitting there and watching me disappear. He knew this would happen. They are too strong to beat, so he is not even trying to stop them. He is sitting there and smiling goodbye. Is this really the end?

Suddenly tears came to my eyes. I am about to lose a friend. My only link to who I really am. I will lose the only person who really understood me and played with me. Today I am entering the world of the adults who are important, smart but also cruel. The world where they argue and fight without a reason.

Ravi walked beside me in silence. Mom didn't even notice my tears until we reached the school. The teacher was waiting there with a couple of new students and their parents.

"There, there, it's not that bad," said the teacher called Anja.

"Ina, what's wrong?" asked my mom with fear when she noticed that I was the only one among first-graders to start the day so dramatically. I was feeling such a strong pain in my chest that I was proud of myself for not screaming blue murder. I did my best to sob as quietly as possible. Especially because I knew I would spend quite some time with those people in the future.

"Everything's OK," the teacher comforted my mom. "This reaction is entirely normal for a child who is entering a new environment. Some children need time to get used to the new people and environment."

Their talk seemed un-understandable. Get used to? New environment? It sounded like they were talking about a laboratory animal. How can somebody so miss the reason for my tears? Ela went towards her class and tried to pretend she was not in the least related to the human water hydrant she had arrived with. My mom and the other parents were served coffee in small plastic cups.

Soon the parents left and mom urged me for the final time to be good. Ravi watched the development silently and looked at me from time to time. His eyes glowed more than ever before. Anja the teacher held me by the hand.

"Let's go to our classroom, children."

My classmates followed her and she dragged me along too. Slowly

we pushed through the door but I kept looking back at Ravi all the time. The front door was made of glass with wooden handles. When we went through, it slowly closed. We went towards the stairs to the first floor and then I couldn't stand it anymore. I wrestled my hand from the teacher's and ran towards the door. I couldn't open it.

"It's alright, kids", the teacher tried to calm down my classmates who had witnessed another outburst of their new fellow student. "Let's go to the classroom and Ina will wave her mommy goodbye one more time."

On the other side of the glass door Ravi was kneeling down. I placed my hand on the glass and he did the same. My tears multiplied as if they followed the weather for it had started to rain outside.

"Don't cry," Ravi tried to calm me down. "We will see each other again."

"Pro-mise?" I sobbed.

"For sure. Some day."

Some day – another word for *never again*.

I noticed he started to disappear and finally he seemed to be just a reflection in the glass door.

"What – is – ha-ppe-ning? Where – are you?" Finally I couldn't see anything through the flood of tears.

Anja the teacher came and took hold of my hand again. This time firmer.

"I've seen many emotional children but you really love your mommy too much. This is not always the best, you know. You must learn to think with your own head", she was saying to me while we were walking towards the classroom. But I was still looking back towards the door. I didn't care in the least why the teacher was saying these things or what my classmates would think when they saw my puffy read face with a huge swollen nose, which stuck out like a slimy poisonous mushroom. I looked towards the door where I saw such total emptiness, rain and tears, the same as I felt inside. When I opened the classroom door and saw all the strange faces looking coldly at me, another shiver went down my spine…

III. DARKNESS

ALTHOUGH THE WALLS OF THE CLASSROOM WERE A LIGHT TURQUOISE green shade, I felt like I was caught in a dark cave where I would be kept for the next nine years. The fact that I was right was even more devastating.

I sat in the only free place next to a blond girl whose hair was braided. She was very quiet but she liked looking around even when the teacher explained what we would do during the year. The girl's name was Renata. Later I found out she had problems concentrating and moving…When I got to know her better, I found out that her most prominent ability was to express her feelings without any shame. She was definitely a rare bird in this respect.

I looked around the classroom. There were about twenty of us. The teacher explained that we were to raise a hand if we wanted to ask something otherwise she would speak.

An unknown girl raised her hand.

"When do we finish?"

I was happy to hear the question because it meant I didn't have to ask it myself. I was homesick and missed Ravi – in the first five minutes of the first school day.

The slightly offended teacher continued, "We finish in four hours. And by that time we will have fun…" She kept talking but I couldn't follow her words anymore. I wanted to be outside. Rain kept falling on the school windows creating a hollow patter.

"Ravi, Ravi, Ravi", I kept repeating in my head. I was calling him like I did before when he used to appear in the next second. First he would crack a joke and make me laugh and then we would go out…But this time my prayers were left unanswered. I could call him as much as I wanted but Ravi obviously was not able to come to this place, this hole full of strangers. I decided to give it another try at home.

I looked around the room. I concentrated and tried to find out what this place was really like – what the chairs were like, what the walls were like, what the big green board with magnets was like (what color they were)… What the things you could *touch* were like. Had I stayed in the stuffy hole, I felt inside, I could have gone mad with loneliness and horror…

It was a middle-sized room, the walls were turquoise green decorated with flowers up to a meter and a half and the rest of them up to the ceiling were white. The teacher gave as the assignment to look for red rectangles in the bags we had brought with us. I did it in five seconds. Ravi had explained the difference between square and round shapes ages ago. But he did it differently, not by sitting in a dark classroom. We watched the trees, the table, houses, the ball I played with…So when I had finished picking out rectangles I could go on observing the room.

Suddenly I noticed a head with dark brown curls like Ravi's in the second row, two desks to the left from where I was sitting.

I let out a scream of joy.

"Is there a problem?" the teacher asked. What was I to say to her? I think I have found purpose to my life? No, she had already misunderstood me before. I suppose I will have to get used to the fact that in the adult world you have to explain everything, every word. Because nobody reads your mind, and much less senses how you feel.

"Everything is fine." These were the first words I spoke ceremoniously in that God forsaken cave. "I'm helping Renata find rectangles." Luckily I had noticed just in time that Renata wasn't pleased with the task at all, grabbed her bag and resorted to a lie.

"OK. But don't do everything instead of her." the teacher said not wanting to argue. Renata and I had one thing in common – neither of us *really wanted* to be here. But different from me, she actually clearly showed that without being embarrassed.

I couldn't wait for recess to start. I didn't have to ask when that was because a girl called Alja had done it instead of me. She was the first one to start this line of questions. Somehow I got the feeling that none of us felt too well in that classroom and I thought that we just might become good friends joined by a common interest.

Minutes felt like hours. I kept looking at the second row. The curls would shake from time to time and then lower over a sheet of paper. But the head refused to turn so that I could see the face.

"I'm sure it's Ravi, it must be Ravi, he always comes when I call him. Maybe he is just playing and pretending not to see me..." And so the years, sorry, minutes went by. And then when I had almost given up hope, the teacher told us to wash our hands because we were to have a snack. I rushed from my chair to the second row. I patted the boy on the shoulder, "Ravi?"

Finally the curls turned. The face couldn't have been further away from what I had expected. There were some freckles on his big nose and they were bigger than mine. His cheeks were round and his eyes closer together than they should have been. Unevenly combed hair was falling to his low forehead. "My name is Miha", the boy said and wiped his nose with the back of his hand.

"Oh, I'm sorry." I lowered my eyes and my water hydrants started to fill up again. Obviously Ravi really wasn't allowed to come here and soon I'll be better than Alja in asking when this finishes. I lined up for my snack and got lost in the hustle and bustle around me. It seemed everybody could hardly wait to eat something. And I could hardly wait for this to finish. All of it. Who would want to live somewhere where nobody respects you and assesses you only on the basis of what you can repeat after others?

And so my first lunch break during which I had to try very hard not to burst into tears came to an end. Because I had already proven that I deserved the title "drama queen", I didn't want to sink even lower.

After lunch we spoke about the other shapes: circle, square…Colors: blue, yellow, green, red…As I did in the morning, I first found the shapes for myself and then for Renata who kept demonstrating my feelings.

A mellow melody came from a loud speaker and the teacher told us that it was composed by Mozart and explained to us it meant the school was out for the day. Mozart had just become my favorite composer.

I ran to where I had left my shoes and put them on quickly. The bag which seemed to be getting bigger and bigger kept bouncing off my right shoulder as if it wanted to tell the others that a big van with poorly closed back door was approaching. I threw my slippers under the bench and ran home without saying goodbye. I was lucky I didn't have to open the front door because the hall was full of students who were all in a hurry to get to the school bus and they were holding the door for each other. I knew I would get home faster if I ran so I set off quickly.

I quickly looked to my left and right and dashed across the road. I could hear Ela shouting after me:

"Wait up, Ina. I'm supposed to take you home!" Then she turned to her friends saying, "I'm sorry, I must go. The little brat has lost it completely."

Ela was running after me but I was three times faster. There is a huge difference between jogging and running to the source, to the purpose of everything.

I was getting closer to home. The house, which always looked so bright and colorful, seemed empty and washed out in the rain. The colors became diluted and the walls were gray. I noticed my face was getting dryer which meant it had stopped raining and I wasn't crying anymore. The only thing that was left was expectation. Pure expectation.

When I opened the door and got onto the house, I took time to take off my shoes – my mom was very sensitive to that and I didn't want any problems – and then I drew a deep breath for something that was more important. To scream from the top of my lungs.

IV. THE REALIZATION

"Raaavi!" I shouted from the front door without any shame. "Raaavi!"

I searched in all the places where I usually found him. Behind the door, under the bed, in my room, the pantry, I checked all the chandeliers, under all tables; I even opened the fridge just in case.

I couldn't find him anywhere. I ran behind the house, up the hill where he had tried to convince me not to attempt flying. Nothing.

When I had already given up hope, I noticed that something moved at the back door. Somebody closed them. Is it possible...

I ran so fast it looked more like teleporting than running. I pressed the doorknob with great expectations and opened the back door of the house: "Ravi?"

A familiar face looked at me but it wasn't the one I had expected.

"If you ever pull that off again and run off like that, I swear, you'll regret it, you little punk," Ela said breathlessly. "You better make sure it doesn't happen again!"

I froze with surprise. "OK."

"And one more thing: it's not cool at all to have imaginary friends. If you can't make friends, just be alone. Stop imagining you have invisible friends. Loonies do that and I don't want a loony for my sister. Get it?"

I collapsed into a chair when she said the last sentence. I felt embarrassed and defeated at the same time. With my last breath, before a watery curtain covered my eyes, I looked around the room for him to smile at me from a corner and prove to her and to me that nobody in this room was crazy. And bring me back to life with that smile.

He wasn't there. My eyes watered up and Ela lowered her tone by a decibel.

"I'm sorry. You know I want the best for you," she tried to apologize, "but you must understand this is not how you should deal with your problem."

I couldn't listen to her anymore. I ran to my room and shut the door. I threw myself on the bed and buried my face in the pillow. Finally. Here I was able to let out a cry that I had been carrying around with me all day. Into the pillow so nobody could hear me.

And I cried. As long as I had the strength to cry. Then I just sobbed. I don't remember when I fell asleep.

I sensed the color of dark chocolate, which was mixed with different shades of golden and bronze rays. In the center, I discovered a dark hole from which I swam and it was only when I got a couple of meters away and was able to see the whole picture from a wider perspective…The circle of brown, golden and bronze rays started to move away and I noticed a totally identical circle nearby which looked like a chocolate fountain. I kept swimming and suddenly I noticed that these two circles were parts of something bigger…Eyes. Face.

Before I was able to extend my hand and touch the face I had already swam too far away. A gorgeous pair of golden-bronze brown eyes, dark brown wavy hair, a heart-shaped face and such a familiar smile were lost to me in the universe without gravity…I realized I wasn't really swimming; I was flying. I wanted to fly back to find the face I had lost but I couldn't. I could only fly forward. So I lounged on to maybe find something that could help me find what I had lost.

I noticed a smaller planet of an irregular shape among other planets. Obviously it wasn't a planet at all. When I flew closer I saw a castle that had been built on a cloud. Although it looked fragile, I noticed how strong it was when I landed there. I landed on some sort of yard that invited the visitor to the castle where a ball was in progress on one side but on the other side there was a bottomless abyss. Obviously it was one tip of the planet. I noticed I was wearing a very suitable silver blue dress for the ball and I decided to go in. The only thing I didn't have was a mask. It was a masked ball.

The two doormen let me in but were not too happy about it so I felt quite unwanted. In the dance hall this feeling intensified. When I entered, people started turning towards me. At first this didn't bother me until what I didn't even want to sense happened. I knew I was different from them and they would cast me out so I looked down. A girl in a glittering black dress pushed me to the floor and pointed a finger at me. She said something to the effect of: "She's the one!" I didn't know what she meant. I only knew I did nothing wrong and that I was innocent. I just didn't belong there, to that court. Obviously.

I knew this would happen so I felt somehow relieved when it finally did happen. *I am different. I will be cast out.*

The guards, who looked quite pleased to take on the role of bouncers, surrounded me and grabbed me by the shoulders. They lifted me up as if they had caught a long sought-after bad guy. The satisfied low chatter of the crowd changed into loud sounds of approval when the bouncers quite aggressively dragged me out. The people wanted to show me one last time that they really didn't like me by tearing pieces of clothing of me, laughing at me and calling me names. I didn't know why but I quickly started feeling guilty. I looked down to see as little of what was going on as possible.

This was clearly a mistake because we arrived to the exit where they let me go and threw me to the ground. Because my eyes were half closed, this change was an unexpected surprise for me. I wasn't able to grab hold of anything or break the fall with my hands.

I was falling and finally hit the ground with my face. It had been raining outside so I fell into mud. People were still laughing and pointing at me and I was thinking to myself that I was alone and that I will probably stay that way. I saw my muddy reflection in a puddle. Alone in my own company. At least someone will always be there for me. Myself. I will always be alone. On the one hand this is good. I won't have to share my muddy puddle with anybody. I felt a strong pang of pain at this thought. I realized I wanted to share the puddle, mud, joy, happiness…And that was just empty consolation.

A shudder went though the noisy crowd and everybody went quiet. People started to draw apart. I started to crawl too to get out of the way because I didn't know what to expect. The crowd made a passageway and a young man whom everybody seemed to respect greatly came through. I stopped. I still lay on the ground supporting my upper body with my elbows to keep my face out of the water. I didn't care. I looked down into the ground where I lay.

Once you have been disclosed when you lie on the ground in the mud and it's more than clear that it can't get any worse, also the wish that people would care disappears. I was lying in the mud and I didn't care. Let him kill me, I don't care. Let me become a prisoner for life, I will find something to do. Let them torture me if this is what they want. It's really just pain in a small body, nothing more than that. I felt relieved because I had found myself in that puddle. It seemed as if I had just made a friend who will be with me in every situation, someone who will always be on my side. If not because of anything else, because she *has to* be. I smiled at myself for being so silly to try to find happiness outside myself, somewhere else.

The young man reached the end of the human corridor and stopped by my side. Nothing happened for a while so I decide to look up. He was wearing a very simple crown (which looked like the crown you can make from cardboard or colored paper – golden, simple with tips cut out). He bowed to me with respect and offered his right hand to me. I accepted it. Soon our eyes locked. Again I was looking into the eyes that I had seen so many times before. It seemed these eyes had changed so many shapes on different bodies and faces, but I would recognize their owner anywhere… He let go of my hand and moved both his hands closer before him as if he was holding an object. And he was. Another crown appeared in the golden haze between his hands. He lifted it up and held it for a while over my head. When he placed it on my head, our eyes locked a second time. This time for a longer period. The people had disappeared or I simply didn't see them anymore. I saw brown, golden and bronze rays, the smile worth a thousand other smiles, the heart-shaped face with a small dimple in the chin…And I knew that this time we were equal. I don't *need* him but I just *want* him around me. I felt loved and loving at the same time. So simple. So equal. So free. As it should be.

Silence. All thoughts amalgamated into one love. We didn't need speech. We knew. He smiled at me and I smiled back. Instead of captivity, I was given the biggest freedom in the world. *Thank you,* I thought. He understood. He reached out his hand and I knew he would do it.

His right hand caressed my left cheek. I felt the happiest I had ever been. That happiness had nothing in common with the happiness you feel when you get a chocolate bar, it can't be compared to the experience of being given anything. This happiness simple *is*, it always has been and it always will be. It had been waiting for me up to that moment. And now I was here, with *him*. In that happiness. Forever.

V. THE CONVERSATION

I FELT A PALM SLIDING DOWN MY CHEEK AND I WAS STILL SMILING. This time it felt more organic, more material. The friction between the skin cells on the palm and those on the cheek. The feeling of absolute peace was substituted with the realization that I was in my body again and that the universal peace and happiness I felt was only a dream. I opened my eyes.

"I'm glad you are feeling better," said my mom. "Ela told me you had quite an adventure."

"What did she tell you?" I asked quickly. I was totally awake.

"Well, only that the two of you came home from school and then a sound…as if somebody was being skinned alive came from your room and it lasted for an hour."

So she didn't tell on me that I had left school without her. I must make up to her for that.

"Mom, I…" I stopped and swallowed hard. I didn't know whether I should tell her the truth or not. She would become very sad when I mentioned Ravi and I began to imagine why. And that he knew why too.

"Your friend *Ravi*…" she said his name the first time.

"…we don't have to talk about him." I wanted to change the subject as if I felt her mood would change again.

"I wanted to say that I'm sorry if I worried too much. It's nice to have friends like this but now you are entering a real world with real friends. You can learn a lot of interesting things that will prepare you for life in school," she continued.

"It is not necessary that we go through our lives dreaming," she added.

"I know, mom. OK."

"Promise me something, please," she said caringly.

"If you had kids, you would want what's best for them, wouldn't you?" she looked at me and smiled like only a mother knows how – warmly and protectively.

"Sure, mom."

"Try to be as friendly as you can at school. If you are good to others it comes back to you. Even if others are not good to you, don't let that make you think otherwise. Maybe it's just a test how many times you can react calmly and lovingly.

"OK, mom."

"Also try to do as you are told. The teachers are there to teach you something so try to be as nice to them as to the others," she pleaded with me. It seemed she was giving me very important instructions; the tone of her voice told me I should listen more carefully than usually. Like I was receiving important instructions how to fly a space ship and I could hear them only once before I'm sent into space.

"If you need help with studying, you can always turn to me or your sister. Remember that learning new things is as exciting as playing but it is even better: you are really discovering the world you are living in. While learning new things you can find something that you will really enjoy doing, you can find new friends."

"OK, mom," I answered. I noticed that mom had changed a bit. I had a feeling she became wiser. That she was talking to me as she hadn't done before. When she spoke about learning and discovering new things, I had the feeling that I had heard that before…and not from her mouth.

"I love you, Ina. And I will always want what's best for you so I must tell you another little thing."

"Yes?"

"You know I don't mind if you cry. I think that with crying we release some of the emotions we keep pent up in ourselves and so we can be kinder and more relaxed with others when we get rid of these feelings.

"You cry too?"

"Sure I do," she smiled reassuringly, "but sometimes it is better if we cry alone because other people might interpret our tears wrongly. They might think we don't like their company, that we feel sick or something else. And there are also people who make fun of us if we cry. I want to protect you, pumpkin, so try not to cry in front of other people."

I knew she just wanted the best for me. She wanted to protect me.

"OK. I'll try."

"This doesn't mean that you can't cry in front of me. You can always come to me when you feel bad." She smiled conspiratorially. "We'll cry together."

That's a sight I'd like to see! Mother and daughter screaming into a pillow together. I smiled.

"I hope you will console me with words and that we don't have to cry at the same time," I corrected her statement. We laughed.

"I'm so glad you are feeling a bit better. The first school day can be quite difficult for anybody."

You can say that again.

"You must learn how to overcome that. You can set additional tasks for yourself to make the time pass quicker. I always used a little trick when I was at school." She winked conspiratorially.

"Trick?" My level of interested shot up. I really wanted to know how to survive that eternity hours others call a normal school morning.

"Mhm," proudly said mom. "What do you do to make the morning at school pass faster than you can say recess?"

I shook my head with surprise. "I don't know." But I really wanted to find out.

She dragged out telling me as if she was about to reveal the biggest secret and she wanted to make sure I really deserved to hear it. Finally she made up her mind and lowered her head towards me. She spoke slowly and ceremoniously.

"So that you become really *interested* in the whole thing."

"Really – interested?" I didn't quite grasp her words.

"When you are really interested in what the teacher is saying, may it be mathematics which will be really useful for you; nature or how to speak another language, the lessons start passing at the blink of an eye," she made a funny face and I laughed.

"Really?"

"Hours turn into minutes, no, seconds," she continued, "and before you know it, the lesson is over. There is only one tiny little problem," she went on.

"What's the problem?" I was totally into it. What could be bad about lessons ending in five seconds?

"You wish they didn't finish so fast. But we can overcome that problem too. That's why there is homework with which you can satisfy you hunger for more at home," she said and smiled.

I had never talked to her like that before and I felt I was gaining another friend. Suddenly school stopped seeming so cruel. If I become interested in what the teacher is saying, maybe I will stop seeing the dark cave instead of a classroom. I will focus my attention elsewhere. I won't have to think about Ravi, I won't have to be sad. Maybe the time will pass quicker without fear and sadness. To be really *interested* in what the teacher is saying…"even if it is only how many rectangles I have in my bag?" I asked mom.

"Even only that," she nodded wisely. "She might give you more tasks later if you ask her. Teachers are not so scary, you know. They really like such inquisitive little people as you are."

I sat up in my bed feeling reassured.

"OK. From now on I will be really interested in whatever we talk about at school."

I decided that more for myself than for her. Because of all the benefits I will get from such behavior.

"Guess what? I picked up some chocolate ice cream with cookies from the store today and I won't be able to eat it myself. Do you want to help me? We can pick up Ela on our way," she smiled.

"Sure!" I got up and started walking not only towards the ice cream but also towards tomorrow, school and a new life.

VI. THE SCHOOL

WHEN I GOT UP AND HAD MY BREAKFAST THE NEXT DAY, I KEPT going over yesterday's events in my head. I wanted Ravi to make contact and I still tried to call him once in a while. I was torn between the outside world and my own world and I somehow knew which one would prevail. Which one would *have to* prevail.

Before I opened the school door that day I promised to myself to do as I was told for the next nine years. I would try the trick of being interested in everything, I would try to do what I was told and at the same time keep negative emotions to myself. But when all this was over I would live as I pleased. I didn't know how at that time. But I knew there had to be more to life than this. Had to be.

The days started to pass faster and I started to mark as much as I could what reality meant to other people. My reality was: my name is Ina Kralj. My parents' names are Amalija Kralj and Zoran Kralj but I call them mom and dad. I have brown bobbed hair. My mom combs my hair but I prefer it tousled. My nose is small and covered with freckles. I'm very small for my age, which really gets on my nerves. My mom says that there will be time when I'll be pleased I look younger. I live in a small village, half an hour's drive from Ljubljana, the capital of this country. We are in the Republic of Slovenia, which is a part of the European Union. I attend elementary school, which seems really huge to me.

I was getting used to being in the green classroom full of my classmates every day. I wasn't too sociable. I liked Renata. She was always rather quiet and people avoided her. But I liked her because she was never afraid to show how she felt. She always expressed exactly what she felt. I was really sad when she moved to Ljubljana after six months. I had a feeling that she never judged me like the others did.

I spoke to the other classmates but I never had the feeling that we got on. I always felt there was a glass wall between us that I wasn't able to knock down no matter how hard I tried. For the first time I felt on my own skin what status in the society, in the classroom meant. The unspoken rules which prevailed in communication. *If you have a new bike, you have many friends. If you dare to insult somebody, you are strong. If you spit on the floor, you are cool. If you fight, you are brave. If you know a lot, you are a dork. If you don't take religious classes after school, you are not part of the crowd…*

I begged mom to enroll me in religious classes. Those who attended religious classes went there directly after school, and the majority went. They always left school early, they laughed as if they knew more than the other kids and there were times when they wore formal clothes of light colors and received big and important presents. Mom always said it had to do with religious conviction and that I would decide for that when I grew up. Today I understand her and I'm grateful. But at that time… No, I didn't understand. Not at all. I didn't understand what hanging out with friends, big shiny presents and one lesson a day had to do – with religion. It seemed they were meeting in some kind of secret society that was very popular. And I could never have that feeling.

But I did start to enjoy the lessons at school. I used the trick of being interested in everything and the lessons went by faster than the recesses. Soon the teachers started giving me additional tasks, which made me very happy. I had to put a lot of effort into not showing too much satisfaction because I soon discovered that learning new things was not too popular among other students. But it was interesting to see how the class grouped up according to who got on with whom. "Pretty girls" (always wearing different shades of pink, their school bags covered with crystals), "popular girls" (they had the power to pronounce you the most popular person and opposite; they liked to speak very loudly and sometimes, as part of the protocol, they would even hit somebody) and "weird girls" (those who enjoyed studying definitely belonged to this group because the other two groups didn't accept different types of people and also not the above described type). The downside of our group was that it wasn't as connected as the others, we didn't stick together and so we were pretty weak.

The boys basically belonged to two groups: fighters (big group) and those-who-are-afraid-to-be-fighters. Fighters risked a lot and they had an adventure waiting for them after every lesson. Either in front of the school or in the classroom itself. They were very popular with the girls who belonged to the first two groups. The third group of girls wasn't in high demand.

It's a pity I belonged to the third group because I didn't think I was weird. More…different.

There were three more girls beside me in the "weird" group: a fun girl with long brown hair called Katja; a quiet girl called Bojana, who was a bit taller than the rest of us and who sat totally still also during the recesses; and Alja, who always wanted to know when the lessons would end.

I liked hanging out with Katja. Her eyes would light up whenever she was telling us something even if it was just every day gossip: " Have you noticed that Melita has a new jacket?" or "The teacher sent Helena to the headmaster." She was simple but fun. The only thing that made me sad was that she would always vanish into thin air whenever an attack of one of the other groups was about to take place. She was nowhere to be found although I could swear I had talked to her only a second before. She was probably afraid because the other two groups were very strong and there was always a struggle for dominance, for survival. If only Katja knew the group would be stronger if we worked together…

In the pretty girls group a girl called Iris stood out. She came from a very wealthy family and you could see that she was different from the other girls. She was very pretty and she liked to accentuate her beauty with pink hairpins, bracelets and heart-shaped rings. She was the leader of her group without being chosen by the other members. This is just how it was. When she first stepped into the classroom, the other girls who wanted to be as pretty as she was gathered around her. And the group was formed. The other members were: Nina, Laura, Tjaša, Maja and Simona.

The popular girls differed from the pretty ones in the fact that they wore less pink items. They were nicely dressed too but they were more verbally aggressive and they enforced law and order. Well, not always fairy. They attacked members of the third group many times. They would tease, taunt, play practical jokes and think up funny names for the classmates. The first and second group didn't attack each other – they ruled in harmony. Tina was the leader of the popular group. She kept repeating one and the same phrase: "C'mon, get lost, will you" whether she wanted to get rid of somebody or just hear her own voice saying that out loud. The following girls liked hanging out with her: Ksenija (who enjoyed hitting people), Katarina, Melita, Helena and Tadeja.

There were only four boys in our class: Tine, Primož, Miha and Domen. Besides being a fighting hero, Tine was also the most handsome boy in class. All the girls were in love with him. He had blond hair of medium length and a baby face. His full lips and blue eyes were the reason why his name was written in heart shapes in so many girls' notebooks. He was really good-looking but he didn't know how to talk nicely. Tine and Primož would have an argument over totally unimportant things, like for example the weather, the color of trousers or whether the lunch was tasty of not. What followed was a fight during which all the pretty girls would smile enthusiastically, and Tina's clan would cheer and clap loudly. Domen was usually pretty laid-back and he enjoyed attending religious classes. He wore glasses and went out of the classroom during every recess to prevent the other boys from taunting him. He and Miha belonged to the "those-who-are-afraid-to-fight" group.

And so the months went by. The mornings passed very quickly because I was really interested in what we were studying. Tina thought up the nickname Dwarf for me and it stuck till the end of elementary school. So when we met she would upgrade her typical catchphrase and it sounded like this: "C'mon. Get lost, Dwarf." It was meant just for me. So I didn't really enjoy meeting her. If I saw her coming towards me, I busied myself with something or went to the restroom. At least there I had my peace. For now.

In the afternoons when we didn't have lessons it was more difficult. Ela was busy with her friends; mom and dad were busy with adult things (work, cleaning, cooking…). Mom did help me many times with my homework and I liked spending time with her. And I could see she also enjoyed being with me. This might have had something to do with her loving teaching. She would drive to Ljubljana every morning where she worked as a teacher. Sometimes we would play games together or she would join me while I was brushing my teeth. She would stand next to me and bump into me with her hip gently as if she was trying to knock me over which always gave me a pleasant feeling of safety.

My dad was pretty quiet. He worked in a lab in Ljubljana and he studied insects. When he came home from work he would hug Ela and me telling us that he loved us. Many times he was really tired and he napped on the sofa, also when he was supposed to watch Ela and me.

Although I knew my parents really loved me there was something missing. I felt what it was but I didn't allow myself to think of it. Think of *him*. I wanted to suppress the memory of him into my subconscious and make him stay there. Whenever I thought of him I started yearning. I felt pain first in my stomach and them in my heart. When the feeling reached my head I had already started to cry. And I was trying to stop that. Why be sad if that wasn't necessary?

Many times I would simply take my color pencils and started drawing. Not very well at the beginning (Iris was much better then me in art class) but I was able to relax in this way. My imagination flew like when I hung out with Ravi. Drawing helped me get through so many rainy afternoons. If the weather was nice, I sometimes went drawing on the hill behind our house. The view of the sun setting and the peaceful settlement between hills always made me feel better although I was alone. I wanted to draw the peace and quiet I felt and the mood I was in when I looked down. I spent a lot of time before I learnt which colors to use and where to shade buildings (it was only later in art class that I sometimes did it correctly). Visiting the hill behind our house was always a special and pleasant experience. Because there was a graveyard below, there were never too many people here. I liked my town although it was small.

And so the school year slowly came to an end. I passed with excellent grades and so I got another nickname – Dork, and now Tina's catchphrase sounded something like this: "C'mon, get lost, Dorky Dwarf. My behavior was marked as exemplary. Because I wasn't familiar with this word I became a little scared. The word sounded strange and suspicious. The smiling teacher explained to me that it meant other people should follow my example. It was difficult to imagine that this would ever be possible in our class hierarchy.

VII. THE PERIOD OF HORMONES

AND SO THE YEARS WENT BY. To prevent myself from thinking about my lost friendship I wanted keep myself busy during my first school vacation. Many times I would grab the hoover and said to my surprised mom: "Don't worry about it. I'll do it," while she just shook her head incredulously. Ela came by, looked at me and hissed, "Suck-up." But I knew this was much better for me than sitting on the stairs and remembering the lovely experiences from previous summer.

Mom would sometimes give me money for the work I had done and I realized my allowance was substantially higher than Ela's. She was really mad about this since I was younger than her. She kept her friends away from me, she simply thought I was too young to hang out with her. She was nice to me only when she wanted money from me. She didn't borrow it from me, I gave it to her. We did a trade off: I would give her money and she would do my makeup or play with me for half an hour. Sometimes she did my nails. I felt really good at such times because she was so nice to me although I knew this was probably just for the money.

The summer passed quickly and soon I found myself in school again. Second, third, fourth and fifth grades went by. Besides going to summer and winter camps where I learned to swim and ski (of course this didn't pass without Tina's taunting me with "Dwarf in water" and "Dwarf on skis") the years were pretty boring. But I did really like the lessons. We learned about Egypt, the Greek, nature, Slovene language, writing, drawing, music, singing and physical education. I attended all extra-curricular activities that existed in our school (the choir, painting, mathematics, journalism, photo, drama, writing, English, dancing and lace-making where we made simple lace). Those classes were available for students from fourth grade on.

The classroom seemed more crowded each year. It no longer seemed as big as it did on the first day. Probably because we were bigger every year. It happened many times that you would have to think for a second or two before you recognized a fellow student after the vacation. I was still the smallest although my mom tried to convince me I was growing fast.

Meeting Tina on the first day of seventh grade was very interesting. By coincidence we came to the school door at the same time but from the opposite directions. I couldn't get out of her way or hide. When I noticed her it was too late. I decided to step through the door bravely and hope she leaves me be. When I took the door handle and started to open the door she hung on it with all her strength making it close with a bang. She squinted.

"Hmh, who might this be…" she pretended she was trying to remember where she knows my face from.

"Oh, that's you, Dwarfy Dork."

She never made the effort use the feminine form of the noun since it was intended for me and I was a girl. Actually she preferred it that way because it sounded even more demeaning.

"Hello Tina," I said. "Can I please go inside?"

She grabbed the handle fast and opened the door making it hit me on the head. When she came through, all I could hear beside the pain in my head was the eco of her always-present greeting: "C'mon. Get lost, Dwarfy Dork."

Otherwise not many things had changed in my class, it was only that the characteristics of my classmates grew with them. Iris looked even better, Alja got used to not bugging the teacher with questions anymore, but she occupied herself with writing and corresponding on small slips of paper torn from the back of her notebook. Katja knew more and more news, who was in love with whom and why. Somebody usually made up such news and then it circulated the school making it easier for the students to pass the time. Tine looked more and more like those jeans models. He was the coolest guy in our class if not the entire school and he enhanced his status with regular arguments and fights mostly with Primož.

What about me? My behavior was still exemplary, I was still more interested in what we were studying than anything else. Except…I noticed changes in myself and others. The world was becoming less and less mysterious and more and more inviting and pleasant-smelling. I would look at myself in the mirror and I had a feeling that a part of me wanted to be liked by the others. To be liked by the boys. I wanted to be pretty too. Sometimes my stomach started to tingle and even hurt when I watched a romantic movie. When I told my mom about that, she smiled and said: "Don't worry, it's the hormones…"

And to make things worse, Ela started to hang out with boys. Soon she met a "serious" boy and they started dating. I felt that Ela was, because of the hormones, experiencing the world in a similar way as I did although she still didn't trust me. She trusted her girlfriends and her boyfriend. In the evenings many times because she was eighteen years old.

For her eighteenth birthday she got a sum of money the parents had saved for her since her birth and a gorgeous and mysterious golden heart-shaped locket. It had two small buttons that opened in a secret way known only to its owner. So Ela and mom went to the goldsmith who showed Ela in private how it worked. Neither mom nor I knew the secret. And soon I didn't even care anymore. Whenever I would broach the subject of what was in the locket, Ela self-confidently retorted it was none of my business.

One night Ela was out with her boyfriend and I couldn't sleep. Snoring was coming from mom and dad's room and it felt like I was home alone. I wasn't afraid at all. I felt like I singe-handedly ruled this fortress at the end of our street. I grabbed a sweater and went outside. Although fall was in the air, it was one of those October nights when it is still warm enough to go outside wearing only your pajamas. Like the nature was saying goodbye to summer and blessing us with a couple of nights which are considerably warmer than they should be. I came through the door and looked out to the street. Our house was a little away from the rest of the neighborhood but still close enough to reach school in five and store in three minutes. There was a graveyard on the hillside behind the house and there was a pleasant glow of candles above it.

I went towards those lights when I heard a car approaching. It was too late to step back inside so I quickly hid behind the back wall of the house from where I could see the entrance very well. The car stopped on the drive and two shadows stepped out. One of them was Ela and the other...her "steady" boyfriend.

"Thank you, Grega, it was great," Ela said and smiled. She was totally different than she was at home, when she was talking to me. It felt like I wasn't looking at her but watching a nice romantic film.

"You are great," he returned the compliment and pushed her gently against the car. He put his hands on either sides of her like he wanted to stop her from leaving. The moonlight and the light on our drive illuminated their faces and I could see that the smile was slowly disappearing from their faces. Soon they became strangely serious. It was only now that I noticed that my heart had started beating wildly. Why? My mom would say it had to do with hormones. I wished I could find these little devils that disturbed my life and played with my heart.

The silhouettes started to move closer. Their lips were totally still and relaxed and waited for it to happen. Without pouting. Soon a pain in my stomach joined the wild heartbeat that seemed to eco around the neighborhood. I felt butterflies in my stomach that no doctor could cure. Every expert helplessly blames hormones, before he is consumed by laughter. Why was I shivering? I wasn't kissing anyone, she was!

Soon after their lips met there was a smack that I heard live for the first time. Usually I saw such kisses only in films, mom and dad didn't kiss like that. The second kiss followed but this time their faces were tilted differently. And another time. Suddenly Gregor's hand was on her back drawing her closer to him. More kisses. And more inexplicable feelings on my part.

He stroked her cheek with his left hand and she went though his hair with her fingers. What followed was a sigh of pleasure and desire. Then she stepped back.

"Good night," she said smiling.

"C'mon, Ela. When will you stop torturing me?"

"I've already told you I want to take it slowly," she said on the doorstep.

"But if you really want to know, our anniversary would make a suitable time. What do you think?"

The boy let out a helpless moan and said goodbye. He sat in the car and Ela was already nowhere to be seen. I was alone again and I started thinking if other animals also had problems with the little rascals and if hormones could be surgically removed.

Soon I went back into the house and creped into bed. Nobody saw me. But I couldn't sleep that night. It was already morning when I fell asleep.

VIII. TUTORING

BECAUSE I WAS STILL SUSTAINING – AT THE EXPENSE OF MY POPULARITY – the state of all-encompassing interest and with it very good grades (sometimes I got a B in a test on purpose) the teacher soon named me the class tutor. In this field I surpassed even Iris. Since her wish to be beautiful prevailed over her wish for knowledge I still had much better grades than her. It's true, though, that mainly boys needed tutoring. That's why I was frequently uncomfortable, especially when I was alone in the classroom with Tine. I knew that all the girls wanted to be in my place when the teacher assigned us to study after school.

Tine showed me a sort of respect, mostly when we were alone. There were moments when he had to lean forward to take his eraser (which happened frequently considering his poor math knowledge) and then, after use, instead of leaving it somewhere within his reach, he put it back near me, like he wasn't going to need it again.

My heart beat much faster when I was with him and I wondered if he could hear it. Sometimes he'd make a joke of some mathematical law and laughter would come from my throat like I never knew was in me! It seemed so strange, phony, nervous and giggling. I knew that *I didn't laugh like that*. Usually I'd be tense for at least an hour after the tutoring ended. And then I'd be totally depressed for four hours at home. I'd wonder if he loved me and daydream about long walks along the beach and him holding my hand. He'd whisper sweet nothings to me and I'd laugh. Not

just my belly, my whole body would ache and radiate in expectation…
And then he'd suddenly pull me close to him and…Unavoidable meeting
of lips…Paradise…

A minute of fulfillment usually followed. Then I'd realize that I was
sitting in my room and how pathetic the whole situation was. Of course
he didn't have feelings for me. After all, it was just me. While Iris was…
Iris. *That* Iris. The most beautiful girl in the world. That's how it was and
that's how it'd always been. I sank low again and was sick of constant
mood swings – from euphoria and giggling to endless depressions.

Soon I wasn't feeling hungry anymore. I couldn't eat on account of all
these feelings, because food was making me sick. I was constantly hurting
all over and it didn't matter to me if I was a little hungry in addition to
that. My mom noticed that I was acting strangely and she couldn't stop
worrying. Ela thought of a new nickname for me – »Sleepwalker«.

She soon – in the middle of one of my personal dramas, when I was
crying because Tine probably didn't like me – knocked on my doors.

»Ina, what's wrong?« she asked without sugarcoating.

After a brief quarrel about there being nothing wrong with me (I
couldn't sell that to the world's greatest dummy, anyway) I briefly explained to her what was going on. I left out those parts about my stupid
daydreaming, naturally. Nevertheless, she managed to understand what
was really going on with me and she sighed deeply.

»This is more serious than I thought,« she said thoughtfully, although
I didn't know exactly if she was really that concerned about me or if she
was just amused like all the others when they see how you're suffering
because of puberty, hormones or whatever that sickness is called.

»Love is a funny thing,« she said and burst out laughing. I knew that
in reality she was amused by all of that!

Before I managed to get upset again she threw a suggestion at me:
»Why don't you simply tell him that?«

She confused me. Until now I've confined myself to beautiful day-
dreams about my Prince Charming, about walks with Tine, about kisses…I

wasn't really interested in reality just yet, because it scared me too much. That's why I've been – except for tutoring – avoiding him like the plague. *Nobody* could know. And now all of a sudden a suggestion I should tell him. Should I tell him? How – can I – just – tell him?

»Maybe you could write to him,« said mom. »It's better to know how he feels than to suffer all your life like that. You could die if you stop eating!«

That was true. Maybe that way I could show those little maggots that there's no fooling around with me. They can't just play with me like that and expect everything to pass without consequences. I'll write a note. A nice, short, pleasant love note that will explain everything.

Mom agreed with me. Having too little experience with writing love notes I turned to her. This time I wasn't the only one awake all night for a change. Now we were awake together. I remembered her promise on the first day of school. She said I could always count on her. And I really felt that. Why did I cry that time? I knew I was missing one little part, an *important* little part, which I couldn't connect into my life anymore. It was so long ago...

IX. THE NOTE

»Dear Tine,
I just want you to know that I like you very much.
If you feel the same, we can talk about it when we study math.
Best regards,
Ina«

MOM THOUGHT THAT LOVE NOTES MUSTN'T BE TOO OBVIOUS. My suggestions were: "I love you", "I keep thinking about you" and "every time I see you, my heart starts pounding"…When we were finished and the million crumpled pieces of paper lying around the bed had been cleared away (apparently a perfectly normal procedure when writing a love note – you're writing to a person you love, you're not satisfied with your first draft and neither with the five hundredth one), it was already dawning. I lay in bed for an hour clearing my thoughts. I couldn't sleep anyway.

When the alarm clock went off I got up and tried acting as if the upcoming day wasn't particularly important. I wanted to find inconspicuous, yet still attractive T-shit, inconspicuous, yet still attractive pair of tight jeans, inconspicuous, yet still color harmonized pair of flat pumps and inconspicuous, yet still present perfume described as: »Musk, the perfume men can't resist«.

And so inconspicuously dressed I headed off to school. Before I went my mom conspiratorially winked at me and said significantly: »Have a *successful* day at school, dear!«

On my way to school I thought about how to execute my little plan. Using a messenger? No way, everyone would know everything immediately. Unfortunately I still haven't found a friend I could trust completely. Should I just hand over the note to him? When? During tutoring? But it suggests talking during tutoring! He needs time to read the note, to think about it…He must get it as soon as possible…What if I simply put it in his bag during recess? During the first recess, to give him more time…That's right, yes. If he doesn't find it, it's obviously not meant for us to be together.

I got to the school. My heart was pounding so hard that I welcomed school hustle and bustle, which subdued my excitement and ensured that my pulse rate remained my secret. I changed my footwear and put my jacket in my locker. I took my books and headed towards the upper floor for our class meeting. Marija, our home-class teacher (otherwise our math teacher), talked about some end-of-school-year program and about summer holidays. Is the end of school year already near? Have I been tortured almost the whole school year? I realized that this year I probably wouldn't have straight A's, because in the second half of the school year something else overtook my primary interest of wanting to know everything. My daydreaming was interrupted by the sound of a name being repeated like a steady ringing of the bronze church bell…

»Ina! Ina!« The teacher tried to establish contact with me while I was obviously asleep.

»Not only have your grades dropped, now you sleep during class?«

Miss Marija tried to be friendly and pedagogic at the same time, because I'd never been insulting or otherwise disobedient towards her before.

»You can still have straight A's, you know,« she continued dramatically. »If you try really hard!« It seemed to me that my success meant more to *her* than it did to me. My regression must've been pretty tragic for her.

»I'll try,« I said not too convincingly just to get her off my back. »I apologize for being…absent-minded.«

»And then some,« said Primož and the whole classroom laughed.

The laughter made me wake up, blush and realize that the class was almost over. Which meant – recess. The teacher made a note about the absentees and asked if anybody had any additional questions. Her question was interrupted by a gentle Mozart melody, which never before seemed so terrifying to me...

X. THREE, TWO, ONE...

THE FAMILIAR MELODY PROPELLED THE STUDENTS FROM THE CLASSROOM. The only one to stay behind was the quiet Bojana, who still liked to remain seated as she did seven years ago. That confused me. I had hoped to *stay alone*. Maybe I would be able to stick the note somewhere where he could find it more easily…And so we remained seated. I looked at her.

»It's nice to have a break,« I started the conversation hiding my nervousness.

»Mhm,« she replied in short.

»It's nice to be able to go out whenever you want to during the recess. To the bathroom too, if you need to,« I tried to steer her out.

»Yeah, great.«

»And it's a much prettier outlook from the other side of the hall than it is from the classroom,« I encouraged her.

»Why don't you go and enjoy it, if you like it so much,« she replied coldly. »I'm not stopping you.«

»Nah, it's O.K.« I started sweating heavily.

Primož burst into the classroom. He obviously succeeded in offending Tine again. He was shoving the desks and the chairs around, blocking his classmate's way. An audience had already gathered around the happening and everyone sure cheered for the class heartbreaker…

That's the right opportunity! I couldn't believe that he was the one enabling me to carry out my plan properly, without being seen by anybody!

I quickly drew nearer to his schoolbag. Even though everything happened quickly, it seemed very slow to me. Like in slow motion. His schoolbag, deliberately torn in several places (giving the impression of numerous victories and thus appearing cool) was leaning against the desk on the floor, slightly open. My trembling steps had reminded me that I was forgetting how to walk from the excitement. All my thoughts poured into the small envelope I was carrying in my hand. I was afraid that my sweaty palm would moisten it, thus destroying the aesthetics. So I held it with just two fingers.

The boys were still fighting, although exceptionally slowly. My hair suddenly covered my face, so I had to move it away with my free hand to be able to see the target. I shifted from one foot to the other and then leaned on the desk. I crossed my arms and aimed the note with the corner of my eye as if dropping a bomb from an airplane. I closed my eyes and parted the fingers. I dropped the work of art my mom and I had been creating the whole night. In spite of the hustle and bustle I was still able to hear the quiet, papery sound of the envelope landing in the schoolbag.

After that everything started to happen extremely quickly. As if a filmmaker would fast-forward a recording, the recess had ended quickly and we were already sitting in the geography class.

I couldn't focus during the entire class. Geography teacher became, like Miss Marija, visibly dramatic every single time he looked in my direction. At one time he cleared his throat and asked me if I knew the answer, to which I replied I didn't. It seemed to me that his eyes were wet. He told me that I could still succeed if I really wanted, but that I had to find interest in our world. Interest in where we're living. Then he generalized the whole thing by saying that he expects from all of us to make an effort to achieve a good result by the end of the school year.

Every time Tine reached in his bag I felt as if my heart and stomach had switched places and then returned to their original positions. It hurt very badly. He sat in the row in front of me during the geography class, so I was able to watch his every move.

When the bell finally announced the end of class, we gathered our stuff and headed towards the arts classroom. We assembled robots out of geometrical forms and drew them. I noticed that Iris smudged the pencil-drawn shadows with her fingers thus making her drawing look like a black-and-white photograph. I had my difficulties – but not only with drawing robots. I shivered every time when the fair-haired boy facing me needed something from his military-green bag…

After the endlessly long arts class we headed for the math classroom. I was almost convinced that the note had fallen from his bag. The panic engulfed me. If the note had fallen from his bag, it could be lying on the floor. It could have been picked up by anybody. It mentions both our names, *his and mine*. That would've made sensational news – not just for our class, but also for the entire school!

Within the next five minutes of recess I quickly retraced the route we'd made that day: the math classroom, the geography classroom, the arts classroom and back to the math classroom. I found nothing. So the note must have been in the bag, in his possession, in the math classroom. We had the double math class waiting, which I wasn't looking forward to at all. Writing the home assignment had been replaced by creating a love masterpiece for a fair-haired breaker of innocent hearts.

After the first math lesson we got a little break. I was almost calmed down, because it looked like Tine was going to find the note at home and will thus have the chance to think about his feelings in peace. I will probably get my reply tomorrow. What is done is done. Now I can't take anything back.

When the next math class began, we sat down and started solving whatever each of us had left from the previous class. The teacher asked if anyone had a question. Tine raised his hand.

»Go ahead, Tine,« she enthusiastically exclaimed. Tine usually didn't ask questions, because he simply wasn't interested in mathematics. If you don't know, what the lecture is about, you can't ask questions. I thought he must be so enthusiastic about math because *I* had been tutoring him. In my euphoria I hadn't had the slightest premonition of what was about to happen.

»I wonder if you could come here for a minute,« said Tine, as if plagued by a slightly bigger mathematical problem.

The rest of the class were doing their assignments and weren't particularly interested in who was asking what. They were happy with being off the teacher's spotlight.

The teacher stayed with him for a while and I couldn't hear anything past a few subdued »Aha«s and astonished »Mhm«s.

Before long I felt a hand on my shoulder. I was startled and I flinched.

»Don't be scared,« the teacher reassured me. »I just want to show you this.« She held a folded piece of paper in her hands. »Tine found this in his textbook and since it has your signature, it must be yours…«

The class went silent. All eyes were pointed at me. Now I was more concerned with the color of my face than the throbbing of my heart. I felt the pulse in my head while the blood rushed even in the tiniest veins on my face; I knew that it must have turned crimson…

»Well?« she lowered her head even closer to me.

»Is this *really* yours?«

Confused I took the paper in my hands. »Mhm,« I muttered. The class buzzed with satisfaction. I just provided them with enough gossip for the rest of their lives…

»Do you know how she blushed?« »She admitted writing the note.« »It said she wanted to make out with him.« »It says she loves him.« »She said in front of the entire class she was in love.« »She's not pretty and now she's not even smart.« »That was the most entertaining math class ever«

In my agony I quickly collected my things and left the class without saying a word. I didn't care if I got detention for it. It can't get worse than it already is. On my way out I quickly glanced towards Tine's desk. He was bent over his assignment and didn't look especially affected. Quite the contrary. It seemed that he was really interested in math. *At least something*, I thought.

I wanted to get out of the classroom before I burst into tears and I managed to do that. I changed my footwear and got dressed in peace. When I hastened towards home the thought of nobody being there gave me some relief. I picked up the pace and soon found myself before the front door. I changed and sat on the bed. On the same bed I sat with my mom yesterday, discussing how it's important to participate, not just to win, how love was interesting and how in this day and age, in the twenty-first century, girls frequently take the initiative. I caught sight of myself in the mirror. The sight of a small seventh-grader with freckled nose and average face. Alone. Completely alone. The sight was getting foggier and foggier... Three, two, one...I took a deep breath and started sobbing uncontrollably.

XI. AWAY!

AT THE THOUGHT OF WHAT LAY AHEAD IN THE NEXT COUPLE OF years, of how much gossip material I had given my classmates and the unenviable situation I found myself in, a flood of tears, worth at least five hours of crying welled up in me. I wasn't keeping track of time, but I knew that darkness had fallen outside when I finished sobbing completely worn out. Mom came in my room during my crying and consoled me, then dad, and even Ela felt sorry for me. I didn't want to be pitied by anybody. I wanted to get away from here. I imagined that there had to be people like me somewhere who knew exactly what I was thinking and how I felt. They knew that human (or hormonal) feelings mustn't and can't be made fun of. They knew that we are all alike and should be friends. We are all human, so why would we want to ridicule and despise each other?

I decided to *try to stand by myself as best as I could*. Mom undoubtedly had my best interest in mind with her proposal and I would probably give the same advice to my daughter if I saw her suffering. But she wasn't hearing the nickname Dorky Dwarf like me every day, tutoring Tine with me, struggling through difficult moments with me when I had nobody to talk to during recesses. *I* was the one going through all that. If I didn't stand by myself now, I would never learn to do that. This is merely about a little girl in a small elementary school in a small town in the world. How many little girls had experienced that, or worse, in the history of mankind? And today – do we know who they were? No, the world has forgotten that it ever happened. The world moves on. So should I.

I also decided to pay no regard to the hormones. My feelings were the death of me and I experienced that probably more than the next person. Tears may very well point to the fact that one is sad, but I became aware of the *breadth* of that feeling. The depth of sadness. All possible dimensions, color nuances, tastes of human feelings that nobody around me could understand. Not even my mom. But there had to be something more than just feelings in this world...*Had to be*.

School subjects. Interest. I could still pull through. That would save and revive me. I firmly believed in myself, that I could really do that. I will stand by myself and divert my attention elsewhere. That is the point, isn't it? The attention. Where you direct your attention, you invest your energy. My energy is much too precious to be invested in unimportant and immature matters. Even if I never have a boyfriend.

Yes, I will be successful. Me and *I*. Best friends. In that moment I tried to figure out who I actually talked to when I was thinking. Is that one voice in my head, two, or is there more of us? How many thoughts run through my head in a single day and how do I slow them down to get at least a little bit of rest? However, I feel that the voice in my head is mostly kind to me. I love myself. I've always loved myself. I just needed to direct the attention towards me. Now it seems that there are no obstacles too difficult for me and *I* in this life...I have myself.

Maybe something good would come out of everything that'd happened. I'd found myself, rediscovered strong desire for knowledge and I simply knew that I wanted to go away when the elementary school finished. It's not that I didn't like my family. I loved them. It's just...I felt that my heart was much bigger than everything I'd known thus far. That my soul may be deeper and older than my small body let to believe. And I needed a suitable place for it.

Before I went to sleep that day I opened a few books in tried to do at least half of my homework. I found out that I was far behind with my subjects, so I used the computer. I hadn't used it too often for studying, probably because it was occupied all the time. We had one single family computer (and four candidates wanting to use it), so it was occupied all the time. Mom was usually the first to come home from work. She sat behind the computer, checked her e-mail and prepared for the next day. The Internet offered a lot of abstracts, images and contacts, and she couldn't imagine her life without it anymore.

Then dad would come home from work, and Ela and I would patiently wait for him too to finish his most urgent business on the computer. He loved Facebook and used it to connect with his fellow scientists – they exchanged the photographs of insects they'd found and categorized, reported about changes and added Latin names. It's usually 8 p.m. when it's Ela's turn and she stays on the computer until ten. She always chases me away just in time so I can't see which is her favorite website. When she's done I can't use the computer anyway, because it's bedtime. Most of the time I can't get my turn and I'm pretty used to that. It doesn't bother me too much. And you can get addicted to it.

It was different this evening. When I eventually came out of my room I discovered that everyone was already asleep. When I politely asked them to leave me alone, they obliged. And they were more considerate than usual. Even Ela hugged me and muttered something like: »It's alright, kid. He's not worthy of you anyway.«

Consequently I didn't even hear when they went to their beds. The whole house was quiet except for dad's occasional snoring. In the living room at the end of the hall the screensaver testified to the fact that the computer had been unoccupied for some time. I felt a quiet satisfaction since I was able to command my own life again. I quietly sneaked down the hall (I took the slippers off on purpose and tried to become one with parquet), first past Ela's room, then past mom and dad's bedroom.

Finally I reached the long-awaited trophy and became aware of the fact that I'd been missing the feeling of having the world at my fingertips. I moved the mouse and the computer awoke. I clicked and Google materialized before me. Miraculous. First, I took care of my homework. I found quite a few useful summaries for my Slovene reading assignments, which I'd been neglecting in no small measure recently. Why should I read stories written by others when my own was so much more emotional and interesting?

Then I cleared up a few mathematical misunderstandings, which had been hindering me during tests. I determined what the problem was – I didn't understand how to connect the calculation of square dimensions of geometrical forms (for example, of rhombus or deltoid) through their perpendicular diagonals. It's very simple, in fact. I found an explanation in colors on a web page, with arrows indicating the course of procedure. Much more understandable than the one in the textbook. The author of the Mathematical Hacker web page in this way helps anybody with any mathematical question. People come up with the most unusual ideas!

After successfully finishing homework I thought about how precious it was that I got the *opportunity to work on the computer.* It wouldn't have been right if I'd miss out on this opportunity, even if that meant an hour or two less sleep.

What else interested me? Which secondary school I should attend after finishing the elementary school? I entered the phrase »high school«. The computer hummed quietly as if it needed the time to think. There must be a lot of information under that phrase, of course...The results for phrase »high school«. A sea of potential high schools throughout Slovenia for those who had finished elementary schooling opened before my eyes.

The Poljane High School, the Ledina High School, local business results for: »high school near Ljubljana«, the Bežigrad High School, the Šiška High School...

After a few clicks I noticed a red button in the top left corner of some high school's web page saying »Seeking wisdom in the wide world after high school«. It looked interesting. I clicked on it. Along the list of the most successful students who continued their education abroad there was additional information about student exchange and links to specific areas of interest. Added was the information that student exchange involves college students. Nowhere was stated that it can't involve high school students. And if I'm interested in…attending high school in America? I clicked on America (button next to Europe, Australia and Africa). They exist, they really exist! Numerous institutions where Slovenian students are studying! On the list of cities I went for New York. Why? Maybe because I'd heard so much about it? Because my mom's favorite song was New York, New York sung by Frank Sinatra? I don't know. I clicked on it. Yes, student exchange is a broad and extensive thing…All of a sudden I was full of questions. Are there *high school students* along college students and how many are there? How many Slovenians are involved in student exchange per year and how long does it take? Is there a certain academic record or a score of points required?

Added was the information: for additional questions call the telephone number…The National Education Institute…I took a piece of paper and wrote down the number and relevant information. I'd find an appropriate secluded spot during the day – maybe I'd go on the hill behind the house – call them and ask them everything I wanted to know…My heart was pounding…Was I dealing with feelings or hormones again, or simple longing for something bigger and unlimited?

I checked the written information once more. I folded the paper and put it in the safe place, in the small pocket on my T-shirt. *And what now*, I asked myself. It was 1 a.m. and I still wasn't sleepy. Maybe I could visit YouTube and check for any videos on student exchange. Watching short clips had always been more entertaining than reading the news. Click.

In the top corner it said in bold type: »Welcome, Ely1990!«. And under that: »Videos recommended for You«. Under that followed videos with titles like: »Jonathan Jackson is sooooo hot!«, »Miley Cyrus interview«, »Enation rocks!«, »The coolest interview with Freddie Highmore«, »Stuart

Townsend is the sexiest man on the Earth«, »Make Up Tutorial – Sexy Smokey Eyes«,…

Interesting. Ely could be my sister's nickname. And she was born in 1990. So *that's* what interests her. She always sent me away because of these videos. My heart was pounding even faster. Maybe I could click on one of them and see if we have the same taste…

I checked if I was still alone. I set the speakers on minimum, just in case. I could still hear what was being played, while the sound was hushed enough so that I was the only one hearing it. What followed was an hour of real relaxation. I went to America and experienced interviews with celebrities, listened to inspiring rock songs and sometimes silently giggled when I saw certain photomontages made by regular people behind computers like me. A girl was enthusiastically explaining and demonstrating how to make an attractive make-up. And do your nails. How did she know to do that? Wow. You can really get hooked on YouTube. I was enjoying an inspiring rock song about how we always have the permission to realize our dreams, when I felt a hand on my shoulder.

I cried out. My blood turned to ice in my veins and I immediately switched speakers to »mute«. It was too late.

XII. SURPRISE

I WAITED FOR THE INITIAL SHOCK TO PASS, THEN TURNED AROUND IN the swivel chair and tried to show as relaxed face as possible. So what if I got caught? I'd never played against the rules before and I'd never been disobedient in any way. Maybe it was time for something like that to happen.

»I forgot to sign out. Doing a little research, eh?«

I recognized Ela's voice.

»And on *my* YouTube profile.« It seemed that all the understanding expressed four hours ago completely faded. Her face was hard and unforgiving. That's the bond between sisters. When someone can make you cry without a reason and with a single grimace just because she is your sister. If a stranger looked at me that way in the street I wouldn't care.

»Please, forgive me,« I started. »I really didn't mean anything bad. I was using the Internet and I wanted to check something out. I didn't even dream about your page still being open...«

I was truly sorry. Ela would usually think of a punishment without hesitation or would go on giving me dirty looks or would ignore me for the whole week. But this time she saw my face and obviously remembered the day I'd had...And thought of a couple of years *still to come...*

She smiled. »Did you at least like it?« she asked in a reconciliatory voice.

»Like it? It was awesome. All those videos, actors, interviews, music *numbers*...« I intently used the expression music numbers instead of songs so I would sound cool. »I didn't even realize that all that stuff could be seen on the Internet. I always used it mainly for school. You really have good taste.«

»Okay. Let's say I believe you.«

I got up and let her take over the computer.

»You can log out if you want.«

I headed towards my bedroom. Even though everything turned out okay I still felt a little embarrassed. Like I'd ransacked someone else's things. And got caught on top of that. What could I say in my own defense? That I was stealing? How could that even happen? I wanted to *know her*, nothing else. At the door I turned around once more.

»Ela?«

»Yeah?«

»I'm really sorry. I shouldn't have browsed through your profile.«

»Mhm.«

I headed towards my bedroom.

»Ina?«

»Yeah?«

»If you want, maybe we could...watch a video together sometime. I could use your comments. Besides, we have a lot of work to do on your taste. I have to teach you how to separate real guys from assholes.«

We giggled. Never before did I feel so connected to her. It seemed to me that she too may have been sad or hurt because of them, but she simply didn't want to show that to me. Now that I had been and was still *going to be* publicly humiliated, she maybe saw a part of her in me. Maybe there was something good in what happened to me...

Just like Ela knew how to awake tears, fear or anger in me in an instant, she also knew how to evoke peace and love. I was extremely surprised and shocked at the same time at how quickly I was able to open up to her. Perfectly self-evident friendship gleamed in my eyes:

»Thank you, Ela. I'd love to. Invite me sometime.«

I went to bed. It's interesting how a day perceived as a total disaster can turn into an evening full of revelations. Firstly, I don't want to tutor Tine anymore. Secondly, I want to excel and redirect my hormones towards where I can benefit from them. And thirdly: I want to discover the world. I want to travel. That need was born so deep inside of me that I could feel how it was shifting my world and the world of all the others. Like a very low and powerful frequency that's creating an earthquake. Like unavoidable rotation of planets. Like universe. *It's urgent.* I love this place and my family but I need to go away for a while. I'll find a way. Two more years.

With such thoughts I set the radio alarm clock. I set it on especially loud, because I sensed that after meager three hours of sleep I wouldn't be especially inclined to start my day happily and lightly. Especially not a day like tomorrow. I closed my eyes and enjoyed the sensation of the warm blanket and the silence, which was calmed me down and lulled me into the fateful school day. The day after the big bang…

XIII. THE DAY AFTER THE BIG BANG

IT SEEMED LIKE I'D BEEN ASLEEP FOR FIVE SECONDS – I CLOSED MY EYES and the alarm clock went off immediately. The calm of a deep sleep was replaced by panic when previous day's events replayed in my head. I knew what lay ahead and I knew it was unavoidable. If I wanted to conclude this schooling I had to face them. Since I wanted to get at least a little sleep I set the alarm clock to the last minute.

I had to hurry up. I spotted the blue T-shirt by the bed, the one I wore the day before. Filled with superstitious fear I put it in the dirty laundry so that the previous day's energy could be washed away.

I hastily selected a pair of jeans and a white T-shirt (I'd heard that white color meant positive energy, which I was in a dire need of), took my bag and headed for the battlefield. *I'm with you*, I thought. *On your side*. Me and *I*.

As I was approaching the school building I could see from afar that it was somehow different. It seemed that there was a spot on the wall. Wait a minute, that's not a spot. Something has been written. I stepped closer. The spot divided into three parts: one three-letter word, a dot in between and another four-letter word. Even closer. I felt it, I knew. Even though I was disgusted, I took one last look upwards, towards the writing. It was quite near the entrance greeting everybody coming to school. I think it was more visible from the road than traffic signs. The inscription that hit you in the face, whether you liked it or not...

INA + TINE

I directed my eyes towards the ground again. In the last second before I opened the school door I thought of asking the principal if I could finish the elementary school online or in the form of a correspondence course. Funny. Who would want to approve such an idea considering that I have a five-minute walk to school...And what reason would I give for that? A broken heart? No, I have to do this with my head held high. I also sensed that the writing wasn't the worst awaiting me that day...

When I entered the school all the eyes focused on me. A few second-graders quickly ran towards the classroom where us seventh-graders had the first period.

»She's here! She's here!«

I couldn't believe it. An intelligence service. What's next? Mafia and interrogation? Probably. Certainly.

I changed my footwear and slowly prepared for class. I wasn't in a hurry. I waited to the last minute, to the last second before the school bell rang and then entered the class. On the blackboard it was written:

INA + TINE

I quietly sat in my chair and acted as if I didn't see the writing. I disappointed ninety-nine percent of the public, except Bojana, who expressionlessly sat in the same place she always did. The good side of the fact that she always simply remained seated in the same spot and was really very still and quiet all the time was that she probably couldn't be thrown off the track. I was slightly envious of that. She would probably never have to confront or fight.

The first thing the teacher noticed when she entered the room was naturally the writing. It was obvious that she didn't envy my situation as she nervously asked:

»Who's the monitor? Clear the blackboard, please. And if I see another teasing remark on the blackboard I'll give minuses to everyone except Ina if the perpetrator doesn't come forward.«

Her incentive speech had quite the opposite effect. My classmates started laughing because the writing hurt *at least somebody's* feelings. They got what they came for. Drama.

That made her even angrier.

»Is that right? Let's see if you find this funny: UNANNOUNCED VERBAL EXAMINATION!«

The classroom grew silent. Unannounced verbal examination meant that she was very, very angry. A measure she hadn't used in a few years. Even though she could have afforded it, she hadn't tormented us with it in the past; she'd always been very understanding towards us. We knew that the questions would probably refer to the subject matter we'd covered recently. I was counting on that. If I wanted to strike, if I wanted to save myself, maybe I could do that now.

»No need.« My voice boomed through the classroom so silent, one could hear the spiders on the ceiling whispering. I was scared. But I knew that after yesterday's studying and according to the hypothesis that Miss Marija's first few questions were always easier than the rest of them, I might have a chance to succeed. At the same time I also had the moral advantage.

»Ina, you know that doesn't apply to you,« the teacher tried to back out.

Somebody snorted and her eyes harshly followed the sound through the classroom. The students quieted down.

»No, really, *I want to take the verbal exam* and improve my grade.«

I was nearly speaking in slang to relieve the tension that dominated the classroom.

»Are...you sure?«

»Yes. I am sure.« To additionally convince the others and myself I nodded my head. I looked around the classroom and came to the conclusion that I may have provided a little drama after all. They were disappointed only because its outcome wasn't as expected.

The examination started. Luckily her tactics was such as I had expected. I had to calculate square dimension, compare forms, draw diagonals and play with formulas. The questions were almost *too* easy. With the previous day's freshly acquired knowledge resting inside me, I even smiled a little every now and then and colored an occasional plane yellow or red for better understanding. The teacher was completely taken by surprise.

»I hope that you all learned something today,« she concluded enthusiastically.

»Ina, congratulations on your courage. I think I don't need to stress that you're done with verbal exams for this year and that you're on the right track to completely improve your math grade. To *A*, of course. I'll enter this into the class register…«

I smiled. I didn't feel particularly brave. Cunning, maybe. My plan worked better than I had expected. And it incited my adversaries even more, of course.

The class was over too soon. When the bell rang I quickly gathered my stuff and rushed to the teacher.

»There's something else,« I said as the school began to bustle with activity, when nobody could hear us anymore even if they wanted to.

»I really want to focus and improve my grades in other classes too. So I won't have the time anymore to…« I swallowed hard, »tutor classmates after school.«

In spite of my pretext the teacher knew exactly what I was talking about and she started answering me as soon as I finished my sentence.

»Of course, that's understandable. If they want the knowledge they'll have to learn by themselves. If they want to pass this grade they'll have to make an effort.« She winked at me conspiratorially. We both knew who she was talking about.

For a second I felt safe even though I knew that friendly relations with teachers wouldn't help me climb the popularity scale. But it was all the same to me. I couldn't have been lower on the list as it was.

During the recess I headed for the bathroom, but there too wasn't as peaceful as it used to be. The boys were chasing girls and knocking on doors, the girls were pushing them away and giggling enthusiastically.

When they saw me approaching it was already too late. They imme-diately open the door, chased the boys out and invited me in. *Maybe I'm not that low on the list after all*, I thought.

»Hey, Ina.« Iris called to me. It seemed to me that she was getting more beautiful every single day. She had a glow the other girls didn't have. »The thing you did yesterday was really brave. You can hang out with us if you want.«

I couldn't believe my ears.

»Well…Alright. Why not.« I truly couldn't refuse such an offer although it seemed a bit suspicious.

»But we have to beautify you a little for our company…« giggled the others. Yes, that was true. They all wore make-up and were perfectly groomed, while I with my plain-old-Ina look didn't belong there. I had to become *that* Ina. Made-up beauty that turned all the boys' heads. *Fatal* Ina. *Model* Ina. In short, something that I wasn't.

They were obviously well prepared for my initiation into the group because they immediately offered me a chair (in front of toilet stalls!) and each of them had a few beauty accessories with her. They must've spent the entire previous day planning such a well-organized initiation.

Five pairs of hands sliding up and down my face and head gave me an interesting feeling. After five minutes I felt like a Hollywood star getting her hair, make-up and nails done simultaneously. During the procedure I briefly considered if I was being the victim of a prank. And if I was, I was in the bathroom anyway, where I could wash the make-up off my face. When they were done I looked in the mirror. I was beautiful even though that still wasn't me. They obviously *truly* want me in their group. *Truly*.

When the bell rang they asked me to walk in front of them, saying they were proud of their new member. I thought that was suspicious but the temptation was too strong. Besides, I was greatly outnumbered so I couldn't put up any real resistance. As I walked towards the classroom I heard the laughter and good-humored disposition of »Pretty girls« walking behind me.

Just before I entered the classroom I felt as if someone had put a hat on my head. Before I realized what was going on they pushed me in the classroom and closed the doors behind me. I discovered that I was wearing a homemade bridal veil.

»Let me out! That's not fair!«

My banging on the door encouraged them even more and they loudly started singing the wedding march:

»Tam, tam, ta-dam, tam, tam, ta-dam…«

When I realized that I wasn't helping myself by screaming since I was already caught in a trap, I noticed the company in the classroom made up of members of all the other groups and non-groups. As if the situation wasn't bad enough, the chemistry teacher, who often came in a few minutes late, was late again for his class. They must've been counting on that.

Directly in front of me the boys were pushing each other around and grinning like fools looking at me.

»Tine wants to ask you something,« Primož said with a smirk and punched the star of the classroom.

The model stepped forward and the classroom froze in expectation.

»I just can't believe that you wrote that note.«

What's done is done. I decided to tell him the truth. As calmly and down-to-earth as possible. Without any embellishments.

»Well, I did. Believe it or not.«

I'll start selling hotdogs and popcorn in a minute. With coke. So they can enjoy the soap opera all the more.

»And?« he raised his eyebrow.

»Well, you're not what I thought you were.«

The boys burst out laughing. Primož took over the role of conductor and led the classroom through a rhythmic chant:

»I-na plus Ti-ne! I-na plus Ti-ne!«

I became sad when I saw how much fun people could have by simply repeating the same syllables over and over. Especially when this repetition is intended to hurt a fellow human being.

While Tine was assaulting the conductor and the classroom got another attraction, I quietly sat in my chair, took off the veil and prepared my chemistry notebooks.

Luckily the teacher came in before long and everybody quickly sat down. Chemistry class went on as usual and luckily nobody had any new ideas how to continue the drama. I didn't have any more plans to improve all of my grades that day. I'll need more effort and luck to do that. And I've grown used to friendless recesses. I'll try to be patient for another month…

Taunting was over for the day, thank God. Except for a few Tina's remarks, of course. She tried to come up with a new nickname for me, the one that would reflect my unfortunate love life. Luckily she couldn't come up with anything that would stick, although she tried really hard.

When the school was over and I closed the school door behind me, I tried to walk away as normally and naturally as I possibly could. I knew that I was still being secretly watched from behind school windows and that they couldn't wait for me to burst into tears. Therefore I served them a dessert: I remembered my plans for the rest of the day: the hill behind the house, calling the National Education Institute, peace and quiet, celebrating the A in math, studying for grade improvements. I smiled happily and jumped in the air.

I couldn't care less who was watching me. With the corner of my eye I noticed the janitor approaching the wall with the writing on it with a bucket of white paint and a painting roller.

XIV. THE MAGIC AFTERNOON

ICHEERFULLY JUMPED ALL THE WAY HOME AND DISCOVERED THAT I was the first one to arrive. I quickly wrote on a piece of paper: *Went for a walk. Don't worry, will be back soon, Ina.* I changed into sneakers, took my mobile phone and the piece of paper I prepared the day before. Then I lightheartedly went out.

Walking up the hill I suddenly felt short of breath; I spontaneously ascended much faster than usual. On the top of the hill I looked downward and admired the beautiful landscape beneath me. It was a pleasantly fresh spring afternoon and the clouds were gathering in the distance. I took the jacket I brought with me, spread it in front of me and sat on it.

"Well, let's do it," I told myself. I called the fatal number. It clicked on the other side and a middle-age sounding lady answered. I could hear that she answered the phone routinely.

»The National Education Institute, how may I help you?«

»I apologize for the interruption. This is Ina Kralj speaking. I'm interested in student exchange…«

»For high school or college students?«

»High school students. I'm interested in conditions, if I need a certain number of points, any references…«

»Listen. I'm very sorry, but…«

It seemed like my life flashed before my eyes in that one second.

»…But the most frequent are college student exchanges. I could provide you with some answers for those, but for the high school student exchange you better call…«

She gave me the number.

»Thank you very much.« I was ecstatic, because the high school student exchange evidently does exist. It didn't matter if it was frequent or rare, what mattered was that it *existed*!

I called the number she gave me. A friendly gentleman answered and explained to me all the details. He told me I would have to finish at least two years of high school in Slovenia before going to America. He recommended several Internet websites and pointed out things I needed to pay my attention to: how to fill out the application, how long it takes for an application to get approved. Since I was still underage, I was going to need my parents' consent and a few teacher references also wouldn't hurt...

When I hung up the phone I felt so empowered...I knew I probably wouldn't have any problems with teacher references and I had four years before I applied. I could still improve my grade point average so that won't cause any complications. It'll be slightly harder to convince my mom why it is in her daughter's best interest to travel to the other end of the world... But if I tell her now, she'll have enough time to get used to the idea...

Dark clouds I was watching before from afar drew nearer during my phone conversation and I felt the first raindrops on my face. I felt so free! Let it wash me, let it wash away my stupid make-up! Let it give me a rebirth! When it came down pouring I still sat on the top of the hill making plans for my future. I thought about the beauty of nature when it rains and watched old women rushing from the cemetery so they wouldn't get caught in the rain. I dismissed everything and lay in the grass...

Rain dripped down my face and I was soaked to the skin. I didn't care; I enjoyed it. I positioned myself horizontally to the hill slope, pushed off and started rolling downhill. I didn't know that was still so amusing. The last time I did I was a small child...I screamed with joy and landed happily at the foot of the hill.

I stopped and got up all muddy. Two women rushing from the cemetery turned around and saw me wiping myself off with a smile whistling

»New York, New York«. Considering the gossipy character of rural women I knew that soon everybody will know about my little adventure and I felt like a celebrity whose every move is being watched by paparazzi. Nevertheless, I enjoyed the moment, as for my reputation…Let's say it was already so low that I wasn't about to concern myself with little muddy news that was about to spread through the village in a few seconds.

I slowly started walking towards home in the rain…

XV. THE FAREWELL

I WAS SITTING ON THE HILL WATCHING THE SUNRISE. I had a difficult day ahead of me but I knew that my effort would pay off. I was already anxious for everything to commence. I'd shaken hands with many people, said goodbye to a lot of them…

Mom's interest in computers and the Internet increased by a thousand percent. When she was outvoted in the family meeting four years ago in favor of my going to New York she embraced the other extremity. She started educating herself, started taking courses, hired a tutor…So much so that on the day of my departure she probably knew more about the Internet, communication possibilities and Skype than anybody else in our neighborhood. And about the city I was going to.

»Mom, if you ever grow tired of Slovenian language, you can always teach computer science…« I joked.

»Go ahead and make jokes but this is serious stuff« she replied. When I saw tears in her eyes saying those words, I quickly changed the subject.

I took one last look at the hills and our neighborhood. The sun in the eastern sky was covered in beautiful reddish and purple shades that were getting lighter by the minute. The church stood quietly among houses watching over parishioners. Birds' singing slowly started filling the silence. I felt that time has come for me to say goodbye and my eyes started watering. Here, in this peaceful spot, I'd always found my happiness…I'd always forgotten about my troubles. Now a great distance will separate me from it…I could still stay at home…

Wait a minute! I'd lived for this journey. I'd been preparing for it, like a bride prepares for her groom. For two years I'd been a role model for all elementary school kids. I'd even made into the golden book of top-of-the-class students. And then I was at the top of my class during the first two years of high school (I hung out with my classmates only in school, but I had my goal and that was what mattered). I really worked hard. I learned everything there was to know about New York on the Internet. I even wandered through the city with the little help from the Google satellite (it's amazing how clearly one can see the streets, the city and its surroundings – as you were *already* there). I gladly and lovingly endured all types of offensive behavior by my classmates during the last two years of elementary school, because I knew what awaits me in the future. The city of my own choosing. The city I even dreamed about. The city that drew me more than I'd dared to admit.

I'll visit during the holidays anyway, I thought. *Just imagine the disappointment if you quit now. No, no. These are needless obstacles. Some kind of denial brought on by fear. Emotions. Attachment. I can't afford that now. Not now, when I am so close.*

I told my mom I was going on the hill behind the house and asked her to give me a sign by waving when she was ready. I explicitly asked her to be punctual because I didn't want to be late for my flight. And she did come out of the house and she did raise her hand. I could see from afar that she did that reluctantly. She really didn't want me to go, but she knew that there was no point in holding me back.

I slowly got up and realized that day had almost fully broken. To chase away needless thoughts I ran down the hill. I was home in fifteen seconds. Ela and dad lined up at the front door while mom waited by the car. I knew that farewell was going to be emotional, so I quickly said:

»Maybe it would be smart to do this quickly…mom's already waiting,« I awkwardly shifted from one foot to the other and hugged dad first. Never before had I seen him so anxious. When we hugged, Ela moved away. They'd probably agreed in advance to give each other enough space for a proper farewell with me. So much about quick parting.

»I'm sorry if I've been…a slightly less active dad than you wanted me to be…« he said when we hugged. He loosened his grip and looked me straight in the eyes, so I could feel that these words were meant just for me.

»I thought that I was doing the right thing, that I had to provide for my family and my kids, when in reality I missed the train on which you are, my youngest baby. And now you're leaving.« His eyes teared up. I never saw my dad cry before. And what was worse, he cried because of me.

»No, dad. You've been great. Really.« I tried to console both of us. I thought it'd be silly to tell him that I was seventeen and that expressions like »baby« probably weren't suitable anymore. Although it felt nice, homely. As if the last piece of our relationship puzzle had fallen into place. I too was aware of the fact how much I'd been missing him all these years. It's true that he used to relax on the couch every evening but I never thought of really connecting with him. It's been so easy to connect with mom, that I forgot about dad.

»We'll see each other anyway. On Skype.« I had that excuse prepared in advance. An injection against sentimentality.

His eyes were still locked in with mine. »I remember seeing you for the first time…I came immediately when I heard what was going on. Because it was so unexpected – you had been in there for scarcely six months and you already wanted out – I didn't even know how you were doing. If you were alive, healthy? I couldn't even caress you in that glass box…But I could see your eyes. You were determined to survive. As you are determined now to succeed…I believe in you, Ina. Take care of yourself.« He hugged me again.

»And now I'm going to give you a present. I'll be very happy if you decide to carry it with you all the time.« He took a small, oval, pink object from his pocket.

»I hope you girls like pink«, he smiled. When he pressed the button I let out a little cry, because out came a blade.

»Dad…« I started to protest. »What a bloodthirsty gift.«

»Let me finish« he interrupted. »It's not just a self-defense tool. It can help you cut the food, open a letter or quickly come to your rescue during camping…« I flinched at the thought of how the *same* knife can be used for various activities…

»Besides that it also has a can opener, little scissors and it looks good. A top quality mechanism that never breaks down. It has a five-year warranty…«

»Are you giving it to me or are you trying to sell it?« I smiled.

»And what's best,« he wouldn't be interrupted, »It's small and handy, in fashionable pink color with glitter and it has a dedication on the back.«

I turned it around. Dedication written in dad's awkward handwriting with a permanent marker said: *I love you, my youngest baby. May this sentinel take good care of you.* And the date.

I felt that I couldn't stand all of this much longer. I wondered how long had they prepared for this and what Ela had in store for me. I hugged him quickly and thanked him sincerely. I wanted to let him know that his present and his feelings *really meant a great deal to me*, while at the same time I knew that I was dangerously close to bursting into tears, putting down my baggage, changing my mind and burying my dreams forever.

When Ela saw that we were done she came closer, while dad stepped aside. *They practiced this without a doubt,* I thought. She said in unconcerned manner from a distance:

»What's up kid, now you think you can just go, or what?« I liked her approach. It was fresher and less theatrical.

»Yeah, I think I can. I've got signatures of both parents, wanna see them?« I joined in. It felt like I was at the border crossing.

»No, no, it's OK. Come here.« She spread her arms and hugged me. I melted in her embrace and soon it didn't even feel like hugging anymore. We just stood there, simply existing in silence. I knew it. I'd miss her too. Leaning against her chest I felt something pressing me. Then I remembered her locket. That golden locket she'd been always so proud of. A little heart whose content was known only to her.

And so we stood there as if in some other dimension. Then she let go of me and said in a strict voice:

»Now close your eyes. And don't dream of peeping!«

I obediently closed my eyes. Nothing happened for a few seconds so I winked.

»Don't even think about it!« she reminded me sharply.

So I stood there and waited for something to happen. Soon I felt her elbows moving around my head in an unusual manner and then something small touched my chest. She wouldn't possibly...

»May I open them already?« I asked impatiently.

»OK, do it.«

She quickly stepped away. I opened my eyes, felt around my neck and gaped widely. My reaction must've been written in Ela's script because her camera went off in her hands. Unbelievable, she took my picture!

»I'll keep this photo as a keepsake,« she said contentedly.

»Ela, I can't take this. This is *your* locket.«

»You will be eighteen next year, won't you? So we won't have to buy you a new one then.« She laughed.

»And now I have to show you how it opens. Now you get to see what was in it these past few years.« She said that like it was never her secret. She took the locket from under my neck, turned one little button 180 degrees to the left and pulled it outwards, then turned the other one 180 degrees to the right and pressed in inwards like one would press a button in an elevator. How simple, I thought. Instead of pushing the buttons apart, one just needs to turn them a little, each in its own direction, and the riddle is solved.

She opened the locket and the little heart halved in two. One half contained a little picture of Ela, the other one...mine?!

I was totally surprised. My mouth dropped open. She should take my picture *now*...

»I was expecting Gregor's picture to be in there, or Mateja's, or Eva's…« I started naming her numerous girlfriends.

»That's OK, but there's only one girlfriend in my life who I can be sure will always love me, no matter how or why we quarreled the last time… That's my little sister. That's you, kid.« It seemed to me that she added the nickname *kid* because she didn't wanted to be too sappy.

This time I wanted to lift the untamable pulleys full of water just enough to show her how astonished and grateful I was. Unfortunately there was too much water and too much emotion. When I let myself lift them just a little they crashed under the weight of the water and my eyes opened like floodgates. I hugged her.

»I've got nothing for you,« I moaned.

»It's you that's leaving, not me« she contradicted. »And anyway, you gave me a photo I can frame. Forget the frame, I'll turn it into a billboard,« she laughed.

»I'll always love you,« she added, releasing me from her hug.

»Me too.«

I quickly tried to compose myself. I have to be strong. I have to. I have to.

When we were finished, I looked at both of them, dad and Ela.

»Thank you. Thank you both. I really love you.« And so that my emotions couldn't get the better of me again, I quickly added:

»I'll see you tomorrow on Skype anyway.«

I quickly turned around, opened the car door on the passenger side and sat in the car. Mom had already been waiting and I could see that she too was moved, even though our goodbye scene hadn't even began yet…

XVI. THE AIRPORT

I SAT IN MY SEAT AND WAITED FOR THE »LAUNCH«. It was one of those moments when people you'd just bid farewell to, stand in one spot and wait for you to drive off, so they can start waving goodbye to you. When mom and I drove off the gravel driveway, dad and Ela started waving immediately. Their innovativeness touched me. In one moment they stood next to each other and waived only with their outer arms; it looked like a single, slightly heavier person was waving. Then dad stepped behind Ela and they waived so that one had his arms up in the air, while the other had them down and vice versa. It looked like one person with four arms was waiving. These lively figures kept getting smaller and smaller until they vanished behind the neighboring house when we passed it.

Mom sighed. Even though she was a strong woman she couldn't avoid feelings of guilt from time to time or feeling like a victim herself. She knew how to change the timber of her voice, so you were on her side in a second, regardless of what you thought a moment ago.

»So, you've really made a decision, haven't you?« she said after fifteen minutes of silence and the steady hum of the engine. I heard that magic change which would've probably had immediate effect on me, had I not known her. She probably didn't do it on purpose. It was more like a subconscious maternal reaction.

»Yes, really.«

Silence.

She took one deep breath and exhaled. I reminded myself how much she'd changed in the last four years. She even learned to meditate, because she was so concerned about my leaving all the time. Her colleague – known for her calm and easygoing solving of conflicts in the classroom as well as in the teacher's lounge – invited her to a meditation group and since then she handled the fact that I was going to live in New York much easier. In the end she even helped me pack, she printed out the plan of New York City subway for me, and was always there for me if I needed her. On the odd morning she even invited me to sit and relax with her.

Without yourself, wash away your thought, she used to say to me. It was nice and homely. It felt like I'd done that in the past. At the same time it connected us. Ela wasn't too interested in meditation. But it helped me to be relatively calm most of the time during the flood of INA + TINE writings, and not to give in to hormones too easily. I can actually proudly say that I've managed to subdue them.

In spite of being calmer now, mom couldn't resist the need to try and hold me back one last time during the final moments of our non-electronic, live communication – whether using the timber of her voice or through some motherly comment…

»Be careful,« she started again. »I've made you a list of streets that are known to be safe, and a list of streets you should avoid. Please, promise me you'll use only the safe ones …«

»Of course I will, mom. Don't worry.«

We reached the exit leading off the highway in direction Kranj, towards Brnik and the Jože Pučnik Airport. I find it interesting that our main airport isn't situated directly in Ljubljana, the country's capital. Mom always liked to talk to her passengers while driving. She said it helped her stay focused. That day I especially loved talking to her. I tried to absorb her presence as much as I could during the drive. I watched her from the side, I watched how the morning sun shined on her face and I thought she was very beautiful.

One of her characteristics was that she wasn't beautiful just on the outside. She had black hair always neatly tied into a ponytail, small and thin figure, angular and fairly symmetrical face. I've always been more enchanted with what radiated from within her. Her soul. Because of her soul I've always had the feeling that my mom was a beauty without comparison. She seemed the epitome of inner and outer beauty in total balance. That glow can probably be experienced only in live contact… While through Skype…Well, better that than nothing.

When she asked me what I was thinking about, we started discussing outer and inner beauty and the drive went by very quickly. We were so immersed in the conversation that I nearly forgot I was leaving. Only when we parked in the airport parking lot my heart started beating faster. We were there an hour early, which is not too much because of all the formalities. Better too early that too late.

When we checked my documents, ticket and luggage (I wasn't allowed to have any fluids in my backpack) we saw that we had enough time for a quick drink. There was the airport bar near the entrance, where we occupied a table and started deciding what to order.

Everything seemed so simple. As if I were sitting in a bar with a friend who supported me entirely in my new adventure. Mom could be so easy-going sometimes that I would forget she was my mom. Her young soul shined through her eyes and it seemed that *she* was the younger one.

When the waitress brought her cappuccino and my aloe vera drink (these juices were becoming increasingly popular – I wondered if that was the case in New York) she immediately asked for the check.

»…so it's settled.«

When I insisted that I would take care of it, because it really meant a great deal to me, she refused me by saying that it was her turn to treat and that she would've never forgiven herself, if it was the other way around. Then she mysteriously leaned towards me.

»There's something else…« she said slowly, as if mentioning a national secret.

»What is it?«

»Dad and I agreed to back you up financially too. So we have a small gift for you…« She took out an envelope.

»O my God,« I said in a subdued voice. »Are surprises never going to end?«

My comment was meant in a positive sense. I really didn't expect such a positive response. The longer I persisted in my decision, the more rewarded I got. Is life the same? The more determinedly and persistently you pursue your goals, the bigger the prize, even if you almost change your mind a hundred times? It obviously is.

»There's a card in the envelope. We didn't think it would be smart to carry the cash around. Especially since Americans love credit cards…« She sounded like a teenager during the last sentence. She put the back of her hand in front of her, as if wanted to indicate this thing was very »cool«.

»You don't have to open it now. You can do it on the plane, if you get bored. The flight from Munich will be pretty long.«

»Well, alright. Thanks, mom. You shouldn't have.« That was absolutely true. During the past four years I'd been receiving a scholarship for specially gifted students on account of all my activities (Miss Marija was the one most adamant about it, saying I set an example for everybody in school, and I wasn't going to refuse it, naturally). After I started attending high school I was allowed by the National Education Institute to keep it. The only thing I needed to do was maintain my high grade average. I opened a savings account and put every Euro I earned in it, including the money I made by cleaning the house. I'd accumulated enough so I could make my ends meet and now I received this unexpected gift. Just in case.

»Thank you, really.«

The departure time of my flight was announced over the speakers. We got up and headed towards the gate.

»So you won't be late,« mom said quite the opposite of what she was thinking. I could hear in her voice that she still didn't want me to go, but she didn't intended to stop me, since I *really* made that decision…

I stopped and hugged her at the gate where the security officers perform the last examination and where we had to separate. So we stood a few feet away from the security personnel locked in the last embrace until my next visit…I thought we would never be able to experience an embrace through the Internet. That feeling of warmth, when two souls decide to open to one another. When one experiences comfort, approval, safety and happiness. I felt I needed to say something to her.

»Thanks, mom.« I looked her in the eye.

»Since I've known you, you've been the best mom in the world. It doesn't matter if you got angry at me sometimes. That just showed that you really worried about me and that you cared. Thank you for always being there for me and for always believing in me, even when I didn't believe in myself. And thanks for the trick,« I winked at her, »that I'm always interested in everything. Without it I wouldn't be here where I am. Thank you for all the love,« I tried to radiate the same warmth I frequently noticed in her, »and anyway, thanks for everything…«. I ran out of words and I hugged her again. Her lips trembled suspiciously and I couldn't tell if she was laughing or was ready to burst into tears.

We were locked in the embrace for quite some time. I wondered who I was going to hug when I got to New York. A taxi driver? People in the street? Teachers? At the thought of how far away my next embrace was, especially the embrace of my loved ones, I felt pain again. I had to bite my lip so I didn't cry. There would be time for that on the plane. Not now. It'd be even harder on her if we both cried.

We looked at each other again and she gave me one last motherly caress. I didn't mind. She was my mom after all.

»I'd tell you I love you, but you already know that,« I smiled.

»I'd tell you you're my favorite youngest daughter, but you already know that.«

I raised my eyebrows. »You've got another youngest daughter I don't know about?«

She recognized the paradox of what she just said and let out a smile that started to twist into its opposite. The security officer watching us couldn't decide if we were laughing or crying.

We said our final goodbyes and my hand luggage was checked again for any illegal stuff.
After the examination I turned back one last time. Mom was still standing beyond security personnel, holding her jacket with one hand and nervously waving at me with the other.

»Watch out for yourself!« she said.

»I will. I promise.«

Our eyes met once again and we smiled. I didn't realize that our saying goodbye took so long. I looked at the watch and discovered that I wasn't that early anymore. People started pouring in from waiting areas and mom disappeared in the crowd. I too was pushed forward and I couldn't stay in the same place. I joined the crowd and went with it.

I repeated the flight scenario once again in my head. *Munich first. Follow the signs in the corridor. They're visibly placed above the crowd so every-one can see them. You'll have two hours to catch the connecting flight to New York. There the transportation will be waiting to take you to the dormitory.*

I climbed the stairs to the plane and found my seat. I was glad to be sitting by the window because I like a nice view. *This is it,* I thought. *There is no way back now…*

XVII. THE JOURNEY

THE ENGINES SOON STARTED HUMMING AND THE PLANE STARTED to move. We taxied down the runway, faster and faster. That was my last dilemma. What sort of a person was I? Was I afraid of flying or not? The sense for flying is supposedly encoded in the subconscious, so flying can be either very stressful or quite pleasant.

When we took off, I became heavier in my seat; the horizontal ground that I saw just moments before through the window, was moving sideways. I felt nothing negative. No fear. Relief maybe.

When the plane was high enough, I saw my country beneath me for the last time…I thought how beautiful it was. Mountains, hills, the sea, the plains, small towns…*God's blessing on all nations, Who long and work for that bright day, When o'er earth's habitations, No war, no strife shall hold its sway; Who long to see, That all men free, No more shall foes, but neighbors be …* Doubtlessly the most selfless national anthem in the world, because it doesn't praise just one nation, but all who want to see peace in this world. Peace, not warfare. The thought of our poet France Prešeren thinking the same things as John Lennon did when writing Imagine, brought a smile to my face. They'd probably get along great.

And there lay Slovenia, all beautiful, basking in the sun. Near the airport a small dot watched the plane. My mom, maybe? I was further and further away…The landscape below me was getting smaller and smaller and when I saw that we were approaching the clouds I looked down for the last time. The sense of flying was exceptionally pleasant, although looking down on Slovenia made my heart sink…I wasn't betraying my country by following my dreams. I was serving it. I'd be much less happy if I had stayed just because I had to. We started rising through the clouds and the landscape below us disappeared in the fog. »I'll see you, my dear,« I whispered.

I relaxed in my seat. The pocket on the back side of the seat in front of me was full of magazine-like material containing information about the flight, timetables, etc. After approximately half an hour a nice flight attendant distributed meals in small plastic boxes. I found it quite unbelievable that we got food on a seventy-five-minute long flight. Like getting a free meal on a train ride from Ljubljana to Koper…I gladly opened the received gift and ate its content. It was just in time for a snack, so I enjoyed bread with several spreads and a salad. The meal ended with – a dessert – little bar of chocolate. Since this was my first encounter with such a special treatment on a journey, I found the gesture to be very nice. Later on I got used to all of that – the meals, the questions if everything was okay, if I needed something…I hardly got used to the idea that I was in the air, when we already started descending. *That was quick*, I thought and started collecting my things.

Luckily changing planes in Munich went much smoother that I dared to imagine. The signs were clear and accurate. Since this airport was much bigger than the one back home (where we walked to the airplane), there was an airport bus waiting on us. From then on everything went smoothly: the luggage check-in, the check-in, the waiting area (I even bought a small fridge magnet as a souvenir), the ticket, the security check-up and I was sitting on a plane again.

This plane was much bigger than the previous one. The seats were divided into several rows (the previous one had only two, the left one and the right one), they were equipped with headphones and there were screens hanging from the ceiling. Flight attendants courteously prepared us for the eight-hour flight. In comparison to the previous flight, where we got *only* a free snack, here, in addition to regular meals, we also got the whole set for a comfortable journey which we were allowed to keep! I happily sat in my seat and discovered that I was again seated by the window. I felt very light. I felt like I had left all the heavy energy of confusion and homesickness behind. All in all it seemed like the ultimate and the best reward for my determination. I felt increasingly more invigorated and dedicated to my goal.

The takeoff wasn't as mysterious as the first time around. I was looking out of the window feeling completely at ease. It was nice watching us ascend. When I put my face close enough to the window, I could imagine that I wasn't sitting in my seat looking out of the window but that *I* was the one flying.

I felt even more at home when I saw the same TV shows, I sometimes watched at home, being played on the airplane screens. They started off with "The Nanny", which I liked because of the main character's carefree attitude towards the world. We could select the desired language on the headphones. There was no Slovenian language available, of course. We could choose between German, Spanish, Italian…I had the most fun while listening to the show in Chinese.

Quiet monotony soon took over the plane. We sailed through a constant, pastel-colored haze…On several occasions we would rise above the clouds and it seemed like flying over a vast white sea. Then we would quickly re-enter the cotton-like whiteness…

I didn't even notice that I fell asleep. The next thing I became aware of was a voice informing us that we were about to land and that we should fasten our seat belts. We were also given the local time and several other details. I prepared for landing, fixed my messy hair and took a look through the window. It was like in the movies. Some of the most well known American scenes unfolded in front of my eyes…The Brooklyn Bridge, the Statue of Liberty…The plane circled towards the airport which was really huge. I hoped that this time too the signs would be clear and accurate…

If they weren't, I might get lost.

We landed without any complications. A bus was waiting for us by the entrance, just like in Munich, and took us to the luggage claim area. When I took my suitcases off the luggage belt I immediately felt safer. Just as I was considering what to do next, I noticed a group of people standing by the exit. Some of them were holding pieces of paper in their hands, with a person's name or a company name written on it.

Near the exit stood a man of average build, somewhat fat, tidy in appearance, wearing a cap. If I had to guess, I'd say he was a chauffeur. And when I saw what his inscription said, I knew I was right. It really was a chauffeur. My chauffeur.

XVIII. NEW YORK, NEW YORK

»I NA KRALJ?«
»Yes, that's me,« I answered in English.
»May I see your ID?«

Wow, he was meticulous. Well, thank God. Now I knew that he really must've been waiting for me and not just for someone who could pretend to be me.

»Of course,« I reached in my backpack and showed him my ID. His facial expression quickly changed from strict to welcoming.

»My name is Jeffrey and I'll be taking you to your dormitory. If you want, I can show you the shortest way to your high school. It'll take you an hour and a half to get there on foot. Or you can take the subway or a taxi. You can find both near the beautiful Central Park…«

»Oh, thank you. I'll be happy to walk the first time and take a look around, Jeffrey. Could you please tell me what time it is? I forgot to set my watch on the plane…«

»It's 3 p.m.«

»Great, thank you.« My wristwatch was showing 8 p.m., which meant that New York was five hours behind Slovenian time. That's why the day seemed so long…

»Just follow me, please.« He gallantly pointed in the right direction and slightly bowed his head. He took the bigger suitcases and carried them for me. We soon reached the road where a big black car waited. He put the suitcases in the trunk of the car while I took the back seat.

We drove for a long time but I'd been prepared for the fact that the city I came to wasn't in the least similar to Ljubljana. If I remember correctly, it is five hundred and thirteen times bigger than Ljubljana. That means it is almost seven times bigger than the country I come from.

Although it seemed huge, I immediately loved it. It pulsed with a special, higher frequency that also powered my heart. It was big, but I wasn't afraid of it. Quite the contrary. I got the interesting feeling that I was at home *here too*. Can a person have two homes? We drove across a really long bridge and got to the other cape. Huge skyscrapers were crowded alongside beautiful beaches. I knew where we were, because I familiarized myself with the city through the Google satellite. We turned right and started approaching the Central Park. We drove past the Empire State Building. Funny. Although the building stood there and passers-by probably didn't think much of it, I felt like a child who got a present on Christmas Eve. I saw it *live* and it seemed magical to me.

When we got to the Central Park we turned left onto 68th Street. *How practical*, I thought. Instead of various names that would confuse newcomers, the streets have numbers here. There are too many, of course, for each of them to have its own, unique name. The streets were arranged in a nice, rectangular pattern. We got to my new high school surprisingly quickly. Jeffrey stopped the car so I could take a good look at it.

The building's front wall was dark gray in color, with lighter shade above the ornamented portals. Different wall colors (light and dark gray) were separated by a white line. The wooden entrance was embellished with golden handles. Three steps led to the gate. The main entrance was divided into three doors: the door in the middle looked almost like a castle gate; the two side doors were smaller. Each door had a small oblong window on the eye-level, with an interesting iron Y-shaped grid on both sides (the same above and below). Round-shaped white ornament above the entrance connected all three doors into one whole. It looked almost oriental with its opulent decoration. Square windows on each side probably didn't fit in as much style-wise. Side doors had the same, although smaller ornaments. On the left side of the door the name of the school was displayed. The glass case contained a few important notices.

Seven different doors led into the building from the sidewalk only. One of these doors was even larger that the main door and had a much prettier ornament. A blue flag, adorned with a yellow lion's head and a learning-stimulating inscription, fluttered over the main door.

The sidewalk in front of the school was made of larger square blocks (some slightly differentiating in color). The trees, arranged evenly every fifteen feet, were planted in the outer third of the sidewalk, so entering the school wouldn't be obstructed. The other side of the street was also lined with trees and the whole surrounding area looked well-kept and green. *The people attending this school surely must be pleasant and cultured*, I thought.

I turned around and went back to the car. Jeffrey was already behind the steering wheel, toying with his phone, patiently waiting for me to soak in my new environment. I opened the back door and got in. I told him I was ready for him to show me the way to the dormitory. I knew that it took only a couple of turns. We'd drive back towards the Central Park, then turn left and go up the Central West Street. After a nice stretch of the way along the Central Park, that is straight on past the museum, we'd turn left. It looked fairly simple on the map. In reality things appeared slightly bigger. That's why I was glad to have a personal guide at my side during my first day in New York.

When we were driving down a long street, I could observe the colorful Central Park on my right. It was thrilling; not only because of its size, but because it changed so much along the way. From the well-maintained park with jogging paths, to hilly parts overgrown with trees. It offered everything: from the forest to quiet picnic areas. The visitors looked satisfied, probably happy because, on this patch of land, they were able to relax in their own way, without being disturbed.

Traffic lights were on our side, so we fairly quickly reached the intersection where we turned left. The way was – in addition to being long – also quite simple. And well populated. I made a decision: I'll probably walk. It'll go by quickly along the park and it'll do me some good. Besides, the streets seemed safe, without any potentially dangerous dark alleys.

Jeffrey parked in front of the dormitory, that is the International Student Center. The neighborhood seemed old-fashioned and well-maintained. The dormitory entrance didn't stick out. I was surprised by the dormitory's interior, which had little in common with its exterior. In a positive sense, that is. If the exterior seemed old-fashioned and theatrical (with its burgundy-red color and some type of decoration consisting of symmetrical rectangles along the sides of doors and windows), the interior was warm and contemporarily furnished.

The reception area was on the left and they knew I was coming. A friendly receptionist asked from afar in a typical American accent: »Ina Kralj?« It was funny hearing my name pronounced in American English.

»You understand, we have so many different nationalities under our roof and each language has its own pronunciation rules…« she apologized.

»Of course, of course. I understand.«

We were being, almost too polite. I was slightly embarrassed because I was so far away from home for the first time and she obviously wanted to express her most heartfelt welcome. When I filled out a few forms and checked in she showed me my room. Jeffrey helped me carry my luggage to my room and then he said goodbye. He told me he worked in the building and that we would see each other all the time. The receptionist told me to freely ask her if I wanted to know anything.

My room was on the second floor, the last door on the left, on the other side of the building from the reception. When I opened the door, a pleasantly fresh smell greeted me. I noticed that the windows on the right were open and that the bed, situated on the right side of the room, was aesthetically made and covered with fresh sheets. A writing desk with a lamp on it stood by the window, with two huge wardrobes next to it. I put down my things and sat on the bed. Although simple, the room was fairly modern-looking and it seemed – appropriate for studying. Without any unnecessary decorations. Even though I was pretty exhausted from the journey, I decided to unpack my suitcases right then and there.

I was fairly quickly done with my clothes. I lined up my shoes by the door. I opened the small backpack I had with me on the plane and a white envelope peeped out of it. That's right, my credit card!

I opened the envelope and took out the contents. Beside the credit card and the little piece of paper with a code on it, saying that I should learn the code and then destroy the paper immediately, there was a short note.

> *Dear Ina!*
> *Although our hearts are broken because you went away, there is a part of our subconscious that is nevertheless happy, because we obviously succeeded in encouraging you to be interested in this wide world of ours. We wish you to be able to always use your common sense and follow your instincts in America too. We love you,*
> *Mom and Dad*

XIX. THE FIRST CONNECTIONS WITH HOME AND THE UNUSUAL ENCOUNTER

NEXT DAY, RIGHT AFTER BREAKFAST, I WAS ALREADY IN THE COMMON room (on the first floor), sitting behind the computer, signing into Skype. I was the first one to breakfast and I found it interesting to be almost the only one in the dining room. It was 7 a.m., which meant high noon in Slovenia. I impatiently sat behind the computer…Not just because I was homesick, but also because I wanted to check out how the connection would work and if we were going to be able to see and hear each other despite being separated by thousands of miles. That experiment always seemed most interesting to me.

I brought my headphones with me and connected them to the computer so the sound from speakers wouldn't disturb anybody. In the screen's lower right corner an icon appeared indicating that »Kraljfamily« was logged in. Because all three of them wanted to talk to me at the same time, they logged in under that name. The ringing started.

I answered and we adjusted the microphones. Being worried that we wouldn't be able to hear each other properly, mom set theirs on too loudly. Then we added video feed (mom naturally instructed both of them, knowing the procedure by heart). When she saw me on the screen she cried out enthusiastically.

»This is going to work, isn't it, mom? We can see each other every week,« I encouraged her.

»This is really incredible,« she admitted.

It's true that we've already made the sound test at home, but this was different. We could *see* each other no matter where we were. She too was completely overwhelmed by this »discovery«. The conversation itself – besides the fact that all three of them kept staring into the screen as if they were looking into space – didn't offer anything special. I told them that the journey was very interesting, that I was alright and that I've already been shown the way to school and back. I even stepped aside a bit so they could see the common room and I told them which way was the reception.

At home nothing changed in a single day other than the fact that I was on the computer screen rather than in my room. It seemed like I'd never left. The age of communication definitely has its advantages. We decided that I should send them a text message or an e-mail in a few days, letting them know when to be available on Skype again. And vice versa, of course, if they wished to communicate with me.

When we said goodbye everyone had calmed down. The distance didn't seem such an obstacle anymore. Under such conditions I could have been anywhere.

It was 8 a.m. when we concluded the conversation. Friday morning. I had the whole weekend to get used to the city, to maybe walk to school a few times and to prepare myself for Monday. Luckily I already had a few books with me and was supposed to be informed about everything else when I get there anyway.

I decided to take a little walk before lunch, maybe to school and back again. If I was quick, I could be back before lunch. And if I wasn't, I could turn around halfway there.

I ran to my room and noticed looking out the hallway windows that a beautiful day had awakened outside. I put my sneakers on, stuffed a few necessary things into my jacket pockets (cell phone, lip balm, dad's gift, MP3 player and some money), locked the room and went outside.

I was right. It was a beautiful day and it wasn't hard to find out which way I needed to go. Towards the greenery at the end of the street. The street too was nicely tree-lined and that greenery provided me with the additional sense of safety. When I reached Central West Street, I crossed to the other side to walk alongside the park I had watched from the car the day before.

I really had a nice, long walk. Walking after such a long flight and sleep was quite invigorating. I wondered how invigoratingly sore my muscles were going to be the next day, as I slowly put behind me 87th, 86th, 85th Street...

The main road was a hive of activity with all the pedestrians, cyclists and cars. Each building was attractive in its own way. The Central Park spread out on my left. I took my MP3 player with me to help me speed up my pace. Ela helped me put together a playlist that would suit living in New York. In the past two years she often invited me to »surf the net« with her. The funny thing was that I often didn't have enough time to accept her invitation, because I needed to study in order to maintain my high grade average.

So I turned on my MP3 player and started listening to »Empire State Of Mind«. It really felt like being in a movie. I got to the museum fairly quickly and I knew that I was approximately halfway there.

Ela had prepared a lot of optimistic songs for me. The walk was passing by so quickly that I thought I went too far on 69th Street. Then, with a sigh of relief, I remembered that I was walking downwards, which meant that street numbers were decreasing, rather than increasing.

I put away my MP3 player because my ears started to hurt a little. At the intersection, where I was supposed to turn right towards 68th Street, I missed the green light by a second. So I waited for the stop light to change again.

Just when I decided to examine the signs on this intersection more closely, so I could be sure where to make a turn next time, something confused me. On the other side of the street stood a random group of people, waiting for the green light, just as I was. They were all looking in their respective directions, mostly somewhere in the distance, past me. All but one man.

He had medium-length, blonde, almost white hair and was at least fifty years old. He was entirely dressed in black – he wore a black suit with a black shirt underneath. He looked very dark and contradictory in the bright, sunlit day. Even though his face was dreadfully serious, it could be said that some of his features were softer than his rigid poise. His sagging cheeks on the edges of his angular face gave away his age, but his slightly heart-shaped chin simultaneously radiated some sort of mysterious charm. He was pressing his thin lips together and after a few seconds I got the distinct impression that he was looking at me. Not past me, *right at me.* Even though we were apart by the whole width of the main road, I saw that his irises, hidden in his symmetrically-shaped eyes on top of a straight nose, were colored differently. His right eye was light-blue, while his left eye was dark-brown, almost black. When I put together the complete portrait of this strange-looking man in black, the street suddenly didn't seem so safe anymore. Even in the light of day.

I was even more surprised by the taste of iron in my mouth. Was that blood? Impossible. Did I bite my lip? I used my tongue to inspect the inside of my mouth, to check where that taste was coming from. I couldn't find anything.

The streetlight turned green and once again I got the impression that the movie of my life was playing more slowly that usual. My heart froze as the dark gentleman kept gazing at me. I decided to keep my eyes straight ahead while crossing the road and pretend not to notice him looking at me.

I made a few short steps on the crosswalk and kept looking straight ahead towards my destination. I almost thought that I made it, when I felt a strong thrust against my right shoulder. The dark figure turned halfway towards me in the middle of the street. I heard a few words in the British accent.

»Mind where you're going!«

And he walked away.

I was so shocked that I stopped in my tracks in the middle of the street.

I came to only when vehicles started honking and the remarks to get out of the way started flying. I was slightly confused for the rest of my way.

The taste of iron disappeared.

I sincerely hoped that this wasn't dark gentleman's everyday route, in which case I needed to find another one. I slowly walked towards my destination and noticed the sign »SCHOOL X-ING« in the road. *This is a sign for people like me,* I thought.

When I reached my destination I wasn't that impressed anymore. I quickly turned around and started walking back towards the dorm. Even though going back flew by quickly, I realized that I was actually late.

XX. THE LAST WEEKEND BEFORE SCHOOL

THAT FRIDAY I HAD TROUBLE SLEEPING. I found it really difficult to relax. I wanted to summon my feeling of happiness that accompanied me upon my arrival to this fair city, the feeling of peace I got when looking at Central Park; nevertheless, the man in black crossed my path every time I closed my eyes.

When I wanted to see a calm sea behind my eyelids, I spotted a boat in the water and in it – a black figure. When I wanted to see a forest, he peeked from behind every tree. When I wanted to see a sandy beach, a black throne arose from the sand with a man in black sitting on it, saying to me in the British accent: »Mind where you're going!«. Even when I wanted to count sheep, he walked among them and stared at me seriously.

O.K., I thought. I'll count men in black, if it'll help me go to sleep. The more of them, the better the result for me. And so I started. One man in black crossing the road. Two men in black crossing the road... And so more and more men in black crowded on my side of the street. When I realized that I succeeded in setting a trap for myself through the sheer stubbornness, the men in black started laughing and pointing at me. They slowly started reaching their arms towards me, like they wanted to grab me by my neck. Horrified I opened my eyes and took a deep breath.

That won't work. I got up and turned on the light. I felt much better with the light on. I looked at my watch. 1 a.m. *Perfect. What now?* I took a piece of paper and decided to draw him as best as I could. I tried to capture any detail I could remember…The chin, the cheeks, differently colored irises, blond hair…

Then I had a nice conversation with him. I held the drawing in front of my eyes and said to him:

»Dear man in black. I've no idea who you are, that's why I'm going to be very happy if you let me sleep. I haven't done anything to you, so you've no reason to be angry with me. Maybe you've confused me with somebody else. Thank you very much for having discussed this in a civilized manner. Have a pleasant evening and a good night.«

I folded the piece of paper and put it in my planner. I went to bed and pretended to have forgotten to turn off the light. I remembered some American movie, where a little girl didn't want to turn off the light when going to bed, because she was afraid of »slimy soul suckers«. I smiled at the thought of having the IQ of a seven-year-old.

I closed my eyes and discovered that he was gone. There was a light behind my eyelids. Maybe there was something to it. I didn't know if the conversation or the light had helped, but the man in black left me alone and I was able to go to sleep.

On Saturday and Sunday I didn't go out much. Partly because of the rain, partly because I wanted to get to know my new home better. The dorm additionally filled up during those two days. I too got two new neighbors, but I didn't start hanging out with them immediately. I decided to give them some time so they could get used to their new environment.

I was looking forward to school. My English was pretty good and I didn't have any difficulties to discuss anything with anybody, be it in the reception, common room or dining room. I enjoyed the atmosphere too. Everybody treated everybody else with respect. Having flown in from all corners of the world prevented the formation of closed groups within the dorm. We had each other and that was it.

Even though I was very pleasantly surprised by the hospitality and the nice general atmosphere within the dorm, I couldn't wait to go to school. I wanted to know what my new classmates would be like, what we would study. Subconsciously I probably wanted to understand why was I drawn here so strongly.

On Sunday evening I went to bed especially early. Now I could sleep even with the light off. I simply imagined that I was sending friendly thoughts to the man in black and he vanished at the very thought of kindness. He obviously couldn't stand for somebody to feel good in his company. So I slipped into dreams easily and looked forward to the day I'd been waiting for these past four years…

XXI. THE FIRST DAY OF SCHOOL IN NEW YORK

Since I knew that I was going to walk to school the next morning, I'd taken two pieces of bread with a spread from the dining room the evening before for the next day's breakfast. That way, after turning off the alarm clock and preparing breakfast, it felt like having my own apartment. A dwelling place where I was my own master. I enjoyed looking out to the street while I was eating. The time when dawn announces the awakening of a new day always seemed mysteriously invigorating and almost fairytale-like to me. The first people were already on their way to work and a few cars drove down the street. I finished my breakfast and put on the clothes I'd prepared the night before.

I knew that we would receive the official school T-shirts, which were optional, though. We were allowed to wear our own clothes if we wanted to. Students even used to wear school T-shirts when there was a danger of staining, for example, instead of an apron in home economics class or as a protective garment during chemistry class.

I didn't want to be too conspicuous anyway. I put on a pair of jeans, a purple T-shirt with white inscription, and a pair of purple flat pumps that matched the T-shirt pretty well. I must admit, I prepared that combination already back home. I stood in front of the mirror for about an hour, holding the photographs of students attending my school, comparing my appearance to theirs. I really wanted to fit in. At the same time I consciously tried to hold myself back, so I wouldn't give the impression of someone who craves the attention…That particular combination made me feel spontaneous and relaxed. Just perfect for meeting new people.

I packed my backpack, took my jacket and headed out. I said hi to the receptionist – her name was Jeanie and she asked us to call her by her first name – and stepped out.

I already knew the way very well, even though it looked quite different so early in the morning. The birds in the park hadn't awoken yet and the old houses looked a bit darker. The disturbing incident from three days ago crept into my thoughts and I started thinking that it might by useful to buy a bike. Cycling is healthy, you don't pollute the environment and you reach your destination quicker.

So that day I started watching the cyclists more closely. The road alongside Central Park offered a good sight distance and cyclists didn't have any trouble joining the traffic flow. That was it. I already had my cyclist's license and maybe I could use the credit card mom gave me… Maybe I could find a secondhand bike at a bargain price…I should ask around how these things work and where you can park your bike. That would be really helpful. I was still slightly afraid of the subway…

The sun was rising very quickly and it started to reveal the streets full of cars. Even though the traffic was quite smooth, some drivers honked their horns or cut each other off. The sidewalks were getting busier and people mostly walked very quickly. The staircase leading to and out of the subway was very crowded. I saw a lot of business people and men wearing ties.

When I got to the crossing on the corner of 68th Street, I immediately remembered the incident from three days ago. I quickly scanned the crowd waiting at the stoplight. There were a lot of people dressed in black but none of them looked at me. Most of them were looking down or staring somewhere across the street, towards the park, for example. They were just businessmen waiting at the stoplight and they couldn't have cared less for delusions of some high school student on the other side of the street. I was glad and felt reassured that the Friday incident was obviously just a one-time event. It just happened so that I came across someone once that gave me an unexplainable feeling of guilty conscience and looked at me with a mixture of anger, superiority and dark charm. Once in a lifetime.

And luckily – never again.

The stoplight turned green and awoke me from my thoughts. The crowds from both sides of the street merged and nothing dramatic happened. No thrusts against my shoulder, no British insults…I turned around one last time and looked back towards the crossing. In my mind I said goodbye to the experience which I couldn't classify either as good or bad. I was glad and proud that I'd experienced something thrilling on my first day in America. Straight out of a movie.

I got to the school and was an hour early. A few students were already entering the main gate and I decided to join them. I knew which floor the administration office was on and I took the staircase just off the lobby. I thought it was funny that I knew so much about this school. If I had enrolled in a high school in Ljubljana, I wouldn't have dreamed about surfing the Internet day after day, making inquiries about its employees, researching on which floor was what…But because I was setting on a journey to the other end of the planet, I *needed* to know everything. If it had been possible to find out where the toilets were, I would have discovered even that.

I waited in front of the administration office and was inexplicably afraid to go in. Blue chairs were lined up in the hallway and I took the nearest one to the door. A few students walked by, each with their own set of problems and they didn't take any notice of me. Waiting in front of the administration office was obviously a standard practice here. Finally, a student with long black hair stopped in front of me. She had dark eyes and aesthetically shaped eyebrows. Her had a fringe cut in a straight line over her forehead and her red lips smiled from her face.

»You're new, aren't you?« she asked in genuine American English.

»Yes, I am. Is it that obvious?«

She smiled.

»It's obvious *enough*, because it's your turn and you're still waiting. There are just two possibilities here: either you simply don't know you may go in, or you're afraid to go in. Or both. So you must be new.«

»You got me.«

I smiled, because I realized that her smart little speech was actually a joke. She was glad because audience's response was positive. She stuck out her hand.

»I'm Hannah.«

»I'm Ina.«

She repeated my name as if she wanted to check whether she heard it correctly. I expected this to happen frequently in the future. Without a word she took my hand so I got up. She knocked, opened the door and said casually:

»Hi, Mrs. Britmann, this is our new student Ina. She wants to know where are we going to get our T-shirts and probably also when and where our first day of school will start. And I want to know if that'll be in the gym this year too.«

»Oh, yes, I forgot to mention in the notice that we're meeting in the gym,« exclaimed the friendly lady with curly gray hair and reading glasses on her nose.

»I'm so sorry, this has never happened before!« she corrected her glasses absent-mindedly and succeeded in calming me down with her apology. Such bursting into the office was quite a shock for me but I tried not to show it. Hannah was obviously a year in front of me and I took it as her favor to me. Such as a friendly shove into the sea, when you are standing on a beach considering painfully if you should jump in or not. Quick and painless.

Mrs. Britmann gave us the requested information and directed us towards the gym. On our way there I learned that Hannah was the editor of the school newspaper. Coming from her mouth it sounded simple and nothing too dramatic. Another year in this school, I suppose. I told her I was from Slovenia and that caught her attention.

»Wow, you speak pretty good for someone from so far away,« she commended me. I sensed that the name of the country I was coming from didn't tell her much, but she found it exotic.

»Say something,« she encouraged me.

»What do I say?«

»Well, how do you say...the first day of school, for example?«

I told her and thought it was hysterical how she almost twisted her tongue trying to learn the sentence.

»What is this, Russian or what?« she protested. I explained to her that some Slavic languages had many similarities, but were sometimes also very different. Some words might even sound similar, but can differentiate in meaning. In spite of the fact that she found it very difficult, she persistently repeated the sentence until it sounded at least similar to how I had said it. Her »r« still sounded English, of course. She proudly repeated the sentence and coming out of her mouth, it sounded like Chinese. In short, like something extremely learned and she was the only one besides me who knew what it meant.

We got to the gym where quite a few students already waited for the ceremony to begin. The hall with the arched ceiling had a very pleasant feeling. It was used for gym classes as well as for various cultural events. There was a space in the wall under the balcony with a set stage. Above the stage was a basketball hoop attached to the balcony. Dark blue sheets, obviously school flags, hung from the balcony. The space was filled with chairs arranged in a semi-circle, with blue padded benches surrounding them.

We separated temporarily, because we had to sit in different parts of the hall due to the sitting arrangement of our respective classes. When I was a few feet away, she called my name again.

»Hey, Ina?«

»What?«

She smiled. »Uspesen prrrvi solski dan,« she said in Slovene and tried to pronounce the »r« as correctly as possible.

I smiled back and said in English:

»Thanks. You too.«

I went to sit in the first row with other freshmen. Just before the period started the speakers blasted the instruction that all students needed to report to the gym without any exceptions. The hall was already filled up pretty good. After a minute or so the bell announced the start of the period.

The faculty was crowded in front of the stage and I watched them with interest, wondering who is going to teach us this year. A nice dark haired young lady – she must've been around thirty-five – was testing the microphone, which squeaked a few times in the large resounding space.

»Dear students, I hope you can hear me well. Welcome to this beautiful school on the first day…« She explained all the details and all the rules we needed to know. Where and when to get the T-shirt, when was lunchtime, how and when to turn to the administration office for help… Then she made an official introduction:

»And without any further ado, let me introduce our school's principal. Please give a big applause for our principal, Mr. Aidan A. Davies!«

Another door opened behind the stage and behind them stood the introduced man. Suddenly, my blood turned cold in my veins. Obviously the story hadn't ended yet, it's only begun. The man in black was looking straight ahead, into the hall, and it seemed like he was looking for something. Looking for *someone*. He calmly marched to the front of the stage and took the microphone. I was glad to be sitting in the second row and not the first. I slowly leaned forward and tried to hide behind the person in front of me. And that was exactly what attracted the principal's attention. He found me in a split second and even though he was addressing the entire hall, it seemed to me that he was looking at me constantly. I could feel the taste of iron in my mouth again.

»I'd also like to welcome you to this school on this beautiful sunny day,« he said routinely. It was obvious that he didn't mean what he was saying, not in the least. He became even more serious after the introductory greeting.

»The rules of this institution have been presented to you. Know that they are clear and final. Whoever breaks them, has to answer to me.« He looked at me sharply and something flashed in his differently colored eyes. »And so you won't be disappointed, your principal also has a sense of humor,« he said unusually rigidly, in stark contrast with his words.

»My name is A.A. Davies. Aidan for friends. You may call me Principal Davies!«

I knew what he was getting at. He took the commonly used manner of introducing yourself, when you state your full name and at the same time explain to the other person that they may call you by your first name, like your friends do. This time he reversed the process and thought it was funny. Even though he smiled coldly, so we could see his slightly askew, but still very symmetrical teeth, the students didn't find him amusing. The puzzled faculty members started applauding him. The students followed their lead with mixed feelings.

The principal gave the microphone back to the event organizer and then he vanished as quickly as he came. The entertaining part followed with the school dance group. I liked them very much because they seemed so relaxed and their dance moves contained a lot of attractive hip-hop elements. Finally I was able to breathe normally again and the blood in my brain started circulating properly again.

So. The man in black was the principal of this school. His name was Davies and it would be really smart if I tried to be a good student and to stand out as little as possible if I wanted to stay in one piece. All of a sudden the school didn't seem that magical anymore. Why was I drawn so intensely to this place? Why? I became homesick…I thought of the small village hidden among the hills, where everything was so simple and small. Here everything was so wide and large. A huge, bright city. A great joy and a big mystery at the same time. Big anger, big happiness, strong feelings…Did I come here just to turn around and go back again? No, there must be a purpose to me being here! I have to get stronger so that meeting people doesn't confuse me anymore. I'll do my best to finish this class. And then? We'll see what happens next.

Two attractive dance numbers were followed by the distribution of schedules, classroom registers with students' names and T-shirts. I checked my schedule and saw that I would meet my new classmates in the English Literature classroom. We were supposed to get the keys to our lockers there.

I ran into Hannah on my way out.

»Would you like to know where the English Literature classroom is?« she greeted me from afar. I got the feeling that nothing could surprise her.

»Yes, please,« I said politely.

She started explaining, then stopped, thought for a second and said: »You know what? I'm going in that direction too, we can go together.«

A few freshmen heard what we were talking about and followed us automatically. On the way to the classroom I noticed several metallic drinking fountains. I found that to be a imaginative idea. I'd heard many times that it was healthy to drink a lot of fresh water during studying – as well as in general. Here that theory was put into practice. On the way, Hannah also showed me that lockers were situated on the third floor and warned me that I needed to be patient there. That was a pretty crowded area during recesses because everybody wanted to exchange their textbooks and other things. I liked the fact that lockers were sensibly arranged so that available space was used optimally. Lockers too were blue, as was the floor. Every locker had a small round padlock in the middle. For easier recognition each padlock had a small dot in the middle and every dot was colored differently.

When we got to the classroom I thanked her, but she just waved her hand: »No problem. It was my pleasure. You're basically quite alright, you know.« Even though she didn't sound convincing I knew that she meant it.

She kept going down the hall and I stepped into the classroom. The first thing I noticed was that there were no desks, just chairs arranged around the room. Every chair – these were also blue – had a wooden arm on its side, which could be moved to the front and used as a desk. Floors were made of parquet, the walls were whitish in color. Neat wooden cabinets were placed along the sides of the room. There were two blackboards: the green chalkboard (for writing with chalk) was installed on the wall, while at the same time the whiteboard (for writing with markers) could be lowered over it.

The majority of the students were already seated and I found myself in one of those moments when you must act upon intuition. You enter a room full of people. Where should you go? Where should you sit? I looked around the room. I wanted to absorb the atmosphere and read the people in the room as fast as possible. I was in luck: nobody knew anybody else from before. We'd have to start from the beginning. In this classroom too – as in the dorm – there were no little groups. People were on an equal footing. They did talk among themselves, but I had the feeling that they would talk equally friendly among themselves even if I switched all the pairs.

That filled me with a pleasant sense of trust. It didn't matter where I sat. I'd chosen a free chair in the second row. A good-looking female student with blond curly hair sat next to me. Her face was very symmetrical, adorned with green eyes peeping from under the bashful fair eyebrows and beautiful full lips. Even though she was really beautiful, one could tell that she wasn't aware of it. Maybe she was even *ashamed* of her beauty. I decided to approach her.

»Hi.«

She turned around.

»Hi,« she modestly smiled back. She was even prettier when she smiled.

»I'm Ina.«

»My name is Jeanette.«

»So you must be from…«

»France, yes. From a small town of Limay. Half an hour's drive from Paris.«

»I'm from Slovenia. I come from a small village. Half an hour from our capital, Ljubljana.« I liked being able to describe where I was coming from in such a similar manner.

She noticed the similarity, the fact that we both lived half an hour from our respective capitals, and she smiled again. It seemed that before that she thought she was the only foreigner among Americans. Meeting me convinced her otherwise. She wasn't alone.

»Do you like it here?« I continued.

»Tremendously. The teachers are very nice and the students were very kind in directing me here. I have a feeling that I would love it here if it wasn't for…«

She stopped and looked at me again. Probably she wasn't sure if she could trust me. I finished the sentence for her.

»…If it wasn't for that sullen principal?«

She smiled again and nodded. I wondered why she was so insecure. If I had her face, I'd already be on the covers of fashion magazines, and in my private life I'd be known for my parties and who knows what else. But she was so simple. In full contrast to her looks, which she didn't emphasize at all. Without the excessive make-up or fancy clothes. Just a T-shirt and a pair of jeans. And I was convinced that she would, like the majority of people in the classroom, wear the high school T-shirt. To show where we belonged to.

The bell rang and through the door – that was, surprisingly, blue – came the English literature teacher. She looked very nice with the blond pageboy haircut and a fair complexion. A few tiny wrinkles surrounded her blue eyes betraying that she was around…thirty-five?

She came gliding gracefully to her desk and put down the books.

»Welcome, students,« she began like she was going to tell us an interesting fairytale.

»Because we don't know each other yet, it would probably be appropriate to ask you to write your name and country on a piece of paper. This being the English literature class I'd be very pleased if you'd take a few minutes and prepare a brief presentation about yourself in the best possible English. It would be nice if you included something interesting about yourself, such as what you like or dislike. I too haven't introduced myself yet, because I too will take a piece of paper and write down something interesting about me…« and she already started distributing sheets of paper.

I thought that was extremely innovative. After such an introduction one would expect us to really try hard to be as interesting as we could possibly be. I thought of secretly writing down the stories I liked best so I wouldn't forget them. I could also write down the names and memorize them at home.

We only had five minutes to complete the assignment. That was pretty demanding. How do I introduce myself to all of them and entertain them at the same time? I looked around the classroom and saw that the rest of them had been sweating equally nervously over a piece of paper as I was. That calmed me down a bit. After five minutes the teacher took a tennis ball out of her handbag.

»We'll pass this around so that the order in which we do this is quite random. When you're finished with your presentation simply pass the ball to whomever you want.«

She took her piece of paper and ceremoniously cleared her throat. »I'll start this to make it a little easier for you. So: Hello to all of you. My name is Lucy Highmore and I'm your English Literature teacher. The interesting thing about me is that I love the Internet, so all of the assigned homework can always be found on Edlin. I also like Facebook, Myspace and YouTube, so be careful about what you publish on these sites. I know your names now.«

»Well, *not yet…*« somebody said courageously and we all laughed.

»This is it for now. As you can see, it's not that difficult…« she said and put her piece of paper back on her desk.

»And to whom may I pass this beautiful ball to?« she asked smilingly.

Ninety-nine percent of my classmates looked down. I was too late.

»The girl in the second row. Catch!«

And I was cooked. I stood up and tried to relax my arms so they wouldn't betray the shaking caused by excessive beating of my heart.

»Hi, my name is Ina Kralj and I come from Slovenia, which is in European Union. The interesting thing about me is that…I also like the Internet,« I finished quickly.

»I forgot to tell you that one of the rules is that we're not allowed to repeat what the people before us said,« the teacher corrected me and the murmur spread across the classroom. It seemed like most of my classmates had a similar plan.

»Well, alright,« I tried to smile.

»The interesting thing about me is that…« I decided to be honest.

»…I come from a very small country called Slovenia. Hardly anyone truly knows of it; those who think they do usually mistake it for larger Slovakia that has a similar name. The interesting thing about Slovenia is that it has plenty of natural riches: the sea, mountains, lakes, the Karst… all that on such a small territory! And yet we Slovenes don't respect that enough. We don't respect ourselves enough. We mostly crave foreign things, thinking they're better. Foreign places, brands, languages…I have a feeling that I've found myself here among you. That I can be proud of who I am. I feel very comfortable here among you. Even though this is the first time that we see each other. I feel like I already know you. I hope this doesn't sound too strange…« I became afraid of being too honest in front of the classroom of strangers. I looked down. What did I expect? Didn't life teach me anything? How did it end the last time I was completely honest? With two years of shame. And now, on the first day of school I make exactly the same mistake!

Be brave, Ina. I looked up again prepared for the consequences. I was facing thirty-one big smiles. Applause developed in the background and spread across the entire classroom. I certainly didn't expect *that*.

I was looking around the classroom hoping I wasn't dreaming. They were really, but *really* impressed. The teacher's eyes were slightly wet. I wasn't that touching, was I? Just honest. Have they felt that so strongly? Was that even possible?

»Thank you, Ina. Pass the ball forward. I expect the rest of you to be more lenient so I won't have to cry all the time…« she smiled.

I decided to pass the ball further back. In the fourth row, in the corner by the windows sat three boys. The one in the middle stood out by having slightly darker complexion and dark hair. I threw the ball to him. He got up and cleared his throat. He spoke in a serious manner.

»Hello, my name is Robert R. Davies…« Murmur spread across the classroom. Only then we noticed a slight resemblance because the boy had a darker complexion than his father. Everyone became serious in an instant and the boy to his left put his hand over his mouth. He must've had a nice chat with his neighbor, not knowing *who* he was talking to. I wondered what they'd talked about...

»Yes, it's true, my last name is Davies. The interesting thing about me is,« he started smiling, »that I have a father with a bad sense of humor.«

The entire classroom laughed with relief, including the teacher. Robert's neighbor to the left removed his hand from his mouth and laughed cheerfully. My neighbor Jeanette also completely relaxed. She surely must've sensed the oneness that dominated the classroom. I was glad that we all shared the same opinion because that meant that taking classes with these people might even be...pleasant? Yes, I confess. I was having a good time.

»Thank you, Robert. That was really interesting. It's nice to see that you're slightly different, although I have the utmost respect for the Principal...« she corrected her thought, so that we wouldn't get the wrong opinion. The Principal must be respected, by all means. Nevertheless, even Miss Highmore couldn't avoid laughing at her own wry remark.

And so we passed the ball around. Robert passed it to athlete John. John (who was also into opera) passed the ball to Jeanette. After she confided to us that she liked singing when she was alone, she passed the ball to a fair-haired boy with glasses, named Ted. Although he excelled in chemistry, he still didn't know what to do with his life. And he also liked being called Teddy. The New York native Elyssa wanted to be a musician. The next one to catch the ball was dark-haired Dominic, who wanted to become a reporter, but his parents wouldn't allow it. After him came the red-haired Kayleigh, who wanted to be a Hollywood actress. The next one was musician Jesse, who wanted to put a band together, so he asked us to think about joining him. Then the ball was caught by black-haired girl of oriental appearance. She told us she was of Chinese descent and that her name was Ching Lan, which meant »a beautiful orchid«. The next one was Ian, who wanted to become a teacher someday and he knew that ever since he got a younger brother ten years ago. The interesting detail: sometimes, at home, they locked themselves in the bathroom and played school.

The next one to catch the ball was Alysha and she confided to us that she wanted to become a painter. In general, I thought that the really interesting thing about my classmates were the very things they wanted to accomplish in life. They've exploited that fact diligently. As has the next one to catch the ball. He was slightly different, though. He got up and hesitated a bit, like he was deciding whether to tell us his secret or not.

»Well, go ahead, Derek, we don't bite,« joked the teacher. »So far we haven't condemned anyone because of their secret.«

»I…I'd like to become a writer someday. To have a crazy idea that'd become a hit.«

He looked around the classroom. When he saw that we supported him in his intention, he exhaled deeply with relief. He sat down while the teacher went on:

»Writing is healthy for the development of imagination. I really hope you'll make it someday. Bravo, Derek.«

I was glad and honored to be a part of a group of such a nice people. For the first time in my life I saw beauty in the word »classmate«. A person that attends the same classes as you and encourages you in what you do. Miss Highmore had – intentionally or not – hypnotized us in a way that we all wanted to let on much more on the first day of school than we even dared to dream.

The next one to catch the ball was Jimmy and he hinted to Jesse that he play the drums. Then Kelly said she liked to cook. Rebecca wanted to assemble a group and stage a school musical. Philip was an enthusiastic physicist and mathematician and wanted to discover an entirely new theory in the field of energy engineering. Kiana wanted to become a model. Sabrina enjoyed watching TV shows.

»I hope you'll also find the time for school,« said the teacher. That was her least approving remark that day.

The ball was in the air again. Rodney said that he didn't know yet what to do with his life, but that he wanted to learn to play a musical instrument. Gina told us that in her spare time she liked to meditate in Central Park and that she lived near by. Francesca was Italian on her mom's side and wanted to become an opera singer. Elliot liked to play »The Glad Game«. It was a game he always played when something bad would happen to him, by trying to think of as many reasons as possible why that was the best thing that could've happened to him. April liked to go to the cinema. Sasha was a big fan of anything connected to martial arts and TV police shows. George wanted to become a surfing instructor. Lilly wanted to cause a revolution in the field of cosmetics. Black-haired Sienna was probably the only one that didn't like this game we'd been playing and she openly said so. Then she quickly remarked that she liked recesses and passed the ball forward. Brian told us that he loved animals and that he wanted to become a veterinarian. Lance enjoyed listening to French chansons. The last one to catch the ball was fair-haired Christy. It was obvious that she was pretty tired of waiting. She spent the entire period repeating over and over in her head what she was going to say when her turn came. She said she liked old movies and hated waiting. The entire classroom laughed.

It took us the entire period to introduce ourselves. When Christy finished her presentation she looked around the classroom to see if someone was still left and then she returned the ball to the teacher. She thanked us and then quickly mentioned a few more rules regarding the monitors and handed out the keys to the lockers. She also revealed that she was our home-class teacher. That explained the sense of attachment she'd been radiating the entire period. Maybe that was the reason we were so smitten by her.

When the bell rang I was pretty sorry that the period ended so quickly. I put away my notebook, which I used to secretly write down the names so that at home I could repeat who was who. I really wanted to memorize my classmates' names as soon as possible.

The following classes weren't as interesting as the first one. At the end of the school day I was pretty tired. It seemed that I'd spent all my energy in the English literature class when I used up a large amount of adrenaline to overcome my inhibition and tell something interesting about myself. When my adrenalin level dropped I felt happy and relieved. Naturally, I tried to concentrate as best as I could on the names and information. After that period my concentration began to wane. And we had to climb so many stairs during recesses…

During the last – biology – class I almost fell asleep. Each teacher made us say our names in our own way, or we just wrote them on a piece of paper in front of us. But the English literature class was the one we mostly remembered. In biology class we wore our nametags pinned to the chest, like store clerks and hotel employees usually wear them.

I sat in the back row and supported my head with my hands. The others were pretty tired too, yet some of them at least tried not to show that to our teacher, poor Mr. Dawson, who was perfectly innocent in all of this.

In addition to his lecture, which struck me as very monotonous, I soon started listening to birds singing. The waves of both frequencies created a pleasant thinking background. I thought it would be entertaining to count all the things in this school that were blue…and so I gradually stopped hearing the teacher's words as well as birds' song. I thought that a shadow shot past me, then turned towards me and said in a laughing boyish voice: »It's really nice to see you«. I heard that voice more clearly than anything before. Like it was echoing in my head.

I shuddered and straightened. As I opened my eyes I saw with relief that nobody noticed me falling asleep or shuddering. The first day of school and I was already sleeping. I straightened again and rubbed my eyes. The teacher had just written the homework assignment on the blackboard and I copied it in my notebook. A few boys sat in my row and I saw that they too had trouble fighting off sleep.

When the bell rang, we were done for the day. I was at my locker putting my last things away when Hannah came by.

»What's up, freshman? Did you have an 'USPESEN PRVI SOLSKI DAN'?« she tried again in Slovenian. This time I didn't have enough energy to answer her joke with another one.

»Successful and tiring,« I replied politely. I just wanted to go home. »Thank you for everything, Hannah. See you tomorrow.«

»You look tired. Do you have a ride?«

»Not really.«

»I've got a car. Want a lift?«

I wondered what I did to deserve such a generous offer. Could I trust her? I didn't know. I knew that I was really beat. If I walked home, there'd be no telling when I'd get there. Or I would fall asleep on some bench along the way.

»Well…Alright, since you're offering. I'm staying at the international student center.«

»I thought so, yeah. Well, come with me.«

The drive flew by quickly. Hannah was relaxed and smiling, obviously used to the school pace. She drove routinely down Central West Street and said playfully:

»Wouldn't it be nice to go on Broadway one night and see a show that is absolutely new, with fresh, unknown faces that have just been discovered?«

»Yeah, that would be interesting,« I commented, although I didn't have a clue where that idea came from, because I wasn't capable of thinking about anything else than the day in school. When I mentioned my idea about counting all the blue things in our school, she laughed out loudly.

»We've already tried that in our class, but it didn't work. There's too many of them!«

Everything was so much easier and faster in a car. We talked some more about our day, she had a few comments about teachers, and we were already at my place. She offered to come and get me in the morning, saying that she had to drive past here anyway.

»Why are you being so nice to me?« I asked.

»Let's just say that I want to treat people the way I want them to treat me. When I first came to this school I didn't exactly receive a perfect welcome.«

Although I was interested in what had happened to her, I decided not to bother her. The offer to drive me to school in itself seemed almost too kind.

»I wanted to buy a bike, anyway,« I said.

»...my offer stands until you buy one,« she added.

»Well...if you're sure...«

»Of course,« she quickly added, »No problem. See you tomorrow at six-thirty.«

I closed the car door and she drove off the sidewalk. I ran to my room and lay on the bed. My fast breathing started to slow down until I got lost in my thoughts and finally fell asleep. I woke up in the evening. I was glad that I had brought home the croissant I couldn't finish for lunch, because I slept right through dinner. Before I went to bed that night I checked what our homework assignment was. I decided to do it right away. I also went quickly through the names of my classmates and tried to recall their faces...

An interesting day, really. Full of everything. New people, new experiences...Where there is a dark side, there must be a light one too. Like yin and yang.

Thoughts were randomly buzzing through my head as I was preparing to go to bed. Before falling asleep I once again thanked the universe for the beautiful day. This time I didn't have any trouble sleeping like during the weekend. I dropped off in a second.

XXII. DAYS OF SCHOOLING AND ANOTHER ENCOUNTER

EVERYTHING WAS HAPPENING VERY QUICKLY IN THE DAYS THAT FOLLOWED. Hannah waited for me in front of the dorm entrance every morning. I insisted I should repay her somehow, but she wouldn't take any money. She said playfully that I could ask her out for a drink sometime, but it seemed to me that she had enough of her own friends for that.

In school I mostly hung out with Jeanette, Gina, Elliot and Christy. I got along fine with the others too, but the class was simply too big for me to chat with everybody during every recess. Besides, little groups started to form. But not as obvious or as exclusive like those from my past experiences. People started connecting based on their common interests.

Elyssa, Jesse, Rodney and Jimmy already formed a rock band. They were looking for anybody that could help them: songwriters, lyricists, practically anybody that would be interested. Derek and Dominic wrote a few lyrics and they would sometimes meet in the music classroom and try to set music to them. Jeanette and Francesca often joined them and I thought they could make a nice trio with Elyssa. Although they had three totally different voices they sounded very good together.

The boys often hung around the girls, especially before those classes when homework assignments or essays were due. Ordinarily they got along great. It goes without saying that there was absolutely no fighting involved; it was obvious that they'd outgrown that a long time ago.

I found it interesting that, in a way, Robert avoided me. He was always friendly and smiling around other people. When it came to me, he was sort of…reserved. If he noticed, for example, that I was coming down the hall, he pretended not to see me and quickly took off the other way. I didn't think that was fair. I didn't do anything to him. He could at least say hello.

Otherwise, I got along great with the boys. Elliot always knew how to make me laugh. He would circle around the classroom looking for positive things in every problem. By doing that he was really helping me to find a solution even when I was depressed. He loved me the most when I was sad. He immediately came to me and asked what the problem was.

Hannah finally found a way for me to help her. She would often need photographs for articles she was preparing for the school newspaper. Sometimes I helped her gather the material and sometimes I would take photos with my cell phone. One day, when she was writing the article about fire alarms, she sent me down to the basement to photograph the devices that produced the sound informing us to leave the building.

I knew that they were by the staircase leading into the basement. I took my cell phone and headed towards the basement. I wanted to do the job quickly because despite rooms and corridors down there being painted white, the basement always seemed to be emitting some sort of darkness. At least it seemed that way to me.

I quickly turned on the camera on my cell phone. Hannah would later process my amateurish photos so they would look pretty decent. This time I needed to photograph three red electric bells of different sizes. First, I photographed them individually, then all three together from different angles.

Suddenly I felt a strange taste in my mouth. Iron again. Maybe I'd been in the basement for too long, inhaling that heavy metallic smell… Then a sharp British accent crept up from behind me.

»What the hell are you doing down here?«

»I'm…err, I'm taking pictures for the school newspaper. The fire alarm,« I tried to explain. A dark figure started approaching me. It was much taller than me. At least a head and a half.

»Haven't you been told that only the janitor was allowed to access the school basement? Besides me, that is. Just imagine how crowded it would be around these devices if everyone was coming down here.«

Then he moved even closer and my back hit the wall behind me. That meant that I had nowhere to run, much less to be able to defend myself. He added in a serious voice:

»People might get *hurt*.«

»U-understood,« I tried not to stutter. I was already shaking. He smiled coldly, faking kindness.

»I'll be merciful this time. You get only a tree-hour detention. And if I ever find you down here again…«

»It won't happen again, I promise,« I assured him.

He took a piece of paper from his jacket pocket and handed it to me: »Take this to the administration office. There you'll get the instructions what to do next.«

I quickly put away my cell phone and started walking up the stairs. At first insecurely, then increasingly faster, and when I was certain that he wasn't behind me anymore, I ran with superhuman speed.

I must've been white as a sheet when I ran into Hannah, because she immediately asked me if I was alright.

»I am, I am. I'll just take this to the administration office…«

She snatched the piece of paper from my hands. When she read its content she turned white too. Tears filled her eyes and it was obvious that she was really sorry.

»Ina, please forgive me for dragging you into this. I really didn't mean to do that. I thought everything would be okay,« she was actually crying now, »I didn't know you'd run into him. I really didn't. I wouldn't go down there alone and I urgently needed the photo…«

»It's only detention. I'll hold out for a few hours. Don't get too dramatic.«

I tried to console her. I've never seen her that emotional and worried.

»And it's all my fault, it's all my fault…« she repeated in tears.
»Would you care to explain to me what's going on if you don't want to be consoled?« I yelled almost hysterically.

»Alright. I'll meet you when you're done with detention. After school. At Rigoletto's.«

At the restaurant near school, where students often went to eat, then. Alright. I handed over that piece of paper in the administration office and was told which classroom served as the school's detention center, so I went there. It wasn't the least bit dramatic. One of the teachers was appointed to keep order in the classroom. And so we sat in silence. I closed my eyes and relaxed. *This could actually be fun*, I thought. Nobody said relaxing was prohibited. I could play with my cell phone like some other detainees, but I wasn't in the mood for it. It got me in enough trouble for one day.

The first two hours went by pretty quickly, the third one little slower. My chair was pretty uncomfortable and I wondered if that was the point of school detention: maybe the punishment was supposed to be educational enough so that you simply wouldn't repeat your offence. I wondered if such a punishment could influence your grades. I couldn't imagine that something like that was possible. If I were the principal, I'd separate such things entirely. One's behavior has nothing to do with one's grades…Of course, if *I* were the principal…Since Mr. Davies was the principal, the situation was probably slightly different.

I needed to read the school statute again so I wouldn't get unnecessary punishment like this one anymore. I hoped that Hannah wasn't being too hard on herself…

And so the third hour slowly passed too. I went outside and headed towards the red-framed display window of the restaurant where we were supposed to meet.

XXIII. AT LUNCH

I WAS STILL IN THE STREET WHEN I NOTICED HANNAH SITTING IN THE darkest corner of the room. It seemed to me that by trying to be unnoticeable she attracted attention even more. As did I when I was trying to hide behind a row of people sitting in front of me on the first day of school. I entered through the red-framed glass door and walked up to her. I talked her into leaving her dark corner - we namely had to go to the cash register to pick and pay for the food and drinks. Only then we could choose the spot where we wanted to sit. I picked a slice of »Maestro« while she chose a slice of »Fiesta«. We both decided to have a Coke with it. The waiter gave us the chosen slices but had to go to the storage to get fresh bottles. He told us he'd bring the drinks to our table. After we paid Hannah still wanted to sit in her dark corner. I refused her:

»Come on, let's sit somewhere bright like normal people.«

»No, thanks.«

»Come on, we're just talking,« I tugged at her sleeve.

»No, it's fine here,« she got increasingly louder.

»Hey, we're not selling drugs!« I snapped at her. In that exact moment the songs changed on the radio and by pure accident my last sentence was suddenly the only thing that everybody could hear. I discharged it into silence. People turned towards us. Embarrassed, I quietly sat on a chair next to Hannah.

»You must be really embarrassed to listen to me, ha?« she smiled.

»You're practically begging for attention in this darkness. Just so you know,« I retorted.

»Let's get to the point,« I continued. »Who was that silly girl crying and dramatizing in front of me in the hallway three hours ago and why did she do that?«

»It's complicated…I swore I wouldn't tell anybody…you don't know what trouble I could get into…«

»You can trust me. You know that.« To get her in a better mood I joked: »After all, you *have to* tell me, because you got me into trouble…«

»Well, okay. But you have to swear to me that you'll never, never, never…«

»I swear I'll never, never, never…«

»…tell that to anybody.«

»…tell that to anybody, except if that somebody could help out in some way…«

»NO!« she almost screamed. People again turned in our direction. »TELL NOBODY. PERIOD.«

»Okay, okay. I'll tell nobody, period. Tell me already.«

She started slowly and insecurely.

»Well, it happened a year ago. I was just about to go home. I had a lot of stuff in my hands, including the slippers I changed out of. I was standing on the staircase when one of my slippers fell over the banister and into the depth. Right down to the basement floor. When I put the rest of the stuff away I went to the basement. I picked up the slipper and then…I remembered the rule that nobody, but nobody was allowed to go to the basement and I really wanted to know why. Since the school had ended, the building became ever more quiet and it seemed that the basement was empty too. I told myself that I'd go down the corridor once and then straight home. I went past the fire alarms. Even though the corridor was white, it seemed spooky. I walked down the corridor opening doors. I saw a lot of rooms. The copy room, the storeroom, the repository…The corridor was getting darker and darker. At the far end one door was left slightly ajar. Through the opening I saw an ordinary white candle standing in the middle of the room and next to it, on the floor, a wooden board with some sort of paintings on it. The room was really dark and there were masks and amulets hanging on the walls. Suddenly, the door closed in front of me…«

»YOUR COKES, young ladies!« shouted the waiter and we jumped. He materialized right next to us.

»Thank you very much,« answered Hannah in a tone of voice that communicated quite the opposite message. He understood and vanished quickly. Hannah confusedly shook her head.

»Where was I?«

»The door suddenly closed in front of you…«

»Oh yes, that's right. So, the door closed. Suddenly, his face arose from the darkness in front of me. He leaned against the door with his hand. A dialogue followed, which I can't remember clearly because I was absolutely terrified. He told me he had the power to destroy me and that I wouldn't be able to get good education in life. In short, that he could completely ruin me. He soon went from words to actions. He brutally grabbed my elbow and threatened me. After much persuading and an oath that I wouldn't tell anyone about the dark little room in the basement, he eventually let me go. I was frightened like never before. Even when he gave me the permission to leave, I was barely able to move from fear…«

She took a few sips of Coke. Talking in such a frightened state exhausted her. Nevertheless, I felt relief. And at the same time a burden in my heart, because I knew what kind of responsibility I'd taken on. I'd never, never, never…tell this to anybody.

We ate in silence. Even though my pizza was very tasty, I couldn't care less about it. I was still arranging new information in my head and replaying a few favorite parts of the horror story I'd just heard…A dark room…A candle…A board…Masks…Amulets…What was the meaning behind all that? Was there a connection with the taste of iron I felt in my mouth every time we met?

We left. I thanked her for everything she confided in me and promised her again that her secret was safe with me and that I would protect it with my life. She drove me back home. We didn't talk much during the drive. I think that we were both preoccupied with thoughts buzzing around in our heads…

XXIV. THE SECRET VISITOR

W HEN SHE DROPPED ME OFF AT THE DORM, WE QUICKLY SAID goodbye and the car drove off. For a moment I stood still in the dim street full of old houses. I wanted to clear my head before entering the world of other people and greeting the receptionist on the way to my room. I watched the houses across the street and thought that they were cinematically old. As I was absorbed in the appearance of the street I felt a hand on my shoulder. Someone was obviously behind me. I quickly turned around.

There was nobody there. Still, I felt I wasn't alone. Someone was near me. Scared I ran into the dorm, quickly greeted the receptionist and rushed off to my room. Even though I generally trust people and hadn't locked my door so far, this time I made an exception.

Being much too awake to be able to go to sleep, I decided to occupy myself with something. I sat behind the desk and tried to find something to do. I took the things from my schoolbag and started doing homework. First I went through my math notes; I marked the spots I didn't understand to research them later on the Internet. Then I read through my biology notes, my chemistry notes…

Since it wasn't too late yet, I went down to the common room to see if I could still use the Internet. As I was walking past the reception desk, Jeanie stopped me.

»Ina! Is everything alright?«

»What?«

»Are you alright? You ran past me earlier like you'd just seen a monster.«

»O yeah, that. No, no, I'm okay,« I tried to calm her down.

»What happened?« she wanted to know.

»Nothing, nothing, I just remembered that I forgot to do something for a friend…« I made a lame excuse. I couldn't think of anything more sensible. Should I have said I was schizophrenic?

»Well, alright. And if there should be something wrong, you just tell me,« she concluded.

»Okay. Great. Thanks. Just one more thing. May I still go online for half an hour?«

»Of course, till 10 p.m.« It was just past 9 p.m.

»Thank you so much.«

I went to the computer and slowly forgot about my worries. I finished my homework and even browsed through a few Slovenian educational websites. The material was more or less similar to ours, but browsing through Slovenian pages made me feel like I was at least maintaining my mother tongue. Lately I'd been speaking so much English that I started to think in it. I was quite relieved when I saw that I could still connect to my roots.

At 10 p.m. I went back to my room. I prepared the things I needed for the next day and put them in my bag. Then I slowly prepared to go to bed. I tried to think about nice things. The occurrence in the street surely couldn't have been real; it was impossible for someone to just materialize next to me and then vanish again. I get too much into it, that's the problem. That's why I wouldn't watch horror movies in the cinema. Because the feeling of horror would follow me home. I simply had to forget what Hannah told me. I couldn't tell that to anybody anyway, so why would I burden myself with it by thinking about it?

No. I consciously started thinking about the following day in school, about my obligations, about how I could invite Gina and Jeanette out for a drink sometime, because there were numerous nice coffeehouses around our school, where we could have a coffee, tea, or something similar.

I laid on the bed and turned off the light. When I closed my eyes, I got the unpleasant feeling of not being alone again. I turned on the lamp by the bed once more. There was no one there. I even looked under the bed and found myself to be silly. Like I was looking for monsters in the closet.

I lay down and turned off the light again. And again I felt like somebody was standing by my bed. *Maybe I am crazy*, I thought, *or maybe I could simply face my hallucinations.*

After all, I was alone in my room, thanks to God. I couldn't imagine what it would be like having a roommate.

»Could you please go?« I said calmly. I spoke out loudly on purpose.

»Maybe you're just a figment of my imagination, maybe you're not, it's all the same to me. Could you please go so I could sleep in peace? Please.«

Silence. I didn't expect an answer, of course. If someone would answer me in the darkness, I'd probably die of fear. Although it's true that all of a sudden I felt a light breeze on my face and then – solitude. Whatever there was in my room, it obviously left. I was relieved. *You see*, I told myself, *you only needed to talk to it*. I fell asleep feeling a weird combination of confusion and relief.

XXV. BLENDING IN

THREE MONTHS PASSED BY AND IT SEEMED TO ME THAT I HAD PERFECTLY blended in with my new environment. In the dorm I'd met new neighbors – Eszter and Rossana, who always knew how to make me laugh. They both sported pageboy haircuts; Eszter had black and Rossana blond hair. They were friends from Hungary and I was very surprised to hear that. They too were happy when we discovered that not only were we neighbors in the dorm, but also in the sense of our native countries' geographic position. Every time we met we would say »Hi, *neighbor*!« in a meaningful way: we liked the fact that the meaning of those words was ambiguous and that we were the only ones to understand it. Sometimes in the evenings they would ask me to join them for a girly gathering.

I talked to my family every week and I saw that they completely accepted the new living conditions. Mom was still the leader of the team when camera and sound were switched on. And she would still turn the volume all the way up – so we would *really* hear each other. I became used to asking her at the beginning of every conversation to turn the speakers and microphone to medium level if she didn't want me to turn deaf. Conversations were mostly filled with interesting things (naturally, I only talked about things that couldn't make them worry about me). Enough interesting details and news piled up in a week, so we would always have lively discussions, be it about my new grades, or about dad discovering important differences between two beetles…

I felt very comfortable in school too. I tried to store the incident with the principal in the deepest part of my subconscious and I really started to study. I wasn't alone in it though, like I'd been before. It seemed that the majority of my classmates already knew about my trick, because they were all really interested in the subjects. It even occurred that we'd compare who had the best notes – not just to compete, but to copy those that were the most accurate and precise, and we'd all learn from them. Even our home-class and English literature teacher, Mrs. Highmore, had to admit that we were a very strong class and that we liked helping each other. Even Sienna softened and smiled from time to time, even though she still got mad when Elliot started brainwashing her with »The Glad Game«. He was actually drawn to unhappy people and Sienna often didn't even *want* to be in a good mood. That was part of her image, her character.

Months were getting colder and before I knew it, it was already December. Mrs. Highmore announced that we would collect gifts and organize a small raffle before Christmas.

I was pleased, because I always found such things entertaining. Especially in this class, in this company, in this environment…I dwelled for a whole week on what to choose as a gift for a random classmate. It would be good if it was something useful, and of course, appropriate for a boy or a girl…I even included Hannah into it. We'd go to the stores together and regardless of what she suggested, I always found a reason why I thought that present wasn't appropriate. Except one time, when the situation was quite the opposite. In a music store I spotted a CD entitled: Christmas Evergreens in Rock Version.

»This could be interesting,« I said.

»What? Christmas rock songs? Hmm, maybe that could work. The only question is what is the teacher going to think if she gets your gift. Francesca also probably wouldn't like it…«

I was almost sorry for telling her so much about our class.

»Okay, okay, I know,« I said reluctantly. I couldn't imagine giving that to somebody as a gift, but I really liked the whole idea. Christmas in a new, playful way. Crazy and likeable. Maybe I could even buy it for myself, to conjure up the Christmas spirit…Hannah put the subject of our conversation back on a shelf ages ago and we headed out of the store.

»And what do you want? Think about what you'd buy for yourself,« she encouraged me.

We were just walking past stalls with crystals.

»For myself I'd buy…for myself I'd buy…« I started looking at some merchandise made of crystals and minerals, »For myself I'd buy a pendant.« I picked up a bright brown pendant above which the inscription read: Tiger's eye.

»Hmm. Interesting. You're right, this is appropriate for a guy and a girl.« She read the attached slip of paper: »It helps with studying, improves self-confidence…it's used for protection or as a talisman against evil thoughts and spells, it shows how to properly use your powers, increases telepathic abilities and clear perception of people…You believe all this?« she looked at me from under her eyebrows.

»It doesn't matter. The thought counts. I believe that something bigger than us exists, yes. A form of energy, surely. And if at least a bit of that energy is caught within this stone…I don't know. Maybe it works.«

Hannah smiled: »So, it's not about the power of the spell, but rather about the power we attribute to the spell…«

»Exactly. I think this pendant will do perfectly.« I immediately waved to the saleslady. I also found a neat little box to go with it. I handed over both items to her and I paid the requested amount.

I was glad and satisfied that I had found the solution in such a nice and original way. And I also needed to thank Hannah somehow. I thought of buying something bigger for her. We'd really connected in recent months. I'd never talked to anybody that freely before. And I also knew what she wanted.

It was already very late when we said goodbye. I was really grateful to her for coming with me. It didn't matter that I was the one picking out the stone; what mattered was that I had her to comment on my ideas, help with suggestions and drive me from one shopping center to the next. My neighbors were also in a good mood. When we said hello they hinted that we needed to get together urgently, because they had a little present for me. I smiled and protested that they needn't have done that. Since they insisted, I agreed to meet with them soon and said goodbye. I tiredly sat on the bed and entered a list of people in New York I wanted to present with gifts into the reminder on my cell phone. Naturally, I also added my neighbors. When I finished, I put down the phone and opened the bag with my acquisition from the stall. Tiger's eye peeked out of the little box and I thought how this stone really must be special. I myself also wanted to add to the stone some secret power and fortunate appeal. Using my free hand I improvised a magic motion with which the stone should receive special abilities…I hoped that Jeanette would get it, or maybe Gina…It didn't matter. The one getting it should have luck in life. I impatiently put it back in its box and started counting minutes to the school raffle before drifting off to sleep…

XXVI. THE LAST SCHOOL DAY BEFORE HOLIDAYS

THAT MORNING I WAS SLIGHTLY TIRED BECAUSE THE NIGHT BEFORE WE celebrated Christmas at my neighbors'. I gave them a couple of gift cards for a cosmetics store and some handmade pralines. Since they enjoyed dressing up nicely from time to time, they loved my gifts. They gave me a friendship bracelet like the ones they were wearing and we had a really nice evening. We compared celebrating Christmas in Slovenia and in Hungary. They taught me to play a few games. That's why I went to bed later than usual. In the morning when Hannah came to get me, so we could drive to school together, I almost overslept. Luckily I already had all my things prepared, so I was ready in a few minutes. I carried the neat gift I bought in a special bag so that the box wouldn't get damaged. I had the feeling that it was going to be a special day…

The school was also festively decorated. Some students even wore red jackets with white fluff. Or they wore red caps with white pompoms. Santa Clause really is a trademark. I myself didn't wear anything red. I was already slightly tired of that color because it could be seen practically everywhere, so I didn't even think of wearing it. I wore a white and green T-shirt and accordingly, the rest of my clothes (winter coat, jeans, shoes…) were matching. Nevertheless I wanted to look at least slightly festive, so I experimented more with make-up and earrings.

The school day slowly began. This time I couldn't pay attention to what we were learning. My thoughts kept constantly drifting to the ceremonial event to be taking place during English literature class that was last on the schedule. That's why I was only half-listening to the other school subjects, regardless of how entertaining, festive or interesting the lecturers were. If someone should ask me something, I'd only be able to mechanically repeat their last spoken words, but couldn't put them in the proper context of the subject matter.

Finally. The bell indicated the start of the last period. I tried to walk slower than I really wanted. I had to hold myself back, so I wouldn't talk about the celebration all the time. Even I didn't know why that period meant so much to me. »It's only a stupid Christmas raffle,« many would say. Every gift will get its number and then we'll draw. The gifts had to be worth around five dollars, which wasn't much.

What am I actually looking forward to, I was asking myself. *A cheap gift? The drawing?*

We entered the classroom and sat in our chairs. All these months we'd been sitting in this classroom just as we did on the first day of school. Probably purely instinctively, because we'd memorized the arrangement and therefore knew where everybody was sitting. I also felt the most safe in this classroom. I didn't know why. Somehow it was most *ours*. The recess – during which Jeanette kept wondering what was in my small box – was over pretty quickly and soon Miss Highmore came in too.

»I hope you're prepared for the festive event,« she said as soon as she walked in. »I too brought my gift, but before that we'll enjoy a special screening of Charles Dickens' A Christmas Carol...«

She pulled down the whiteboard, which hung above the green one and turned off the light.

»I think we're never too old to watch a quality animated feature,« she said in a relaxed manner.

The classroom buzzed with surprise. Some of my classmates were against it, the others laughed. The girls were mostly for it, except for Sienna, of course.

The teacher ignored those opposed and turned on the projector that was prepared in advance. We watched Disney's adaptation of A Christmas Carol and I thought it was quite entertaining. And moving. Right at the end, when stingy Ebenezer Scrooge already softens, gives presents to everybody around him and hugs little Tim, I almost started crying too. I looked around the classroom and saw that I wasn't the only one. Dissatisfaction with having to watch a cartoon had subsided long ago and everybody absorbedly watched the program right to the last minute. Even Sienna. Elliot sat next to her. At the most moving moment he took her hand that rested on the desk. For half a second her face reflected Christmas idyll ecstasy; then she suddenly became serious and moved her hand away indignantly.

»I hope you've enjoyed yourselves, like I have,« said Mrs. Highmore, »and just so you know, A Christmas Carol is one of the most important works of English literature. Today you saw its more entertaining adaptation. It's never too soon or too late to become carefree as children again. Especially at Christmas.«

She was right and no one contradicted her anymore.

»And now we have a few minutes left for…presents!« she announced festively.

It happened quicker than I expected. We all put our presents on the desk by the blackboard. Before that we glued on the numbers that were also prepared on the desk. Then each of us would draw a piece of paper and take the present under the drawn number from the table. If somebody drew their own present, they were allowed to return it and try again. My present was under number 14. I was on a constant lookout to see who'd get it.

I looked to the last row towards the boys and was surprised to see that everybody wasn't as excited about the raffle as I was. Some of the boys were sitting and talking, while Robert even dozed off leaning against his arm. I was pretty disappointed. I thought they'd find raffle more interesting and absolutely wasn't expecting people to be sleeping. Mostly girls were gathered around the teacher. In spite of the lack of interest in winnings from the last row I was still on the lookout. I *was* interested in what's going to happen and I wasn't going to miss the raffle just because of some bores in the last row.

Jeanette got the present prepared by Lance. Gina drew George's present. I drew the present under number 5. It was angular as if a CD was wrapped in a wrapping paper. I obviously got music, which was alright. I kept on looking who was going to draw my Tiger's eye. There were only three presents left on the desk. As she did with all the other drawn numbers, the teacher read out loudly this one too.

»The drawn number is...14!«

I immediately looked towards the person receiving my present. Our eyes met. He obviously didn't care about dozing anymore. His look was calm and confident. He nodded towards me like he knew exactly whose present he got. He smiled at me and I looked away in surprise. How could he have known that he got my present?

Robert took the small box without words and sat back in his chair. He opened it and hung the stone around his neck without thinking. I don't know why I blushed and suddenly became very hot. To relieve the tension I also opened my present. A CD came out of the wrapping, with the cover that was very well known to me: Christmas Evergreens in Rock Version.

And that wasn't all. When I opened it, there was the CD on the right and the cover with a dedication on the left that said:

> *I wish you an exceedingly Merry Christmas, Ina.*
> *Best regards, R.*

I stared in disbelief and closed the CD. I remembered I was in a classroom full of people and that it would be smart to hide the dedication. I'd talk to him later. I opened the plastic box again and took the cover out. I put it in a slightly bigger pocket in my jacket. If somebody should ask me what I got, I could show them only the CD.

The first one to turn towards me was Jeanette. I quickly showed her the CD and I got away with it. In reality she was so preoccupied with her own present that she barely looked at mine, said how inventive it was and focused on her present again.

The period went by pretty quickly. Robert was the first one to get up and leave when the bell rang and although I rushed behind him, he was gone when I got to the hallway. I didn't even see in which direction he went. Students poured out of the classrooms and it'd have been senseless to look for him. He obviously had a good reason for leaving. In any case, he needn't have bothered with magic tricks just to leave the classroom. I found that sort of behavior especially offensive, also because of the approaching holidays. He could've taken at least a minute of his time.

I remembered I was meeting Hannah outside so I quickly wished a Merry Christmas to my classmates and Miss Highmore one last time and headed towards the exit.

Hannah already waited impatiently by the door and greeted me with: »Where have you been? Recess is already over!«

»I'm sorry, but…You know how it is, we were wishing each other Merry Christmas and it dragged on a little…«

»It doesn't matter. Come with me.« She tried not to smile. It has probably something to do with presents, I thought. I wasn't worried, because I got a surprise for her too…

We went around the school corner. She was obviously having a problem with finding a parking space. She proudly showed me her car and yelled: »Ta-taaa!«

I didn't know exactly what she was getting at, until I saw something attached to car's rear end…Something pink, metallic, with two wheels…

»You didn't!« I screamed and looked at the bicycle neatly tied to the trunk of her car. A big bow was attached to it in the middle.

»Before you get upset, let me explain that the bike is secondhand, but in great condition. I bought it off a friend, who won't be needing it anymore, because she got a car. She kept the bike in great condition all the time anyway…And it didn't cost very much.«

»Hannah, you really shouldn't have…« I contradicted. My present was a drop in the ocean compared to hers.

»You know what your problem is? You're too modest. You say: Thank you.« »Thank you,« I repeated rather reluctantly.

»And don't ride it in this cold. I'll drive you and your bike home right now.«

If I hadn't known her as well as I did, I'd have found her uncompromising kindness suspicious. I had got used to it by now and found it quite acceptable. I hugged her.

»Thank you.« This time I said it with the biggest possible amount of warmth. I was also grateful for getting a true friend, who was always prepared to help me – beside the company of wonderful people who made up our class – in just a few short months.

I sat in the car. Before Hannah was able to start the car I turned towards her.

»I have something for you too…I admit that my present is little smaller. But I hope you'll like it. It's a novelty basically, with fresh names of Broadway stage…«

I handed her the envelope. I saw that she was sincerely pleased and also surprised; she obviously didn't expect a big present from me either.

»Now we're even,« she admitted. »I think that you paid even more for these tickets than I did for the bike…«

We laughed and drove off. Hannah turned on the radio. That afternoon the streets were especially busy. But we expected heavy traffic. The sidewalks were full of people, the traffic was moving slowly. The weather wasn't of service either. It was overcast and dark, even though it was still daytime.

When we were halfway home, I suddenly felt a hit on my head. Like someone had smacked me slightly with a hand on top of my head. I froze in my seat while Hannah still drove and listened to the radio. I knew that the thing from a few days ago obviously wasn't a onetime event. The thing from my horror movie came back. I felt that something was sitting in the back seat. *Oh no, not in front of Hannah*, I thought. I didn't want to spoil her holidays.

It was still in the back seat. What was It waiting for? For me to talk to It again? In front of my friend? I tried to remain calm even though I was seething inside. I had enough of everything. Was I crazy? Why didn't It leave me alone? Before I could realize what was going on, my face was already covered in tears. I tried to sob quietly to keep my crying to myself for as long as possible. It was still sitting right behind me in the back seat. I felt a hand on my shoulder. When I looked back, there was nobody there. The tears started running down my cheeks even harder and it wasn't until the last intersection, where she had to look both ways before turning left, that Hannah noticed my swollen face.

»For God's sake, what's happened to you?«

I needed to focus for a moment. Should I tell her? Will she understand? It'd be difficult to invent something in a second, something so huge that'd made me cry out all my bodily fluids.

»You…won't make fun of me if I tell you?« I asked all seized up.

»No, of course I won't. I entrusted you with a secret, remember? It's your turn now.«

»Well, alright.«

I told her everything I knew about the thing that visited me. I didn't know what that was. I also told her that It vanished the last time after I pleaded with It to leave.

»Do you think I'm crazy?« I asked her.

»Not at all.« She sounded very convincing. »Maybe you have an ability that you're not even aware of. I sometimes…*dream* about what is about to happen,« she told me. If I didn't live in a crazy world of hallucinations, I'd be making fun of her. This time I took her dead seriously.

»Really?«

»Yes, really. I even dreamt about *you*, even before I met you. I also dreamt what you were going to wear on your first day of school.«

I stared in amazement. Was that even possible?

»Some things are obviously predetermined,« she smiled. She took the entire conversation much more calmly than I had expected.

»I hope that we can at least prevent some wrong decision with a positive outlook on the world. I've no idea why I dream about those things and I've stopped asking myself that. I was also convinced that I was going crazy. Those weren't just dejá-vus, those were huge shocks for me. I thought I was crazy. Then I tried to look at it more positively…like it was a gift. Maybe it'll come in handy someday. Your perception of the world might also be a gift.«

I'd never thought about it that way. She really calmed me down even though I was uncomfortable talking about it in the company...of a third person if the immaterial visitor on the back seat could be called that.

I hugged her once more, this time sitting down, in the car.

»Thank you. Really.«

»Should I walk you in?«

»No, it's alright. I must face It alone.« I said that to put her at ease. In reality I wasn't entirely sure what awaited me...

We untied the bicycle from the trunk and stored it in the basement and then she said goodbye. I was left alone in the street...Well, almost alone.

»Well, let's do this!« I said. I slowly went up the stairs and entered the dorm. The thing followed me, naturally. I acted like I didn't feel It and said hello to Jeanie. I told her I was probably going to go to bed early that evening, then wished her good night and went upstairs.

I slowly prepared for bed. I wasn't in a hurry. The invisible thing was always with me anyway and I felt like a death row inmate. I knew that something important was about to happen and I felt that this time It won't go away just like that, upon my request. It had its *purpose* for coming back. Before I really went to bed I sat behind my writing desk. It sat on the bed and I could feel its presence ever stronger. The feeling of unavoidability made me cry again. *Obviously good things really don't last*, I thought.

I quickly took a piece of paper and a pencil, wrote a short message and sign it. I left the paper in the middle of the desk, so it was clearly visible and went to bed.

I turned off the light on purpose; I *felt* It anyway, whether the light was on or off. As I lay I could feel its presence even stronger.

»WHY are you here?« I tried to be as hushed as possible. Nevertheless, the question arose from deep within my heart...

XXVII. THE VISIT

I STARTED TO SHIVER INSTEAD OF ANSWERING. I knew that the invisible thing was still there, that it was watching me, studying me, not going to leave at all. I lay in my bed. Suddenly I felt the thing had sat on the edge of it... *What shall we do now?* I thought. *Am I going to die?*

I felt pressure on my chest as if somebody had placed a hand there. The same as before, in the car when that thing hit me on the head.

Suddenly I felt peace descent on me. I started to disappear. First I lost my legs. Then arms. And before I could start panicking, my torso was gone. I felt how different my soul was from the body to which it has been attached for the entire 17 years.

Was that – *it*? Was I going to die? Luckily I had written a note and left it on my desk, just in case...

> *Please let my parents Zoran and Amalija Kralj and my sister Ela*
> *know that I love them very much and that I am extremely grateful*
> *for all the support they have given me in my life. I am sure I am in*
> *a better place.*
> *Best regards, Ina Kralj*

It had to happen.

Suddenly an even stronger whirlwind came over me. The only thing I felt was the weirdo beside me...I knew it...Obviously I was leaving.

His hand glued itself to my chest and I felt I got lifted. It was as if he was lifting a weight which was feather-light. I could see his silhouette which was totally white more and more clearly. White dots which looked like very high frequency started coming from his white hand which was still glued to my floating body. My body started to buzz from the chest outwards. There were more and more white cells in my body and they were pulsating faster and faster.

Although this sensation was new to me I felt totally at home. Also the fear disappeared completely. There were no emotions, rules, norm…I had left all that behind me. Then my whole body filled with the light of a higher frequency and I was left in complete silence. There were no thoughts left anywhere and everything was very simple.

I don't know how long we swam in silence but I felt no negative emotions towards the friend beside me. There were no emotions at all. They dissolved completely in the buzzing of the high frequency…

Suddenly I felt how separated I was from the Earth. That the frequency of my body was different from the frequency of this planet. I felt as if I had, in a way, *defeated* this planet. As if all tests and relationships here had been an illusion. As if *really* everything was possible.

Then pictures started speeding past my head. When I looked at them more closely, I noticed they were really films…Because I was vibrating a thousand times faster than before, I was able to grasp all of them in a second…

MY BODY IS WHITE AND OBLONG. The vibration of my body is equal to one of the highest frequencies in the universe. I live on the planet which is on fire all the time. I don't feel the heat because I vibrate with a much higher frequency than the temperature. There are creatures beside me who move around with the power of thoughts. Everything is happening quickly. I and another similar creature are the fastest. I know we were created from the same vibration, split from one body. Then: the decision for work on the planet Earth. To awaken one of the most beautiful but also one of the darkest planets and make it brighter. Create harmonized balance. Me and the creature that looks like me are momentarily in the Earth's magnetic field. We observe the movement of the planet and notice the difference in the height of the vibration of the planet. This planet vibrates with lower frequency. We knew it would be like that although we couldn't feel that before. When gravity and an accelerated frequency drop take their course, it's to late to change our minds. We fall in the strong gust of a narrow tunnel and immediately become very small and sticky. First I squeeze out of the narrow capsule and then you. We have landed in the middle of a cave, there are 28 hairy Earthlings dressed in skins around us and they are clapping and dancing excitedly. Because of the shock we use our voices and start shouting. They become even more excited. With years passing we learn their language and way of life. We take over the low frequency of the planet and go hunting together and become members of the tribe. In the period of growing up we find partners for reproduction. Two families are formed. The tribe expands with the addition of a couple of children. I die in the attack on a saber-toothed tiger and then remember again why I am here. You follow me twenty years later when you accidentally fall into an abyss and remember again why we came.

THIS TIME I AM BORN INTO A POOR FAMILY THAT LIVES IN A WOO-DEN HUT. People are dressed in sheets of cloth; some women have a red dot in the middle of their foreheads. This time I am born a man. Since there are too many of us to survive, I leave home early. I come to a monastery where everyone wears red and smiles all the time. It is here that I meet you. A distant memory is awakened in me and I think I know why I came. I recognize the meaning of life and I surrender to spiritual learning. Before I can awaken and utilize my knowledge, strangers attack our monastery and kill its inhabitants. Including us.

WHILE WE ARE SHAPE AND LIFE SHIFTING, WE FIND OUT THAT A LOT OF HIGH FREQUENCY BEINGS HAVE JOINED US IN THE EARTH'S ORBIT. We are glad they help us although they are largely unsuccessful. Even if they immediately remember their task, even if they share their knowledge of high frequencies with the Earthlings, it's usually in vain. The Earthlings fail to understand their demonstrations as lessons but rather pronounce them to be miracles. They lack trust and strength to identify with the high frequency so they step on the other side and worship it...

I'M WAITING FOR MY DESCENT AGAIN. This time I was born into a wealthy family. I can see I am a girl. People teach me to behave myself and sit up straight. They don't tolerate different thinking so I do what they tell me. At a party I meet an interesting poet and I immediately recognize you in him. It seems that the life before didn't exist at all. I don't remember the task we were given, I only know you are my only friend here. I fall in love. I secretly meet you several times before we get caught. Because our relationship is forbidden, you are thrown into jail. Soon I fall ill with the disease that has spread all over the world. You find out I died of plague. Again I remember why I came. Soon you find a way to leave your body too but the way is utterly inappropriate. You undo your existence through suicide and your substance is covered by darkness. Your vibration becomes too low for me to meet you ever again...

I AM BORN IN A POOR HUT AND IT'S VERY COLD. Mother and father explain life in nature to me clearly; by observing animals, plants and stars my eyes open more and more. In a few years I become the master of the house and realize at the same time that something unusual is happening in my life: people ask for my help more and more frequently. And what's even more unusual: when I focus on the solution their troubles and illnesses disappear. I begin researching. Yoga attracts me the most and I share it with my students. I accept people of all castes, races and religious beliefs. I'm growing up in the highlands and when I turn fifteen I remember why I came. I find out that I will not find the right knowledge on the farm. I have to connect myself with my frequency, which will help me raise the energy level of the planet. For a long time I live in the caves of the Himalayas and I remember every single message I receive from the universe. One day while walking in the mountain I meet you and despite the knowledge I've been given I cry like a child. You tell me how you became friends with low consciousness but managed to overcome it and so earned your way back, which only rare people manage to do. Together we train ourselves and repeat the knowledge which keeps coming back to us. We use body motions to enter the new messages into the Earth's frequency and we call these movements Yoga. We have more and more disciples but we notice we are not strong enough to turn around the frequency of the whole planet. We decide to leave our bodies and try again on the other side of the ocean.

I WAS BORN IN EUROPE, YOU WERE BORN IN AMERICA. I am a girl and you are a boy. My parents are Slovenian and yours are British and Indian. Your mother dies in childbirth. You have kept the majority of knowledge we have gathered and because you know the secret how to travel from your body, you visit me regularly until I start elementary school. I have forgotten most of the knowledge because I was born too soon and the shock was too big. Because you have more experience with low frequencies than me, such fluctuations as birth do not throw you off balance anymore. In your visits you try to remind me who we are and why we are here. Because you know I am the only one who can see you, you fear the people around me could be afraid of that and try to stop my progress. You decide to leave me but at the same time keep sending me telepathic messages. I decide to travel to America. You follow and protect me all the time. On my first school day, during a biology lesson you even quickly travel out of your body to welcome me. Every day you hurry home to a relaxed state in which you can travel to me. You used this little trick of yours when you traveled out of your body during the raffle and guided my hand to catch the number of your present. But when it was your turn to draw, you turned your physical body away during the shuffling of the slips and you closed your eyes, but your soul was turned towards the hand that was moving through the numbered slips and you chose the right one...

When you become too entwined in my thoughts and feelings I can sense you and became absolutely terrified because I can't recognize you. Just now we are one in the white vibration of our original frequencies. Our task is to make people aware that a new dimension of life is coming to the Earth that they were already familiar with once and prepare them for the period of peace, which is not an easy thing to do. For this reason there are more and more beings on this planet who help us. The majority of people will soon have to recognize the existence of a higher frequency of love and the state of permanent happiness. The era of peace is coming.

I already found out that those were not films but memories. The visitor put me on the ground again, this time so that I was standing next to the bed. I saw my sleeping body as if this wasn't me.

"Before you say anything, I must show you this." He pointed to a line of light connecting me to the sleeping body on the bed.

"Hold it carefully and look where it leads." I could feel it and it seemed like an umbilical cord. I could feel the heart beat of my body, the breathing and the position of my body through it. The line connected my material and immaterial left legs. Very close to the body it was tied around my leg.

"Now gently loosen the knot. Be careful the string doesn't tear, this is very important. You need to *undo* it and it really helps if you imagine having already done it", he explained clearly.

At first the string was really tightly knotted around the leg; I couldn't undo it in any way. Then I put the advice I was just given into practice. I tried to feel the victorious relief of having succeeded easily. And believe it or not, the knot started to loosen. It really followed my thought. It became undone momentarily all by itself. Suddenly I was holding the other end of the glowing umbilical cord in my hand and I was not attached to my body anymore. I could go anywhere.

"It is very important how you protect the end of the string because it is very sensitive," he said and showed me his left leg. There was a glowing string tied around his leg from his ankle to his knee as if he wore a shoe with laces tied around his calves.

"Try to tie it around your leg like shoe laces. Turn the ending inwards to protect it. Imagine," he emphasized again, "that the ending is really safe."

I followed the instructions and I succeeded immediately. Only now, when the danger was over, he could relax.

"Shall we go for a walk?" he asked me playfully.

"Where to?"

"The sky is the limit."

He took my hand and walked through the closed door. It took me some time to get used to vibrating with a much rarer and higher frequency than other materials on the Earth. He put his head through the wooden surface of the closed door and said, "Are you coming?"

I made a brave step forward. After a split second of darkness while I was getting through the wood, I found myself on the other side. Quite simple. "So, how should I call you now, Robert or Ravi?" I said when we were walking in the Central Park.

"In school it would be better if you called me Robert but here I prefer Ravi," he said with a smile.

"Thank you for everything you have showed me," I said. Somehow I didn't know how to begin the conversation. I wanted to tell him so much but at the same time I had a feeling he already knew all that. We walked in silence for a while. It was interesting to walk without hearing or feeling the ground under your feet.

"Ravi?"

"I really missed you."

"You can't even begin to imagine how I missed you."

We fell silent again. We were walking in the park and I noticed there were more people around us than I would expect in the middle of the night.

"Don't be afraid but all these people are not...bodies. Some of them are souls which are waiting to be born again, waiting to descend."

I also found it strange that some of them could see us.

"Let's get away from here," he said and offered me his hand. I extended my arm and he put it behind his back sliding the other one under my knees and lifting me up. Of course I was light as a feather. He closed his eyes and collected his thoughts. Suddenly we lifted off the ground. I twitched out of habit even though I felt nothing could happen. The Central Park below us got further and further away. Instinctively I closed my eyes. When I realized there was nothing to be afraid of, I opened them again. A starry ground glittered below us. The lights of the nighttime New York were so...magical. We flew above the city and I felt very cozy and warm. I would feel the wind in my physical body but now I was feeling only peace and safety. The further away we got from the city the bigger and brighter was the carpet of lights below us.

There was a dark spot in the middle of the pool of lights and I knew that was the sea between the capes. We started to get closer to the city again, this time he flew straight towards the dark spot. A light appeared in the middle of the spot and I immediately recognized the island with the Statue of Liberty. He landed on its head where there was no one. Neither material nor immaterial beings.

"I asked for some privacy in my mind," he said mysteriously.

"I think that tonight no one has thought about hanging out on the head of the Liberty," I said joking. The view was spectacular. It was a clear night and from this distance the city seemed quiet and peaceful. The lights were moving in the streets, but the sound got lost in the night and didn't reach us. I felt the time has come for us to talk.

"I'm sorry I waited till now," he said as if he felt what I was thinking.

"I wanted you to get used to the new environment. I was avoiding you because I didn't want you to recognize me at once. Luckily I was able to make you forget me entirely by leaving at the right time years ago…" I felt the frequency of his thoughts. He was sad because I hadn't recognized him immediately on the first school day.

"How can you say that? I *never* forgot you. I *consciously* repressed the memory of you. You know how painful it was for me when you left? And how do you think I felt when I wasn't sure if you were real or I was losing my mind?" The ten-year wounds were reopened, the feelings of disappointment and confusion came back to me. I remembered the hope and horror I felt when I realized he wasn't coming back.

"I know. I know. Sometimes I would visit you and try not to get involved but it was too painful for me too…So I stopped coming. But I kept thinking about you every day. When I was meditating I talked to you and invited you to come here. It will be easier for us to do our work here. The world is bigger and more open."

"Were you inviting me just…because of the task?" I tried to stay calm. I was surprised I could still be so emotional if I wanted but my excitement was not manifested by wild heartbeat. Because I didn't have my heart on me at the time being.

"Do you remember the dream you had after I left?"

Sure I remembered. I remembered everything that night. How I came running home from school and looked for him. How Ela told me to forget him because he was imaginary. How I cried and wailed into my pillow. And how I sank into dreams. A ball in the castle…cast out. Accepting the fact that I really only had myself. Then – the meeting of soul mates. Love which is brighter than any infatuation, it just exists silently and irrevocably forever. Happiness. Equality. I don't *need* him, I only *love* him. Deeply happy to have him by my side. Sure I remember.

"Exactly…That's exactly what I feel for you. I've *always* felt that."

The memories kept flooding back. I knew that *always* meant a very long time. Since our creation on a star somewhere in the center of the universe, a billion light years away.

A silence descended on us, we looked at each other holding both hands. He let go of my hand and touched my cheek with his right hand. I felt peace and deep happiness which creates all good vibrations in the universe. The drive which transforms darkness into light. We embraced each other. I really love my family and Hannah whom I hugged last, but this embrace felt totally different. As if that was the first embrace in my life. And at the same time…an indescribable feeling of discovering who I really am. In the union with him.

That embrace made up for all the years of waiting. And if I had to go through all the tests, ridicule and accept all social and genetic believes one more time to be on my way with him again, I would gladly do that. I would know what was waiting for me in the future and would be totally calm.

Now I also understood why I was looking forward to visiting this city so much. Somewhere deep down I knew where I was going but I was afraid to admit that to myself. I was afraid to admit who I was. I was afraid to be disappointed when the veil of oblivion lifted and I discovered who I *really* was.

But the opposite happened. I experienced the moment as the feeling of being able to breathe again. As if I had put down the heavy rock of believes, ego, norms and values. And what was left was me. And Ravi. We were still embracing and becoming one. Soon I couldn't anymore feel where my body ended and his began. As if I had fallen into him and melted with him. I opened my eyes and all I could see was white light. Everything around us was bright. The all-encompassing silence that contained our essence was so real. Not to think about anything seemed so simple.

The beam was shrinking gradually and we reappeared in my room. We were still locked in the embrace and bright. He touched my forehead with his and I felt a deep sense of gratitude to be able to be here with him now. To be able to exist in this vibration. I realized I couldn't remember when we left the Statue of Liberty.

"How did we get here?" I asked.

"Actually, we have already covered two topics today – flying and tele-portation," he explained to me with a smile.

"But I didn't do anything by myself."

"This is how you start. With demonstration and copying. It might be too much for the first time if we had studied everything at the same time…What are you doing tomorrow at this time?"

"I can't make it tomorrow because I'm learning how to fly," I said jokingly.

"OK. So it's the day after tomorrow then," he said. Although it was a joke I decided to stop.

"No, no. It's fine. You can come tomorrow because I actually need an instructor."

"All right then. Flying lessons. I'll send you the invoice by mail."

We laughed. We hugged again and I thought to myself if kissing was possible in this state. Anyway I decided that we had covered enough ground for one day. I didn't want to force him. I didn't even know what his opinion was regarding that…

I lay on the bed, to be more precise into my body. I retied the glowing string and collected my thoughts. Gradually I began to feel my heartbeat and even breathing pace again. Before I could completely assume my body, I heard Ravi whisper, "This is my opinion regarding that…" I could feel a light tingle on my lips. "Good night."

XXVIII. CHRISTMAS HOLIDAYS

WHEN I WOKE UP IN THE MORNING, I FELT COMPLETELY REFRESHED. My body was overflowing with health, I felt light and it seemed like I sprung out of bed. That morning something drove me to sing constantly, even though that wasn't my habit in the past at all. I had the feeling that everything really was possible and that all the bad things in this world were just tests, trials.

I felt my heart beating differently than before. With much less weight. I could breathe in more air and it seemed fresher than before, even though I was still in my room (which wasn't aired). I knew that the event from the day before didn't happen just in my dreams, because my body was changed too. It was so fresh and healthy! *Only I* was in it, without thousands of problems. And I was normal. Then it struck me: there was nothing wrong with me. I was okay. I was really okay. After a decade of wondering what was wrong with me, all the burdens disappeared. Truly. *I was great.*

I felt so good that even if someone was to tell me that everything was just a dream, I would still cheerfully dance away to the breakfast. And that was exactly what I did. I met Eszter and Rossana in the dining room and they couldn't be more surprised at my change.

»Which cosmetic product do you use when you wake up? Because I want the same one!« joked Eszter and shook her black hair.

»What happened to you, *neighbor*?« asked Rossana and I wondered if it was really that obvious. It probably was.

»Well, I had…a really nice dream.«

»Was it…a romantic dream?« Eszter raised her eyebrow. Why should I spoil her fun?

»Hmm,« I replied meaningfully.

»Was there any…kissing?« asked Rossana.

»There might have been…« I feigned ignorance.

»Was there any…other activity?« Eszter said meaningfully and imitated the key act of procreation of living beings with her hands.

»Hey, I'm not discussing that!« I refused her. The joke almost went too far.

They told me over breakfast that they slept excellently too and that it must've been related to weather. I looked out and saw it was snowing. And as if I didn't feel fairy-tale-like already, »I'm Dreaming Of A White Christmas« played on the radio. When we finished breakfast, they told me they had a lot of errands to run, call their families and sort out a few other things. I cheerfully waived them goodbye and wished them a Merry Christmas.

They reminded me that I was planning to talk to my family that afternoon too. This was going to be my first Christmas away from home.

I spent the morning in continuous admiration of the beauty of New York – the beauty of the snowbound Central Park, to be exact. I went out just so I could watch people and the beauty of the world. I felt like being reborn. Like this was my first day on this multicolored planet. The green landscape was gone and footbridges, small hills and trees were covered in whiteness…I remembered the previous day's whiteness, the glowing energy Ravi and I were embraced in most of the time we were together, and my heart raced again. I could tell it wasn't used to these new feelings yet. Nevertheless, I knew it was strong enough to stand all the new vibrations coming to this planet. *It had* to be.

This time too I felt more *people* than bodies in the park. It seemed that I'd become much more susceptible and sensitive to frequencies surrounding me since the day before. I removed snow from a nearby bench with my hand and made some space so I could sit down.

I watched people passing by for a while, then I relaxed and closed my eyes. I tried to open my *spiritual eyes*, the ones I was using the night before. Supposedly they were also called the third eye, but just on account of the spot they were placed at. I saw the same landscape in front of me like I did before, only more people, more souls were present. They looked like clusters of energy walking – or flying – within the area I was watching. Each soul had its own thought vibration. I couldn't perceive these vibrations clearly enough to be able to say word-for-word who was thinking what. I sensed them more like colorful hazes. Some souls were very bright; they were mostly floating above the ground. The others pulsated in various colors and every possible shade. The darkest souls mostly nested in bodies and it was obvious that they were worried, or were in a hurry, or were thinking very strongly about not so positive things.

I also noticed a soul walking down the path and based on that concluded that it must be coming together with a body. It was orange for a while, then yellow, and when it came near me it became light pink and almost white in the end. Golden-white. It sat next to me.

»Meditating, are we?« it smiled. »I didn't know you too liked relaxing in Central Park, or were you just copying me?«

Earlier I already thought it was her, but now I was certain.

»Gina, how nice to see you on a snowy day like this,« I said with calm delight and opened my eyes. »It's true, I'm copying you.«

She laughed. »And what do you feel when you do that? I mean, do you just relax or does anything…happen to you?«

I recognized the predicament she felt in her voice, because she didn't know what she could discuss with me or which level I was on… I understood her. I too would be slightly embarrassed if I didn't know whether I was talking to a first-grader or a PhD holder. Or whether they were studying this for entertainment and a little relaxation or this was a serious matter for them. I smiled at the thought of Gina being obviously pretty serious about the whole thing, since she asked me such a question.

»It seems that a lot is happening to me sometimes,« I replied absent-mindedly. She exhaled with relief, probably sensing that she had finally, *only now*, found a genuine classmate. We obviously didn't discuss this sort of knowledge in school. Those interested in it oftentimes appear to be strange in society's eyes. And to have somebody to share this with was simply…invaluable.

»Really? What happens to you?« she immediately wanted to know. I decided to keep the whole incident with Ravi, flying and teleportation to myself for the time being.

»I mostly see colors,« I started. »Sometimes when my eyes are closed I see people as hazes and they're not necessarily physical beings. Today I've been watching the energy of this park and you walking. At first you were orange, then yellow, then light pink and finally, when you sat next to me, golden-white. I don't know yet what that means, but…Does that tell you anything?«

Her eyes were wide open. I obviously said too much again. How was it possible that I was so open? Why was that happening to me so often? She needed a few seconds to compose herself. When I raised my eyes she looked at me admiringly.

»Where have you been all this time?« she answered in surprise.

»How long have you been practicing this? You've got to tell me!« she insisted.

After some persuasion and pleading I mentioned that during a meditation I had experienced a memory about where I was coming from. I left Ravi out of it, of course, and I described the experience quickly and simplistical-ly, thinking: it may be true and it may not be true. But she was much too sensitive for me to fool her. She *sensed* the truth of what I told her. After a few moments of silence she slowly started to speak. I felt that she wanted to confide in me and share something she hadn't told anybody in school before.

»O, my God,« she said in amazement. »It was only a year or so ago that I found out why I was so disappointed in life. Did you know that I used to take drugs?«

»No,« I said simply. I didn't want to create a scene around this piece of information.

»That's right, yes. When I was born, I too had a strong sense of people around me. And I was totally disappointed with the majority's low vibration as well as with my own powerlessness. That disappointment followed me most of the time during my schooling and I reconciled with the feeling of constant pain. It seemed like a way of life. And then one day, in this big city, I got an offer to try grass. Since I was disappointed with life anyway, I thought grass might be helpful in some way. Soon I was smoking it regularly, because it gave me the pleasant feeling of being able to see people, my friends in other dimensions, I couldn't reach otherwise. Everything snowballed from then on: I started mixing all possible substances, heroin, cocaine, various mixtures, sometimes good, sometimes not so good. Memories of happiness, high vibrations, the fact that everything was possible, they were all awakening inside me. Sometimes I could feel all over my body like my cells were made of pure light. That *I was* the light, the energy. That all the people were good. When the physical reaction in my body eventually wore off, I fell back into this world and I felt increasingly more disappointed. I was terrified that I lived in a world where I actually didn't want to live. I felt like an alien.«

»Don't we all?« I smiled. »After all, we're just souls living in these bodies. It is quite likely that we had inhabited some other planet, and completely taken over its identity and wondered what the inhabitants of the Earth looked like. Although in that case the inhabitants of the Earth would be aliens to us…« We laughed at that interesting and at the same time funny philosophy.

»And what happened then?« I wanted to know.

»The logical thing happened. For visions, which I was getting less and less frequently – you have to understand that drugs immensely tire the body – I was prepared to do anything. To kill, to prostitute myself, to steal…I'm really not proud of certain things I've done in my life… Until my mom had enough of it. One night, when I wanted to steal the last remaining valuables from our house, the police were waiting for me there. I was so disappointed that I screamed some of the worst things to my mom that you can possibly say to someone. I felt like she didn't understand me at all and that she turned against me. In reality she did the best thing for me that she could possibly have done, and nowadays I try to show her that every day. She saved me from death and hell.«

»From hell?« I wasn't used to the use of such final and threatening words. Especially not on such a lovely day.

»Do you know what happens to you if you commit suicide?«

I didn't, but Ravi did.

»No, I don't,« I played ignorant.

»You voluntarily reject the most important law in the universe. You attempt to condemn the divine creation, that is yourself. And that's definitely not our domain, to judge others or ourselves…Therefore you fall very, very, *very* deeply. You fall into such low and unavoidable vibrations that it's almost impossible to escape them. That's why I used the word hell.«

»How do you know that?« I was curious.

»Because I *almost* experienced that a few times during my drug taking days, but it obviously wasn't meant for me, thank God,« she tried to smile and then realized that it was time for our discussion about sad stories to end. She quickly straightened up and concluded: »Well, in the following few months I went through agonies I wouldn't wish on anybody, went to a few closed treatments, and got introduced to meditation in one of former drug addicts' meetings. We're all looking for a flux of energy that we've lost anyway and the idea that such a flux could be achieved naturally, without the intake of illegal substances, completely enthralled me. In a positive sense, I mean. Not long ago I experienced a sense of memory during meditation, I really *knew* why I was here. And that living on this planet is actually a gift.«

I really didn't expect to hear such a detailed and profound story. It seemed like life was constantly sending me gifts. This time it totally unexpectedly brought me another colleague. I felt that she could help Ravi and me a great deal. I needed to talk to him first, though.

»I can also answer your question,« she said with a smile.

»If I recapitulate in proper order: It's nice to walk in the park by myself! I like that some people take care of holiday atmosphere here too! Is that Ina on the bench? And: all of a sudden I feel so peaceful."

»Excuse me?« I said.

»You caught the colors of my thoughts and they perfectly matched their content. If you'd devote more attention to these vibrations, you'd be able to *hear* the frequencies, like on the radio,« she explained.

»And you catch them?« I asked.

»No, but I'd give anything for you to teach me what you know« she said sincerely.

I was surprised. I didn't even realize that seeing a few colored lights was some special *ability*.

I looked at my watch and realized that I was late for lunch. I thanked her for the discussion and her trust. We wished each other happy holidays and I slowly went home.

»Ina?« she called my name again.

I turned around.

»You will think about it, won't you?« she asked with a smile on her lips.

»About what?« I played ignorant.

»You know what I'm talking about.« Yes, I knew. About learning how to see auric colors.

»Of course I will,« I told her.

»Have a nice day.«

We waived goodbye one last time. I thought about how different yet similar paths will bring us in the end to the same revelations. I picked up the pace, because I wanted to be on time for lunch. The snow creaked under my boots and it felt like I was hearing the sound in my throat.

I made it. After lunch I cleaned up a bit, changed and sat behind the computer. I logged on Skype and thought about what to talk about.

It rang soon and for a change they had already set the volume of the microphones. When we added the video, I saw all three of my family members dressed in red. Mom quietly said: »Ready, steady, go!«

All of a sudden they all raised their hands holding glasses of Coca Cola and shouted: »Merry Christmas, America!«

My surprised laughter stimulated them as well and it was like an avalanche coming down the mountain. I thought they were so funny and entertaining that I couldn't stop laughing. After that if someone produced a sigh or a giggle from time to time, it caused a new fit of laughter. Eszter and Rossana passed by and stopped. When I noticed them I wiped off my tears of laughter and invited them in English to come closer. They too were heading towards one of the computers to call their families and were dressed nicely in a Christmas tradition.

When the merry atmosphere quieted down, I asked my family if they were up for some practice in English, because I had a small surprise for them. They agreed and I brought Eszter and Rossana in front of the screen. They were glad, honored and in a good mood for being able to meet my family. And I was silently grateful to them, because that way my parents could see that I was having a really nice time and that I was surrounded by relaxed and cheerful people.

When they went off to make their own calls, I learned that my family had bought a puppy, a cocker spaniel. Mom said that even though she seemingly never wanted to have an animal in the house, she desperately needed someone younger that Ela around her in recent months. Ela was, after all, already a young woman and mom didn't have that feeling of being urgently needed anymore. Which was also okay. When she talked about it, her eyes slightly teared up. Even though she saw me every week, it wasn't quite enough to satisfy her maternal instinct. And when dad suggested buying a dog, she was suddenly all for it. Now that was the most spoiled animal in our neighborhood.

I smiled at the thought how I wanted to have a dog. Obviously wishes do come true, but only when we let them go. When we give up all hope, in a sense, and throw that wish into the universe. Well, at least I'd get a chance to play with him in the summer.

»What's his name?«

»Ludvik,« said mom. »Or affectionately: Ludo.«

»It shows that you picked the name…« I commented. Dad replied:

»She wanted to name him Ina, but in the end we convinced her that wouldn't be the right decision. Because the puppy is a boy…«

I laughed. I was glad that they were having fun. Ela sat quietly next to them and spoke out more decisively for the first time:

»Now I have a Christmas wish. Could I have a few moments with my little sister?«

Mom and dad realized that they instinctively pushed forward and kept their daughter in the background. They were crowded in front of the computer screen so somebody had to yield. Ela was the one waiting in the background. My parents moved away and let her have the seat.

»We'll leave the room, but call us when you finish so we can say goodbye!« said mom attentively.

When the door closed, Ela sprung to life.

»What's happenin' sis?« she asked lively.

»What do you mean?«

»I think you know what I mean. The whole screen glows from your infatuation. There are little hearts around your face. Well, tell me who he is,« she wanted to know.

I was considering what to tell her. It's true that I loved talking to her, but I wasn't convinced that she could understand. I decided to give her just a hint.

»I think I like one of my classmates,« I smiled uncertainly.

»Yes, and…?« she encouraged me with interest.

»But I don't know what to do, because he's the principal's son…«

She laughed like she had just read the most interesting piece of yellow news.

»Tell me more, tell me more…« she continued hungrily.

I mentioned that I had a feeling that the principal doesn't like me very much.

»That's normal. That's how fathers-in-law are. We all have our problems with them,« she replied calmly.

Then I told her, how by pure chance I drew his present and he drew mine, and how he smiled at me when that happened. Naturally, I left out the details about soul mates and the dedication inside the CD. Basically, I told her just about those things that I was *certain* really happened. About the events that happened when I was in my own body and he was in his.

She enthusiastically listened to what I was saying and she opened up to me as well, as much as possible in such a short amount of time. She told me she and Gregor were together for five years now and that they were – despite ups and downs that every couple experienced – very happy and were even considering getting married. Which was a secret for the time being. I felt honored.

»Thank you for such great news, congratulations,« I said enthusiastically.

»You know, you can't tell that to anybody over here anyway, being on the other side of the world,« she was evasive. I could still feel love in her words.

The line behind my computer was growing longer and longer and we had to say goodbye. Obviously everybody wanted to talk to their loved ones on Christmas Eve. Ela called mom and dad and we wished each other happy holidays once more. The line got disconnected and I left the chair behind the computer to others.

I left common room immersed in my thoughts and remembered what was in store for me that evening. In the middle of the staircase I suddenly started walking faster until I was almost running. I probably set the record in quick showering and teeth brushing that night. I was much too fast. I went to bed at 8 p.m. and it was quite logical that Ravi wasn't there yet. I laid on the bed and relaxed. As I sensed I was slowly drifting off to sleep, I decided to try something.

XXIX. THE FIRST PRACTICE

I WANTED TO LEAVE MY BODY, BUT ON MY OWN. I wanted to surprise him. I thought about the previous night. How did I feel, when Ravi lifted me above my body? I imagined myself floating above my own body. My breathing rhythm was getting more and more peaceful…And suddenly I was hanging above my body.

It was hard, because I had to *imagine* each next step. Like training a muscle I never knew existed. Then I *imagined* standing by the bed. I was there immediately. The law of teleportation was absolute and always executed in an instant. I carefully tied my silver umbilical cord to my left leg, like the night before. And I was already free. Soon I sensed his vibration and hid under the bed. I used my own body as a cover, so he wouldn't immediately notice me.

»Ina?« he asked. He materialized right next to my body.

»My God…Ina. Ina! INA!«

I decided to end the dramatic scene immediately. I stood up without any crawling and put the upper part of my body right through the bed.

»What's the matter?« I smiled.

»That's not funny at all. I thought you were dead,« said Ravi seriously.

»Dead?« I asked slowly.

»Do you realize what a dangerous procedure you've performed today? I wouldn't be able to forgive myself if something went wrong…«

»Wait, wait, what are you saying? I thought it was quite entertaining.«

»If the cord should tear or get damaged for whatever reason, you'd be in a very serious danger. Tearing the cord is the same as committing suicide. You get sucked into very low vibrations in an instant. I'm not saying that some of them aren't entertaining, but…Once you're there, it's almost impossible to come back.«

»Okay. I'm sorry.«

»I can't lose you again. I'm sick and tired of constantly loosing you and then looking for you.«

»I know. Me too.«

He remembered that he must maintain the state of happiness and corrected himself. He straightened his back and asked proudly:

»So, are we going to fly?«

I placed myself closer to him and said seductively:

»I'd love to, mister pilot.«

As he stared in amazement I already vanished through the door. He followed me and asked: »So, you've been practicing teleportation as well? Without me?«

»You understand how it is with me and learning. I want to know everything. Maybe I'm…I'm obviously a bit too eager,« I remembered my bold venture. And anyway, I had this feeling that some old memories had been awakening inside me and that sometimes I simply *knew* what I had to do.

I told him about my splendid physical feeling. He laughed at me.

»Do you like it?«

»It's magical. I've never felt so good before. What happened to me? With my body, I mean?«

»When you leave your body…How do I explain this? It's like cleaning service. You leave your apartment and call a cleaning service company to come in and clean it when you're gone. When you come back, the apartment's clean, aired and absolutely fresh. The same happens with the body. While you're gone the energy cleanses its structure. When you come back the body's exceptionally fresh, clean and well rested...«

»Thank you for such a vivid explanation,« I smiled.

Then he took my hand and transported us out of the dorm. Since Central Park was crowded again, he took my hand and said: »I propose that we practice flying where we started from.«

He transported us...to a green hill. There was a forest on top of the hill, a cemetery at its bottom. Little lower and to the left was a house. *Our* house.

»Is that even possible?« I asked in amazement. Until then I teleported myself only around my dorm room, but now I discovered that it works equally fast when traveling much greater distances.

»*Anything* is possible,« said Ravi convincingly.

And as if that wasn't enough, the dawn was already announcing sunrise. There were no clouds in the sky and the birds started waking up.

»How do you think I would visit you ten years ago? By airplane?« he smiled. I knew that, because everything was clear to me in theory. But when I tried to do that in practice I got confused. It was really fast. I thought I was *further* away from home.

I thought about watching my family. I realized that I saw them the day before, but...I was so close. Ravi caught my thought.

»You can go in if you want, but remember that we came here to practice.«

»We can go together and see the puppy,« I said almost childlike. He saw that I was smitten by the abilities I'd been given.

We went together to see the puppy, whose sleeping space was arranged in the living room, but nevertheless slept in my parents' bedroom. Wherever he wanted, mostly in bed. When we entered the bedroom, he woke up and growled. We were strangers to it, naturally, and it couldn't know that I was his owner's daughter. He barked loudly.

»What is it?« said mom. »Why are you barking? Did you have a bad dream, Ludo? Was it something else?« she kept asking softly. Dad went immediately back to sleep.

We backed away towards the door and the puppy calmed down.

»A good watchdog, huh?« I said to Ravi and Ludo raised his head again.

»Maybe it's time for us to go,« said Ravi and stepped through bedroom's closed door.

I followed him. When I came through the door, I couldn't see him anymore. I looked out of window and spotted him on the hill. I went quickly through the other rooms and checked if my things were still where I had left them. My room was more or less unchanged. Ela's room was still in the morning dimness. I went past her bed and noticed various colors of blurred moving pictures above her head. She was obviously dreaming. I wasn't inclined to investigate her dreams. It seemed like invasion of her privacy. I quickly caressed her goodbye and went outside. I materialized on the hill, next to my instructor. He was serious and it was obvious that I did something wrong.

»There's one more very important thing,« he began as we sat on the hill, watching sunrise.

»Certain abilities are received based on one's state of consciousness, based on one's high morals. That's basically a safety fuse, so one can't use them for evil purposes. One can use them only to benefit mankind. In the opposite case they simply don't work.«

»Is it wrong to simply visit people?« I asked.

»Basically…yes. If you don't visit them with a powerful intent and a wish to help them, the ability doesn't work. Today we didn't intend to help anybody and Ludo sensed that. We were like a couple of intruders in that bedroom. I sensed the inappropriateness of our doing and left. It would've been different if your family *really* needed you today.«

I tried to understand what he was saying. So, I need to be very sensitive about myself to be able to determine if I really had *people's best interest* in mind every second. I didn't imagine that my own ego could tempt me that easily. I thought I was a positive person.

»How did you feel when I paid you a visit for the first time after ten years?« he asked.

»Very frightened.«

»So you see. That's why you don't help anybody with such visits. You

only frighten people. And fear attracts extremely negative vibrations. Once you're afraid, the thoughts that stimulate that emotion only multiply. Since most people don't know that in such cases they should awake the feelings of happiness – to imagine and realize them – such visits could be pretty harmful.«

He stepped on my ego. »Then why did *you* visit me?«

He smiled. He knew I was going to ask that.

»Because my intension was still good,« he explained. »I wanted to show myself to you. By doing that I'd raise your consciousness and help you to find the original vibration of your soul again.«

»Okay, okay, your intention was good,« I admitted.

»I wanted to wait for you to go to sleep, when you asked me so sweetly to leave. Because of that I had to leave that night. You can never change a person against their will. I was glad when you didn't send me away the second time.«

I thought about how blocked we human beings are. We're afraid of anything we can't understand. I wouldn't send him away the first time, if I dared to look the truth in the eye. If I *knew*, *who he was.* I'd welcome him with my arms open. Basically I believed that *he'd* have to run away from me. He laughed.

»Do you really read my every single thought?« I got angry for a moment.

»It's not that difficult. You'll learn to do that too, because you're already sensing their colored hazes. You just need to adjust your antenna,« he was practical.

»Soon everybody will learn to do that and it'll become the basic form of communication,« he said seriously. »Like cell phones. Of course, only those firmly convinced within themselves that they wish to use the ability for good intensions *only*, will actually get it.«

That made sense. I didn't feel that weak anymore for being connected with him every second. I even liked it. I couldn't keep any secrets from him anyway, because it didn't seem natural. He always knew everything and I wasn't ashamed of it. My thoughts weren't that special anyway. I didn't plan any mass murders or something similar that needed hiding from the world.

»It'll soon be like that, yes. When all the people put their egos aside, as well as worn-out fears passed on to them by their ancestors, suddenly there'll be a lot of free space in our heads. We'll start using a bigger percentage of our brain. And we'll know that our heads are totally clear and our intensions are good. It won't be hard anymore to let somebody else into our thought frequency. These things will be perfectly natural.«

Everything again made perfect sense although the majority of people would be horrified hearing something like that. I looked around me. It was already daytime and it looked cold. I didn't feel the temperature.

»Wouldn't it be appropriate to finally start talking about today's subject matter?« he said teacher-like. His way of talking entertained me very much. We were sitting on a hill on the other side of the planet and the sky was opening above us. I realized that I was standing in the daylight for the first time and I saw that we were both slightly transparent. I got up.

»Of course, let's start.«

Ravi began teaching me. It was basically good that I already knew how to teleport, because that was the basis for flying. The first thing is just a combination of two different images, two feelings. Firstly, you see that you are here. Then you *imagine* that you *are* there. And you already are there. Flying is similar to a film. You have to imagine every frame, every step.

»That's impossible!« I shouted as I was trying to imagine every single frame. The furthest I got was materializing three feet above the ground, and then I was again down on the ground. I was angry.

»Don't worry about it,« he calmed me down. »Try to relax your mind. The movie reel rotates in a relaxed manner, nobody's trying to stop it, nobody's trying to rotate it. It rotates spontaneously. Relax.«

Well, okay. I sat in dry grass and relaxed. He too started meditating sitting down. I slowly fell into a strong flux of light. My mind quieted down completely and my thoughts powerlessly became silent. Silence became self-evident, a fact. I placed a reel of film in that silence. I was in that film, in the same position, sitting on the hill. The reel started rolling and the movie Ina started rising.

I took off the ground. When I was fifteen feet in the air I thought: »Great, I did it!«
I was down on the ground again in an instant.

Ravi was immediately by my side.

»Are you okay?«

»Of course, I'd just like my flying adventure to last a little longer,« I replied slightly disappointed.

»I think we've accomplished a lot today,« said Ravi proudly. »Shouldn't we go home?«

»Yes, we should.«

He took my hand and we materialized in my dorm room. I remembered that I had something to tell him. I felt that such a question wasn't a taboo anymore.

»I have a question for you before you go.«

»Yes?« he said. I could clearly see that he knew what I was thinking about, but I pretended not to know anyway.

»Did you or didn't you kiss me yesterday?«

»Yes, I did. I'm glad that you managed to remember that event.«

I knew what he meant by that. When he kissed me, I was already in my body and at that time the communication between souls can be obstructed. Because the soul is already integrated in the body it often can't sense things as they really are. And then there are also our personal limitations how much we *allow* ourselves to sense.

»If by any chance you have a similar intention today, I'll be very pleased if you're done with it before I'm back in my shell again,« I said like I couldn't care less what he did. I turned away and he took my hand and pulled me to himself. Our lips united.

When one experiences a kiss, it's usually on both levels. Physical and spiritual. Even though I experienced it only on a spiritual level, I didn't miss anything. Again I started becoming one with him, who was a part of me and knew me from the very beginning of my existence. Who *was* me, in a way. The kissing, like I experienced it with Ravi, could hardly be called kissing. It was more like merging into oneness than uniting of lips. This time we rose without trying. Embraced we became one in a kiss and stopped in midair, approximately a foot above the ground. Silence surrounded us again.

I don't know how long the kiss lasted, because time stopped anyway. I thought, *what a kiss goodnight*! He smiled.

»Just so you know, I've been thinking a lot about seeing you. You know, when we are…in our *shells*,« he used my expression on purpose.

»But, I'm going skiing with my dad for a whole week.«

»Really? *He* skis?«

»He's not such a bad person once you get to know him. He just…had a…difficult past.«

A shadow went across his face and I sensed that he didn't want to talk about it. I was satisfied too, because I didn't want to talk about him either.

He courtly thanked me for a nice evening and I knew he meant it. We agreed once again to meet the next day, and I cheerfully thought that it was probably going to be like that every evening during the holidays.

I lay into my body and repeated the process of tying. I sensed wind on my lips one last time…

XXX. A WEEK FOR LOVE AND LEARNING

THE FOLLOWING WEEK I COULDN'T HAVE BEEN MORE SURPRISED AT myself. Even though I »toiled« all the nights, each morning I woke up full of fresh energy, like I was reborn. I came to sense more and more that the rule about »leaving the apartment« was very real.

»Soon we won't be needing sleep anymore,« said Ravi one evening.

Great. I was already accustomed to having my convictions about life on Earth constantly shattered. Now I already knew how to get to the real truth. I simply needed to collect all the information I'd learned about the basics of living here and turn them upside down. The perfect formula.

»That'd be an excellent theoretical explanation for textbooks,« he added. I smiled.

»I'm glad you like it.«

I managed to learn to fly pretty successfully within a week. I remember that I chose to visit the Statue of Liberty for my first longer trip. It seemed like a nice spot for a practice. A training in concentration and a reward at the end of it: a divine view. When I succeeded to land on the head of the statue, I breathed with relief. I knew that breathing reaction was just a habit, because in this dimension I didn't need oxygen at all. And I felt a lot stronger than before. I missed something though. The feeling of pride and self-praise because I succeeded.

»Those feelings slowly disappear,« Ravi told me.

»Slowly all the emotions will melt away in your ethereal body.«

I got alarmed. Some of the feelings were quite alright and I didn't want to lose them. They were proof that I existed, while the exchange of pleasant and unpleasant feelings added much needed contrast to the painting of my life. If I was sad first, I felt a huge difference after I was happy again. That gave me the feeling that I was better off than before.

»What if there was a formula which enabled you to stay in that state? That you never had to cry again? But not because you wanted to repress that feeling but simply because it didn't existed anymore. What if you were able to raise your physical body to a level, where it could completely follow your soul? So you could accomplish this thing we were doing in this dimension also in your physical body. Isn't that a challenge?«

»Does that mean that...I mean, if I didn't have feelings anymore, how would I...feel love?«

I had difficulties with the formulation of that question and Ravi was able to observe its formation. The setting of words and commas, deletion, the new formation of words and only then the sentence emerged.

»Of course not,« he put my mind at ease. »Do you remember your life on the burning planet?«

Yes, I remembered. Interesting, because I had the feeling that I remembered more things from my previous lives each day this week. The information was dripping into my – now already very spacious – consciousness. I remembered the planet hotter than the Sun. I remembered the beings that had inaudible, high frequencies. Our birth planet was this burning star, but we were, as one of more important posts of that species, controlling the balance in the universe. Nowhere was supposed to be too much darkness. Where beings – not necessarily inhabitants of the Earth, but inhabitants of any planet – forgot their role in the Universe, we came to help. For the past four thousand years we'd been dealing mainly with the Earth, because mankind started completely forgetting the true purpose of its existence and the existence of this green planet...

»Your memories are getting clearer. They're almost as clear as mine,« he was satisfied. He continued.

»Do you remember us having feelings on that planet? I mean, did we get angry, did we cry, or did we treat each other in some other inappropriate way?«

I closed my eyes to focus more easily. »No. At least not that I can remember. But I do remember the constant state of...profound peace and happiness. And powerful love. But it wasn't as superficial as this infatuation the bodies of people on Earth can feel. It was present as... profound state of each individual being.«

»I think you've just answered your own question,« he replied.

I was reassured and satisfied. Each day I could feel the melting of old messages trapped in my body since who knows when. Ravi said that the most entertaining thing about human bodies was the fact that they carry within them the genetic record of all previous generations. That's why those who didn't monitor their behavior, frequently started acting as their parents or close relatives. That's where the attachment was coming from. The attachment to everything: to people, objects, memories, events, feelings...That's where our fear that we may find out we're not at all who we pretend to be comes from.

That week I was learning and learning. I absorbed the knowledge I once already had, which made it easier to remember. Like I was studying for some sort of graduation.

My love life blossomed too. Throughout the whole week I felt perpetual state of love, whether my loved one was by my side or not. I knew that everything was possible and that my physical body was getting used to ever higher vibration. I was absolutely healthy and felt great. It all went by too soon though. On the last night, before we said goodbye, I felt slightly insecure for the first time. It was Sunday, the last day before school started again.

»See you in front of the school tomorrow?« he asked with a smile. I felt that he looked forward to that and couldn't wait for his body to embrace my body in reality too. Even though all that happened during the week, it couldn't be more real. For me those nightly practices became much more important than what happened during daytime. Since days were short, I frequently went to bed as early as 6 p.m. First I would practice for a few hours, then we went together around the world. We practiced at various locations: India, Egypt, Australia, South America...

On some locations we were actually seen by people in their own bodies and I knew that such masters will increase in number. They won't be masters at all, but normal inhabitants of the planet.

I swallowed hard when I asked this question. »How do I know that this...is real? I've been thinking...«

»That's your first mistake.«

»What?«

»That you've been *thinking*. You shouldn't have any thoughts.«

»I know, I know.«

»If you doubt only for a second whether this week has been real, just take a look at your body and its response to the work we've been doing at night. You were light, healthy as never before, singing or dancing all the time...«

»At this point I'm not exactly sure whether that was caused by sleeping too much or being in love...«

We both laughed.

»Could you please wait for me tomorrow, I mean today, in front of the school?« he asked cheerfully and chased away my dark thoughts.

»Would you meet me?« his eyes glittered divinely.

»Of course. I'd love to.«

»Quarter past seven?«

»Okay.«

He kissed me. Again I forgot who I was. I was one with him.

When I reconnected with my body, I again felt enormously pleasant awakening of material existence and every muscle in my body was ready to be of complete service. This way I could be a top athlete, a mountaineer...I could be anything. Once again I felt the power of those words: anything is possible. Truly. Everything is possible.

XXXI. BLIND DATE

I GOT OUT OF THE BED LIKE I WAS SHOT OUT OF A CANNON. When I felt fully connected to my body, Ravi left too (he always stayed with me till the end of the procedure, just in case).

I got straight into the shower and did the entire 'general cleaning'. I washed my hair, I used scented and slightly spiced Indian soap I bought during the week, and after showering I rubbed in a skin lotion. In the end I looked in the mirror and saw that my body was beaming with health. I smiled at the face in the mirror: »You don't need beauty creams anymore.«

Then I focused on my wardrobe. I had prepared the clothes the previous evening before I went to bed, but felt like wearing something different in the morning. Instead of a pink combination I chose a white one. I felt clean (physically as well as spiritually) and happy. I wanted my image to reflect the way I felt. I chose a fresh white collared shirt and a white pullover.

When I was ready, I took one last look in the mirror to check if I could do something with my face. I felt really…nice. I thought the skin on my face radiated exactly the same glow as all cosmetics companies wanted to conjure up in the retouched photographs of their models. But they were doing that in an artificial way, on the outside. My face radiated *outwards*. And so I came to an easy decision to stop using make-up.

I took my backpack and went to the dining room. I thought the breakfast was excellent and I lovingly nourished my body. When I finished, I looked at my watch. Ten to seven.

I went to the front door and saw that Hannah had already arrived. I ran out, waived at her and sat in the car. We hadn't seen each other the whole week and when she saw me, she was utterly surprised.

»Okay,« she started, »it's not a new hairstyle, you're obviously not wearing any make-up although I could swear you went to a beautician, it's not about new clothes…You smell nice, but that's not it. WHAT HAPPENED TO YOU?!« her enthusiasm bordered on euphoria.

»I'm sorry if I got a bit too much into it, but you have to understand. I've just seen a miracle embodied, a goddess,« she explained.

»I don't look that good,« I joked, although I sensed in the tone of her voice that she was telling the truth.

»You're right. Not that good. You look *even better*.«

She started the car and we headed towards the school.

»You're in love, aren't you?« she read me straight away.

»Well, yes, I mean, no. It's complicated. I don't know if he feels the same way.«

That was true. He hadn't expressed his love for me present in his own body yet. After all the painful experiences in my life, I wanted to make sure everything was real before making an announcement about anything to anybody.

»If I was in such a situation, I wouldn't glow like that,« Hannah insisted and I decided to turn the conversation in another direction.

»And how did you spend the holidays?« I asked her.

»Oh, we're changing the subject. Okay,« she saw right through me. »I was at home a lot, at my parents'. We decorated a Christmas tree, ate enormous quantities of food and received visits from relatives.«

I remembered that I missed that parade this year. My family surely had a similar traditional string of visits. Customs were obviously alike all over the world.

The traffic was surprisingly light and at ten past seven we were in front of the entrance.

»So, why did I have to be so early at your place?« she asked. When she called me the day before to make an arrangement for my pick-up, I explicitly asked her to be punctual or even a little early.

»I'm meeting a…friend before classes.«

»Aren't we mysterious. It works for me,« she shrugged stoically.

»You know I'll tell you everything when I'm…really sure. I always confide in you.«

»Yeah, yeah. Hurry now, you don't want to be late,« she lovingly sent me out of the car.

I opened the car door and stepped out on the sidewalk in front of the school. More and more students were pushing their way through the entrance. Nobody was waiting in front of it.

Take it easy, Ina. It's not even a quarter past seven. He surely wanted to be punctual. I stood in the most visible spot in front of the entrance. Since I was – except for my jeans – predominantly dressed in white, it was impossible to miss me. I was wondering if maybe I was too noticeable and looked at my watch again.

Fifteen past seven. Maybe my watch was too fast. The crowd in front of the entrance was getting bigger as students hung out, joked and discussed the holidays. Then they went inside and a new group of people gathered in front of the entrance, discussing similar topics.

While I was waiting I could hear the questions: did you have nice holidays? Where were you? Oh, you went skiing? It was quite resting…Every assertion made me remember my experiences and I tried to convince myself that everything I experienced during holidays was *real*. God couldn't be so cruel to play a joke like that on me.

I remembered what happened on the last day of school. The raffle…That was real, because I had a *proof* for it. He'd surely come. He had to come.

Twenty past seven. I felt a too familiar taste of iron and this time it was especially distinctive. I looked in the direction of the smell of blood and spotted principal Davies. It was more than obvious that he was enraged, as his eyes were drilling holes in me.

»How are you, student? Did we have nice holidays?« he said faking kindness.

»Why are you standing in front of the building? Knowledge awaits inside. It really wouldn't be wise to miss the first day of school after holidays,« he continued coldly.

He smiled coldly when I assured him that I was waiting for a friend and would be in right away.

»*I wouldn't wait for too long* if I were you,« he said with a special emphasis before he entered the building.

What a strange conversation. But then…when did I have a normal communication with the principal anyway?

At seven twenty-five Hannah walked past me and gave me two thumbs up, as if saying: »Go get them, girl!«. She wished me luck and went up the stairs in the building.

Seven thirty. I heard the bell ringing inside the building and the atmosphere slowly quieted down. I too considered going in. I obviously dreamt about the whole thing. It was too good to be true. Thinking that I was obviously crazy enough to experience such genuine appearing hallucinations at night made me cry automatically. Again I felt the pressure of feelings which were unknown to me during the whole week. I experienced a strong sense of sadness and a state of mourning. I cried in front of the school entrance, being thankful that nobody was there anymore.

When I succeeded in entirely ruining the »divine look« of my face in a single minute, I decided that it probably wouldn't be too smart to go into the classroom. I'd deal with the principal later. He probably couldn't expel me just because of a single day of nonattendance. I intended to leave and go home. This would be the first day of school that I officially cut class.

I took five steps and stopped. I turned around towards the door. It was past 8 a.m. for some time now and I knew he wasn't coming. Nevertheless, a part of me completely and utterly believed that I wasn't going crazy; that the week I had spent with him was real. I stood in front of the door looking at notices. Silly. Like they'd announce on the notice board: "*Hello, Ina. Robert isn't coming today. We're very sorry that you've imagined everything, but it was real fun watching you all the same.*"

I stared towards Central Park and thought about going home once more. Slowly and with rigid steps I set out towards the park. Time: eight fifteen. This time I stopped after ten steps as someone had pulled my arm from behind. All of a sudden I got turned around. A warm body pressed me against itself. He smelled good. Without any perfume, just *him*. I couldn't notice that before when we weren't in our bodies. I felt the accelerated beating of my heart as my life once again turned in the right direction.

»Please forgive me for the delay, I really came as soon as I could…«

I sensed sincerity and care in his short-winded voice. He held my face in the palms of his hands and looked me in the eyes.

»And what have we here?« he said and wiped away the tears from under my eyes with his thumbs. He sensed my thoughts. »Because of me? What about the state of happiness we've been discussing?«

»For now, I'm not doing very well if I don't know whether you exist or not. It's deeply rooted in me; a childhood trauma, I guess. Some people get frightened by a spider as children and consequently they're afraid of spiders all their lives. And I'm afraid that you're not there. That you don't really exist. That you're a hallucination…«

He silenced me with a kiss. This time our bodies participated as well and beside the union on the energy level I felt a strong need for physical one too. I felt the pleasant rubbing of his thin yet soft and relaxed lips against mine all over my body and soon I didn't know anymore whether I was vibrating from desire or New York had been hit by an earthquake. We were lucky to be alone on the sidewalk, because Ravi got into this physical experience as deeply as I had. I felt his heart beating through my pullover and although it seemed impossible until now, I felt that even our hearts were beating as one, although in a frenetically fast tempo. I opened my body completely and it was perfectly soft. My hands were, as were his, clinging to the embracing body, like they were holding on to dear life. I knew that it was worth waiting for the first kiss all my life. Especially because it was with *him*. And because it was so…celestially beautiful.

»I hope that this is a big enough proof that I'm real,« he said short of breath, »although I really didn't expect something like this.«

»Was I really that bad?«

»My body was…shaking with desire. My every cell wanted you. And they still want you,« he concluded.

»I was already afraid that I was the one with Parkinson's disease…« I smiled.

He kissed me again and the world shook once more. I wanted to ask him something but it was too late. The whirl of passion washed away all my thoughts and I found myself in divine love again. It was so simple. I don't know how long we kissed, but it tasted like enlightenment. The entire street glittered, partly from snow, partly from the light surrounding us. After approximately the fifteenth kiss I started sensing all sorts of vibrations, although I was still tied to my body. I had the feeling that there were no obstacles anymore; that everything weighing on me melted away in Ravi's embrace and that it didn't matter at all why he was late…Why he was late, of course, that's what I wanted to ask him! He sensed my thought.

We reluctantly broke the embrace and went for a walk, hand in hand, of course. He interlocked his fingers with mine and that seemed to me like the most natural and familiar thing to do. On this day, the first day that we could really be together in our own bodies, the school had to wait. We went to the Central Park, which was so well known to us and so big, that we could walk for days and still wouldn't see all of it…

»Why I was late? It's very simple, really. I told my father that I really liked you and he got very mad. And because I was still in a good mood in spite of all that, he locked me in my room. When I realized that by objecting loudly and beating on the door I was only enticing him further, I got quiet and waited for him to go to work. Then I escaped through the window and called a cab. In the meantime I kept asking you through my thoughts to stay by the school entrance. It's high time for you to give me your cell phone number, so I can call you. Well, even though we saw today that telepathy was working in our case pretty nicely. And it's cheaper. But you can give me your number anyway, just in case.«

He smiled at me, and I stopped again and hugged him. I remembered my turning around on the sidewalk in front of the school and I knew that the time was near when I would throw away my phone. If I hadn't been stopped again by human emotions, I might've caught his message in its entirety, maybe even *heard* it. That way my body responded only to one part of message: *stay in front of the school*.

»Thank you for running away from home just for me.«

»I escaped for myself. You can't imagine how I would've suffered by knowing that the other part of me was wandering around the city thinking I didn't exist.«

»The other part of you had a very interesting conversation with her future father-in-law,« I told him. It only seemed fair that I mentioned that part of my waiting too.

»At least now I know why he was so angry,« I added. »Do you ever talk about that? Does he treat you the same way?« He answered with a question.

»What way?«

I told him everything I knew about his father and how we ran into each other when I first came to New York. I described every incident in detail: how he looked at me from the other side of the street; how I dreamt about him; how I thought I'd never see him again, when I discovered that he was the principal on my first day of school; how I always, when I met him, got the unmistakable taste of blood in my mouth; how we met in the basement and I got detention.

»And Hannah also…« I stopped there. I remembered I'd *sworn* to her. I couldn't say anything she entrusted me with that afternoon. Never to anybody. Ravi immediately sensed my blockage.

»Is anything wrong?« he asked.

»As a matter of fact…it is. I promised her I wouldn't tell anybody ever what she confided in me, because that's a really dangerous piece of information.«
»You don't have to tell me,« he smiled.

»What do you mean by that?«

»Did you also promised her that you wouldn't reveal that information to anybody telepathically?«

»No, but…«

»So technically, we're not breaking any rules. And believe me, I'm one of only the few who can help with the mentioned problem.«

»This is not about you. I'd tell you in a split second. It's just…Are you quite sure it's okay?«

»Let's try. If I catch the message, it's certainly okay, because otherwise such an energy flux wouldn't open between us. And if I don't receive the message, I'm obviously not suppose to know.«

I agreed. We were just walking past one of the wooden benches. Ravi wiped the snow off of it and prepared it for a comfortable sitting. He took off his jacket, spread it across the spot where I was suppose to sit and politely gestured: »Mademoiselle…«

»Oh, thank you. What about you? Won't you be cold?«

»To be perfectly honest, I couldn't wait to take it off. I'm getting less and less cold. Probably because of the additional energy. Or because of you; I'm not quite sure yet.«

I sat down smiling. When he joked I could feel my heart. I could physically sense freedom. When I was with Ravi, all the armors and bonds that were restricting me, melted away. My heart was glowing like a free star.

»Try to think just about that event,« he said. »Like you were really there. I suppose that Hannah described it vividly enough to you.«

Yes, she did. Her description was more than vivid *enough*. Every time the waiter interrupted us, I had the feeling that Mr. Davies was going to materialize in front of us and pierce us with his dreadful eyes. I almost felt like all of that happened to *me*.

I instinctively became serious. When Ravi sensed the vibration of my thoughts, he said with satisfaction: »Well, okay. Time to relax.«

XXXII. THE TRANSFER

I TRIED TO RELAX. In the beginning I was afraid of betrayal. I still had a bad feeling. Then I thought of Hannah. How she was afraid. And how very dark and harmful feeling fear was. What she could attract by being afraid. Was I really helping her if I didn't tell or show that to Ravi? Or was I just keeping her in a narrow space of fear she had locked herself in? Would she even understand if I asked her for permission?

Then I thought of the solid laws of the universe If you wanted to harm somebody, you simply couldn't act anymore. You couldn't use your body, your abilities…At least not if you wanted to be in a high frequency. Then everything was okay, one way or the other. If the flux was released, that would obviously help her, and *I* wouldn't be the one deciding about it. I wouldn't judge it. I realized that I didn't have the right to judge anyway. I had the right to simply exist and act in accordance with the laws. And the right to really have fun doing that. It had been selfish of me to think that *I* was the one deciding who was the traitor in this situation.

I came to a decision and relaxed. *Really* relaxed. I'd thought before that I was relaxed, but only now did I discover that I'd actually been sitting tensely.

My muscles gradually became softer. I was sending the energy to where the tension was. Such an approach was like a gentle vibration massage to my body. Each individual muscle was slowly becoming ready to submit to my will. Soon I was completely relaxed. My thoughts became less and less frequent and eventually they quieted down completely. In silence I surrendered to the light with my entire body. It was even stronger this time and I felt the ability to leave my body should I wanted to do so. I was surprised at how quickly I was able to reach that state.

Soon something even more surprising happened. In addition to the light, a pleasant glimmering droplets started falling from the sky. It looked like tiny stars were dropping right at us. When they touched me, I had the feeling that they were breaking my body apart, although it was a very pleasant feeling. Like I was able to experience some sort of depth showering. Fireflies were penetrating me, creating a new vibration within my body.

Soon I felt that I was more filled with myself that before. Like I'd put together both parts of my self. Like I even wasn't a woman anymore, but some sort of hermaphrodite, although I didn't sense my body or my sex. I knew. Ravi successfully entered my magnetic field, my thoughts and my consciousness. We obviously succeeded. *It was meant to be.*

Then I firmly decided for the last time that the universe *knew better* what was right than I did.

I thought of that incident. I really put myself in her shoes. I imagined the school down to the last brick. Its interior…Staircases. Classrooms. Windows and blue window frames. I materialized on top of the staircase… The image was becoming more and more alive…

I HAVE TO PUT MY THINGS IN MY BACKPACK, SO I CAN GET HOME AS soon as possible. It would be nice if I helped my mom in the yard today. Since I carry too much things at once, I accidentally drop one of the slippers. It bounces off the railing and flies away into the deep. I look down and see all the staircase levels and the square-shaped floor at the very bottom. Down there, where the staircase ends. Down there, where nobody is allowed even to set foot. Down there, where all the punishment begins. In the basement.

I think, I'm going to pick up what I dropped. Is that such a sin? I walk down to the basement and pick up the lost object. I straighten up and look around me. I really want to know why nobody is allowed to come here. I look around once more. There's nobody anywhere. What if...I went down the corridor once and then home. I walk past the fire alarms. A white, spooky corridor. I'm opening doors. Here is the copy room. This is the storeroom. The repository. The corridor gets darker and darker. At the far end one door is slightly open and I see a flickering light through the opening. I get closer. There is an ordinary white candle in the middle of the room with quite a few drops of wax accumulated around it. It's probably been burning for some time now. There is a wooden board on the floor next to it with some sort of paintings on it. In the middle of the board is a circle with arrows pointing in different directions. The board contains a small wooden object that looks like a button. The room is very dark; masks and amulets hang on the walls. All of a sudden the door closes in front of me.

Suddenly, his face appears from the darkness in front of me. He leans against the door with his hand. His differently colored eyes get even closer to me and I stiffen in fear. His face is supernaturally dreadful. His thin lips smile coldly and his slightly askew, but still very symmetrical teeth, sparkle in the darkness.

»Who have we here?«

»My name my name is Hannah, Principal.«

»And what is such a young girl, like Hannah, doing in such an obscure part of the school? Do you remember what the school rules are?«

»We shouldn't go to the basement...?«

His disposition changes from cold kindness to impatience. He starts walking past me, up and down the corridor, like a cat deciding how to consume the captured mouse. Is mouse going to suffer? Is it going to die quickly or in pain? His speech becomes slower and more emphasized.

»And why in God's name would you then even consider setting a foot on the basement floor, much less coming all the way here?«

The reproaching British bass voice echoes thunderously through the corridor. He obviously knows we're alone. So the cat won't be disturbed during its chosen game. I could at least pass out or play dead like a mouse in the given situation. But I froze so deeply that I can't even move, much less fake death.

»My sl...slipper...f-fell...« I try to explain and I realize that it's pointless. I shouldn't have come here, full stop.

»Do you know what I can do to you? What power I have?« he asks calmly.

»I can see to it that not only you don't finish this school, but also don't get accepted anywhere else. And without a high school diploma Good luck finding a normal job. That way your life will become a bad foundation for anything you might want to accomplish: to have an education, a family, a suitable job Your life will be a hell without goals and meaning. An average existence, if not poverty. An eternal torment worse than death. Is that what you really want!?«

»Nnno, of course n-nnot,« I stutter.

»Then WHY did you come down here?!«

I feel tears filling my eyes and like a genuine mouse I wait for the end.

»Please, forgive me, I'll never come down here again. I swear on my parents' lives, on my life.«

»That,s not enough,« he says coldly and lowers his voice. He's into the game again and starts singing to himself: »Hmm, hmm, hmm, what should we do with you...?«.

»I won,t tell anybody that I was here, just let me go home. I promise. Really.«

»Do you know how much a promise of a little girl, who has just reached puberty, is worth? I can tell you. Nothing. What did you actually see in the room?« he asks, like he's looking for a reason why would anybody even want to look into the dark basement room.

»Nothing except a small candle. And it's not my concern why it's there.«

»You're right. It's not,« he brutally grabs me by my elbow until it hurts. On the one hand I'm glad that the thing I've been expecting anyway finally started.

»Please, let me go. I'll never tell...«

»Anybody, yes. I,ve already heard that« He decides to let go of my arm anyway.

»Okay. Have it your way. Never to anybody. It'll be our little secret. And if I find out otherwise...You know what will follow. To tell somebody such a foolishness and to ruin your life, that would be really stupid.«

»Yes, really, yes.« I even try to smile. Is it possible that the mouse walks away at the end of the script – unharmed? A tad softer British voice answers me.

»Go home, Hannah.«

»Yes. Thank you, Principal.«

I want to run, to be home as soon as possible. To be safe. As I try to move my legs I realize that I should be happy if I manage to move at all. I'm still numb and I slowly walk away with great difficulty. I can hardly feel my legs, but I still try to move them. As I get out of the school and realize that I am outside, that I have enough room for running, my body relaxes a little. I start running. All of a sudden the adrenalin comes rushing into my blood and I start running with supernatural speed. Like I've got death on my heels. As I arrive home, I'm hardly breathless at all. I really decide not to tell this to anybody, ever. I'll do my best as long as I'm attending this school. And I'll really avoid him and the basement...

Suddenly, a whirl of light caught me and banged me against the bench. I jerked and opened my eyes. I felt like I had a really vivid dream. Next to me Ravi awoke too.

»Did you see that?« he asked with excitement.

»How did that happen?« I asked in amazement. »I saw *more* things than she'd told me that time.«

»That's the whole point. We weren't browsing through your memories. We connected with hers and the universal knowledge. We saw what *actually* happened.«

»Is that possible?«

»It obviously is. Although for now, only the most clairvoyant souls have that ability. You were always among them.« I was astonished.

»How? Aren't you…«

»Stronger? Of course I am. But you're more clairvoyant.«

»Aha.«

»Yet another reason why we make such a good couple,« he smiled charmingly and brought me back to reality.

XXXIII. THE SECRET CLUB AND THE KNOWLEDGE ABOUT DARKER CREATURES

I SNUGGLED UP TO HIM AND FELT SAFE AGAIN. It seemed to me that we really worked very well together and he knew that. He was leading the way when power was needed and followed my lead when the power of intuition was called for. I remembered all the fluxes, the energy rain and all the dimensions I witnessed during the last event. I realized that it really had to be my specialty.

The thought of how Gina reacted to my perceptions made me smile. We met close by that time, not far from here. Ravi caught my thought vibration, but didn't know exactly where to place it.

»What about Gina?«

»She wants us to teach her how to see thoughts.«

»Since when?« he was interested.

»Right after our first night together I came to the Central Park in the morning and ran into her...«

I told him about our meeting and ultimately I didn't know anymore what I was saying to him and what I was showing him. All these images were also in my thoughts and Ravi received information from both sources. Video and audio. We were like a couple of portable transmitters. Soon he absorbed the event like he was there.

»We could teach her that, why not,« he encouraged me.

»After all, you know why we're here. To prepare the planet for the new frequency. It's only reasonable to start with those who are particularly sensitive to it. In the end all of those you'll be teaching will...«

»…*we'll* be teaching,« I corrected him. »After all, you are the stronger one, remember?«

»Of course. Those we'll be teaching will help with the unavoidable spreading of the new awareness.«

»And the thing will spread like wild roses…« I continued poetically.

»Where did you hear that?« he said. One could feel that I wasn't the one who came up with that sentence.

»It's from a movie I like. It's about the future too, about a little girl and how she saves the world with her innocence.«

»We're truly the most innocent as children. And *we know exactly*, why we came here,« continued Ravi thoughtfully. Suddenly he stood up.

»Let's form a club!«

»What?«

»Let's form a secret club that nobody must know about except its members. What do you say? We have to start somewhere.«

»Are you sure?«

»Of course. Where there is a strong negative pole, there has to be a strong positive pole.«

»Strong negative pole?«

»I admit, I still think about a scene I witnessed. My father is obviously in a bigger trouble than I thought. Believe me, I know a lot about these vibrations, because I nearly became one of them. Boards and buttons, amulets and candles, that's just a few entryways, through which lower beings come in. A lie is their virtue and when you're the weakest, they offer you help. You have the feeling that there, on the bottom, you found real friends. A few stronger ones among them know how to perform a few tricks, which completely entrance you in your powerlessness. Those beings promise you their help and love, *if* you promise them your loyalty. I was lucky. I twitched when I heard the word *if*. A distant memory awoke within me that high vibration beings never set any conditions. Where there is an »*if*«, there is no true friendship. I was right. I accepted their game and swore to myself to be loyal only and exclusively to myself. I started lying. I started pretending to be powerless, so the beings would still help me, while at the same time I kept promising them that I'll surely swear them my loyalty. They helped me to regain my inner strength, and I secretly started reconnecting with my original vibration. I was lucky, because the majority of low frequency beings mostly don't have the ability to read thoughts. That's why lying is even possible…«

»And what happened then?« I asked impatiently. I was uncomfortable imagining him in the middle of the negative pole of the universe.

»I always performed my vibration tests in private. The beings soon gave me my privacy, since I was loyally helping them with their every mission. They had to believe that I was a part of the pack, even though we sometimes did truly loathsome things. A lot of people on Earth bow to them from day to day, simply because they don't have the knowledge. Since in my point of power I tried to calmly swallow the fact that I can't help people who swore their loyalty to low frequencies, it was easier on me, even though I was sometimes severely tempted to at least try to prevent all those horrors. I knew that by doing that I would disclose myself and thus my path would be sealed. So I pretended to laugh when in reality I wanted to cry when they were torturing somebody. My alleged friends liked me even more after that and they were prepared to help me even more, regardless of what I asked for. Of course, I was promising them all the time that I will soon join them entirely.«

»I didn't think it was so complicated…«

»Then one day I felt that it was time to leave. I thanked my friends for their help and simply started vibrating on another frequency. They bewilderedly watched me disappear. They tried to hold me back with guilt one last time. *Look everything we've done for you and you're leaving. We murdered just for you and this is your gratitude*, they screamed. I knew that lying was the language of that area and that the things they were screaming at me, were in reality a praise for me. They were defeated. I smiled and replied:

everything is fair in love and war. My case is special. It involves both... Soon
after I reappeared in the Earth's orbit I waited for a new descent.«

I was shocked. Ravi also explained that he was never able to show me
that story that clearly, because I wasn't involved in it and I didn't have the
access to such a low vibration. If I was *shown* such a sequence of events,
I'd be in danger of summoning these beings since they responded to
thoughts. Like everything in this world.

»So there is a chance that we summoned Aidan today?« I referred to
the principal by his first name for the first time.

»Well, there's always a chance. But I sincerely hope he was occupied
enough with his work not to have the time to notice us. He ought to be
really relaxed and connected to the collective consciousness of the universe
to even sense us. And also clairvoyant, like you are. I think that there's
almost no chance that he saw us. But I'd really like to know what he's
got against you...« he started to think.

»I'll probably never get to know that...«

»Please promise me that you'll continue to avoid him, okay? These
being are truly dangerous and I'll try to find out how we could save him.«

»I've already promised myself that. Every time I meet him I renew
that promise.«

»Okay,« he said in a reassured voice.

»The first step is surely our secret club,« he continued. »Are you for it?«

»If people will be for it, so will be I.«

»Of course they will. We already have our first member and then the
thing will spread like...«

»...wild roses.« I used the movie expression again.

»Wild roses, yes.« He smiled and embraced me around my shoulders.

»Here, in the middle of the Central Park I proudly announce the in-
augural meeting of the secret club,« he said proudly and started to ponder.

»Do we have an official name or are we just a *secret club*?«

I smiled. After all, the name wasn't that important.

»I don't know. We could be the Secret Club of the Eternal Light!«

»That maybe sounds slightly funeral-oriented…« he teased me.

»What about…the New Frequencies Club,« he thought out loud.

»That sounds like remedial physics class,« I reciprocated.

»Then you think of something better!«

»I'm trying to!«

We came to the next bench. People had obviously already sat on it since it was completely clean and dry. We sat on it and I leaned against his shoulder. We closed our eyes. My thoughts suddenly dispersed and we sat in silence. I already got used to that feeling of silence…

We both opened our eyes and said simultaneously:

»The secret club.«

XXXIV. PROBLEMS

RAVI LOOKED AT HIS WATCH AND REALIZED IT WAS LATE. »If I want to get home before my father does and meet you again in the physical form, I must hurry,« he said.

»Okay. I'd rather spend fifteen minutes less with you now than to be unable to see you again,« I consented.

We went back to Central West Road and Ravi waived his hand. A taxi came in a few seconds. Ravi opened the car door.

»I'll see you, colleague,« he joked. The kiss followed and the world stopped again. Since we knew it was the last kiss of the day, we clung to each other even more tightly.

The taxi driver honked the horn.

»Are you coming or not?«

»In a minute,« Ravi answered smilingly. I could see that other people couldn't resist his charm either. They simply *had* to be friendly with him and *had* to do as he asked. I noticed that heavenly power he was given for wanting only and irrevocably good for people. He could control the entire world if he wanted to. The beauty of this rule of acquiring such an ability lay in the fact that this ability wouldn't be given to him at all, if he wanted to used it for *himself*. If he thought for a second how to take advantage of this power, he'd lose it in an instant.

He kissed me once more and then sat in the taxi.

»See you tonight?«

»Of course,« I replied freely. The day unraveled completely differently than I had planned. A thousand percent better. I headed home with a spring in my step.

Luckily I arrived just in time for lunch. The events simply kept composing a perfect mosaic, but I knew I wasn't the author of this beautiful emerging picture. I was just…participating in each piece of the puzzle. I was a tool for something higher. I realized that *my* wishes weren't important at all. If the arrangement was such, I'd get what I wanted and deserved. Like I got the opportunity to be with *him*.

When I finished lunch, I headed towards my room. I touched the cell phone in my jacket pocket that I had bought after living in America for several months. It wasn't one of those state-of-the-art phones, but it enabled communication. I was able to talk to my classmates through an American operator, which was less strenuous on my wallet. I remembered I had forgotten to give my number to Ravi. But there'll be another opportunity for that, surely.

The phone rang as I entered the room. I checked who it was and cheered up. It was Hannah and she couldn't wait for me to tell her what had happened.

»Hannah? You won't believe what happened…«

»Ina? Finally. Where are you?«

»I was waiting in front of the school quite desperate because he obviously wasn't coming…«

»The Principal said today you were the worst role model…«

»And then Robert came after all, although an hour late…«

»He said he saw you waiting in front of the school…«

»And he explained that he got into an argument with his father because of me, can you imagine? And then, when he got locked in his room, he escaped through the window…«

»He allegedly spoke to you and you said you would come in…«

»Then we went for a walk in the park and…I think I got a boyfriend.«

»…and his conclusion was, that it was a case of intentional insult of the school administration. You're facing expulsion!«

»What?« Only now did I start to listen to her more closely.

»Is that even possible?« I asked again.

»When principal Davies is involved, anything's possible...« She sounded scared.

»He can't do that! No, no, there must be a solution,« I said more than convincingly. I was in love with his son, after all. What a paradox! God really is a joker.

I changed the subject.

»What about you? Did you hear what I said?«

»Wait, let me think...« there was a few seconds of silence as she tried to remember what I was saying on the other side of the line. The sound of my words echoed in her mind until she shouted almost euphorically.

»Whaaaat? You and Robert? Really? It worked?!? Awesome! Tellmeeverything, tellmeeverything, TELLMEEVERYTHING!!!« she quickly demanded.

So I described a few of that day's moments for her. Since I didn't want to exaggerate, I left out the part where we meditated and exchanged information via a thought flux. I could sense, though, that Hannah was going to be a member of our club someday. Maybe even its strongest part if she succeeded in getting rid of her fear. She ought to let it melt away. She would be surprised at how fast such an emotion disappears when one focuses on the positive result.

She shrieked in delight once again and wished us all the luck. I was radiant like never before and she said she could feel that even over the phone.

»See you tomorrow!« she said, »I can't wait to hear all the details!«

»See you, yes. If the principal allows me to enter the school at all.«

»You know what? What if you checked online how to deal with these things? There surely must be some kind of a high school association or something like that. There *has* to be.«

»Great. Thanks for the suggestion.«

I realized how much easier we solve problems when we're not involved

in them. Hannah was solving *my* problem with the Principal with feathery ease. But as soon as she'd remember *her* relations with him, she'd freeze. If we knew how to distance ourselves from our problems in every single moment, solutions would come *immediately*. But we mostly prefer to submit to the feelings of fear and hopelessness of a situation, without realizing how *dangerous* such feelings really are.

We cheerfully said goodbye and I immediately went to the common room to use the computer. There was a long waiting line there. It looked like I wouldn't get to the much-needed Internet for quite some time…

I sighed and thought to myself: what other choice do I have? I chose a line and went to the end of it. I wondered if the laws I was using outside of my body also applied when I was just a normal student in the middle of the common room. Ten people ahead of me waited for a computer. I closed my eyes and remembered that our sight was often the least appropriate sense since it gave us information about a situation *such as it was*. Thereby it convinced us that it would never be any different.

I focused. I thought of the common room where the line in front of my computer didn't even exist. I felt joy because I was able to get to the information immediately in such a nice and simple way. I stayed in that frame of mind for some time and then redirected my thoughts elsewhere. I thought of Ravi. Suddenly a shriek interrupted my thoughts.

»Fantastic, girls! Tomorrow's examination has been cancelled! Party!!« said one of the girls standing in line and I noticed that the rest of those waiting were also girls. The entire line was shouting and they started to walk away. I got to the computer *immediately*.

Was that possible? I was shocked. Was it possible that their professor received urgent obligations exactly when I was visualizing an empty line? Did it really work that fast? I wondered what would happen if I was imagining the world peace…Would that also happen instantly? I'd probably need larger quantities of energy for such a feat. Even my little miracle seemed amazing anyway.

I opened Google and started to investigate. I felt like a detective about to solve an important mystery. I took it as a challenge. I surfed for about three hours and found some useful information. I decided to discuss this with Ravi and was glad that we were blessed with such a special method of communication. What we couldn't discuss during daytime, we'd finish during nighttime.

I cheerfully picked up the bunch of papers and took them upstairs. Since it was already getting dark, I intended to go to bed soon. Although I did discover that the association existed, I wanted to solve this problem in a more refined manner. I also looked forward to the night I was going to spend with Ravi…

When I got to my door, my Hungarian neighbors stopped me.

»Where are you off to, *neighbor*? We hardly see you anymore…« said Eszter disappointedly.

»Yeah, why don't you come over and we'll have a girls' night…« added Rossana.

I thought about what meant more to me: hanging with the girls, playing a few board games, or…? No, no, the other option was much more appealing.

»I'm sorry, neighbors but today I really have to go to bed early…« They interrupted me before I could finish my excuse.

»You've been going to bed early the whole week! You vanish into your room at 7 p.m. and you don't come out till morning,« protested Eszter.

»We really want to know what you're doing, because it's impossible for somebody to need that much sleep,« added Rossana again.

»Really, what are you doing in your room?« asked Eszter meaningfully.

What was I doing? Oh, no. I'll get disclosed, I told myself. No. I needed to keep my head cool. I'd surely manage to explain everything in a nice and understandable way…

»Me? Oh…I…STUDY.« And it was true, too.

»I study. I'm a foreigner, as you know, and they expect the same level of knowledge like I was one of them. There are no exceptions.« That was also true. There really were no exceptions. The only thing I left out was *what exactly* I was studying and *with whom I was studying*. And I really didn't think it was the right moment to start discussing that.

»Well, yes. Alright. If you should change your mind, just knock, neighbor.«

They wished me goodnight and we went to our separate rooms. I wiped my sweaty forehead: whoooo. I'd have peace for now.

I prepared for bed very quickly and lay down. I was so impatient that I decided to practice a little. I practiced teleportation, flying…everything within my room, of course because I expected Ravi the whole time.

This time he didn't come for a very long time. When he still hadn't come at midnight, I knew something was wrong. It wasn't just the delay. *I felt* that something wasn't right. I calmed down and tried to relax completely. Maybe now I could finally start to trust my feelings. Maybe I could calm down and not jump to any conclusions. To just be. If it was meant to be, I'd receive Ravi's message. Again I was sorry for not giving him my phone number.

When I managed to calm down my thoughts, I started feeling some kind of twitching. My soul was engulfed by a sphere of colors that wasn't mine. The colors were mixing and I realized that what I was seeing was a blurred colored film. The more I wanted to see it, the more I struggled and the less I saw. When I lost all hope and relaxed, the picture began to clear up. So I tried the distancing tactics. I tried to observe the haze in front of me as objectively as possible and without any feelings. I was right. It was a message. *His* message.

He was sitting on the bed in his room, taking to his father. I saw that his father was very upset and that Ravi tried to calm him down. His father would sometimes get so involved in the argument, that he screamed his lungs out. When he lost control of his emotions, he was unable to see that his son quickly closed his eyes and sent a very powerful telepathic message. I could even hear his voice.

I won't be able to come today. My father found out that I had escaped during his absence and I also think that he knows what method we use to meet. Maybe we'll be able to talk tomorrow, during classes. Nobody will get suspicious there if I take a little nap in the last row…

I could even hear his laughter.

I love you, Ina. I hope you can hear me.

This was the first time that he said to me in this lifetime that he loved me. And he chose the most beautiful way. I had to overcome myself to be able to hear his message but it was worth it. I heard him more clearly than anything else.

I concentrated on the picture he sent me once more. I was drawn to him. I wanted to go there and find out what was happening. I decided to try. Although I didn't know where exactly he was, I concentrated on the room they were in. In my mind I put myself in the left corner of the room, near Ravi's bed...

I was engulfed by the light. I got there quicker than I thought was possible. His father was still there and they were still engaged in a heated debate. Ravi twitched slightly and quickly looked in my direction. So, he noticed my arrival. Luckily, his father didn't see that.

»What do you even like about her!?« he raged.

»I've already told you. Besides being heavenly beautiful, smart and kind, her presence fulfills me more than I ever dared to imagine. And sometime in the future, when we're both mature enough, I'd like to marry her.« He said these words with such a conviction that I was completely taken over by them. I knew he was serious about me. After spending several thousands of years together, it probably wasn't too early to consider marriage. But I also knew that he was upsetting his father even more with that. Still, I decided to respond.

How about asking me first, before you go and shout that from the rooftops? He smiled for a fraction of a second. I saw that he received my thought.

I'll ask you as it befits, he replied. *What are you doing here, Ina?* he added with care. *It's dangerous. My father's not alone.*

I looked around and saw three beings of smaller stature walking around him, encouraging him. They were distinctly dark and I sensed their low vibrations; it was like listening to a very low-vibrating bass.

Don't look at them, Ravi warned me attentively.

I came to see if I could help in any way. That's how I found you. You know, if I wouldn't want to help, maybe I wouldn't find my way here. It's my duty to be here.

You got me, answered Ravi. I was admiring his immense spiritual power, for while he was answering me, he was also calmly talking to his father. *If you really want to,* he relented, *you can send light to these beings around my father. I think they still haven't sensed that you're here. And I also think they can't see you. Try closing your eyes. Don't look at them, because...there's nothing to see.*

I relaxed and sat on the bed. I noticed that Ravi and his father merely passed the ball to one another and that conversation wasn't going anywhere. It seemed to me that Davies was in the room just so he could control his son. I imagined the light and the room was full of it instantly. I heard the muffled screams of the dark creatures and then they were gone. The conversation too died down. The room stood still in silence.

»What did you do?« asked Davies.

»Nothing, father,« said Ravi calmly and I could see that he was telling the truth. It *really* wasn't him.

»She's here, isn't she? *She* is here!« Davies started to pace around the room, looking for me.

It's best that you leave now. I'll deal with him. See you tomorrow at school.

Is everything going to be alright? I asked with concern.

Of course. I'm okay. The creatures will need some time to recover too. You gave them pure love.

I know, yes. I've learnt from the best, I smiled.

See you tomorrow. Thank you for this.

You're welcome. See you.

I left as I came. I was in my room in an instant. As I was preparing to reconnect with my body, the thought occurred to me that I had missed a good opportunity to check where Ravi lived. But I immediately answered myself that that again wouldn't help anybody and that he was going to invite me himself when the time was right.

I reconnected and calmed down. Since there was still some time left before my alarm clock started its morning ringing, I decided to lie in a little longer.

XXXV. THE DAY OF THE TRIAL

W HEN I WOKE UP MY MIND WAS FULL OF THOUGHTS. After the events of the night before I didn't really know what I should prepare myself for. Who was I fighting against? I decided to drop by the school. It was the right time for the principal to be there and at the same time early enough so Hannah wouldn't wait for me for too long. She still insisted that it was too cold for a bike and that she wanted to drive me to school. I had the feeling that she too could feel my *energy*. She was very fond of me.

I sat behind my desk and relaxed. I decided to leave my body for a while and check what was going on in school. I left my body in a sitting position. I quickly untied myself, tied the umbilical cord to my left leg and materialized in school. *If I could go to school this way, Hannah's gas mileage would be much better,* I thought.

I walked through the school and found principal Davies. He looked around himself and I got the feeling that he could *sense* me. I tried to remain objective and not to get involved in his fear which was very strong.

He went to the administration office and gave the instructions:

»Let all the students know that today's first period has been cancelled.«

»For everyone? Even if they have examinations…« asked the secretary. He interrupted her rudely.

»FOR EVERYONE, of course. All students should gather in the gymnasium.«

»Very well, Principal.«

Davies closed the door and mumbled: »So they can see what expulsion looks like…«

He left the administration office and I also didn't intend to stay there. I was in my room and in my own body in an instant. This dangerous procedure became a matter of routine for me.

I quickly dressed and prepared my school bag. I wrapped up some food in the dining room and took it with me. When I came out, Hannah was already waiting. I sat in the passenger seat and bit into the sandwich I brought with me. I wanted to think about the hopeless situation I was in, but I quickly chased those thoughts away. *I will surely make it*, I thought, *even though I don't know how yet.*

As we drove off towards the school, Hannah asked me whether I had found anything on the Internet. I quickly answered that there indeed was an association for these things and that the rulebook clearly stated that you couldn't get expelled from school just like that. That calmed her down and we talked about other, more important things. About Ravi, for example. That is, about Robert.

»*So, how are you?*« she asked meaningfully.

»Great, thanks, and you?« I played dumb.

»Just so you know, I think you two are a great couple.«

»Thank you.«

»And there's something else…And please don't be mad because I didn't tell you this before. A week or so before holidays…I dreamed that someday you'd tell me you were with him. And I thought that was really nice. You two really belong together. Well, after that dream I went to school and watched you and nothing happened. You weren't even saying hello to him. And after holidays, a sudden »boom« and you're together. How did that even happen?«

I sighed again. Another test. Someday she'd find out the truth anyway. But that morning I had to save my strength for something far more important…

»I've already told you. It started with the Christmas card. He did a little trick during the raffle and so I drew his number. I got a CD with a dedication meant only for me. We agreed to meet after the holidays, sparks flew and that's it.« I told the truth, basically. More or less. Maybe I exaggerated using expressions like sparks flew, only for me…But it worked. She believed me although it wasn't easy.

»Okay, okay. Today you'll probably focus more on how to get rid of your father-in-law,« she burst out laughing.

We arrived quickly. I jumped out and she drove off to park the car. I met my opponent already at the entrance and I immediately started sending him love. When I did that I was automatically protected. I approached him totally calmly and without fear for the first time and even the taste in my mouth was normal.

»Good morning, Principal Davies!« I greeted him smilingly. He became red-faced with anger but still managed a wicked smile and re-turned my greeting:

»Good morning, former student Ina!«

I stopped and looked at him again. He wasn't scary anymore. More… sort of scared. He wasn't alone, naturally. I sensed that he was surrounded by three little dark hazes. I had the feeling that he didn't have control over his life or body as he'd wish. As I sent him love, the beings disappeared again. I decided to try to talk to him *now* and not in the gymnasium, in front of a thousand students.

»Is there a chance we could talk?« I asked friendly.

»I'm afraid not,« he replied in the distinctive British accent.

»You're right, I cut class,« I was honest. »But is that really the reason for me to say goodbye to an education forever and ever? I've been an A-student throughout school and I intend to be one this year. You can check my certificate…«

»It's not that. It's about you explicitly insulting the top school official,« he stressed pompously.

»Before I entered the school you kindly assured me you were coming in and then you very shamelessly broke your promise.« I thought he was saying such nonsense that he hardly believed himself. But I decided not to judge him because I hardly knew him.

»Well, okay. May I redeem myself somehow, so I wouldn't get kicked out of school?« I negotiated. I was perfectly relaxed by then.

»You could break it off with my son,« he said quickly. I could feel that only that condition would really suffice for him to drop his unjust charges against me. So, he thought that a threat would suffice. He was wrong there. To exchange love, which had lasted for thousands of years, just so I could be a student at his school – that would be nonsense. I decided to fight. And if I was meant to go to school somewhere else, I'd simply go. Never, but really *never* would I be prepared to give up a person had searched for, waited for, and loved for thousands of years. *Never.*

»If I understand correctly: you'd like to throw me out of the school. But what you really want to let me know is that you don't want me as your daughter-in-law.« I smiled. It was obvious that what he'd been doing was senseless.

»You just come in, Ina. I'll see you in the gymnasium,« he said and I sensed that he was expecting a surprised look on my face.

»Okay. See you in the gymnasium,« I replied like that was perfectly self-evident. I wanted him to know who he was dealing with and that I intended to fight.

When he recovered from surprise, he shouted after me: »One more thing: there will be no opportunity for defense!«

So, I wouldn't be allowed to defend myself at my trial. Interesting, and there I was thinking we were in the twenty-first century, where freedom of speech was recognized. When I broke through the crowded locker area on the second floor, I quickly prepared. I left my bag in my locker so it wouldn't get in my way. I only took my cell phone with me, which I had set to silent mode, and the small locker key. I put both in the pocket of my sweater, which I took with me.

Walking to the gym I checked a few times if Ravi was perhaps waiting for me, and wondered if this morning his father by any chance – besides locking him in his room – also chained and tied him, so he'd really stay at home. But if something like that had happened, he'd surely have sent me a message.

I entered the gym where a lot of people were already sitting. They quieted down immediately. I spotted a few chairs on the stage and their arrangement reminded me of a courtroom. I stepped closer and noticed Miss Highmore standing beside the stage. She too stepped closer.

»Please forgive me, Ina but I think you'll have to leave. I'm truly sorry.« I could see that she was telling the truth.

»It's alright, Miss Highmore. It's not your fault. If someone's to blame, it's me. Or Davies. But certainly not you.«

»Please, call me Lucy. I hope that we could meet again sometime and have a chat over a cup of coffee. You've been my favorite student, you know,« I noticed tears in her eyes.

»But I'm still here,« I comforted her. »And I'll give my best to stay here.«

»Anyway,« she said like she didn't really believe in the positive outcome of this story, »please know that I really love you. Well, the Principal ordered me to show you where you'll be sitting.«

Of course. In the center of the stage. On the bench for the accused. In a minute the principal would probably start distributing rotten tomatoes and eggs and ordering students to throw them at me. I really didn't have anything to lose. He was like an...absolute ruler of the school. Like a tyrant, feared by all. Well, *almost* all.

The bell announced the start of the period. Even the students who came last to the expulsion spectacle sat down. I couldn't notice Ravi anywhere. Instead I saw Davies, who came to the gym through one of the side doors like everybody else. He was in a good mood and rushed onto the stage.

»Thank you for coming,« he said over the microphone.

»I wanted to show you a brief procedure, namely what happens, if you simply disregard the rules for one reason or another.« He still thought the whole world was at his mercy. He smiled mercifully.
»And so you won't think I'm a cruel man, I'll let you go for the remainder of the period after this event. You'll be free to go anywhere or hang out with your friends until the next period starts.«

A murmur of surprise spread across the gym and it felt like he really

did something very generous. It seemed that he'd done something like that for the first time. He really must've been in a good mood. The students applauded him for his generosity and I understood them. Who could blame them? I too applauded with them and kept sending them love. Luckily, principal Davies had his back turned to me.

»I thank you for your sincere approval,« he said cheerfully and I could tell he saw himself as a moral winner of this event. He pointed at me.

»This student here insulted the top school official yesterday, therefore I propose expulsion. Does anybody oppose?« he waited for a half of second and continued: »I didn't think so.«

He brought an old school rulebook with him and started reading from it: »In accordance with the School Code, article 23, paragraph 45, I pronounce you, Ina Kralj...«

I was still sending him love. I couldn't do anything else. His reading was interrupted by a thunderous voice.

»NOT SO FAST!« An older, stocky gentleman with a bald patch in the middle of his head stood at the door. He wore dark-green corduroy pants, a vest of the same color and a white shirt. He looked very well groomed. I didn't know who he was but I saw that the principal swallowed hard.

»Oh, what an honor. Dear students and teachers, we have among us a honorary guest of the trial and the president of the Associated Secondary Schools Commission: doctor Emil Barnes!« smiled Davies in embarrassment and pompously introduced the guest. The students applauded and dr. Barnes quieted them down. Right next to the newcomer I noticed Ravi. So, *that's* what he'd been doing...

Dr. Barnes walked up to the stage. He quickly looked me over from head to toe and turned to Ravi. He gave him thumbs up as if saying: *she is pretty* and turned to the principal.

»What have you here?« he asked him. He took the book from his hands and read: »The School Rulebook, 1947. Don't you think that the time has come for you to update your methods a bit, Mr. Davies? We are in the information age, after all. And you basically live in the previous millennium.« He threw the book away, in the backstage.

The students giggled quietly. It seemed that they finally became aware of whom the principal was afraid of and it was very…refreshing. I think that in that moment nobody wanted a free period. Everybody was watching the happening on the stage with great interest.

Barnes turned towards the audience and took a book from a handy, black briefcase. It was totally different from the old rulebook. It had a bright red cover with gold-trimmed edges. He formally announced:

»This is this year's rulebook. Maybe you'd recognize it, if you didn't cut every single annual meeting of secondary school principals.«

Davies seriously bowed his head and I started to send him love vibrations even more intensely. Not only did this act empowered me, I also wanted the others to show…mercy for him.

»Let's see: *cutting, cutting* ... It's probably under the letter C, what do you think?« The students laughed, while dr. Barnes enjoyed his delighted audience. He was much more relaxed than many scholars of his age. It could be said that the older gentleman obviously met wisdom. He read from the rulebook.

»If a student is absent without a reason, he will not receive academic credit missed during this absence…« Again he turned towards the principal: »Not a word about expulsion.«

Principal Davies was still silent. He was obviously really afraid of dr. Barnes.

»This is like,« the heavyset man burst out laughing, »like receiving a death penalty for stealing an apple!«

He said that in such a funny way that the entire gymnasium started laughing immediately. Davies was still standing in the same spot, pressing his lips together. He certainly didn't expect this.

»…To get…an electric chair for stealing one single grape!« Barnes intensified the comedy. The gymnasium was echoing with laughter that needed some time to die down. The newfound comedian indicated with his hand for the audience to calm down.

»Well, now I have a question for you, Principal. What did the young lady do to *insult you?*« He quoted Davies on purpose and that amused him very much.

The asked man cleared his throat and said quietly: »Because she without a reason...«

»Without a reason? Without a reason? Without – a reason?« Barnes repeated dramatically. »*Nothing* happens without a reason, Principal. There surely *must've been* a reason. And quite accidentally I know why the young lady didn't come to school yesterday...« he looked at me and winked at Robert.

»Have you ever been in love, Principal? I presume that the answer is affirmative, otherwise you wouldn't have a son and raise him with such love. What if I told you that young lady was detained by love yesterday? Is love and infatuation of two young people something bad?« he turned towards the elated audience and encouraged them: »Please raise your hand if you've ever been in love in your life!«

Naturally, they all raised their hands. It looked like a scene from a rock concert. The speaker continued.

»Therefore, as the president of the Associated Secondary Schools Commission, I propose for this case to be dismissed. The accused shall not be punished, by way of exception. We have already tormented the young enamored hearts enough. Those for it, please applaud!«

The students heartily applauded and shouted. The entertaining judge quieted them down for the last time and turned towards Davies.

»While we're at it, maybe now would be the appropriate time to put *you* under the microscope, Principal. But I'm in a good mood today. I don't want to ruin my day. Just make sure that such an absurd situation doesn't happen again.«

When dr. Barnes left the stage, another spontaneous applause broke out and the students joyously waived him goodbye. It was like in the movies. When the main attraction, that successfully managed to frighten even Davies, left the gymnasium, all eyes turned to the stage again. I sat there by myself because the principal obviously left the place during the thunderous applause. Miss Highmore took over the microphone.

»So, there are ten minutes still left in this period. I hope you'll make a good use of them and celebrate nicely. See you in the classrooms!«

I wasn't clear on what she meant by celebrating but the atmosphere seemed suitable. As if the school started breathing again after a long time. The students started getting up. Robert ran to me and hugged me. He gently kissed me in the center of the stage and all the students started looking at us again. Another roaring applause and loud approval followed. We slowly left the stage and the students laughingly started leaving the gym.

»Why would I hide my feelings for you?« he said smilingly.

»Maybe…because of your father?« I asked. »Today he patently let me know that he didn't like me very much. Basically, he doesn't like me *at all*. Not in the least.«

»Maybe he likes you too much,« Robert smiled. »I can't imagine that somebody wouldn't like such a beauty. Have you seen yourself in the mirror today?«

»No, I was too busy trying to stay in this school. When I didn't find you, I simply didn't know what to do,« I reprimanded him.

»My little surprise,« he explained. »I didn't want you to come after me again and spoil it.«

I smiled. He was right about that. Sometimes I was *too* eager to help.

He contentedly put his arm around my shoulder and walked me to the school lockers. On the way there we were running into students who cheerfully greeted us, thanked us and congratulated me for staying in school. Standing by my locker, I felt the phone in my sweater and immediately told him:

»Don't you think the time has come, after all those thousands of years, for me to give you my number?«

XXXVI. THE FIRST CLUB MEMBERS

W HEN WE CAME TO THE CLASSROOM, OUR CLASSMATES IMMEDIATELY started applauding us. They were really surprised, because nobody even thought that we might be together. Absolutely nothing had happened in front of their eyes and they were almost disappointed.

I was surrounded with girls and he with boys. We were the first couple in the class. Luckily, the bell rang before long and there was only enough time for me to shortly answer just a few questions. My answers were very short, for example: »Before holidays«, »With Christmas card«, »Yesterday«, »Yes« and »No«. I had the feeling that he was doing the same. The girls were crowding around me and laughed heartily. I had no idea that they were so in favor of us. Even Sienna smiled from time to time. I noticed that one of them was missing. Jeanette was standing in the corner and I saw that her eyes were red from crying. I wanted to go to her, but at the same time I felt that she wanted to be alone.

Since our first period, the English literature class, was cancelled, we waited for the biology class. Mr. Dawson was punctual as usual. I felt my boyfriend's gaze on the back of my head. Now I could officially call him *my boyfriend*. I relaxed and we immediately found ourselves on the same frequency.

When do we start with our club?

I don't know. I'm still in shock because of the expulsion, and you're already thinking about the club, I joked.

Of course. I never believed you were really going to be expelled.

You didn't? When I talked to him this morning, he was pretty convinced.

I wanted to say, that he didn't have enough strength for that.

Thank you for bringing Barnes. You didn't have to do that.

I didn't do that for you. I did that...

I know. For yourself. Thanks, anyway.

And what about the club? He was still curious.

Great, thanks, I joked. *And you?*

Don't you think the time has come that you started receiving first students? Because you're pretty good at it.

I didn't know what to answer.

You don't have to answer anything. Just say the word YES.

Well, okay. YES. I'll ask Gina.

And I'll ask Elliot. We need male members too.

Okay. Shall we meet after school?

We could.

Where?

I'll let you know. First we have to find out if our honorary members are up for this thing.

Okay. I can't wait for this class to be over.

Me too.

See you.

Funny statement, because we ALREADY see each other.

I smiled. Dawson looked in my direction.

»Any questions, Ina?«

I looked at the blackboard and saw drawings of single-celled organisms.

»No, no, I was just imagining how we would look with so many appendages,« I replied calmly.

The class laughed relaxingly and it was obvious that they were still under the influence of dr. Barnes. I too was grateful for the way things had turned out. That couldn't have happened more perfectly. Strange and

211

full of mysteries are ways…of the universe.

I tore a piece of paper from my notebook. Since I wasn't paying too much attention to the class from the beginning anyway, I exceptionally decided to do the same for the rest of the period. After all, I had more important things to do. I wrote on that piece of paper:

> *Hi, Gina.*
> *I've considered your request.*
> *I want you to know that I'm ready.*
> *We could meet after school.*
> *Robert and Elliot will probably join us.*
> *Let me know if you have time.*
> *Regards, Ina.*

I folded the paper and wrote *for Gina* on it. I tried to bend backwards as unnoticeably as possible and sent it away. When I was looking backwards, my eyes stopped on Robert. I saw that he was writing something, but not in his notebook. On the desk, next to his notebook, he had a torn piece of paper. I knew what he was writing and I smiled. He passed that piece of paper towards Elliot. When Elliot received it, he unfolded it and smiled. He started writing immediately and sent the paper back. Again I heard Robert's voice in my head.

The answer is affirmative, he said to me. *I didn't think Elliot also had experience with meditation. Well, that's not odd considering his constantly good disposition. How are you doing?*

I'm still waiting.

You won't be waiting for too long, he warned me.

Within a second my neighbor from behind tapped me on the shoulder. I received the answer. I unfolded the small piece of paper entitled in Gina's handwriting: FOR INA.

Finally.

I had to wait the whole week for an answer.

I was already afraid something was wrong.

OF COURSE I'll see you after school.

Can't wait. The more, the merrier.

My answer is also enthusiastically affirmative, I smiled.

We could meet in front of the school and go to the Central Park, he suggested.

We could, yes. Great, I agreed.

Excellent. And now only four more classes to go, he thought wearily.

We have to attend four very important classes, if we don't want to be expelled from school, I replied in a nerdy tone of voice.

After today? I don't think so. Quite the opposite. I think my father will really think twice before engaging in something like that again. I think we can cut class now at will and nobody's going to complain...

Is that right? Now you're going to cross over to the dark side too? This lapse from yesterday was an unique experience.

Yes, well, I know. I mentioned that thing from before just as an example. I definitely intend to regularly attend my scholastic obligations, he thought in a learned manner.

Well, that sounds better, I smiled.

And when I do that, I'll just have to imagine what else we could be doing together, if you by any chance ever wanted to...be absent from school with me.

I felt a tingling sensation all over my body...Was that possible? To telepathically send an injection of hormones? And I already thought I was done with them.

ANYTHING is possible, Robert smiled.

It really is, I agreed.

XXXVII. THE CLUB'S FIRST PRACTICE

AFTER CLASSES, WHICH LOOKED MORE LIKE FREE CHAT ROOMS BETWEEN Robert and me, we met in the hallway. There was no sign of principal Davies the whole day. Like he hid somewhere, nursing his wounded pride. After a long time Robert actually talked to me instead of sending me thoughts.

»We're getting pretty good at this, wouldn't you agree?«

»Are you sure this is good? I mean, talking like that constantly? I'm afraid I'll lose the power…«

»We're not hurting anybody with it. We're just practicing a new way of communication, which will be extremely important in the future world. That's why this ability isn't diminishing but is only getting stronger.«

»Aha, well, okay.«

»Basically – by practicing telepathy we're *already* helping others.«

»How do we do that?«

»Soon we won't be that alone in this connection anymore.«

I realized that I'd be sorry to lose this precious little part of privacy. What is it going to be like when the whole classroom is able to listen to what we have to say to each other?

»Don't be afraid, this method of communication is intended only for people with high morals. Nobody will eavesdrop or otherwise ill-use that knowledge. They'll connect to us only *when they need us*. Just like with cell phones. The message gets to the person that was meant for. If you wanted to send me a message using the cell phone, you probably wouldn't send it to everybody in your phonebook but just to me. That's also how telepathy works.«

»Thank you for the answer.« I felt how selfish I'd been. I wanted to protect our love by any means possible. After so many years of waiting that was somewhat logical. He felt me.

»I know. I panic sometimes too, especially when I think about how long we haven't seen each other and how dangerous our path was...« he became serious.

We came to the exit and it seemed appropriate that we changed the subject. Jeanette quickly ran past us. A few seconds behind her followed Lance.

»Jeanette, wait!« he shouted.

»I didn't mean anything bad by it!«

»What is it?« asked Ravi.

»Basically...I'll appreciate it if you don't tell this to anybody...But I asked Jeanette out.« He sighed desperately in the middle of the school hustle and bustle.

»Her reaction certainly wasn't what I was hoping for...« he smiled sadly.

»Don't worry, Lance. You're quite alright, you know,« I said encouragingly. »Maybe you're simply not her type,« I joked.

»Okay, I'll see you around, you happy couple,« he bid us farewell almost enviously. I could feel that he really liked Jeanette. Unfortunately her beauty, which was so distinctive during the first few months, started to fade slowly. She had dark bags under her eyes and she looked tired.

We looked after him and headed towards the exit ourselves. I could feel that Ravi knew more about this matter than I did.

»I'll show you what that's all about pretty soon. Now we have to focus on our first lesson with the members of our secret club,« he changed the subject. I too didn't want to discuss dark topics anymore and my mood improved, which was quite alright, because Gina in Elliot were already waiting in front of the school.

»Just follow us,« said Robert. We picked up the pace just in case. It'd be really uncomfortable if our little club ran into...a wrong person in front of the school.

I also sent a text message to Hannah saying I didn't need a ride home for the day, but that I'd be very happy to see her the following morning.

We soon found ourselves in front of the Central Park and we went straight down the path. We had to go deep enough into the park, so we wouldn't be visible from the street. We strolled for a while and then stopped by one of the benches. Our students were absolutely ready for the first lesson. They were glowing with curiosity.

»So, welcome to the first secret club meeting,« began Ravi.

»My name is Robert Ravi Davies and I'll be your lecturer…Next to me is Miss Ina Kralj, who'll be my assistant today…« he pointed at me and smiled. Gina and Elliot applauded enthusiastically.

»For starters we'll relax a bit.« He sat on the bench facing them and invited me to sit next to him. »Try to…think about nothing,« he added.

We relaxed and soon decided to leave our bodies. We came to our sitting classmates and saw that they were trying as best as they could to stay focused…And of course to think about nothing.

»We'll have to help here,« said Ravi.

I knew what he meant by that. I focused and imagined the light. And it soon came. It was getting brighter. Ravi connected to my vibration and I could feel that he created even more powerful flux from it. The entire park bathed in the light, like some kind of lake. We had created two poles and directed the flux into a couple of tubes – one leading into Gina, the other into Elliot. Such a powerful injection made them simultaneously breathe in deeply. I knew what they were feeling. Pure love. Suddenly, I noticed two powerfully conscious souls standing up from their sitting positions. They were still covered in cells of light, just as I was when I left my body for the first time.

»Carefully,« said Ravi.

»Can they see us?« I asked.

»Of course,« said Gina lightly and I could see that she wasn't quite clear about what was going on. She was looking around perfectly normally until she noticed that our bodies were still sitting on the bench behind me. »O, my God. Elliot, look at this,« she said totally confused.

Elliot looked at our bodies in utter amazement and asked: »Where are we?«

»Please, stay where you are,« calmly said Ravi and they calmed down immediately. Again I witnessed his absolute power.

»Where are we? We're where we'd already been, only maybe we weren't aware of it that way,« he explained.

»Wow.« Gina was thrilled.

»Now an important part follows, so please, pay close attention to it. What I'm about to show you is pretty dangerous, so you need to be extra calm and focused…« continued Ravi.

A lesson followed much like the one when I was learning the ropes. Gina and Elliot were really good at visualization and they absorbed the knowledge pretty quickly. They watched the glowing string through which life was flowing with interest and treated it with love and respect.

Soon after they succeeded in detaching themselves from their bodies, Ravi warned them not to try to do that at home for the time being. He also acquainted them with the most important rule: that these special abilities may only be used for good intensions, which is to say, for the benefit of mankind. He told them that any violation of that rule, such as the use for one's own benefits, was strictly forbidden; in such a case the ability would be simply – lost. They understood.

To let them get accustomed to this state of being, we initially just strolled through the park. They had a lot of questions. We observed people and hazes around them. It was pretty entertaining. Gina and Elliot enjoyed themselves immensely and I could feel that they'd been waiting for this their entire lives.

The lesson was over in a flash. When we got to the end of it, Gina and Elliot sat on the bench, while Ravi and me helped them untie their »shoelaces«. A few moments later we woke up and opened our eyes.

»Wow, I feel so good!« said Gina. »So well rested!«

Elliot was thrilled too. Ravi explained them why they felt that way.

»See you again tomorrow? Same place, same time?« asked Elliot excitedly. We looked at each other. The first lesson obviously turned out far better than we thought it would.

»Of course,« I said.

We said goodbye. Gina and Elliot just couldn't put a curb on their enthusiasm. They hurried off home and I saw that they couldn't wait for the next lesson.

Ravi and me headed towards my dorm.

»I'm not to keen on going home, you know?« he said absorbed in his thoughts.

I can imagine, yes, I thought.

»You can, can't you?« he smiled. He continued by sending me thoughts.

I'm thinking that maybe it's the appropriate time for me to see where you live…with my own eyes.

I hope you won't be disappointed.

Why would I be?

Because this time they're all going to SEE you.

At least they'll know you're already taken. And that your boyfriend isn't imaginary, but flesh and blood…

Maybe it would be good to let your father know you'll be late, so he doesn't worry…

I've been thinking that he maybe doesn't even deserve this, but you're right. I'll send him a text message.

He put his arm around my shoulder, we walked in silence and smiled occasionally. I was happy like never before…

XXXVIII. THE OFFICIAL VISIT

WHEN WE ENTERED THE DORM, JEANIE BEHIND THE RECEPTION desk saw that I wasn't alone and that I was positively blooming. When she took a better look at my companion, she became thrilled too.

»Hi, Jeanie. This is my boyfriend…Robert.«

He shook her hand and introduced himself. She did the same and smiled.

»He came by to visit me today. There's nothing wrong with that, is there?«

Jeanie looked at Ravi, smiled again in embarrassment and I immediately felt his power.

»Of course not,« she said kindly, like she'd been hypnotized. »He can stay as long as he wants.«

We quickly went upstairs to my room and vanished behind the door before we could run into my neighbors.

»So, this is where you live,« he said ceremoniously, like we hadn't met in this room at least a dozen times already. I knew he was kidding.

»Yes, this is my room,« I joined our little game and pointed around me.

»A writing desk by the window, nice, nice,« he commented like seeing it for the first time.

»A nice and spacious closet…« he was describing the space again.

»And, interesting, a bed slightly bigger than one person would need. Curious. Is it French? Is it decorated in accordance with feng shui?« He was asking like he intended to buy the room.

»May I try it?« he asked innocently.

»Please, please,« I politely pointed towards the object of his interest. He calmly said:

»Thank you very much.«

He quickly seized my hips and threw us both on the bed. I got scared and cried out a bit. When we fell on a soft bedspread, he embraced me and we both laughed loudly.

He rolled on top of me and interlocked his fingers with mine. Then he stretched our joined arms over the pillow above my head. I felt so... caught and pleasant at the same time.

Now you're mine, he thought joyfully.

I've always been, I answered.

His face was close to mine and I could hear his heartbeat from afar again. He slowly moved his lips closer to mine. Just before he could touch them, he stopped and I could physically sense the electricity between our lips. If someone should put a light bulb between them, it wouldn't just light up, it'd burn out.

Finally he pressed his mouth against mine. He unclasped his arms and merged completely with my body. We started rolling on the bed and his hands clung to my body like they were part of it. He was sliding them down my T-shirt, my pants and my hair, while simultaneously holding me tightly and decisively. I felt a strong sweet pain that spread from the bottom of my belly all over my body. In a certain moment we became completely locked together and we felt the fusion. We merged completely without thoughts and soon there were no boundaries. We were still kissing, but during that kiss we existed in silence.

Suddenly, a loud sound ripped through the silence. Somebody knocked loudly on the door. We heard giggling coming from the other side of the door.

We got up quickly and I opened the door. My neighbors were standing outside.

»Well, now we know how you study!« they caught me.

»Hello ladies, I'm Robert,« my boyfriend peeped from behind my back.

His hair was slightly ruffled and he was blinking a little, since we'd been just awoken from the state of rapture. He was so indescribably handsome that my neighbors immediately apologized.

»We're really sorry to bother you but for a week and a half now our neighbor has been much too busy to take some time for us. At least now we know *with whom she's been studying*,« said Eszter smilingly.

»Robert, let me introduce my neighbors: Eszter and Rossana.«

»I'm pleased to meet you,« he said and looked at his watch.

»We really hope we didn't bother you too much,« apologized Rossana once more.

»It's alright, I was leaving anyway,« he said and sadness washed over me.

»Take care of yourself,« I said quietly. He knew why.

»I will.«

He kissed me and left quickly.

We were looking after him and he turned back once more in the hallway.

»Have a nice evening!« he said again and winked at me. In his thoughts he added:

See you soon, my love. As soon as I fall asleep at home.

I smiled and waived at him. He walked down the stairs and soon I couldn't see him anymore. My neighbors waived at him too and I found that almost slightly unnatural. After all, he was *my* boyfriend.

Jealousy is a perfectly normal thing, but it's not healthy, I heard in my head. *You know I'm WITH YOU. Most of the time we become attractive to other people too, because they sense larger quantities of energy.*

I was surprised that I could still hear his thoughts so clearly, since he wasn't near me anymore. I heard him like was standing right next to me.

Are you still with me? Does this work so well even from a distance?

We can try it sometime. When you're not so busy with your friends…

Suddenly I heard voices in the distance getting closer.

»Ina! Ina!«

»Look at her, she's totally lost in reverie.«

»So it is true that love is deaf and blind!«

»INA!« Eszter almost shouted again.

»We were already afraid that we've lost you,« said Rossana.

»No, I was just absorbed in my thoughts.«

»Hey, this boyfriend of yours is cute,« Eszter attacked me.

»Is this the one you've been dreaming about?«

»Yes,« I said quietly, still under the impression of my thoughts. »Yes, he is.«

»Oooooo,« they said in unison, like they'd just heard something touching.

»Thank you for introducing us,« Rossana quickly finished the conversation.

»You're welcome.« Well, I didn't have any other choice.

»Goodnight, *neighbor.*«

»Goodnight, *neighbors.*«

I laid on the bed hoping that Ravi would be okay. After a short reflection I got up, quickly prepared to go to bed and went back to bed. As I put my head on the pillow I sensed his smell. Sweetness took over me, followed by pain because he wasn't beside me. I quickly focused and went into alpha state. Soon I left my body. I moved around my room, practiced floating, but most of the time I was just thinking about him. I sent him a message:

I'm thinking about you and hope that you'll come soon. I received the answer within seconds.

I called my father and he was surprisingly calm. I'll come soon. I'm looking forward to being with you. Today we have an important thing to do.

XXXIX. MISSION – ALMOST IMPOSSIBLE

I WAITED FOR HIM ONLY A SHORT TIME. He materialized quickly and very brightly, so I knew he provided himself with additional energy. »And why is that?« I asked.

»Because today we'll check for the first time how well we've practiced until now. We'll try to use everything we've learned so far.«

»Okay,« I said. I knew I didn't have to be afraid of anything with his power around.

»It's not just about that. We'll have to use *just* our thoughts.«

I'd noticed that there were two methods of communication available in this dimension. The speech, as we're used to it when we're in our bodies and a higher frequency, i.e. thought travel.

Like this? I asked.

Yes, like that. From now on, he thought seriously. I could see that he was preparing for something bigger. I decided to really focus completely.

Thank you, that'll be really necessary, he continued.

Where are we going?

To Jeanette's. She lives a few blocks away. We're in luck, because lower beings can't hear our thoughts. At least not those that are with her. Your main task is: you mustn't look at nobody, not at all. If you do, look at hazes in the corner of your eye, but never focus on the fact that you want to SEE them. That might just happen. And when you see them, they see you too. Than the thing becomes dangerous. Otherwise, I'll be happy if you follow my thoughts and your intuition.

Okay. I'll do my best.

Are you ready?

Almost. Just tell me one more thing. What are they like? I mean, these creatures?

Disgusting. You don't want to know, he said quickly.

He embraced me and in an instant we were in a small bedroom. I saw the bed on which Jeanette slept. I could see that she had a very vivid dream, which was – considering the dark image floating over her – very unpleasant. She was tossing and turning in bed and sometimes let out an almost inaudible sigh.

These dreams have been tormenting her a few years now, he told me.

How do you know that?

When you're in her consciousness, you simply KNOW. And because she's very scared now, she attracts them even more, he said and nodded towards the corner behind us. With the corner of my eye I spotted four dark hazes in that corner. Three were smaller and one was bigger.

First, we'll deal with them and then we'll proceed with her dream, he decided.

I knew what I had to do. With the power of my thoughts I needed to attract enough light to cover and fill the room with it and thus defeat all four shadows. It would have really been of big help if I'd had at least some idea what they looked like. I could hardly imagine a fight, during which you couldn't see your opponent. I heard a very low, muffled vibration behind my back.

They're starting to sense us, Ina, Ravi said quickly. *Hurry.*

I imagined the light and thus brightened the room. Low vibrations were becoming louder and louder. Ravi joined me and gave me strength.

Carry on, I need more, he said.

How can I defeat them if I can't see them? I thought.

Give everything you've got.

On one side I sensed Jeanette's fear, on the other dark shadows. The biggest roared loudly.

Hurry, Ina! he almost shouted in his thoughts.

I sent even more light.

More! I know you can do more! Quickly! he encouraged me.

I can't do it if I can't see them, I thought almost in panic.

I heard increasingly louder roaring, then Ravi pulled me towards the bed. A thickened mass of energy formed into a shield in front of his left arm and he held it in front of the three of us. The creature bounced off of it and I looked at it involuntarily. It resembled a large three-legged animal, it stretched two crooked paws towards us and it had deep wrinkles and scales all over its body. A brown liquid oozed from its pores and dripped in all directions. The head on top of the body was small and wrinkled. Uneven large tusks protruded from the pig-like snout. The image was really disgusting. It went mad and started feverishly banging against our shield.

Ravi felt immediately that I made a mistake. Since he knew the danger we were in, he didn't waste time with accusations. He quickly calmed me down.

Now you know what they look like. Now you know how much energy you need. He used all his power and thought: *look me in the eye and START!*

As if he hypnotized me, I fell into a state of relaxation. In front of me I saw only light and absolutely nothing else. All of a sudden I didn't see anything and I didn't hear anything anymore. I just stood still in peace and absolute light. Ravi stepped into my light and increased it tenfold. The creatures vanished in an instant.

You see, you can do it, he thought with a smile.

It was a bit harder than I expected, though.

The universe always presents us with tests slightly above our existing capabilities, so we can constantly evolve. Another one of indisputable laws of the universe, he smiled.

What does that mean?

If you're faced with a test that seems too difficult and you think you won't be able to solve it, you can stop worrying. The universe obviously KNOWS that you're capable enough to solve it.

I really felt reassured. In the beginning I was almost certain that this test was too difficult for me. And then I passed it with honors. The monsters were gone. Jeanette was still breathing hard next to us.

We didn't get rid of everything, he thought seriously.

Do you remember the feeling, how it was when I sent you the first telepathic message? The film that played in front of you? In what way did you have to watch it?

Of course I remember. The more I wanted to see it, the more it shifted away. The more I was objective, the more it got closer.

That's the exact technique we must use now, he thought.

Isn't that...invasion of privacy? I remembered seeing Ela's dreams for a few moments for the first time.

Not in our case, he smiled. *You'll see.*

Well, okay.

Let's start.

We started watching the haze over Jeanette's head. I tried to distance myself as much as possible from the wish to get to know the story and from the deliberation why I was here. Soon I was so into it that I watched the reception like a program on television, which I wouldn't normally choose myself, but was watching it anyway, since I was sitting in front of the television set. Suddenly, the picture sharpened completely and grew bigger. Two figures stood in front of me. One small and one big. I established that the scene was happening in a stable, only the horses weren't in the stalls.

The bigger figure was an older gentleman, a few pounds overweight. A few millimeters long beard, partially bald head with unkempt hair, incorrectly buttoned shirt and a bad odor clearly indicated that he didn't pay too much attention to personal hygiene. A little girl in a red dress stood next to him. She was approximately six.

Look at her. REALLY look at her. Reflect yourself into her, thought Ravi.

I saw. That fair-haired girl was Jeanette. The picture in front of me was becoming clearer and clearer, we were engulfed by the light. All of a sudden I was standing in the middle of a stable, with uncle Perrin in front of me...

WE'VE COME TO SEE THE HORSES. I can't wait. Life on this planet is really beautiful. Such large animals and so powerful…Just one look into the eyes of my favorite horse, which is brown and named Shochli, is enough for a person to be happy all her life…How nice of uncle Perrin to offer to drive me to them…Mommy would never let me go alone. Where are they?

»Horses obviously went to have some exercise,« says uncle Perrin with disappointment in his voice.

»However, I can show you something that is even prettier.«

What could be even prettier than these beautiful animals?

»I can show you something that the whole world really wants.«

»What?«

»But you have to promise me that you won't tell anybody« he says solemnly.

»Not even to mommy?«

»Especially not to mommy!« says uncle.

»Is that something forbidden?«

»No…it's just too precious,« explains uncle mysteriously.

»like a hidden treasure?« I ask.

»Yes, yes, like that, yes,« he says eagerly. »*A hidden treasure*, how nicely put.« He laughs and I'm not completely sure why.

»What is that?« I ask.

»You won't tell anybody?«

»Not even to my daddy?«

»For God's sake, to no one! This secret is so important that only you in the whole world can know about it. And me.«

I feel important, because he chose me to carry the secret of the world inside me. Maybe I'll pass it on someday, when I'm old. Like uncle Perrin.

»Okay, I won't tell anybody. I promise.«

»Do you swear?«

»I swear.«

»Do you swear in front of God?«

I went to church with mommy many times. I like shiny pictures and statues the most. I just don't know why they're so serious…Mommy told me that the one on the cross is our savior. And that he is Son of God. And that God is the mightiest and that he sees everything and knows everything.

»But God knows everything anyway. I can't keep secrets from him,« I try to think logically.

»Exactly because he knows everything, he will also know that you've sworn to him, that you won't tell anyone… And if you ever break your promise, he will punish you more awfully than you can imagine! You'll never see your mommy and daddy again…«

»Then I don't know if I really want to see that treasure. I love mommy and daddy very much and I always tell them everything…«

Uncle Perrin turns around, like I'm not worthy of his trust the way he thought.

»Well, okay. Nothing then. Come on, let's go.«

I stop. What if there really is a treasure that everybody wants? A secret that has been offered to me today and maybe never again? Maybe I could stand not to tell my parents. God, whom I love infinitely, knows everything anyway.

»Uncle Perrin?«

Uncle calmly turns around. »Yes?«

»Okay. I swear to God.«

»Excellent,« he is thrilled immediately. »Follow me.«

He takes me down the corridor and opens the door where the fodder for horses is kept. A smaller room. A storeroom.

»Are you ready?«

»Mhm,« I nod. I am truly ready.

»This treasure is called... love.«

»Love?« The word sounds really familiar. I mostly heard it from cheerful and smiling people.

»Yes. And every man keeps it with him, so he can give it to a woman. Like your daddy gave it to your mommy.«

»Then this is not a secret?« I ask all confused.

»That is their secret. This will be *our* secret...«

»May I see it?«

»Of course...« uncle Perrin starts unzipping his pants and I think how nice it is that men can always have love with them. Out comes a weird, skin-colored thing. The tip of this mass is slightly bluish. I take a closer look and find out that it smells really badly.

»Are you sure everybody wants that?«

»Of course. Usually they even lick it, like an ice-cream...«

I get near it one more time. I become nauseous. I accept the fact that love stinks. When I'm quite close I realize that I won't be able to do it. I withdraw and tears fill my eyes.

»I can't.«

»Try and you'll see then!«

»I can't!« I open the door and start crying. I hear a voice behind me telling me to come back, but I start running.

Love stinks, love is ugly. Love stinks, echoes in my head. *That's not right. God isn't just, if he let love be so ugly. Does my mommy suffer like that too? And I mustn't tell her, because I swore to God...Love is ugly and it stinks...*

I hear a young man's voice in my head.

That is not your experience, he says. *Change it. Illuminate it.*

I stop in the middle of a meadow. In the back of my mind I realize that that's not *my* experience. I recognize the voice. Ravi. I know what the truth is. I know that love is beautiful and good. God is just and good.

I recognize that I need to be grateful for the test I was given, because I'm obviously, surely, capable of solving it.

I stop and look one more time towards the stable. I go back with slow steps. Uncle is still waiting in the storeroom. Two dark shadows are near him.

I try not to look at them. I close my eyes and imagine a powerful light. This light is joined by absolute power. The storeroom fills with light and unconditional love in an instant. Dark beings disintegrate in a hundredth of a second.

In this light I see uncle Perrin as a neutral being that was too weak at the wrong time. He sees me emitting the light and he immediately becomes embarrassed. He quickly zips his pants all the way up and cries near me. I feel absolute love for him, as I do for all living beings. And for horses.

»Please, forgive me, Jeanette... I didn't know... I wasn't aware «

Perrin falls down on his knees in front of me and I find that most unusual. There's nothing to forgive. I'm not here to judge him. I'm here to love. And to pay a little more attention to beings surrounded by dark shadows. I have to love them even *more*.

I laugh lightheartedly in this light and I tell myself one more time: yes, God really is good. Love is beautiful.

My head is full of light and I can feel absolute truth take over my body. *Everything is love*, echoes in my every cell. *God is just...* I'm engulfed by the light and before long I don't think about anything anymore.

I remained seated in front of Jeanette's bed and noticed Ravi in front of me.

He hugged me happily. »We did it! You were incredible!« he congratulated me.

I was slightly tired. I experienced a wide spectrum of emotions.

»Thank you for your help,« I said. »I'd be lost in there without you.«

»You're welcome. You were...great. You got so deep into her, that

her consciousness completely took you over. Your visualization ability…
When you imagined the light…I bet that they ran out of electricity in
heaven,« he smiled joyfully.

Even I managed enough strength for a smile. »Now I also understand
why all the bad things in the world happen…Like everything, but *really
everything*, it's just a test.«

»That's true. But the majority gets lost in accusation, regret and other
emotions…« Ravi added.

I noticed that our intervention lasted for quite some time.

»Are we going home?«

»Okay. I can't wait for you to return to your rested body. Today you'll
be especially well rested,« predicted Ravi.

»I'm glad. I need *rest*,« I joked.

We thought of my room. We were there in an instant. Ravi embraced
and kissed me. We said goodbye.

»I can't wait to see you again. And…congratulations once more.«

I lay on the bed and tied myself. When I opened my eyes, I tried to
move my body very slowly. My every joint was connected with divine
lightness, my muscles gratefully responded to my every movement. My
head was light and empty. I truly felt like I was reborn. This night's
cleaning was obviously extra intense and deep-reaching…I got up light
as a feather and prepared for the new school day…

XL. A NEW DAY!

I LIGHTLY LEFT THE BUILDING AND SAT IN HANNAH'S CAR. I cheerfully realized that I almost wasn't sure which part of the day I liked better, daytime or nighttime. I enjoyed both immensely. In school with my classmates – and with one of them in particular – teachers and school subjects, which were easily dripping into my memory. And at night, when I helped other people with my loved one.

Hannah looked at me sideways.

»Now you have to tell me what you've been up to, because this is more than just infatuation,« she said.

»You're right there. It really isn't just that...«

»There's something more. Something bigger.« She stepped on the accelerator and drove off.

»Such as?« I played dumb. I wanted to tell her about our club, but I didn't want to rush things...It'd be right if she was really ready when she joined our club.

»Such as, why you didn't need a ride yesterday. Or...I don't know. Maybe it'll sound weird...«

»What?« I eagerly asked.

»I don't know. It's just a stupid dream...« she waived her arm. And I couldn't be *more* interested.

»Tell me, tell me, please,« I became impatient. Hannah was surprised that I was suddenly so interested in her dream.

»Look at her, Miss Infatuation. Just a few seconds ago the world still revolved only around Robert, but now we've changed our tune…« she joked.

»Please tell me. And…then I'll tell you what you want to know.«

She found our agreement to be fair.

»Well, alright. Three days ago I dreamt that…me, you, Robert and two of your classmates went to the Central Park. There we sat on some benches. Then…I can't. You'll think I'm weird.«

»No, no!« I encouraged her. »You – weird? I do know you, you know! Please continue!«

»No, you've heard enough.«

»Come on!«

»No, and that's final.«

»What were we doing?«

»I'm not telling you.«

»Did we sleep?«

Silence.

»Did we talk?«

Still silence.

»Tell me, come on.«

»No, I've told you the basic fact. The rest you can imagine for yourself.«

»You know I wouldn't judge you. Even if you told me that we stepped out of our bodies and started flying,« I said like it was nothing.

She hit the brakes and the car stopped with a sharp jerk. She almost caused an accident. The car behind us honked.

»What is it?« I wondered falsely. »Was it something I said?« I asked with a smile. I couldn't pretend anymore.

»SO IT'S TRUE?!?« She was so beside herself that she couldn't even drive.

»Yes, it's true. Please, drive on so we don't cause an accident,« I calmed her down.

She slowly turned on the engine again and drove off. Soon we made up for the lost time and merged with the morning line of vehicles.

»Tell me everything!« she demanded. »How, when, why, who ...?«

»You don't need an explanation,« I smiled. »I can show you.«

I knew she was ready.

»When do you finish with classes today?« I asked.

»Today I have five classes…«

»Great. So do we. We'll meet after school at the entrance.«

We arrived and I stepped lively out of the car. I could see that Hannah was still preoccupied with what happened and I decided to leave her alone so she could settle down. I could feel that she had a million questions, but decided it'd be faster if she simply experienced the answers. The explanation would take up too much time.

When I entered the classroom – we had math in the first period – I saw Ravi laughing heartily in the last row. I connected with him.

What is it?

Look over there, he nodded his head towards the windows.

Jeanette and Lance were standing by the windows, engaged in a relaxed conversation. Lance smiled and looked love-stricken. Jeanette glowed. She was beautiful. It was obvious that she felt the same way about him and that her fear dissolved like old soapsuds.

I ran to Robert and hugged him. I pulled up a chair next to his and said:

»I think I'll be sitting here from today on.«

He smiled and kissed me. Our kisses were always shorter in public than when we were alone. But we internalized them all the more for it. Only we knew what was happening to us when our souls merged into one…

»Khm, khm, I hope I'm not interrupting,« said Elliot and sat next to us.

»I was just wondering if…*we're still on for today.*«

»Yes, we are,« I said lightly. »And we're getting another member.«

»Great,« said Elliot and went off to break the news to Gina.

What was that? I heard a voice in my head.

Sorry, I didn't have an opportunity to let you know, one way or the other…
And who is this…new member?

Hannah. I'm certain that she's ready, because she already dreamt about everything we're doing...

Aha. Well, okay. I'm sorry. I should've trusted you more.

You're forgiven, I smiled.

Our math teacher, Mr. Haynes, entered the classroom. I liked the fact that Robert and I simultaneously decided to pay attention to the lecture. Basically, he was helping me when I didn't understand something. Everything went very smoothly inside our heads.

This way we could cheat on our tests, I thought. *You'd solve the test and the rest of us would connect to your thought frequency...*

Telepathy is intended...

For people with high morals. I know. I was just kidding, I smiled.

So, from then on I was sitting next to him in all classes. Consequently, I understood the school subjects better, and had much more free time on my hands, which I devoted entirely to my new projects...

I felt a new power. And I had such a strong need to help others that I didn't feel the need for vacation. What I had with Ravi fulfilled me so much – physically as well as mentally – that I wouldn't trade it for anything in the world.

That day Hannah joined us. She was the first who *knew* what lay in store for her, because she had dreamt about it. She already *saw* us. After the lesson that Elliot and Gina went through the day before, she too absorbed new knowledge extremely quickly. It seemed like she had known all of that stuff once, because she wasn't all that surprised about it.

We had immense fun practicing teleportation. Elliot could finally fulfill his need for constant movement. His specialty was exceptional speed. It could almost be said that he materialized in two places simultaneously. He was everywhere. Gina immediately included teleportation in her wish for flying. She wanted to put the frames together so much that she succeeded in it even faster that me. She relaxed and...she was already above the park. When Elliot saw her, he materialized a few times in the air next to her, but didn't manage to stay there. Hannah quietly practiced teleportation in the lower parts of the park – on trees, benches, in the snow. Ravi and me sat in the middle of the training ground and supervised the practice.

After an hour of practice we headed back. We sat in our bodies and before we connected completely with them, I asked that we relax a little bit more and watch people. After a short time we could all notice that each person was enveloped in a haze of different vibrations. I asked them to disregard the hazes as much as possible. I purposefully used an example that worked best for me: "Like watching a television program you didn't choose yourself."

The hazes around people slowly started to disperse in every possible color. Club members laughed enthusiastically. They were witnessing such a colorful comprehension of the world for the first time and I was glad to be able to lead them down that road.

People vibrated from very light to darker shades. The hazes slowly started changing into images. I looked around and I was happy to see that we were doing so well. I noticed a person surrounded with three dark shadows entering the park. They were approaching quickly.

»Oh, no,« I moaned. »Stay calm. I suggest that we reconnect with our bodies as quickly as possible.«

Ravi helped Hannah, then he quickly reconnected himself.

We awoke in the last second before principal Davies could suspect that something was wrong.

»Oh, whom have we here?« he asked with false kindness.

»Hello, Principal,« I said almost lovingly.

»Hi, dad,« greeted him Ravi.

»Shouldn't you young people be sitting behind books right now? It is the middle of the week, you know,« said Davies sternly in archaic British English.

»We were headed there,« I explained. »We ran into each other in the park and started chatting away.«

»I see,« he replied.

»Well, alright, young people,« he said and moved on. »See you to-morrow in school.«

We took deep breaths and felt relieved. He was the last person in the world I'd tell about our club. At least not until he was in…such company. We said our goodbyes and agreed to practice on the other side of the park the next day, even though that meant walking a lot further. Despite the unpleasant incident we relaxed and cheerfully went our separate ways. Hannah offered to drive me home.

»May I have that honor today?« courtly smiled Ravi.

»Of course, you two go ahead…« Hannah withdrew with a smile. It was obvious that he used his loving absolute power again, which so far convinced everybody. I gave him a surprised look and asked: »You have a car?«

»Yes.«

»I beg your pardon?« I pretended not to have heard.

»I'm sorry, but…I didn't have the time to let you know one way or the other. And besides that, Hannah urgently needed you until now…« he smiled and I realized that I too couldn't resist his charm. I followed him to the parking lot, where a blue Chevrolet Electron Blue waited for us.

XLI. AN UNOFFICIAL VISIT

WHEN I SAT IN THE CAR, I WAS SO BUSY CASTING GLANCES AT THE driver that I didn't notice where we were going. When I finally looked out, it was already too late.

Would you mind going to my place? he thought bravely.

Just like that? What about your dad?

He won't be home for a while. I saw his thoughts. And he usually doesn't come home till evening.

Look. Maybe that's not such a good idea. Breaking into somebody else's apartment.

It's a house, actually. And it's not any type of breaking in, because I invited you. You were invited by a resident of the house. It'd be rude to turn down an invitation, don't you think?

Half an hour, not more, I thought weakly. I too couldn't resist him. In that aspect I was equally powerless like everybody else.

He parked in front of a really nice and bright house. The lower part of the house was paneled in wood; upstairs the windows, made of smaller triangular parts, composed interesting geometrically accurate shapes. The doors matched the windows and gave almost an outer-space-like impression. The driveway was made of stone, while the staircase was boldly archaic. It almost didn't appertain to the building.

»That's because the staircase remained, while the building was built anew...seventeen years ago. Back then this was one of the finest and most modern houses in the city,« he answered.

Come on in, I don't bite, he thought holding the front door wide open for me, while I was still sitting in the car. *And neither does my father*, he finished the sentence.

I slowly crawled out of the car and took him by the hand.

Are you sure we're doing the right thing?

Weren't you the one wondering where I lived? he joked.

I blushed. So, he caught my thought that time.

I'm sorry, I didn't mean it like that. I couldn't invite you then, could I? You know that I would have if the circumstances had been different…I'd have kidnapped you on the first day of school, brought you here and introduced you to my father…

»Alright,« I used words. Sometimes he was too nice.

He unlocked the door and invited me in with his hands.

»Mademoiselle…«

Immediately upon entering the house its entire interior spread out. Without any anteroom or something similar to an entrance hall, we immediately entered the central part of the house, which was round, like a reception room. It was surrounded by rooms on all sides, and above the floor, two stories up, was a glass roof through which a ray of sunshine was penetrating.

I liked it very much. A fusion of contemporary lines and round architecture.

Show me only those rooms everybody is allowed to see, I thought. For some reason I preferred to be quiet. I still had a bad feeling.

I'll show you the things I can see, he responded.

He took me through the rooms that stylistically matched the round reception room: the contemporary blue kitchen with smooth lines; a couple of guest rooms; we didn't go into Davies' room; a couple of green bathrooms; finally we got to Ravi's room on the second floor.

He lightly opened the door: *Ta-daa…*

The room that opened up in front of me, was different in my memory.

You mustn't forget that at the time I also had to tolerate uninvited visitors

– my father's "friends"
That's right. That was it.

That's why the room seemed so dark. But now the warmest room I had ever seen in my life opened up in front of me. Even though it was simple and size-wise much like mine, it was completely different from the rest in the house. The bed was covered in colorful Indian motifs. A few paintings by Indian masters hung on the walls. His writing desk was divided into two halves. On the one side were schoolbooks, on the other a few incense sticks with a holder and a few scented candles.

I bought that when we started dating, he admitted.

Just in case you came to visit me sometime…

I felt honored. He took the lighter that was prepared by the candles and lighted them. Then he took the remote control and pushed »play«. Pleasant, tranquil music filled the room. Sounds of gentle basses intertwined with chimes and violins. A rustle of sea waves could be heard in the distance. He embraced me.

Once again I felt safe. In his embrace I found a home I'd been looking for. I sensed strongly that home was a state, not a place. That happiness was a state, not an emotion. He leaned his forehead against mine. I could feel falling into him again. If the feeling hadn't become so familiar, it'd have frightened me.

And so we existed in silence. The room was pleasantly supporting our vibration. I could feel that it was completely different energy-wise from the rest of the house. Like someone had subsequently built it into the building.

He started to breathe deeper and I followed his tempo. I closed my eyes and before long I could sense what he was doing. In his heart I saw the source of energy of his power. In my heart I sensed the spark that had guided me through everything I had been witnessing. The energy of wisdom and intuition. When he exhaled, he presented me with his power. My heart was brimming over in the ocean of absolute good. And when he inhaled, he was ready to receive. I presented him all the knowledge that I'd gathered through the millenniums of my existence on Earth. His heart beat gratefully and admired the infinite beauties of ancient truths. While breathing, we completely surrendered to each other. My heart was becoming more and more his, and at the same time I felt closer to him than ever before. It seemed like the things that were already present only intensified, even though I didn't know if that was even possible. The connection between us soon became one heart. One body. One vibration.

I heard voices in the distance...My loved one put my heart back where it had been before. I awoke in an instant. When I came to myself, we were standing in the middle of the room, talking to Davies. Ravi had turned off the music long ago.

»How is it going, young people?« he asked indifferently, not surprised at all.

»Hi, dad. We're good. I was just showing Ina my room,« calmly said Ravi.

»Could you please escort her out? I would greatly appreciate it if her next visit was announced,« he said abruptly. I was surprised, because I expected him to be much ... angrier. Did he at least slightly soften after the incident at school? I looked him in the eyes and saw the truth.

His differently colored eyes were flashing dangerously on the inside. I flinched. The anger I attributed to him was very much present, only waiting for better conditions. For conditions in which his son wouldn't be so much involved and powerful. My confrontation with Davies was obviously imminent. And when the time came, he'd make sure that I was alone.

Ravi and his father agreed that he should take me home. I tried hard not to think about my confrontation with him. I didn't want Ravi to worry.

Soon we arrived to my dorm and in spite of everything I thanked him for the illicit invitation. We said goodbye. I knew that I'd see him in a couple of hours – which had almost become a habit for us – and that filled me with indescribable happiness.

XLII. A SEED OF DOUBT

AFTER A MONTH OF PRACTICE THE MEMBERS OF THE CLUB BECAME very connected. There were no secrets among us, because we didn't need them. That much was clear to all of us. Hannah soon stopped dreaming about events, and started living them. She sensed the more important events a few moments before they happened. That way she saved my life once, by pulling me off the pedestrian crossing. I began crossing the street when the 'walk' sign came on and a car jumped a red light at high speed. Had Hannah not pulled me away, I'd have surely died. Luckily I was the only one in the street; she couldn't have saved more people.

One afternoon Hannah, Ravi and me were left alone. Elliot and Gina had just said goodbye and thanked us again for having such a great time.

Hannah and me were walking towards the car and Ravi was escorting me.

I wish more people had this knowledge, thought Hannah.

Why? I asked.

Because we'd be stronger that way. Maybe we could even help…

Davies? Asked Ravi. The image of the dark room at the end of the basement corridor appeared in his head.

»DID YOU TELL HIM?« Hannah turned towards me with a horrified look on her face.

»No, absolutely not. You can see that we're not talking here. Once, during meditation, we went…there. And we saw the incident as it really happened. I didn't tell anything to anybody.«

»THAT'S even worse!« she was horrified. »And that image is now in his head and everybody can see it!« she started to cry.

»Only those who want to help can see it…« started explaining Ravi. She interrupted him.

»EVERYBODY CAN SEE IT!«

»We had to do it. If we want to help my father, we need to know what he's doing down there. And that incident is of great help to us…« But Hannah couldn't care less.

»I thought I could trust you.«

»Hannah…« I tried to explain.

»I thought we were friends.«

»We are…«

»NO, WE'RE NOT! I confide in you and then some Indian comes along and you forget everybody! Everybody!«

She didn't care that Ravi was still there.

»Hannah, take it easy…« he said calmly. I could feel that he was putting all of his power into his words.

»No, you won't. I've had enough. I'm going.« Hannah got intimidated by his power. She sat in her car and quickly drove off. My heart started aching. I knew that something like that would happen someday.

Take it easy, Ina, Ravi tried to soothe me as I was looking after her. *Everything is just a test, remember?*

It was hard to comprehend that at that moment. I'd lost one of my few true friends and the guilt gnawed at my heart.

You didn't show me the way to that incident, it revealed itself to us. It was obviously meant that way. Look at me, he turned my face towards his. *Everything will be okay. I'm here. Hannah will come back. How could she live in her former way, after she got to know all of this?* Ravi pointed around himself, like we gave her the entire universe. And he was right.

We were *truly* living without any limits. We could really travel anywhere we wanted to. If we wanted to go there with good intentions, of course. He slowly managed to calm me down. He escorted me home and we talked all the way there. In the end I went to bed almost satisfied. The scale of guilt and happiness was balanced, but if somebody blew, it could lean either way…

XLIII. THE CLUB'S ALMOST GOLDEN MONTHS

THE FOLLOWING THREE MONTHS PASSED BY IN A FLASH. Our secret club almost wasn't that secret anymore. Most of our classmates soon started showing interest in becoming members.

Gina inspired George. Sienna realized that Elliot somewhat withdrew from her and she started looking for a connection with him. After hours of pleading, he finally told her where we had been meeting and invited her to come along. She was very pleasantly surprised and she completely changed. She exchanged her dark clothes for light and pink colors, and she gave up the accentuated make-up she was used to. She began shining in an entirely new light and all the boys started noticing her. Too late though, because she had chosen Elliot a long time ago.

The class gained a new freshness. Soon the majority of club members mastered telepathic communication. Even though there were more contacts on our frequency than before, everything happened exactly like Ravi predicted. They tuned in on our frequency only when they needed some information, such as:

George: *Hey, Ravi, are we still on for today?*

Ravi: *Of course.*

Sienna: *Did I miss anything?*

Ravi: *No, today everything is like we agreed.*

Sienna: *Well, okay. Let us know if anything changes.*

And then silence again. They called in like they each had their own walkie-talkie. But it got even better. Each of them started exploring their own capabilities and their own soul structure.

Sienna became an expert for low frequency recognition. Since in the past her image was based on attracting dark shadows and listening to dark music, she could sense them faster than anyone else. So, we were able to practice peacefully in the Central Park, because we had our guard: Sienna.

Elliot was extremely fast, even in combat. If Ravi needed someone to quickly respond to a thought stimulus, he took Elliot with him. Dark shadows often didn't even know *when* he defeated them.

George became a flying expert. He glided through the air in the same way he surfed. He liked the energy even more than he liked the sea, because – like he said it himself – there was more of it and it behaved exactly like he wanted to. And besides that, he felt useful. With his »surfing« he directed the waves exactly to where we needed them. Moreover, he told us smilingly that in the summer he was going to invite us to the beach and teach us how to surf properly.

Jeanette joined us as soon as she noticed that the pulse of the class had changed. She became very brave. She became an expert for injustices. Like me, she too liked to project herself into other people's consciousness and turn unexplainable experiences from their past into pure love.

Soon she invited Lance to the club. He joined us only because of his love for Jeanette. But soon he grew fond of our socializing so much that he started seriously researching himself. He had always liked the serenity and love messages of French chansons and that was exactly what he found in himself. The power to decide to be purely happy at all times. Even if demons of all colors were dancing around him, he happily danced in the light.

Teddy discovered us purely by accident. Hannah often said that there were no coincidences, because everything that happened to us, held a key. She still kept to herself and I missed her dearly during those months… Anyway, Teddy was walking through the springtime Central Park and suddenly he spotted one third of his class sitting on a picnic blanket in the middle of a meadow. We were sitting totally still and although Sienna and I noticed him, we didn't get scared. He was enveloped in a yellow aura and we thought he was ready. When we awoke that day, he was already sitting among us, asking us what we were doing. We explained it to him laughingly and invited him to join us.

Later on Teddy invited Alysha, who was mostly thrilled about colorful hazes. She saw more than the rest of us. She could distinguish color frequencies more precisely and consequently feel people more clearly, deeply, more thoroughly. When we were done for the day, she would often be bursting with ideas how this and that could be painted. At home she would often start painting during meditation. Within a few months she gave each of us a painting, and every single one of those paintings would, seen through our respective eyes, literally glow and provide us with additional stimulation.

The first one among musicians to sense that something was going on with our class, was Francesca. The laughter and muffled shrieks during our telepathic little talks were almost impossible to hide anymore. When she asked me what was going on, I openly told her that we were relaxing in the Central Park and that she was invited to join us. She came that very day. She was the only one among souls who was hiding her true power elsewhere. In her body. She started creating her own music and she enriched her voice with vibrations that she came to know during meditation. Thus she was the only one among us, who managed to transfer those vibrations to the physical world, although she didn't have any special abilities outside her body.

She invited other musicians to join us: Jesse, Jimmy, Rebecca, Rodney...

Philip sensed the change too. When he joined our club, he discovered that our theory was the one he had been waiting for all his life. He was one of the most zealous researchers. He decided to enact and physically define new knowledge. We were thrilled to have even a future physics expert in our midst...

My duty was to sustain concentration. My passion for concentration strengthened even more. In addition to that, Ravi kept sending me his loving power and it seemed to me that I was truly stronger. I realized why we were meant to work in pairs: to chose a soul that perfected us and helped us. He was helping me, I was helping him…

And so our class slowly became one. We started inviting students from other classes. Soon we were meeting in several different groups. Each one had up to ten members. Ravi chose the leaders of other groups.

Principal Davies was rarely seen in school. I had a constant feeling that he was somewhere in the building, but I could never determine his exact location. I didn't want to be too much preoccupied with this. I was hoping that we were safe. After all, dr. Barnes had silenced him months ago…Still, deep inside me I knew that something was up…something unexpected.

XLIV. AN INVITATION YOU CAN'T REFUSE

SCHOOL YEAR WAS NEAR THE END AND I WAS TRULY HAPPY. I felt that I was finally doing what I came to America for. I helped people of all ages, alongside a boy I loved with all my heart. As for the physical love, we decided to wait until July, when I turned eighteen. Ravi wanted that experience to be something special for me and here too his power prevailed.

I pulsated as one with the big city, although I frequently thought about my family. They too had noticed the changes in me and I also told them that I had a boyfriend. They were happy for me. Ela announced that she was getting married in the summer.

»Be sure to bring him along, so we can see him!« she ordered me laughingly.

Everything went smoothly until May. At the beginning of May something unusual happened. Ravi stopped coming to school. He wasn't answering his phone and his frequency was also inaccessible. We all wondered what happened to him. Nobody could reach him. Once I even – allowed or not – materialized in his room. It was empty. If he didn't want to cooperate, he certainly had the power to disappear into nothing. Nobody could find him. That wouldn't worry me so much, because I irrevocably believed in him; what worried me more was the fact that principal Davies disappeared too. The teachers had long since gathered their courage and decided to select a new principal. Thus Davies had nothing to lose anymore. I wondered if they moved away. Where would they go!? Every investigation led to another blind alley.

We were like soldiers without their leader. I myself had many abilities, but I didn't have Ravi's power. His frequency vanished too, like somebody had deleted it. Club members realized that he was the one who charged us the most. Slowly fewer and fewer of us came to the meetings, also because the energy wasn't powerful enough to enable proper practice. I was disappointed, because I didn't feel capable enough to lead people who wanted to help. The ability for leadership and power always came from him. The fear of losing him slowly started awakening in me again. It was so powerful that I unwillingly started falling to a lower frequency...And I was making somebody very happy with it. One afternoon I heard a voice in my head, for the first time in such a way.

Hello, hello? It mocked me. *Can you hear me, hello, hello?*

I knew who it was. I'd been expecting him.

Of course I can hear you. Tell me immediately where you are and where Ravi is. I was irritated and angry. He didn't have the right to separate us again.

We're angry now? I obviously stepped on somebody's toes, Davies mocked me.

It's not an appropriate time for joking, I said abruptly.

I think it's more than obvious that we need to talk. Your sweetheart had some outstanding debts with friends from lower frequencies...

You didn't...!!! What did you do to him? My whole body was shaking and I was left speechless. Was it really possible that his hatred for me was bigger than his love for his own son?

What did I do? What did I do!? What have you done to him? He was constantly obstructing me, putting obstacles in my way. Because of you he even wanted to ruin me professionally! Who else betrays his own father except the one whose head is turned completely by some brat?!?

I realized that he had gone completely out of his mind. He had been playing with dark vibrations like he wanted to check what a forgotten lighted match could do to a gas station.

In the distance I heard voices...I thought that someone was calling me. A woman's voice. *Ina! Ina!* The voice soon disappeared.

Actually, I didn't have any choice, continued Davies. *I knew it was all your fault. Ravi was just reminding me in one way or the other of my – if I may admit – not so pleasant past. I exchanged him – for you.*
What? I'm nobody's property! I shouted.

But they don't know that, he cheerfully summed up, *and if you want to help him, your only chance is to meet me*, he sang joyfully. His dreadful voice echoed in my head like it did in the stuffy basement corridor.

Do you like it? I'm adding effects, he let out a belly laugh, *so it's a bit creepier…*

Okay, I quickly interrupted. *Where and when?*

Oooo, he feigned surprise, *Ina is all for it! Great. Meet me tomorrow after school. Wait for an hour so the building clears up a bit, won't you?* He gave me instructions with fake care. *Then join me in my little room. You already know where that is…I'll deal with Hannah too – later.*

Leave her alone! And Ravi! You can take me, just leave them alone! I screamed almost out of breath.

It's a date then, he determined. *I'll see you, my daughter-in-law never-to-be…*

And then silence. Like a disconnected phone conversation.

I was still shaking and tears filled my eyes. *Not again, not again…* echoed in my head. I buried my head in pillows and cried. I could feel my entire body freeze up at the very thought that something might have happened to Ravi…Each cell in my body seemed to be dying, my soul was shrinking in much too low – for it – vibrations…I mourned…An important thought ascended to the top of my subconscious.

The entire year I felt subconsciously that something awaited me in the future. That I needed to deal with something…with my OWN fear of loosing him again.

I won't solve anything by crying, I thought. I tried to calm down and remember the things that were perfectly self-evident to me in the last six months…For example: I won't be able to solve anything with anger. I laid on the bed and tried to relax. I couldn't. My heart was still beating like an uncompromising wall clock, counting the minutes to the next day's confrontation.

I started collecting information in my head…What actually happened? I remembered that Davies was under a strong influence of lower beings. Nobody in their right mind would do something like that. So he was just their puppet. He had to promise them something in exchange for slightly higher abilities, which are always only temporary in their world. What else did I know about them? I tried to remember everything Ravi told me. Their language was a lie. Was it possible that Davies didn't tell me everything as it really was? Was it possible that Ravi was still alive?

He obviously discovered our weak point, which really wasn't too difficult: to break us apart. Because that fear lasts longer than ordinary human life. But where did he find out how very sensitive we were in this area? Even more sensitive than we dared to admit to ourselves. How did he discover that we all drew energy from Ravi? He must have gained insight into our activity somewhere. Did he acquire the ability to sneak into Ravi's consciousness? Impossible, his son was too strong, he would sense even the very thought leading him up to it. Where did he find out and how?

I felt that this was all the information I could gather for the time being. My heart slowly calmed down. I decided to try at least a little to withdraw from my life…From my fears…I tried to summon all the wisdom and all the memories I had accumulated in the past months…They were rising in front of me, like I was there again…

I will go into my consciousness, I decided. *Maybe there is something that will help me find a solution…*

The hazes were increasingly turning into a medley of films and I started feeling happiness…I was most delighted when I realized that with the help of memory I could bring back to life…*him.* Even though he was just a projection in my head…

W E'RE STANDING ON TOP OF THE HEAD OF THE STATUE OF LIBERTY…*I asked for a bit of privacy,* he whispers to me…His voice is so real. So soft. He's by my side again and I'm fulfilled…

T HE FIRST KISS, WHICH I SENSE AS A LIGHT BREEZE ON MY LIPS… *DID YOU OR DIDN'T YOU KISS ME YESTERDAY? I'm glad that you managed to remember that…*

I'M FLYING ABOVE A MEADOW AND I LOSE CONCENTRATION...HE'S immediately by my side...*Is everything alright?*

IN DESPAIR I ONCE AGAIN WALK AWAY FROM THE SCHOOL ENTRANCE, when he unexpectedly presses me to himself. Is that possible? Does he really exist? *I hope that this is a big enough proof that I'm real...*

IN THE EVENING I GO TO BED, I LEAVE MY BODY AND HE'S ALREADY waiting for me at the desk. I embrace him and I'm fulfilled again with my whole...I feel so powerful again, even though I still know that I'm only watching a memory...

WE FIGHT JEANETTE'S DEMONS TOGETHER. In the end I really feel that everything, but really everything, is just a test. Ravi smiles at me. *It's true...*

THE CLUB. Ravi leads people of which everybody gets to know their own uniqueness. It's a permanent state of happiness. It's interrupted by a conflict with Hannah...

I opened my eyes. Everything was just a test. If I wanted to defeat Davies and his »friends«, I couldn't possibly yield under the weight of human emotions. Because exactly *that* was their weapon…Emotions. Guilt. Anger. Fear. I couldn't and mustn't give them that satisfaction, that weapon.

My strength usually stemmed from Ravi's. But I've always been very good at visualization. So I reached for an additional weapon: now that I rummaged through my consciousness and reviewed my memories, I felt stronger just by looking at him. I would *imagine* that Ravi was alive, that he was saved. That way I'd automatically become stronger and at the same time I would attract events that'd convert my thoughts into reality.

Everything was just a test…That was the hardest thing to accept. Was it really possible that a test existed, where they'd kill my other half just to find our how quickly I'd be able to stop mourning and learn to stand on my own two feet? How could any test in this world be so cruel?

I remembered Jeanette's memory. That event also seemed cruel to me. Then, with Ravi's help, I realized that it wasn't my job to judge what was cruel and what wasn't.

It was good that I managed to relax a bit. *Let's say that everything is just a nice test. Smile. Pull yourself up. Come on, get in a good mood,* I encouraged myself. *You still have yourself…Tomorrow you'll fight alone anyway…* But I was going to be armed with an ancient knowledge and fight for the highest purpose so far. I wanted to summon to life one of the most powerful beings of light…

I hadn't seen Hannah since our conflict…Was it possible that she had given Davies the information that armed him with additional knowledge? After all, she knew *everything*. She was my best friend. It was also true that she quickly yielded when she was scared…

I decided that night was going to be the busiest night of my life. I had to prepare myself, arm myself. First I intended to pay a visit to Hannah. If she was asleep, I'd easily ascertain if she had taken part in the conspiracy. Then I was determined to practice, practice and practice some more. All my thoughts merged into one: into next day's battle with a bright and positive outcome…

XLV. HANNAH

I LEFT MY BODY AND I WAS BY HER SIDE IN AN INSTANT. I saw images above her bed and I knew she was dreaming. She was tossing and turning in her sleep and let out a sigh from time to time. I could sense that she was having a hard time. I sat next to her bed. I prepared to immerse myself into her consciousness and her dreams. I remembered how Ravi used to save me in critical moments and gave me strength, so I could finish my task. This time I had to do that *by myself.* With the strength that awakened in me every time I thought of him.

I shall awake the power. The power that I *know* is in me. Ravi sent it to me every time we embraced or kissed…I thought of some of our most intense moments…Like when we merged as souls into one for the first time…

O N THE HEAD OF THE STATUE OF LIBERTY. He asks me if I can remember my dreams from ten years ago. I remember how much I love him just because he exists. Because he's one with me. Not because I need him, but because I simply love him. *That…that is exactly what I feel for you. I've always felt like that.* His words are echoing in my head like a balm that covers and illuminates all feelings of sadness and horrors of loss. They melt away like soapsuds and my heart is suddenly restored, whole. Found. I merge with the light and the absolute power I received from the other part of me. I know that I'm in the place of power.

I was sitting again in front of Hannah's bed, feeling reinforced. *I'll make it*, I told myself. *I love myself. Myself too, not just him.*

That was my first mission I was about to embark upon by myself and I had to talk to myself...*If I didn't love myself, I couldn't love him either, at least not that boundlessly. But I already know that.*

I took a deep breath, just for the feeling's sake. I didn't need oxygen as a soul anyway. But I did need peace.

I started watching images above Hannah's head. At first I just played with the hazes. Then I completely withdrew within me. Like that wasn't my program. I relaxed my eyes and tried to look past the images. Suddenly they became perfectly clear. The screen above Hannah suddenly grew a bit bigger and created a film. I saw the street that led to the school...And suddenly I was standing in it. Suddenly I *was* Hannah.

THE END OF THE SCHOOL DAY. Oh, how I miss afternoon meetings with Ina and Ravi! I feel like my whole body is aching. Cramps are becoming ever stronger and I can't imagine my life without all the riches we used to share. It was like paradise...I know that I'll have to go back. I'll have to forgive...I spot principal Davies ahead of me and he starts waving at me. Oddly enough, he is smiling. I look around me. He really is waving at me!

»Hannah! Hannah!« he's all smiling.

»Principal Davies? What's going on with you?« I ask, surprised.

»Ha, ha« he smiles relaxed and looks away for a moment, like I told him a really good joke. »What's going on...well, it doesn't matter. I was just looking for you. May I invite you for a cup of...what do young people drink these days? For a cup of hot chocolate?«

»I don't know «

»It'd be perfectly seemly, in a public place, no worries,« he explains with well-mannered care, which demonstrates his British descent. I've never seen him in such a good mood, although something still feels odd but I don't know what.

»Well...Okay.«

Right behind the corner there is a nice and peaceful spot where we sit behind an old-fashioned table. When the waiter arrives I order hot chocolate. That's what I was invited to.

»It's really nice to see you, Hannah« he says smilingly after a long pause.

»You...too?« I'm guessing. He smiles again at my astonishment.

»Let's cut to the chase, why I actually invited you here, okay? I really find it funny, how you're astonished the whole time. You should take a look in the mirror...« he laughs. The more he laughs, the more I find the situation to be funny. His smile reveals his slightly askew teeth and his lips curve upwards in the interesting shape of a boat. I too laugh and his eyes flare up strangely.

»I wanted to apologize to you. What I did to you a year ago really wasn't right. It wasn't right to scare you like that. It's true that what you saw down there was a secret, but nobody in this world has the right to intimidate a fellow human being, isn't that right?«

»Yes, but...How «

»Ravi opened my eyes completely. Now I know that I shouldn't have judged you. Thank you for helping come to that realization.«

The waiter brings my hot chocolate and I start sipping it immediately. I'm slightly nervous and I want to consume it as quickly as possible, so this meeting can be over as soon as possible.

»You don't have to be nervous, Hannah,« he warns me smilingly.

»I just want you to forgive me. May I ask for your forgiveness?« he continues charmingly in British English.

»Of course...« I'm confused.

»Excellent. Please know that I'll never want to hurt you again, no matter what happens.«

»Okay. Thank you...« I'm still astonished.

»That's why I decided to...offer you a gift as an apology. What do you think about,« he pulls an envelope out of his pocket, »fourteen days of excused absence and a two-week vacation with your parents in a spa? I know you're a bit tight with money, so I said to myself: it's never too late for a small gift.«

»I don't know what to say.«

»Say YES. I'd be very sad if you refused my gift. The good news is: you leave tomorrow!«

»I have to ask my parents...«

»They already know. I called them today and they were most pleased. I wanted to inform you in person...« he smiled playfully.

»Do they know about...?«

»No, no, they don't know about our unfortunate incident. I told them you were really one of the most hardworking students in school.«

»Thank you,« I say absent-mindedly.

»Aaah, how good it is getting it out your system,« Davies says enthusiastically. »Isn't it like getting a new lease on life?«

»Aha.« I say shortly.

»You're surely wondering why I was like that at all. So strict, angry and unfair. I've had a very hard life, you know,« he says seriously.

When I left school today I imagined my day could continue in a lot of different ways. But surely not like this, with principal Davies telling me his life story over a cup of hot chocolate.

»I too was in love once,« he tells me.

»What happened?« I ask.

His eyes flash unusually. »It didn't turned out like I was hoping...«

»Something similar is happening to Ravi and Ina,« I remember.

»What do you mean by that?«

I realize that I might have said too much. Then I remember that Ina told our secret to anybody who wanted to know. I summon my courage and summarize quickly.

»The two of them too have really found each other only now, in this life and they're most afraid of being separated again. We can all see that, anyway. I mean, how they love each other,« I quickly explain.

»That's true, yes. They love each other very much,« states Davies, like he just invented a new formula, which will change the mankind. »Very – much – indeed,« he says to himself in the most British way.

I just scoop the last teaspoon of hot chocolate. »Thank you for this,« I say and start to say goodbye. I've never seen Davies so lively. Never.

»You're leaving already?« he winces. »Okay, you obviously have to go. Have a good time, Hannah. I enjoyed sharing these important moments with you very much.«

We say goodbye and I slowly walk away. I'm walking towards my car and as I get there, it hits me: *Ina and Ravi are most vulnerable when they're not together; Davies has just found out about that – Davies goes to Ravi – Ina stays alone – Ravi receives some horrible news and surrenders to dark shadows – Ina faces Davies alone – dark room at the end of the corridor is full of dark shadows – I can't help anyone…*

Oh, no! What have I done!? How could I?

My stomach cramps with guilt. I rush back to the coffee house, but he is already gone. How am I going to live with myself if something happens to Ina? My God, this is horrible. *I* am horrible. *I* betrayed them, more than they can ever betray me…

I run to my car and drive to Ina's dorm. I'm jumping over stairs and I'm in front of her room in an instant.

»Ina! Ina! Open up! I've got to tell you something!«

I try to connect with her.

Ina! Ina! The connection is shut down. I collapse in front of her door and burst into tears. I'll obviously have to leave without wishing her luck for the last time, much less being able to help her with that…

Then I remember *who I am*. This is not *my* experience. This is not *my* fault. This is *Hannah's* experience. And now I'm in the projection of Hannah's body, her consciousness. I illuminate it with light. I forgive myself, I say. The light is in me. I couldn't know, I couldn't grasp what Davies' good mood meant. From today on I'll be more careful…I love myself. I forgive myself. I smile…There is nothing there for which I should blame myself or what I should forgive myself for…My/Hannah's soul lights up in pure light of love.

I sat in front of Hannah and noticed relief on her face. At the same time I felt relieved too, because I knew what had happened. I understood.

XLVI. THE MOST IMPORTANT PRACTICE IN MY LIFE

WHEN I HAD FINISHED AT HANNAH'S I IMMEDIATELY HURRIED off to Central Park.

Great, I thought. *There are plenty of memories here. And many people I can practice on. Let's start.*

For starters I had to find the right person. I glided around the park hoping to find somebody who needed my help. When I had almost given up hope, I saw a homeless man curled up on a bench who wasn't sleeping very well.

I got close to him and saw how many worries went through his head at the same time.

I'm cold. I knew I wouldn't make it. Since Helen left I've felt even more depressed. And now I can be happy to be alive. I wonder if they can find me here. They will look for me at home, probably. And when they realize I can't pay them back, they will look for me all over the city. Why wasn't I able to get approval for my project at that time? Why did I take the risk in the first place? I should have stayed where I was…

I immediately realized I wasn't dealing with a regular homeless person since he was way to tidy under the blanket, but a person with huge worries. More and more shadows kept gathering around him who reveled in his worries and tried to enhance them further…

This is exactly what I need, I said to myself. I knew that more power than I had will be needed to deal with that number of shadows. I will have to turn to energy that protects this planet as well as empowering memories…I went through my consciousness…

"*I'LL SEE YOU AROUND, COLLEAGUE*," HE LOOKS AT ME PLAYFULLY. An earth-stopping kiss follows. Because we know this is the last kiss for today, we cling to each other even more closely.

The taxi hoots.

"Are you coming or not?"

"I'll be right there," he answers smiling. I can see that other people cannot resist his charm either.

His presence filled me with power again. The power was greater than before. I felt stronger every time I repeated the procedure. The energy I imagined got a new frequency of focus. I felt I was just a big pipe channeling this energy. I sensed a big and powerful flow. The light materialized from the air with great speed and piled up in me.

The dark creatures started moving around impatiently. I knew I mustn't look at them under any circumstances. I focused on the energy flowing into me. The creatures realized where the light was coming from and they started to growl...

I felt I needed to strengthen myself even more. I thought of Ravi's support when we took Gina and Elliot to the park for the first time...

I VISUALIZE THE VIBRATION OF PURE LIGHT. Love...I feel Ravi gently stepping into this vibration...The vibration becomes a thousand times stronger. The entire Central Park becomes lighted up, like a big lake...The light flows in two streams, one rushing into Elliot and the other into Gina...

The whole park became brightly illuminated. I became a medium channeling the energy of light into the man on the bench. The monsters around him dispersed screaming. Everything happened very fast and simply. I felt absolute power in my hands. All my old messages of mourning were dissolved in a second. I was alone in my body enjoying the silence.

The homeless guy on the bench got up and put away his blanket. I could see he wasn't cold anymore. He left the blanket on the bench and went home. It wouldn't be right to call him homeless anymore. More... Jim the businessman.

I was surprised how powerful memories can be and I thought again: *if Ravi is a part of me, his power is a part of me too. It MUST be. And it IS.*

I knew I had passed the test. The procedure lasted for a couple of hours and I returned into my body. I was calm and lucid. *I'm sure everything is at it is supposed to be, there must be a reason for the tests we have to face even if we can't see it at the time.*

Momentarily I found myself in my room watching my body on the bed. I looked at it lovingly as if I was seeing it for the first time. It was lying very still in deep sleep. It was beautiful and totally peaceful. I expressed my gratitude for being able to be on this planet; to be trusted with such an important task. I will not do my best, I will do more than that. I will give all of myself, if necessary.

I thanked for the challenge one more time and lay back into my body. The reconnection was effortless and automatic.

I woke up feeling light and full of energy. It was a bit like Christmas holidays. I lovingly remembered Ravi again and this memory was enhanced with a new force of acquired power. The emptiness was crisper, the happiness more pervasive. I was well-equipped for the fight. The feeling that nothing could resist my own and the universe's light. The feeling I could put all low vibrations in a bag, tickle them from outside and have a great time doing this.

I sat on the bed and relaxed one more time. I lovingly became aware of my body and expressed my thanks for it again. I really liked it, I loved it because it had always selflessly and effortlessly helped me with expressing and reaching my goals as well as touching the person I loved.

A constant vibration of happiness that was faster than my heartbeat covered my body. It felt like every cell in my body would feed on this light and rotate around its axis with evident enthusiasm while doing so. I vibrated in a totally new wave. My body became one with the new strength and the new vibration of my soul.

I sat quietly and I felt the now so familiar silence again. Instead of being afraid I surrendered even more. I had realized that was the key to solving all problems. The oncoming fear is the sign that you should let yourself go completely. If you want to control the situation, you should actually let it go. When you want to see, you should relax and move away and do your test as a test – with enthusiasm and without straining...

I felt new vibrations flowing through my body on the top of my head. Like somebody was playing with my hair at the very top of my head. I felt the presence of a large number of beings in my room and I knew those were my friends who had come from all possible dimensions. They all had higher vibrations than the Earth. I saw that what we had in common was that we all originated from the burning planet...

You have our loving support, I heard in my head; *in the sense of energy of course, not power. You have proven that you are really stronger than all of us. We believe you will make it because you believe it too more than ever before. The more power you gain, the harder the tests become. So a really difficult test is really a compliment for you. Accept that.*

The visitors danced around me in the play of the light and it was absolutely magnificent. I really felt supported by the universe and I knew that I would fight for the higher frequency today, so I would do exactly what I was supposed to do here. To raise the level of the planet.

Not for myself; not for a little college girl who had lost her boyfriend. I will do this like a smiling soldier of the new era, new frequency. For the level of the universe, nothing more. I moved away from my character and my personality entirely. I became just a soul in the body. Just a being. Just material which entirely belonged to something higher…

The perception of my body changed somehow. I felt pins and needles all over my body and I couldn't feel the bed beneath me anymore. I opened my eyes.

While the beings were dancing around me, my material body was hovering above the bed. It was so charged with the new frequency that it completely forgot all the old messages including those connected with gravity. I was hovering in a circle of light and I could feel my absolute power and love. I knew everything was as it should be. The only reason why I was given the test was to gain more self-confidence and realize I was capable enough of solving it…

I slowly descended back to my bed and thanked my friends for visiting.

I will be happy to see you anyway, I thought.

We will always be with you. Once you have overcome such a huge blockage of human emotions as you did tonight, the support of the universe becomes absolute and unlimited…

I lay on the bed. Then I put on clothes. I carefully placed Ela's locket around my neck. I really wanted to wear it that day. I put on white clothes. Jeans, white T-shirt and a white sweatshirt. White sneakers. I could feel dad's present in my jacket pocket…A pink knife. *Well, let it come with me today, then…*The jacket I had chosen was white and sporty too. I will be dressed more dynamically, I guess. That was the only color that expressed my feelings and mood. Pure whiteness.

XLVII. THE DAY WHEN THE UNIVERSE STOPPED

I SET OFF TO SCHOOL. I cycled and I enjoyed the feeling of the wind playing with my hair...The Central Park was on my left and now and then I looked towards the greenery. Too many times, apparently, because suddenly I hit something.

"Look out, miss!" I heard and then I saw a man in front of me and I braked hard. I saw that both of us were deep in our thoughts although they were positive.

"I'm terribly sorry, are you OK? I should have been more careful." I heard. I looked up. There was a businessman standing in front of me, he was smiling and carrying a briefcase and he was in an exceptionally good mood.

I checked to see if I was OK and discovered I couldn't be better. "Don't worry about it. I'm fine, thanks. I looked at his face and I recognized him.

"I'm Ina," I smiled.

"I'm Jim," he said and smiled too.

"Can I say something to you, Ina?" his eyes started to shine.

"Sure," I replied.

"I'm sure it's no coincidence that we've had this little accident. I must tell you that I realized today that life offers us an unlimited supply of new opportunities. I experienced a miracle in this park yesterday and I realized why my superiors had turned down the project I had presented to them. I saw everything. The sequence of events, my mistakes, my life...There was this distance, like I was seeing my story through the eyes of another person. I went home immediately. The people I had feared before were nice to me and immediately gave me another opportunity. I'm on my way to work and I know I'll nail it this time. I've never been so sure in my life. Remember, Ina, life is filled with miracles. If we are able to see them."

"Thank you, Jim. I hope you will make it. Actually, I *know* you will," I replied with a smile.

"Have a great day, Ina! Isn't life wonderful?" he said.

"You are right. Have a nice day," I replied in goodbye.

I rode on and smiled again. Life really was wonderful. The sun came through the clouds and I had the feeling it was shining only for us. To notice it. To become harmonized with the vibration of the stars…

The classes went on as usually. The teachers checked homework in every lesson and I enjoyed yet another ordinary day at school. Everybody noticed I was in a really good mood and was totally relaxed in my company. Gina even asked when we would see each other again.

"Not today," I said as if I was arranging a routine meeting. I knew I was able to lead them with my own and Ravi's power that rose up in me. But on that day it was important for me to save all my strength for the fight. I really knew and believed it was possible to bring Ravi back to life with *his own power* that was in me now.

"I can hardly wait," she said and smiled. "I've been missing our time together."

It felt like the class came back to life again. People started treating me as they treated Ravi before. I felt that his charm, ease and absolute power came into me. All the boys kept looking at me and I knew they liked me because I had so much energy. I tried to remain focused. I really didn't need that kind of attention at the moment.

I managed to reconnect in my mind with some of the members I felt closest to. It was a test to see if we could still do it, and the notice that we were probably to continue with practice the following week. They were thrilled and they told me they couldn't wait for us to meet again in the park.

After school I said goodbye to everybody like I would see them again tomorrow. I believed everything would be all right. The universe was on my side. The power of the dark shadows was limited. But the power of light, my power, was eternal. Absolute. Limitless.

I left the majority of my things in the locker, as I did before when I had to attend an interview about getting expelled from school. I left my cell phone there too. It couldn't do anything for me anymore. The only thing I could turn to was the universe and the energy…When everybody left I decided to find an appropriate place to leave my body. I settled for the ladies' room. I locked the door behind me, put down the toilette seat and sat down. I relaxed and left my body. I materialized again in the basement.

It was the first time for me to walk in the hall I had seen months ago in the projections of Hanna's experiences with Davis. From time to time a dark shadow would dash past me but I paid no attention to it. If I didn't look at them, they couldn't see me either. I could feel a rising number of dark vibrations and it seemed that the way to the room where I was to meet the headmaster was getting more and more crowded. I could feel a strong resistance at the door that lead to the room as if it was protected with a black wall of low frequencies. I moved the wall apart and peered inside. Davis was sitting in the middle of the room and everything around him was black. I closed my eyes to keep myself from having to look at the crowd of about 30 dark creatures of all shapes and sizes. In one of the corners of the room I felt a weak shimmer of a small lamp. Dark creatures were crowding around the lamp and jumping on in. They were laughing and talking as if what they were doing was some kind of recreation.

I materialized in the wall very close to the lamp. I pushed my head into the room in order to get a good look. I found out the dark creatures were not jumping on the lamp but on a small string of light. It was tied around something…I stepped back from my emotions to get a sharper picture. The string of light belonged to Ravi. It was his body lying there in the corner of the room. I saw that his soul was not in the body; the string of light he usually tied around the left leg of his spiritual body was tied around the tiger's eye pendant and disturbed the dark creatures with its light.

He had to leave his body, I knew that. But I didn't know what it meant if the cord was tied around the pendant. Was he able to return?

I looked at his body again and wondered if I could see his memories.

A dark spot appeared above his head. I realized it was a delayed telepathic message that was left in his body. Only I was able to trigger it with my presence. The dark blue haze floated in front of my eyes and I saw that the dark creatures couldn't see it. I stepped away from it and a picture started to appear. Ravi and dark background.

Hello Ina, he said and smiled.

I'm leaving this with my body, just in case, in the pendant that carries your love. Even though I know I must obviously look for you among the lower frequencies. I will save you, don't worry. I can't wait to see you, he said with conviction.

Just in case, I'm leaving also some of my last memories. See you, my love. I'm sure we'll make it…

A warm feeling came over my heart when I realized that he remained focused and positive despite the almost impossible test we'd been given. He knew he shouldn't give in to the low-vibrating human emotions. I was overwhelmed with his strength.

The picture was coming closer until I became one with it…I was becoming permeated by his presence until I was totally consumed by it. I became him…

THANK YOU FOR BEING BLESSED BY PEOPLE WHO PULSATE WITH SUCH A NOBLE *positive vibration*, I think, when I'm returning from school. *And especially – thank you for her. Finally we can be – together. Finally we'll be able to finish the task that we'd been trusted with.*

I'm unlocking the door wishing I had Ina's power of intuition. I can namely sense something is wrong but I don't know what.

I enter and I see my dad in the middle of the round parlor. He looks different. I want to go to the relaxed state as soon as possible to connect with Ina and find out if everything is OK. Before I can do that, dad comes up to me and hugs me. I can't check what he is thinking about and I find this really strange. Is he stronger than me?

"Forgive me, son," he says to me.

"I'm sorry for not liking Ina. She really is a lovely girl and I don't know what was wrong with me that I didn't want you to have true love. I was in love once too and I guess I was afraid you'd get as hurt as I had been…"

He hugs me. I hug him back. I can feel my frequency has dropped a bit lately but I'm not sure why.

"You can feel it too, can't you?" he asks me deeply touched.

"Are you reading my mind?" I'm surprised.

"Yes, I've decided to act for the well-being of humanity," he says enthusiastically. When I look into his face I'm not entirely sure. He makes a face.

"It's about Ina," he says worried.

"What about her?" I ask unsure.

"The girls is naïve, you know and she found my *room*. In the school basement. She came across some creatures she shouldn't have and…you know how vulnerable she is, and not used to their power at all. They promised her eternal union with you if she signed something…and…She promised them…" His face contorts again and I cannot bear to listen to him anymore. I pace around the room and try to picture what happened. A horrible feeling comes over me. I realize it has been a while since I've felt something as negative as this and an unexpected convulsion comes over my body.

"Do you happen to know how we could save her?" he asks me.

"I must go there," I'm determined. I'll think of something when I meet them again. I must save Ina! I sit down and try to relax. Maybe it is still possible to connect with her…

"DON'T!" shouts my dad. "If you connect with her, your connection will be visible to everybody. I've checked. If she is not strong enough and she can't find the place to be alone, everybody will be able to see your messages. At least at the beginning."

"You are right," I realize. "I must go to her."

"But that's dangerous, Ravi," he tries to stop me. Although he loves me and is very attached to me I know what I must do.

"I *must* go to her. This is good for all of us," I say. I know I'm right.

"Take me there. To that room." Although the thought disgusts me, I know this is the only way.

We set off immediately. I'm glad to see he is willing to help me. He unlocks the back door of the school and leads me to a small door along a side corridor. When he opens it I can see there are many dark creatures inside. But her body is nowhere to be seen.

"I took her to the dorm and told the receptionist she was sick and sleeping. It seemed the right thing to do. If they had found out she was gone, they would probably have called the police…"

"You did the right thing. We really don't need panic right now," I express my agreement.

The body is not even that important anymore. The soul is what really matters. If she managed to untie in the right way, maybe I can save her…

I lie on the bed and relax. I know that the dark creatures have plenty of data now. If they caught Ina, they know practically everything. It'll be hard…And the hardest part – my cord should be destroyed during the disconnection. I should surrender to them – completely. The cord mustn't be connected to my soul or my body…I disconnect and hold in my hands the glimmering cord. My life. I'm looking for an alternative that would help me survive. In front of me I see my own body with the pendant around my neck.

As I'm about to say goodbye to my body I realize that the tiger's eye that I got as a present from Ina slightly changed its color...Of course, she built her love into it. An idea sneaks into my mind...I realize it's going to be difficult, but not impossible. Luckily, there's a detail the dark beings aren't aware of.

Ina attributed a special power to the tiger's eye hanging around my body's neck. I could tie the cord I should otherwise destroy around this pendant. If I leave it here, next to my body, I leave the essence of my soul in it (as well as a short message and a memory). The creatures to which I'm about to surrender to might think that I left my body completely since the cord will no longer be with me. Maybe I can return anyway. Maybe both of us can return. The cord is being increasingly drawn to the pendant and when I put it even nearer it coils tightly around it.

I surrender to the dark frequencies. I start to observe them. They can see me much better too and they grab hold of my arms. I can feel their violence and surrender to it. My vibration is dropping fast. I gladly let myself go, because I know I will meet *her* there...

Again I found myself outside Ravi's body and quickly hid in the wall. I didn't want to get emotionally involved. I quickly materialized in the ladies' room. I tied myself to my body and let out a deep sigh. I knew exactly how things were but I didn't know *why*.

Why did Davies stain himself with so many lies? Why did he trap his own son? Why did he receive some special abilities which he used to disable Ravi and me...?

I relaxed. I thought of all the nice things that had happened to me that day: the feeling of unconditional love and power...friends from other dimensions...my body floating among them...their quiet blessing...I could feel them beside me again. They were tremendously happy. I felt they were even a bit amused at my questions...

Have you ever stood in the middle of the road, looked at the car driving towards you and asked yourself: "Why?" I hear in my head. I smile. I must do the test. It's not important why. I know.
Thank you, goes though my mind. I felt the time when I had to go to the basement was coming. *I must become even stronger.*

I sank into my consciousness. I looked for the most precious moment which will again carry me higher...

H E QUICKLY GRABS ME BY THE HIPS AND PUSHES BOTH OF US ONTO the bed. I become scared and I let out a scream. When we fall on the soft pillow he hugs me and we laugh together.

He rolls on top of me and entwines her fingers with mine. Then he pushes them against the pillow above my head. I feel so...limited but so good at the same time.

Now you are a part of me, he thinks enthusiastically.

I've always been, I answer him.

He brings his face closer to mine and again I can hear his heartbeat from afar. Slowly his lips get very close to mine.

Finally he kisses me...He untangles his fingers from mine and our bodies merge totally. We start rolling on the bed and his arms hold me very tight...A sweet feeling coming from my stomach spreads all over my body. In one moment we become totally harmonized with each other and we feel total merging. Without any thoughts we merge into one and soon there are no boundaries. We are still kissing but we become frozen in that kiss, we become frozen in silence.

I can feel that his strength become mine again and the high frequency beings strengthen it further. *I'm merged with him*, wherever he may be. I've always been. Nothing else matters anymore.

I opened my eyes again and I felt more powerful than ever before. The absolute power I was feeling in the morning, merged with the power of the universe. I felt almost like I was at home again. On my planet. With him. If I didn't hear the song created by the Earth rotating around its axis, I could become one with the feeling of my home star.

I got up. Slowly but determinately I started walking down the stairs towards the basement. I knew exactly where I should go. When there were no more stairs, I thought: this is it. Like before when I was out of my body and I could feel the dark shadows I could feel them now too. I was surprised to find out that my perception of the outside world was totally identical to when I walked around as a soul. I was able to feel the immaterial world with the same intensity as I did when I was out of my body.

This means that you are very strongly connected to your original frequency, highly vibrating beings explain to me. I can feel them all over the school. *The presence of your own body can't fool you anymore; you see things exactly as they are.*

I paused in front of the room. I knocked. The door opened and closed again immediately after I got in. It was pitch dark. I couldn't see anything beside the glimmer of the string of light around Ravi's pendant and I could see it was getting thinner. When I was looking at his small, frail connection to this world, I realized I had forgotten to remain focused. I felt the presence of dark creatures; the room was still full of them. I felt a pair of strong hands squeezing my neck and heard these words said with absolute fury:

"Let's have it out, then – without unnecessary stalling."

I became totally soft. I wasn't prepared for a physical showdown. Davies' hands squeezed my neck tightly and it yielded completely like soft butter. I didn't have the strength to defend myself. I felt the knife in my pocket but my hand opened up all by itself...I wasn't able to resort to violence, even in self-defense...I left my body momentarily.

But I still had my absolute power of love that I had gained with patience and thousands of years of practice and gathering of knowledge. I could feel that the cord connecting my two bodies was growing weaker and weaker. I focused…

I visualized the planet Ravi and I came from, the source energy that vibrates faster than the earth. I imagined I wasn't on planet Earth but on a star. I remembered the high temperatures which were so familiar to me, the joyful explosions and volcanic eruptions Ravi and I used to fly over. The memory of our source vibrations was so familiar to me…I let the memories take me away…

The Earth yielded to the star's vibration and the tone of its rotation became a little higher. I shed some light on it and some of the dark creatures moved away. As if the majority of the low vibrations stepped away from the vibration of the earth. The room I was in lighted up too. I could feel a very strong connection. The vibration of our star was so close. All the events that had led me here now made perfect sense.

I looked towards my left leg and found out that the string linking me to my body was getting thinner despite the light in the room. I decided to try to make it stronger. I leaned towards it…

"Don't," I heard a gentle woman's voice say. I turned around. A kind, gentle-looking woman came towards me in the glow of the illuminated room. I sensed I knew her. She had a darker complexion and she looked a lot like me. She was wearing a sari that was a golden-red color.

"If you touch the string in this state, you will break it," she said smiling. I noticed that besides looking Indian, she also spoke with an Indian accent. I looked at her and I realized that I *did know* who she was. I saw her when Ravi and me had been preparing for the descent, for birth…

"Rashmi?" I uttered totally astonished.

"Ina," she smiled and came to me. She hugged me gently.

"I'm glad to be able to really meet my daughter-in-law finally…" she turned her face slightly away from me and smiled. Her love was shining on me gently like sunrays and I could feel her real happiness.

"Me too," I said back although I knew it was not necessary. She could *feel* me.

"I must help you," she said when she saw that my string was getting thinner. "I must help *us*," she corrected her sentence. "Finally I am able to be here again and this is all thanks to you, Ina. Thank you."

I didn't understand completely what she meant by that.

I will show you, she thought. *You must understand what is happening. How it happened. What is behind all this. You couldn't see this up to now because too many dark creatures guarded the secret...Relax*, she said to me and then a haze appeared next to her.

I knew what I had to do. Put the feelings aside and look calmly into that piece of colorful smoke...The haze cleared into a film. I saw Rashmi and it seemed like a very vivid memory. The picture came even closer and suddenly I was in her body. I was sitting on a lawn on a beautiful sunny day...

XLVIII. THE STORY OF RASHMI AND AARON

I'M SITTING ON A LAWN IN CENTRAL PARK AND I'M ENJOYING THE SPRING SUN. I feel its loving light heat every cell in my body. We should really be grateful for every moment we spend on this wonderful planet. I can feel myself becoming one with the environment and I don't feel lonely at all although I'm alone. My panjabi* is light enough to allow the air to touch my body and I feel very cozy. I feel am not so alone anymore and I open my eyes.

"I'm really sorry for staring, but it is really you who is so celestially beautiful," say a playful voice with a British accent...

My eyes gradually adjust to the light and I see a young man in front of me with brown hair and white complexion. He is tall and lanky but there is a special energy emanating from him and I can feel it immediately. Pure love shines from his blue eyes and I feel something special towards him – like I know him from somewhere...

I can see a strap around his shoulders and I realize he is carrying a guitar. He says charmingly: "You don't mind if I join you, do you?" and sits down without waiting to hear an answer. I can't say no to him. We look at the sky for a while.

He decides to break the ice and says: "My name is Aaron." He offers me his hand. I smile.

"Rashmi."

"Is this an Indian name?"

"Yes."

"Doest it have a special meaning?"

"It does…" I stop and think for a while whether it's appropriate to talk about these things with a random person you meet in the park. But somewhere deep down I can feel, I know that this boy is much more than that. "Sun rays," I say.

"Really?" he looks at me like he isn't sure whether I'm telling the truth.

"Really," I say seriously.

"For I moment I thought you were joking. The name you've been given couldn't reflect your essence better…That's why I'd been drawn to you. You *shine* too brightly."

He smiles one more time. I notice that his teeth are somewhat irregularly placed but still very symmetrical. I realize this smile seems very familiar. I feel I have finally arrived home…He takes his guitar and starts jamming like this is the most natural thing to do. His fingers are touching the strings of the guitar like this was a dance and not playing music. He looks at the sky curiously as if he was looking for something up there. Then he looks at me again and his blue eyes draw me to the essence of being…All my past experiences suddenly become absolutely meaningful. Everything that I've experienced has led me to this moment. To meet *him*.

He nods like he was reading my mind. He is still playing the guitar. His voice glows with pure love and he starts singing gently:

Tra, la, la

tra, la, li,

you and me,

Aaron and Rashmi…

I smile because the lyrics are so simple but…so…meaningful.

Suddenly I start using my rational side again. It's not really possible that I should meet my soul mate in the park, that he would bring light into my life and then I would live happily ever after. I remembered the rules. I mustn't fall in love. And it is very likely that this charmer here goes through thousands of young girls every day. Using this technique. "Do you always insert the name of the girl you have just met in this song of yours?" I ask.

He stops singing and his face becomes serious. "No, this is the first time. I'm sorry, I thought you felt it too…Oh, it doesn't matter. Enjoy the day." He stands up with a jerk, and I want to vanish from the face of the earth. He turns away and I shout after him:

"Stop! Please wait! I'm sorry!"

"Excuse me?" he turns to me.

"It was not my intention to offend you. It's just…What would you think if you were me? Suddenly a person who completely overwhelms and charms me approaches me. It seems like I know him. I don't know if all this is true or is he is just…on the lookout for innocent girls. What am I to think?"

He slowly sits down again. "I think the best thing for you to do is stop thinking," he answers slowly.

He comes closer to me and I sit still. We look at each other for a while without saying anything. He leans his face closer to mine…I feel I can't resist him. My body stays where it is no matter how hard I want to protect my honor. I look into his eyes and dive in the ocean of happiness…I can feel that he is honest. His narrow lips are really very soft when they touch mine. For a while we only touch each other with lips. Soon I can feel a fire rising up in my body, a fire that even his ocean-blue eyes can't extinguish. We merge in a kiss and I discover how lonely I had been all this time. When I merge with him into one love, one being I realize how much I had missed him. He stops kissing me and holds my face in his hands. He puts his forehead against mine. We both have our eyes closed and we feel a special connection between us…

"I've missed you. I also feel we…*must* be together."

A thought comes to me how funny life really is. Half an hour ago I was completely satisfied with myself and my life, and now being without him in this world seems so…pointless. Worthless. Like a veil of oblivion slowly descended on the period of my life when I didn't know Aaron, which seems like some kind of previous life. One more time I yield to his kisses and realize I will stay with him regardless of all the trials I will have to face at home…

ALTHOUGH MORE THAN A YEAR HAS PASSED ALREADY I'M STILL blissfully happy with him. I can be totally honest with him. Our arguments usually last 30 seconds and then we smile, settle the matter and let ourselves go to the ocean of happiness coming from his eyes…

We secretly meet in his dorm. I told him that being together is unacceptable for my family. He doesn't care. He seems to enjoy it even more.

"I'm your Romeo, then, so what?" he says and smiles.

Soon I cannot stand his fiery kisses that fill me with a sweet feeling and give myself to him completely. We finally experience a complete merging of our bodies and souls. We feel we are one with the universe and that we've been waiting for that since we've been together. He is so gentle and loving to me that I have a feeling I'm being caressed by Shiva himself. By God. I firmly believe that what I'm doing is right. My family says otherwise. Our love is a fact, a divine ceremony. An unavoidable event like the eruption of a volcano that has been asleep for too long.

He pulls a small box from under his bed quickly and decisively. He opens it and I can see the glitter of a gold ring with sapphires arranged in the shape of a flower.

"Marry me," he says firmly and I can feel his loving power. I couldn't say no even if I wanted to. I smile sadly.

"What's wrong?" he asks "Don't you want to…?"

"Of course I want to," I hurry with my answer. "But you know…my family; I have been promised to another man…"

"It doesn't matter. Let's got to Vegas. And then they will have no choice. They will just have to accept the fact that you are already married. That you are *mine*." He emphasizes the last word. I can feel his competitive spirit and I know how that happened. My hands are tied and he tries to untie them before it's too late.

"Marry me," he repeats.

"Marry me, Rashmi."

Two scenarios roll out in my head. Life with him and life without him. Without him I die anyway, I think. I make a fast decision.

"Yes," I nod. "My answer is YES! I'd be happy to."

He starts to kiss me passionately and we roll onto the bed together. We laugh; I feel that all things in life are so simple…you just have to make up your mind.

WE ARE WAITING IN A SMALL LOBBY THAT IS ARTIFICIALLY PINK color. He is wearing a snow white suit and a white head cover. When I showed him how the grooms are usually dressed in our weddings, he became almost obsessed with this. He had to get the right wedding attire. I bought a golden sari`. I also went to a beauty parlor that day and everything was perfect. Although we didn't have any guests beside the best men and matron of honor. I invited my sister Shanti who prepared me as a bride should be prepared (she braided my hair, decorated my hands with henna`, put at least 50 gilded bracelets on my wrists, glued a shiny bindi` to my forehead and covered me in flowers) and while she was doing this, she kept telling me I was stupid and I should change my mind. When I lovingly told her it was possible to buy a matron of honor here, she fell silent for a moment and then changed the topic.

Aaron invited Jones, his friend from university. They hung out all day and they called it a stag party. Without alcohol of course. My groom insisted he wanted to be completely sober during the ceremony.

The door opens and there is Elvis in his golden and white suit.

"Who's next?" he asks carelessly.

Shanti says calmly: "Just a moment, please," and disappears into the room. She closes the door behind her. When I hear speaking, I become curious. I let go of Aaron's hand and lean my ear against the door. A joy comes over me in the expectation to disclose a mystery. I hear my sister's strict voice, she tries to keep it low, but her tone is very clear.

"Listen, Elvis. You will kindly take off your stupid wig. The two people who are getting married now actually love each other, not like the other idiots who come here. We paid more than the others too because we have special requests. So you will very kindly do as I tell you. Put this on! And when they enter, play this music. You will read exactly and only what is written on this sheet of paper. Without any of this rock 'n' roll crap. It's a sacred event, do you understand?!?"

I can hear the swishing of cloth and the soft creak of an audiocassette. I'm moved to realize that Shanti also believes in our love. I hear her footsteps getting closer and I move out of the way. It seems that the boys have heard the exchange too because they snigger at the same time.

Shanti smiles pleasantly and says: "We'll just wait for a while for the photographer to arrive."

The photographer really arrives five minutes later and I find out that my sister had put more effort into this event than I asked her for. I become emotional and my eyes water.

"You needn't have…" I start.

"Hush, hush we don't want you smudging your make up; you don't want to have to explain to your kids why did you end up spending all your savings to look like Alice Cooper on you wedding day."

I smile.

"That's better," she says.

I can hear knocking on the inside of the door. It appears the civil registry officer is ready. Shanti opens the door and holds my hand. The room smells of incense. She leads me to the middle of the hall. Although he looks a bit awkward, Jones also holds Aaron's hand and leads him to where I'm waiting for him. Jones and Shanti join our hands and they do it effortlessly as if they had practiced that before. My sister's enthusiasm amazes me again.

We start walking towards the civil registry officer together and I realize he is dressed like a Hindu monk. There are white lines and a yellow dot in the middle of his forehead, he has natural brown hair. He doesn't look like Elvis at all anymore. And there is more. He is sitting cross-legged in front of an altar pouring yellow dust into in the incense bowl in front of him using a small gold ladle. There is a gilded water bowl next to him. I look at Shanti and she nods at me. A mellow music from my homeland is played, and hearing the familiar sound of the sitar* makes me relax even more.

When I'm walking across the room with my loving groom I notice that the room is decorated with small golden statues. There is a bigger golden statue of Ganesh* decorated with garlands in the middle. The room looks like it was created for a wedding. With the love of my life.

The ceremony is just as I have always imagined it would be. My groom is almost glowing and I ask myself if he can see it in my eyes too how much I love him. From time to time we become illuminated and hear the "click" of the camera and I became aware that I will remember this day with fondness for the rest of my life…When Aaron is washing my feet… as the custom demands and gently kisses the water in his hands, I realize how devoted he is to me. He would do anything for me.

Everything that the monk reads makes perfect sense. It doesn't matter if he is really just a civil registry officer. He acts out his role to perfection. I look at my groom and realize we are one…All three of them throw yellow rice at us and bless our love…There are no obstacles for us. None. Everything becomes happiness. I become fully aware of this.

After the ceremony Shanti thanks the registry officer and he greets us with a peaceful *namaste.*

What follows is a joyful lunch and then our guests accompany us to the hotel.

"Take some rest, you two," Shanti orders us to our hotel room. "We'll tidy everything up, won't we, Jones?" she nudges Aaron's best man who says "Sure" under his breath.

When Aaron carries me across the threshold into our hotel room I smile at the thought how our ceremony was a successful combination of Indian and European traditions…He gently puts me on the bed and starts kissing me. He slowly takes of my wreath. His also lands on the floor. We yield to each other. This time with even more certainty. We know our life is perfect. Now we are one.

"MOTHER?" I call her immediately when I see she has finished with her morning meditation. She is usually in the best mood at that time. My heart is beating like a broken tarabuka*. I know this is because I intend to fight with the power of the family. The struggle against tradition is similar fighting with the windmills. Tradition always wins. I hope this time will be different…

"Mother?" I say again, this time louder. She sighs deeply.

"Yes, my dear daughter?" she says lovingly. I become braver.

"I must…tell you something."

"You know you can tell me anything. Go ahead," she is still calm.

"I don't know how to say this…Mother, I'm pregnant."

Her face becomes totally pale although her complexion is chocolate brown. Then she calms down.

"Impossible," she says. "The wedding to Haatim…"

"There will be no wedding with Haatim," I say timidly.

"I've married the father of my child and his name is Aaron…"

Her face changes completely and she starts shouting. I don't know if it looks more like crying or recrimination…She starts pushing me out of the house when Shanti comes.

"It is true, mother. *I* was the matron of honor."

How I wish she hadn't said that! I wish I could have protected her, taken the responsibility. Mother throws her out of the house too during wild recriminations and we find ourselves in front of the door. Cast outs.

"You shouldn't have said you had anything to do with it," I tell her off because I'm worried about her.

"I organized the whole thing, have you forgotten? And I'm proud of it…" I'm glad that I have such an optimistic little sister.

"It doesn't matter that we've been thrown out! It's even better; it means we are free! We are free from tradition! We can start anew!" She waved her hands and jumped around me.

"Don't you think it was about time you visited your husband? When was the last time you saw him? Last weekend when we went to the market?"

I realize how much I miss him.

"Now you can finally live with him," she enthuses.

"Why are you helping me," I ask, "do you have a reason beside the fact that we are sisters?"

"Because I'm a believer in happy endings. I've been suffocated by what's been happening in our family too. We are in America, aren't we?" she exclaims.

"Can you come with me?" I'm still a bit uncertain.

"Sure."

"Where will you stay…?" I ask worried.

"Don't worry about me. I'll be fine. I have some friends; maybe I'll get a job as a waitress…I must admit," she bursts out laughing, "I've been planning this for some time. And I'm pretty satisfied with how it all worked out…"

We go to the subway station together. She gives me the ticket, and I realize she had really thought this out. In a couple of minutes we get to the right station. Then I have the feeling that the train takes ages to get here. I feel terribly sick the whole time. When we get off I run to the restroom. I manage to hold it in until I reach the toilet bowl…

I'M HAPPY. Aaron and me have been living together for a couple of months and nothing in this world seems more natural, more self-evident than living with him. I don't mean the routine but the lightness of being. Everything is so simple. I carry our baby and he is very affectionate to me all the time. He always washes the dishes. He asks me several times per day if he can help me in any way. When we need groceries he goes to the store with me and does all the hard work. He has the scholarship for the specially gifted students (his average grade is very high) and some savings from home so we get by normally. He tells me he's been promised a good teaching position at a high school near Central Park...

"It's not decided yet, they are still discussing it, but I'm sure we'll make it," he smiles charmingly. After a year and a half we still love each other very much and I can feel that Aaron is even more in love with me than he was on the first day! He hugs and caresses me with joy every time he returns home to me. It seems like he could hardly wait to leave his family, although deep down he respects them, despite everything.

Shanti took care of herself as well. She really got the job, even better than what she expected. She works at the local post office. She jokes sometimes that they hired her because of her looks...

"It doesn't matter why I got the job," she smiles, "What is important is that I have it." She met a nice colleague at work; he is Spanish. She admitted there was something going on between them...

I decide to surprise Aaron this morning. I'll go shopping alone and prepare a culinary surprise for him at home. Although I'm clumsy with the 8-month baby inside of me, the idea is to good to discard it for practical reasons. I set off...

When I'm doing my chores during the day, I pat myself on my belly and talk to the happy-go-lucky baby growing inside of me. I can feel it is a boy and that he is full of energy just like his daddy. This morning is no exception. When I'm walking in the street I gently pat the current abode of my son and talk to him in my mind. I'm so engrossed in the chat with him that for a moment I forget about the world around me. Something hits me on the shoulder. Suddenly I realize I've been surrounded.

"Somebody is really sleepy," says the first person. I see that the group who has surrounded me has the same complexion as mine. Because there are more than ten of them it's impossible to run away. Not with my belly. "Or dreaming," sneers another one.

"Or...in love," the third one says with an undertone.

"Please let me go," I say calmly. "I don't even know who you are."

"That's not important now. What's important that we know who *you* are, Rashmi."

I'm surprised. I've never had anything to do with any kind of violence. And this group looks so organized...like some kind of mafia.

"You know...the word gets around pretty fast..." starts the first one. "When you ran away from home..."

"I didn't run away, my family renounced me," I correct him calmly. He starts speaking again with the same carelessness.

"I'd really appreciate it if you didn't interrupt me," he says pulling out a small switchblade. I can hear a gun being cocked behind my back. The black-haired Indian guy continues:

"So, when you *ran away* from home, your family was very worried. They called Haatim at once and they explained the whole thing to him with utter embarrassment and humbleness. Your marriage to the foreigner was clearly a mistake and a too hasty decision. Haatim is even prepared to forgive you everything if you get a divorce in a week."

The offer is ridiculous.

"I swore to him before God," I say calmly.

"Yeah, before the god of rock 'n' roll in Las Vegas!" says someone and everybody laughs out loud.

"It's none of your business what the ceremony looked like so I'd appreciate it if you didn't make fun of it," I say still calmly.

"So...if I understand you correctly, you refuse to get a divorce?" says the first guy and puts a knife to my neck.

"Yes," I'm trying to stay calm. "I'd really appreciate it if you stopped making threats. I'm pregnant." I'm hoping this fact will make them think twice. I can still feel the knife on my neck.

"Let her go, Jairay, you see, it makes no sense…" says somebody in the group.

"It makes perfect sense!" shouts Jairaj. "Do you realize what Haatim will do to us if the girl doesn't change her mind?!?"

"Who cares; she is pregnant," says the third guy. "We'll think of something…"

The knife is still on my neck. While Jairaj is fighting an internal battle with himself about what to do, I'm sending loving thought to the goddess Kali* to keep at least our baby alive. Two of my captors start pushing and fighting for dominance over the gun behind my back. Somebody pushes me by accident. I fall to my face and Jairaj's knife jabs into my neck.

"Look what you've done, you moron!"

"What shall we do now?"

"Hope you're happy now! You've saved your own skin and killed the poor girl."

"The knife severed a vein!"

"Let's get out of here before the cops come…"

I collapse to the ground and try to hold in the gush blood with my right hand. If I come home fast, I can call an ambulance. I'm not far from home anyway. I crawl backwards and I can feel my legs won't carry me very far…I'm just a few steps away from the entrance and manage to somehow crawl to the door. I'm leaving a trail of blood behind me. When I try to press the doorknob, I can feel my strength draining from me fast…I reach it somehow utilizing the last drops of strength I have left and I notice it is locked. Of course, I'd locked it before I left…I feel for a key and suddenly I don't feel my body anymore…

I STAND OVER MY BODY AND CALL MY HUSBAND IN MY MIND. I can see
I'm attached to my body with some kind of string which is getting
thinner and thinner. I feel that the life in the belly of my body is still
there. I feel so helpless. There is nothing I can do anymore. The pool of
blood my body rests in is getting bigger and bigger…

Finally. I can see him getting closer…*Hurry*, I think. *Please, hurry.*

He is smiling and his head is full of thoughts. Like he has good news
for me. Suddenly he stops. He has noticed my body.

"Oh, my god!!! Oh, my god," he keeps repeating in the combination
of crying and horror while he checks what happened to me. He runs
to the apartment and desperately calls the ambulance. He runs back to
me and presses his fingers against my severed vein. He has blood all
over himself but he doesn't care. He tries all possible techniques he's
heard of in his life…heart massage…CPR. He is covered in my blood
and I can feel him tasting it when he is performing mouth-to-mouth.
He is doing all this very fast and I can see he fights like a lion. From
time to time he checks the pulse on my wrist which is getting weaker
and weaker…

I STAND BESIDE HIM AND I FEEL TOTALLY HELPLESS. I see his tears, I feel
his suffering. I hear his prayers. When I touch his face, he lets out a wail.
He is holding my body in his arms still trying to bring it back to life…
When the ambulance arrives he tells the paramedics he is my husband
and he is not moving away from me. They take me away and I follow my
body all the time. I really want to keep the thin connection with it…

I STAND BY MY BODY, IN THE HOSPITAL. I'm hooked up to several ma-
chines and the monitor next to my bed shows my weak heartbeat. A

being that is very light appears next to me and I can feel his vibration is higher than mine.

"Are you saying goodbye?"

"Why? Should I be?" I'm surprised.

"Actually, you should," the being says decisively.

"But I *love* this person. I can't leave him! I can't leave my baby either. They were barely able to save him."

"Sometimes there is a higher purpose to the things that happen and people can't always understand it."

"So why do I have to leave them?"

"You will discover this by yourself. Your...transformation is a part of a bigger plan." I noticed that the being of light didn't use the word death. "Death doesn't exist. There is just perpetual transformation," he informs me. So he can read my mind.

"It's time to go," he says to me.

"Let me just say goodbye," I say quickly. Aaron is asleep by my bed. His soul is clinging to the bed I lie on and can't see beyond the body.

"We'll meet again," I whisper to him. "Stay as good as you are, love our son...Can you hear me, my love? *I love you.*"

"He can't hear you, he is too worried. Even in his sleep," says the being and cuts the cord.

I go over to him and kiss him anyway. He wakes up and the machine beside my body emits a beeping noise showing that I've left.

He jumps up and presses the red button by my bed. He holds my body and starts CPR. Doctors and nurses come to the room. They try to get him out of the room but he refuses to leave. When the fifth electroshock fails to do the trick, they tell him they've lost me.

"TRY AGAIN!" he orders them. After the tenth try, they tell him they couldn't save me. Aaron hits the doctor with his fist and runs outside. When he reaches the main entrance he collapses and starts crying. I can see two dark shadows near him that have been invited by his anger and sadness...I can't reach him...He can't hear me...

The light being holds me by the hand and consoles me: "You'll come back and visit him when the time is right. Come along now, don't focus on the pain..." We start to disappear...

I VISIT HIM AGAIN AFTER FIVE YEARS. He looks totally different. His left eye became dark and his hair is yellow white. The light being that was with me when I was leaving explains to me why his eyes are a different color.

"He's decided not to have feelings in his life anymore. Not to see love anymore. The left side of the body represents emotions. The right is reason."

I feel bad seeing him that way. There are quite a few creatures with low vibrations around him. He enters the high school. He must have got that job. I'm happy for him. I feel that our son is healthy too and that he has a lot of positive power.

When he enters he turns right on the staircase and goes to the basement. He walks to the end of the corridor. He reaches a small door and opens it. I can see a place where more dark creatures wait for him and I get a bad feeling. He sits in front of a wooden plate and starts with some kind of ritual that I don't know. I realize he is calling the spirits. I want to talk to him but he doesn't hear me. The low frequency beings encourage him and promise him to be able to talk to me and in return he promises his soul to them...

"It's necessary to perform these rituals regularly to harmonize with the frequency of her soul," says the biggest among them. What a lie! I can see Aaron becoming their puppet, a tool. I try to speak louder and look the liar in the eye. The light being is still with me and he positions himself directly in front of me.

"What's wrong?" I ask.

"Looking at those creatures is lethal. I can't let you do that."

"But you said there was no death!"

"You are right. There is just...transformation. And also – a deep fall," he says and takes my hand. Again I start to disappear powerlessly in a beam of light…I guess I won't be able to talk to him as long as those creatures are here…

Again I became aware that this was not my experience. It was Rashmi's. I stood before her looking her in the eyes. It all became very clear to me. I finally understood even why the taste of blood was always present, when I saw the Principal.

"You senced his pain, the way it really was," she said to me. "Please tell him that I love him immensely," she added. The cord connecting my body and the body of the soul slowly started to become stronger. "Will you do that for me?"

"You can tell him *yourself*," I ensured her, "if only we manage to save Ravi…"

I showed her how to do that using projections in my mind. She agreed and hugged me.

I saw the headmaster sitting next to me and trying to bring me back to life. Obviously he was succeeding because I was more and more drawn to my body…

I lay on the floor and tried to connect to my body as much as I could. To feel the heartbeat, to feel the breathing pattern…I started to feel the ground under me and I knew I would make it.

XLIX. THE AWAKENING

I OPENED MY EYES SLOWLY AND I REALIZED I WAS STILL IN THE BASEMENT. Davies was standing before me covering his eyes with his hands. Tears were coming through his fingers. He hadn't realized yet that he had actually succeeded. That I wasn't dead.

When I felt I wanted to test my voice I coughed gently. I was still lying on the floor. "Rashmi sends her love," I said quietly.

Davies moved his hands away from his face. I could feel how he opened his heart entirely. "Ina! Ina! You are alive!" He hugged me.

"Ouch," I squealed when he pressed me close to him. My body had been lying still for quite a while and his strong squeeze was a shock.

"Please forgive me," he said to me as if he was looking at the most precious being in the world. "What did you say before?"

"Rashmi is here. She will help us bring Ravi back."

All the feelings he had been running from came flooding back. "Where is she? You've got to tell me!"

"First we'll save your son. Then there will be time to talk," I tried to calm him down. He let me go obediently and allowed me to lead.

I pointed at Ravi's body in the dark and we carried him to the middle of the room. The string of light was already very thin. I asked Davies and Rashmi to relax and imagine Ravi's soul in his body again.

I felt my power again. This time only one of Ravi's sentences I played in my head was enough: *"When you imagined light…I bet that they run out of electricity in heaven!"* I merged with absolute power I had awakened this morning. I imagined him in perfect union with me. The events were so vivid…We were at school again, I introduced him to my parents and sister, we danced at Ela's wedding. *This is possible*, I thought without a shadow of a doubt. *May it happen*!

I felt Rashmi's and Aaron's power too.

In the middle of the room in Ravi's body it was getting brighter and brighter too. Each of our thoughts harmonized with one wish. Rays started trickling from our bodies and they were all focused to the center of the room. *Stronger*, I thought. *More light*!

The creatures of light from the entire school suddenly found themselves in this room. We received the universe's absolute support. Light came through the room with a frequency that was a thousand times higher than I was able to summon.

"Cooperation is also power," I heard and I answered gratefully: "I know. Thank you."

When the beings of light realized I no longer needed them they dispersed again. Ravi's body was floating in the middle of the room and his soul was glowing in it. Slowly he descended. He just lay there for a while. Then he opened his eyes.

He got up and looked at us. Davies got up and turned on the light. Ravi blinked at the light. The three of us got up too. Slowly he connected all the events. He recognized us.

"Ina!" he ran to me and hugged me.

Davies and Rashmi looked at us lovingly. I saw the manifestation of what I had already seen in my head with my own help and the help of the universe and a feeling of extreme enthusiasm came over me. I had to *become* Ravi to be able to bring him back to life. Now he can play his part again.

"There are so many things I want to say to you," he starts.

"I know. Me too. But first…what do you think we make your parents happy?" I said pointing to Rashmi and Aaron.

You mean we show my father the way out of his body? thought Ravi.

Exactly that, I answered. *I'm glad to see this mind line is still working…*

L. CONCLUSION

AARON HUGGED HIS SON. "Forgive me, my son. There is nothing I can say..." tears came to his eyes again. "I was a puppet in their hands..."

"I know how it works, dad. I forgive you completely," Ravi said calmly. "Hi mom," he waved to Rashmi completely relaxed.

I was surprised. And I expected him to be surprised even more.

"Mom and I often hung out and talked especially before I met you again. She was the one to inform me you were coming here. But soon afterwards dad became so very...different that she wasn't able to keep seeing me. Sorry, I haven't told you that yet. I haven't had..."

"I know. The chance. I forgive you. I think we really got to know each other well today," I said and winked at Rashmi. She smiled.

"Can somebody please explain to me what's going on?" Aaron said enviously.

"Sure. Immediately. You just need to relax and Rashmi will explain everything to you..."

Ravi and I worked together as a team again and it seemed like a child's play now that I didn't have to do everything by myself. Davies left his body momentarily, bathed in light. Ravi showed him the procedure how to attach and detach. When he saw that his father got the point very quickly he left the two lovebirds alone. We attached to our bodies again and told them we were going for a walk. I felt they were so engrossed in their happiness they couldn't perceive anything else. Just as well. It was the same with us.

He took me by the hand and led me out of the house. We ran down the stairs and stopped only when we were in the street. He put his arm around my shoulders, as he used to do, and we walked slowly along the tree-lined path. Suddenly we heard a voice in our heads. It was Hannah.

Ina! Ravi! Can you hear me?

Sure, he answered her calmly like his life didn't hang by a thread only minutes ago. Literally.

As soon as I got the vision I tried to connect to you.

We're fine, Hannah. Thank you for everything, I smiled at her.

Oh, you're saying goodbye. So I guess you need a little privacy. I understand. I'll see you at school on Monday…and AFTER school! Yeah!

Sure, said Ravi. We were alone again.

We walked around Central Park slowly and enjoyed the fact that we had bodies. I thought I had only one question left.

Ravi?

Yes?

How did he do it? I mean Davies. How come you were not able to read his mind? How did he catch us?

This is not the most romantic question for an evening walk, is it?

I'm sorry but…I need to know. To prepare for the future.

He was just a puppet, remember? There was a special kind of contract. Davies promised three very powerful light worriers to the low frequencies: me, you and himself. And in return he would have contact with Rashmi. It was a lie, of course. My father would never have seen her because they just didn't have her. But they really wanted the three of us. So they gave him some power temporarily and disabled us for a short time. I destroyed the contract immediately when I found it. But I didn't have enough energy left to come back. I started to disappear. Suddenly I found myself in my body again…I still don't know how I did it…

We are responsible for that, I explained proudly. Then I told him, or showed him everything that had happened to me since I last saw him.

He was surprised and moved.

That means you don't really need me anymore, he became lost in his thoughts. *Now you have your vision and my power…*

But I don't have YOU, I shouted. *Sorry, I shouldn't get so excited. What I want to say is that we have managed to do exactly what we wanted.*

What do you mean? he asked me.

How did you destroy the contract?

I imagined…

Oh, so you had to use a vision?

You were not there so I had to.

So my power of vision is also in you. That means that you don't really need me either.

He realized what I was getting at.

Well, that's true.

You don't need me but you still love me.

I do. Even more than before if that's possible. More freely, he realized.

And we work together because we like that not because we have to.

*You are right. You see, now I'm learning from you…*he admitted.

*I have to pay you back somehow for all the tutoring you've given me…*I smiled, *you haven't invoiced me yet.*

Suddenly we laugh out loud. We'd just walked past an older couple who were very surprised why we were laughing when nobody said anything…

The last week of June. I had so many great things waiting for me. I finished the year with honors and so did Ravi. Hannah said we had to keep in touch during the summer. Our classmates were sad to say goodbye to us. Sienna made a table with the addresses, numbers, e-mails, birthdays and other data and gave a copy to everyone.

Davies kept the job of the headmaster and nobody recognized him after that fateful event in the basement room. His hair turned back to brown. At the beginning it looked a bit strange: like some sort of colored roots. He soon cut his hair short. His blue eyes started to sparkle with energy again and I could swear he looked ten years younger. The teachers started to enjoy coming to work and Davies asked everybody at the closing ceremony to call him Aaron. He decided to delete the name Aidan from his personal documents because it reminded him of some darker moments. "Who needs two names," he said joking. He started to attend the meetings of the Associated Secondary Schools Commission and Barnes had to admit he was a changed man. He welcomed him to the staff.

What about us? We were planning to leave straight away and surprise my parents. Eszter and Rossana flew to Munich too and we bought the air tickets together. They were pretty inquisitive so we got to talking during the 8-hour flight. Ravi spoke about the energy and the miracles of the universe. It sounded like poetry coming from his mouth. The girls said they will definitely enroll if there is a club formed next year. I winked at Ravi. I smiled at them when we landed in Munich.

"Now we have made up for the lost time, haven't we, girls?" I said. I knew I'd neglected them in the last couple of months.

"Now we are even, you're right," said Rossana.

"But not for long!" Eszter finished the exchange.

We looked for our luggage, waved goodbye and went our separate ways.

Ravi and I arrived at the Slovenian airport almost too fast. The plane was small and cozy...I remembered how big it seemed when I first sat in it. But after the entire year I spent in New York it really seemed small... But still very cozy.

When we flew over Slovenia I thought: *This is your first time here by plane, isn't it?*

Yes, it is, he replied. *It's beautiful to see the view with your own eyes.*

When the taxi drove us to the spot where the view spreads over the village I grew up in, I calmly took in the beauty of the tranquil village life. All resentments were gone. The place was beautiful – like someone had drawn it. I remembered my classmates, the events from elementary school and I felt happiness.

If I had known then what sort of life awaited me I wouldn't have been sad, I thought. *Not for a second.*

You acted that way because you didn't have the knowledge, added Ravi. *Nobody is evil, bad, sad or scared because they want to be, but because they lack knowledge about life.*

When we drove past the square with the church I noticed a group of people standing by the store. I recognized Tine among them. As we drove by somebody pointed at our taxi and everyone turned around. They recognized me and waved cheerfully.

I smiled and felt relief. Things have changed. The past has remained where it should be. In the past. Now is different. Completely different. I calmly waved back.

We stood in front of the door giggling. We knew we were going to surprise them, but we wanted to agree on the details of the scenario. We asked the taxi driver to let us off on the main street so we could walk up the gravel driveway trying to be as silent as possible. We chose the simplest of options. They will be surprised enough as it is.

We rang the bell. We heard footsteps; my mom's. We could hear the patter of small feet too. So Ludo was with her. The door opened and my mom's jaw dropped, her lips stretched in an astonished belated smile, her face sort of froze. Ludo barked at us and I could feel he recognized us.

"Hi mom. This is my boyfriend," I said with a smile.

"I'm Ravi. Pleased to meet you," he introduced himself charmingly.

"Oh my god! Ina! Ravi! To surprise us like this!" my mom managed to exclaim. I had a feeling she got some kind of internal connection, like she could see the events unfold from my childhood on.

You're right, Ravi thought in a way of an answer.

We were still standing at the front door – but now Ela and dad came too. What followed was joyful hugging, kissing and introductions which finally moved to the inside of the house.

FOREWORD

Janja Srečkar's first novel is definitely a book one cannot put down until reaching the last page. On the one hand, there is a perfect fusion of the author's feelings and experiences with that of the main protagonist, and on the other hand it contains deep spiritual messages for the young about how to live, what to learn and how to set goals. The experiences of a child who must conform to and rely on the limited information provided by the five senses shows a void present in an average person's life.

The author offers a possible way how not to remain passive observers of the events around us but become active participants through our inquisitive nature already as children. In this way the book represents an excellent manual for the young and also the not so young. It leads us along the path we are not used to, the path of senses which we refuse to embrace.

Although we live in the middle of the sea of energy, we do not accept it as an inseparable part of us. The five senses and the mind have a limiting effect on us; and the story opens the questions and offers answers to what lies beyond our limitations. We refuse to acknowledge the energy world which Einstein defined almost a hundred years ago in his famous equation about matter and energy. In the technological filed we have recognized some forms of energy (electricity, light, nuclear energy...) and we have used them more or less successfully although we cannot feel, see, hear, taste or smell it. The human mind has this incredible ability of denying itself.

The book The Frequency offers solutions with simple explanations for the energy world which all religions have been trying to explain for centuries. The story is captivating, the main protagonist is easy to identify with. It speaks about special abilities some children and also adults have, that is the ability to sense energy and use it. We are increasingly being given messages as well as actual children who master this art. And for this reason, works like this should be welcomed for they raise the level of awareness and make us face the fears that do not really exist.

—*Jože Žmavc*

ACKNOWLEDGMENTS

My deepest thanks go to my loving husband and also my agent Jan Sebastian Srečkar who has always provided the strength I needed when life challenged me with a test. He helped me with some ideas and with introducing the book to its first readers. He also put extremely large effort for this book to see the world, for which I am eternally grateful.

I am grateful to everybody, who have led me on the path to knowledge: Polona Sepe, Slavko Mahne-Shyama, Foster Perry, Luna, Matej Škufca; Eros with his book [psi], Rhonda Byrne with her book The Secret and Vladimir Megre with his book collection Anastasia.

I thank my mom, friend, proofreader and artist Anka Kolenc. Thank you for your unlimited trust and support. You have proven that you will always act for the development of your daughters and pour your unconditional love on us.

My thanks go to the other members of my family: my father Zvone Kolenc, sisters Mojca Sosič and Špela Kolenc. I thank my mother-in-law Metka Zadravec and father-in-law Ivan Sečkar for their support and trust.

I thank also Marjana Kramer, Andrej Primožič – Primzi, Benko Mrđanović and Jože Žmavc for all the support and also Janja and Jaka Petrič for their numerological advice.

If it wasn't for Edis Talundžič and Sara Mrđanović, the book would never see the world in this e-book form. So I also thank them, for their persistent effort to launch this project to the world. I would like to thank the translators Mojca Lober and Alan Horvatič, who provided the English version of the book.

I am also very grateful to Pia Rihtarič, the designer of the wonderful pictures and ornaments for this trilogy and Katja Pirc for graphic design.

I wish to thank the authors: Gustav Šilih, Charlotte Bronte, Bogdan Novak, Richard Bach, Stephen Turoff, Paramhansa Yogananda, Shirley Maclaine and Stephanie Meyer whose works have touched me deeply and encouraged me to start writing.

I thank a very important group of teenagers who were first to read and assess my work: Alisa Memič, Jasmin Kurtić, Nika Vučko and Tim Rupnik. You were the first to become a part of this story and I will never forget the time we spent together.

Last but not least I thank all of you who have supported this book with your thoughts or opinions.

GLOSSARY OF TERMS

PANJABI: everyday Indian item of clothing for women consisting of a top and trousers.

SARI: Indian article of clothing for women consisting of a top and a sheet of cloth wrapped around the body in a special way.

HENNA: dye made of natural ingredients Indian women use to paint their bodies.

BINDI: a round ornament Indian women place on their foreheads.

SITAR: an Indian string instrument with a hollow pumpkin attached to it.

GANESH: Indian god with an elephant's head, symbol of happiness.

TARABUCA: an Indian drum.

KALI: goddess of death and transformation.

ABOUT THE AUTHOR

Janja Srečkar is a versatile artist (author, poet, director, actress, dancer, singer; a music teacher by profession) and a fan of science-fiction literature. She is especially drawn to the protagonists with special powers. She has a wide array of favorite authors and their main quality is that they strengthen the message they wish to convey with the use of love and humor. Among her favorite authors are Vladimir Megre, Eros, Charlotte Bronte, Gustav Šilih, Bogdan Novak, Richard Bach, Stephen Turoff, Paramhansa Yogananda, Shirley Maclaine, Rhonda Byrne and Stephenie Meyer. In author's own words her mission is "to mask" positive messages - that benefit our everyday life as well as our future - into packages of art (printed publications, theatrical performances, poems...) that people accept, understand and possibly even have fun with."

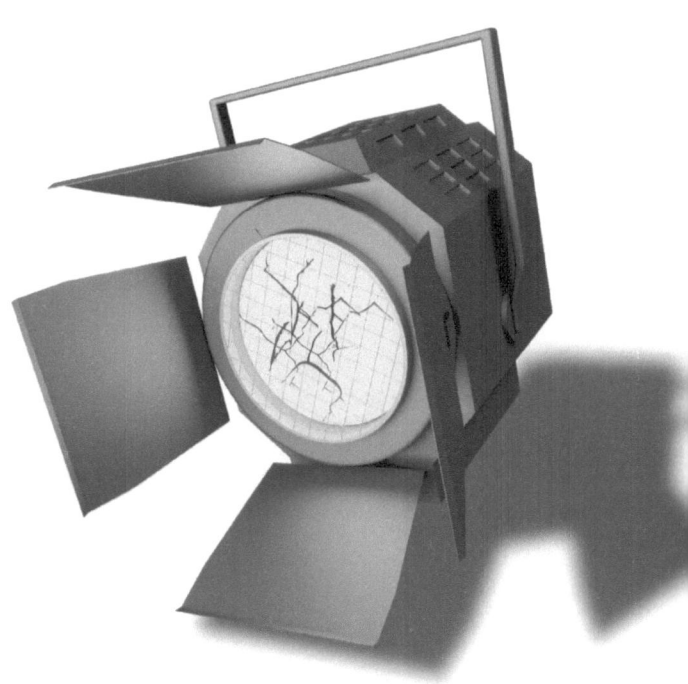

www.ingramcontent.com/pod-product-compliance
Lightning Source LLC
Chambersburg PA
CBHW020725210626
46807CB00016B/94